An

AJ Mark

Angelic?

To be held captive and unable to pursue your own life is slavery, and it's worth fighting against.

There are thousands of slaves in the UK.

www.unseenuk.org

Angelic?

Prologue
February 2015

Robert Sefton Estate Agency
St John's Hill
Battersea
London

Robert Sefton grunted something that could have been goodbye as he left the office. I shot a grin at Harbinder. We only ever laughed at his rudeness. He gave us both a job and that was enough, but it was a good place to work as well. Harbinder made it fun and I got to meet different people, which I sometimes enjoyed these days.

Her face told me there was something she wanted to gossip about. She put a newspaper on my desk and pointed to an article. It was surprising and worrying. The journalist had somehow connected together a whole series of incidents. An SAS operation, the death of a Russian mafia boss, gunfights in central London, multiple arrests, gruesome killings and trafficked women. A few names were mentioned.

Harbinder pointed at one of the names. James Hecketty. He hadn't been seen by anyone for weeks. She asked:
- You knew him didn't you?
I shook my head:

Angelic?

- I didn't ever meet James.

James Hecketty had been part of a small company called SafeNet that sold Internet security software. They had been involved in all this mafia stuff according to the paper. She pointed to another name. Tavi Mansur.

-     I know you knew him.

He too had been a member of the SafeNet team. The article said he had been beaten to death. I only said:

-     We went out a couple of times. He was nice. I liked him.
-     Did he like you?

I nodded my head and my throat tightened as I held back tears. My regret and despair found me again. Harbinder noticed, she knew the signs. I heard her say quietly:

-     I'm sorry.

Then I felt her hand press gently on my shoulder. I put my hand on hers and pressed a little more.

The phone rang and Harbinder took the call. Somebody was enquiring about how much we charged. She had got the message. Tavi and SafeNet weren't mentioned again that day. I tried to sound cheerful as we talked about her daughter's birthday party and the completion of the new extension to her house.

The bus was early, or I was late. It was more likely that I was late and I rushed across the road but stumbled when something seemed to hit me in the back. I ignored it, jumped on the bus and swiped my Oyster card. I sat down where there were two spares. The bus set off and a scruffy lad who had just got on the bus chose the seat beside me. He had seemed a bit anxious but relaxed as he sat down and breathed:

-     OK. OK.

I started to feel cold. The lad next to me stood up, peered

around at the floor then wailed:
-   Oh God No!
He looked at me:
-   Miss! Miss Alex, you're bleeding very badly.
That made sense. I hadn't stumbled catching the bus. I'd been hit by a bullet. I looked down and saw the blood on the floor and felt the wound in my waist. Stupidly I wondered how I'd get the stain out of my beloved tweed skirt. I started to keel over, my strength was going. I could hear a woman screaming and a man calling on his mobile. The bus stopped in a hurry and I was vaguely aware that two men were boarding the bus and shouting things.

I wondered if it mattered if I died. My life was so muddled. I wasn't sure who I was, what was normal or what was real. I only pretended to be Alex.

The world had started to become distant and I slumped onto the floor. Lying down my brain got a bit more blood but nothing was working well. I was in trouble, feeling very cold and already too weak to move. The lad was kneeling over me putting pressure on the wound; trying to keep some blood inside me. Someone was holding my head and stroking my hair.

I could feel nothing and I could only see the floor of the bus inches from my face. My eyes wouldn't move. I thought I heard my mother talking softly to me.

The world slowly went out of focus, blurred into nothing and then, finally, fell silent.

Angelic?

Part 1
James Hecketty

Angelic?

Chapter 1
London
October 2011

Sun House
Brixton
London

Source:	Kyriacos Papandreou, Geoff Gudrun, Police reports
Date:	Friday 21st October 2011
Time:	16.25
Present:	DC Kyriacos Papandreou, DCI Geoff Gudrun

Papandreou and Gudrun took one last look around the scene of the crime. It was the seventh murder case Papandreou had been involved in and the first where they had got nowhere. He wasn't disappointed. It was the only case where he hadn't personally wanted to catch the murderer. Professionally it was different, this was a failure for the team. Gudrun, the SIO, had been one of the rising stars. His luck ran out when they finally pulled the plug on the Sun House case.

Papandreou recalled the first time he had arrived at the Sun House block. A residential development that had been creatively named to appear a better place to live in than it was. When he got the call to go there to investigate a murder with the team, he had assumed it would be a domestic because of the location. Just one victim. Probably the wife killed by the husband, or a lover. Humdrum.

When he had arrived, a little later than he should have been, he found the scene outside the flats already crowded with ambulances, police cars, pathologist's vans and the other support vehicles that go with a major crime. He saw women wrapped in blankets being taken to vehicles comforted by police women. So it wasn't a domestic.

He had been beckoned in through the front door by DC Wilson. This was a brothel. It had the decor, the sofa, the only just over the top pinks and reds. And it had that smell. An expensive brothel. Perhaps it was a gang killing. Automatic weapons and round eyed pumped up young hoods. He asked Wilson:

- What's this? A revenge killing?
- No, we don't think so.
- What then?
- Come upstairs.

Papandreou followed Wilson up the stairway and past a dead body covered in plastic sheeting. There were scene of crime officers busily moving around and Papandreou nodded at the few he recognised. At the top of the stairs was a corridor with rooms off to either side. One of the rooms was set up as an office. A pool of blood on the carpet outside. Two more dead bodies inside. A room at the end on the right had another covered body just outside. He followed Wilson in there.

The room was a typical bedroom in a brothel. Dark red curtains, subdued lighting, a mirror on the wall with curtains to cover it on request. An en-suite bathroom stocked with sex toys, creams and wipes. Another body on the floor. Blood on the wall behind the bed. The room looked like it had been hit by a whirlwind. There was a stench of bleach and the bedclothes were gone. All the drawers had been emptied.

In the room were two other police officers in polyester suits who were waiting for Papandreou. He recognised both of them. The senior man was DCI Geoff Gudrun. He looked round at Papandreou:

- Good to see you here Yak. We already think we know what happened. We'll do a walkthrough next.
- Why's this place such a mess?
- The other girls didn't want the shooter caught. They've done everything they can to mess up the place.
- Are you saying the shooter was one of the whores?
- Yes, we think so.
- Sorry Geoff. I'm missing a piece here. There are eight dead men? How many injured?
- There is an injured woman. We don't think she shot her... Take a look at that body, Yak.

Yak had lifted the plastic sheeting on the body. The man was naked and slumped on his side. The back of his head no longer existed. His forehead contained a single neat entry wound.

The police had worked out the timeline. Neighbouring flats had reported hearing shots fired. They could tell that the girl had got the gun from the man she had been with. Then killed all eight men, most of them armed and shooting back, in less than a minute. Not much later she left the building.

Now, four months on, Papandreou and Gudrun stared down the road in the direction she had gone. A few security cameras had picked her up after leaving the brothel. She had calmly walked down that road through the rain and the lightning. They had followed every vague lead and every possible sighting. Four months. Nothing. No one would help them.

The girls at Sun House said as little as they could, they didn't even want to give her name. They wouldn't describe her at all. Or they described one another. They messed up the forensics and refused to give DNA.

The Russian thugs who ran this place didn't offer much help towards the investigation either. They were clever and well organised. Or dead. They pulled one man in for questioning. He said exactly nothing.

Even the punters weren't coming forwards willingly to help. They got three good descriptions. All of different women. She had dark hair. Most of them had dark hair. Was it black or dark brown? But the punters weren't there to study hair colour.

They had learned a little from the brothel chief. A man called Bronislav Adaskin. He had been gruesomely killed and was still in the process of dying when the paramedics had scooped him up. He'd groaned some comments when they first arrived, fallen unconscious in the ambulance and died in hospital. She spoke good English. That only made it harder to find her. He said she was called Angelina.

There had been eleven women in the brothel. Their problems didn't stop when they were released. It was impossible for them to just forget and start their lives again. He knew that one of them, Margarita Pavlovicha, had already made an attempt on her own life. All the girls were young and their enforced life in the brothel their first real experience of the world as adults. Aspiration, joi de vivre and innocence smudged over by captivity, forced intimacy and violence.

Gudrun turned to Yak:

- Best guess. What do you think happened to her?
- She got help. If she had turned up on my doorstep I would have helped her.

Gudrun nodded:

- Yeah. But we knew that when we were looking for her.
- She got help from someone clever. Cleverer than us.

They both looked hopeless. They had tried hard enough. Gudrun said:

- Sod it. It's not our job anymore.

He shut the door to the brothel and they replaced the 'Police Line. Do Not Cross' tapes. Gudrun was still interested in Yak's thoughts:

- So how do you cope with having been that? How do you cope with having done that?
- No idea. I can't imagine. You struggle. I guess you have to just pretend that it hasn't happened. Pretend it wasn't really you.

They walked slowly back towards the car as Gudrun contemplated his stalled career:

- Fuckin shit! Absolute fuckin shit!... It doesn't matter. I'll go home, drink coffee, get my pension, watch my kids grow up.

When they reached the car Gudrun stopped to look at Papandreou:

- You know what, Yak? I'm bloody glad she killed those bastards. I am glad. I hope she's well. And I hope she dies aged at least a hundred and ten with her loving family around her. And I hope she's pleased that she killed those bastards too.
- Well. Amen to that. But we'll never know.

They both got in the car and slammed the doors shut. Gudrun started the engine and put the radio on. Then they drove away from the drab block of flats.

Chapter 2
London
January 2014

Outside Harvey Nichols Department Store
Knightsbridge
London

Source:	James Hecketty
Date:	Saturday 4th January
Time:	10.25
Present:	James Hecketty, Toby Smithson, Katya Khrushcheva, Katya's Bodyguard

There were so many people. Perhaps being here in Knightsbridge on the first Saturday morning of the January sales wasn't the best idea. The Christmas decorations were still up and the illuminated Santas, snowmen and reindeer floated over the road. Toby and I tried to make progress through the crowds on the pavement. The road seemed just as busy and I noticed we were moving not much slower than the traffic.

Among the private cars, taxi cabs, red buses and delivery vans was a big black Bentley, pristine, chauffeur driven and with a high saloon for comfort rather than elegance. I tried to peer inside, but all I could see was my own reflection in the polished black glass. It passed us, then stopped only a few strides ahead of where we were. Out stepped a beefy bloke and then the most beautiful young woman. She looked in our direction. Then I heard her say something before she glided up the steps into Harvey Nichols. Toby wanted to check:

- Did she look at me?
- Yeah, she did.

Her eyes had seemed to rest on Toby for a few moments. I made him even more optimistic:

- She said you were cute.
- She was talking Russian wasn't she?
- I heard her say you were cute.
- Come on!

He followed her up the steps. I went with him.

She was not too tall, slim and shapely. She looked wealthy and gorgeous and the thick-necked bloke escorting her was not her boyfriend. He looked at everyone while everyone else looked at her. She floated through the busy store as if it was almost empty, everyone turning first to see what others were looking at and then seeing her. Occasional interruptions to her progress were managed with grace and no impatience. A small child impeded her. She crouched down and spoke briefly to the boy and softy touched his cheek. He smiled at her before his mother reclaimed him. The young woman moved on.

We were moving parallel to her past the jewellery and perfume counters. Trying to get through the busy shop and move ahead of her.

She met with a man in a suit who welcomed her to the store. They got into the elevator and we lost her after that. She had looked so beautiful. Every detail immaculate. Everything just as it should be. We talked as we made our

way back through the shop. Toby was smitten:
-   She's just gorgeous. She's perfect.
-   You don't even know her.
-   She's the only girl I'll ever dream of
-   Dreaming is all you can do and she'll seem all the more perfect because you'll never dream any faults. She's just a girl.
-   She didn't look a dope. There were signs of life there. I'd love to find a girl who at least had more feist than gush... What is it with you...? Just a girl? Jesus!
-   That's the problem. You don't want a female human with faults and flaws. You want someone who's perfect. I'm sure that girl has just as much mess in her life as everyone else. I bet she even makes mistakes, has arguments, worries about stuff and gets pissed off occasionally. Like the rest of us. Even the Queen.
-   The Queen has arguments? You're sure? Hmm. You could be right though. I think there was a sadness in that girl.

We had left Harvey Nichols and were walking along the road when I thought aloud:
-   Imagine what it's like being her. All those eyes staring at you.
-   What? Imagine what it's like being her? That girl puts all sorts of ideas into my head without that being one of them. Sod that.
-   Have you never wondered what it's like being beautiful? Her view of the world is so different.
-   Blimey. Where are you on this? You'd rather be a girl?
-   Hey?.. No!.. I'm not saying that. But how does the world seem to her? She's still human, about our age, but things are so different. Every man who sees her stares at her. Every man she meets wants to nail her.
-   OK I get that last part, believe me. But I can't look at

her and think that other stuff. I mean blimey that thought might get there sometime, when I'm 98 years old perhaps. Meanwhile I'm stuck with far more engaging and practical notions. Thanks.

Toby tried doing some research later, though the ill-informed would have thought he was chatting up one of the shop managers, but he failed to find the name of the young woman.

After meddling on the internet for a while I discovered that Toby's ideal of feminine beauty was called Yekaterinya Khrushcheva. He was speechless with thanks when I passed the news on to him. Then he recovered and repeated her unfamiliar name over and over again to himself, almost as though he was casting a spell.

Many things start small. We are told that the tiniest eddy can cause the largest storm. We didn't know it then but our fates and many others had just been stitched in place alongside that of Miss Khrushcheva. Maybe if we'd known all that would happen we wouldn't have taken the next few steps. Then again, knowing Toby, maybe we would have anyway.

He was a tall good looking guy. He had humour and charm in abundance. Girls were attracted to him but he had never yet sustained a relationship beyond a few weeks. Perhaps this Russian girl would be the one for him.

There were three of us who ran a company called SafeNet. After we had finished college Tavi Mansur and I had produced the software and started the business. We knew the software was brilliant, better than any competitor, the reviews all said so, but no one seemed to buy it. When Toby joined the SafeNet team, he created an effective marketing strategy and then we started to sell in quantity.

Angelic?

We were doing very well.

Toby's philosophy of life was interesting. He thought it was everyone's duty to do something unusual and truly adventurous. The whole globe had been visited so you couldn't be an explorer like Shackleton or Scott. That shouldn't stop you doing extraordinary, strange or even bizarre things. We had all signed up for this philosophy. We liked a challenge. We liked to do things that were different.

We'd once spent a week on the streets living homeless. That had been an eye opener. We'd started with one set of clothes and no money. Staying warm and hunger free had been a real challenge. It wasn't fun, but we'd learned a lot. After that we spent the weeks leading up to Christmas working for a homeless charity and Christmas day we spent in a shelter giving out food and clothing. We had a big meal with Tavi's parents on the day after Boxing Day.

All three of us had applied for intern jobs at an investment bank, just to see what would happen. Toby had been successful and managed four months before being ejected on the grounds of lacking the necessary commitment. Which made sense as he'd only attended about twenty days in that time, having rung in with some remarkable excuses for not being there. These had included getting lost on the way, a spider in the bath and not having any clean socks. Tavi had been unfairly locked up in prison for three months and we tried to treat that as though it had been a challenge. It was generally agreed that I was behind on the big challenge list.

Fox's Tarn
Scafell
The Lake District
Cumbria

Source:	James Hecketty
Date:	Sunday 12th January
Time:	11.05
Present:	Toby Smithson, Tavi Mansur, James Hecketty.

It was a good cold bright day. We had all our winter kit with us and had just come up the small rocky gully where we'd briefly made use of our ice axes and the front points on our crampons. We stopped to take a breather.

We'd arrived at Fox's Tarn which sits just below the summit of Scafell, right in the heart of the Lakes. This place collected snow in winter and the wind sculpted it into flowing feminine curves. We admired the shapes and the view of Bow Fell in the distance.

Tavi had something to say. It seemed that he and Toby had been talking about me:
- We've got a challenge for you. We think you'll be up for it. It doesn't look too hard on paper.
- OK. I'm listening. What is it?
Toby took over:
- You just have to be a different person from who you are now.
- What like pretend I'm fifty?
- Something like that. You have to be this person for a

whole month. You live as them, go out as them and work as them. No time off. Even we have to treat you like you're this other person.
- Okay. I'm thinking there must be a catch. This person's wheelchair bound or something. Or they work in an abattoir or live in a tree. Have they got an extra leg?
- No fully able bodied, your age, all faculties intact. You'll have to find your own job. Doesn't count unless you do.
- Ok so far.

We started up the last few steep meters to the summit. Tavi and I got there first. It was windy on top, as always. Tavi had to shout to be heard:
- We create a whole false ID, everything. Credit cards everything. We even share the costs.
- Costs?
- Clothing, housing, phone, etc.
- There's still something missing. This sounds too easy.
Toby arrived, breathing hard. He'd heard enough of our windblown conversation to be able to continue:
- It's something I know you've thought about. You'll probably have to do some training and lessons in all sorts of shit so you can appear to be who you're supposed to be, but you shouldn't find it too hard.
They went quiet for a moment hoping that I'd work it out. I thought I had:
- You want me to act like I'm a woman for a month? Oh flip! Flipping hell.
- It's not just the month you have to do. You learn how to dress properly, move in a feminine way, do makeup and wear a skirt and high heels. Right and nice and girly. You train for all of it. Make sure you can walk and talk the part. You never know you might find that you like it.

- Piss off.
- That's not a no is it? You know you want to really and you're a long way behind us two on the challenges.
- Shit. Oh shit.

We made our way south from the summit, down the long smooth ridge to Slight Side. Toby was grinning from ear to ear. Exultant at selling yet another deal.

- Yes. Yes. Yes. You're thinking about it. Physically you're not too far wide of the mark so you should be able to make it work really well.
- Remind me. How is it that you can tell when you have friends?

Toby negotiated a patch of large boulders; he slipped a bit and sat down rather than fall:

- Lunch here?

We ate our sandwiches admiring the view south towards the estuaries on Morecambe Bay and the Duddon. Then made our way back down to Wasdale Head. Tavi and I threw our rucksacks into the back of his Freelander, Toby kept his and we all went into the pub to order beer. We sat down at one of the partitioned off table areas at the back of the bar.

Toby hadn't finalised the deal yet:

- Now here's the really good part. I've found Katya.

Tavi:

- Katya?
- Yeah, pet name for Yekaterinya, my yet to be met Russian babe. I've got tickets for a charity do that she's going to be at. They're real expensive, but it should be worth the cost to meet the world's most gorgeous girl.

Toby showed us the tickets, he'd carried them all the way around the walk with him:

Mr Tobias Smithson

Angelic?

Mr Tavi Mansur and guest

- You want me to go as a woman? As Tavi's date?
- You've got it!
- I haven't said yes to this deal yet.
- But you're going to.
- Ten days?

Toby was shaking his head:

- Not enough.
- Twenty days?

He was adamant:

- Four full weeks.

It wasn't such a bad idea. I relented:

- Two conditions. You guys can't take the piss all the time. You have to be helpful. And this puts me ahead of you both on all challenges.

Toby nodded:

- That's good for me.
- Deal.
- You bloody star!

Toby was delighted and quaffed his beer in celebration.
Tavi was half pleased and half amused:

- You're going to do it! Shit man! Shit...

I had an idea and suggested to Tavi:

- It'll do wonders for your love life.

Tavi looked hopeful for a moment:

- How's that?
- I'm your date for the party!

I pouted, kissed the end of my finger, and put my finger on his cheek. Tavi swiped it away disgusted:

- Sod off! Shit. Oh fuck. Did you two plan this whole thing just to yank my handle?

Toby was chuckling. He'd thought it all through:

- There's just one more thing. Jim's a brave adventurer trespassing in dangerous territory. This won't work if we start blabbing about what is going on. If anyone knows that this girl is James then it won't work. He won't ever pass. That's apart from all the other shit it might rake up. So we tell no one. Not a rabbit, canary, person, the dog next door or visiting aliens. That's the deal and we all have to stick with it whatever happens.

Tavi was entirely in agreement with this suggestion:

- Cool with me. Why in God's name would I want everyone to think I was going out with a bloke?

Angelic?

Madrid Road
Barnes
London

Source: James Hecketty
Date: Wednesday 15th January
Time: 15.00
Personnel: James Hecketty, Brian

Brian's website claimed that he was the person who had advised Dustin Hoffman in the making of the film Tootsie. I'd seen the movie. It was a very different kind of romantic comedy where Hoffman's male character befriends Jessica Lange while pretending to be a woman.

I gave him a call and turned up at his house in Barnes. He mentioned an hourly fee. It was a tidy sum, but well within my means and the costs were being shared. We set up regular sessions and he gave me a more thorough examination. He looked at the shape of my head and my neck. He compared my shoulders and my hips and studied my hands and arms, rolling my sleeves back. He raised a single eyebrow and grinned:
-    Well you won't have too much trouble looking the part.
-    I won't?
He went on:
-    Appearance is often the easiest thing though, it's everything else that's difficult.
I had no idea how much everything else there was.

We spent time out on the high street observing the differences between men and women. He started to give me an idea how hard this might be going to be:

-    We give off signals all the time about what sex we are. Gender is at the most basic level of human interaction. You'll notice someone's gender before their age or race. Usually before you notice what they are wearing. You have to learn to give off these signals. Every movement you make has to be done in the right gender.

He stood in a queue at a shop and became a woman just by standing differently. It was so subtle. When he got to the till you could see the confusion cross the girl's face as she looked at him properly, she'd expected a woman.

We looked at every gesture that men and women make. Brian had me rehearse male and female ways of doing things so I could go back whenever I wanted. His teaching made me understand how to appear more masculine as well as more feminine. I developed both roles and became more characteristic in each of them.

He showed me YouTube videos with all the techniques that drag-artists use to make themselves appear female. For instance how a man can make his least feminine bulge effectively disappear so he can wear close fitting trousers or even a swimsuit without giving the game away. I saw the steps to take to hide facial hair, how to make an Adam's apple less obvious and just how realistic prosthetic silicone breasts can appear. These were things a man would have to know if he was serious about passing as a woman.

I started looking at my face in more detail. You have to if you want to put makeup on. I noticed all the tiny blemishes and looked up ways of covering them up. As time went on I would emphasise the role I was in using make-up.

As a bloke I'd always looked a bit wimpish. Most people probably saw me as a skinny geek with glasses. I made myself look more masculine when James by adding some shadows and making my eyebrows look thick. I added some stubble and then took to wearing a false beard.

At Brian's recommendation I saw a voice coach twice a week as well. That really helped too. Pitch and pace vary constantly in feminine speech. Masculine pace is more constant, pitch less varied. Again, the difference in my speech became more distinct as I got better and better.

Both my teachers kept saying how impressed they were with me. It was a good technique for a teacher. I gained a lot of confidence. It was like training to be a person as well as a woman. I found out ways to behave such as if I wanted to appear happy, interested, angry or sad and ways to keep a conversation going or start one off. People's reactions to me began to alter. I had more options and felt more confident and less awkward in company whether I was taking on a male or a female role.

SafeNet Office
Battersea Park Road
Battersea
London

Source:	James Hecketty
Date:	Thursday 16th January
Time:	09.00
Present:	Tavi Mansur, James Hecketty, Toby Smithson

Tavi was making the coffee at the office. We would be drinking a lot of it over the next few days. He handed me a full mug. We both had that feeling of excitement. A bit like when we set up SafeNet. We were going to do what we did best. We knew we were good; this was our speciality and we were the best. We were footballers at the world cup final, the favourites for the 100m relay final at the Olympics.

We were going to screw with other people's data. We were going to hack the hell out of every database we could get into, not to get data out but to enter false records. My feminine character was going to become a real person, with a history, bank accounts, credit cards, academic qualifications, school records, photo album, parents, boyfriends, medical history, holidays, shopping history, mobile phone records, jobs, homes and everything else. It was important everyone was convinced she was not James.

Tavi sat opposite me. Each of us worked with six monitors. Two were shared. There was a joint screen where we both stored the results of changes we had made. We both had an action screen where we could see what the other was doing. The other monitors showed the progress of our data searches and password cracking algorithms.

The easiest way to create a false person is not to. You find a real person who's dead and use their ID. That gets you a starter. It took us a day to find the right person – Alexandra Elisabeth Harewood. From there on everything else fell into place. Our brains buzzed with all the options and possibilities.

Toby came in at one point on day one. He saw we were busy and knew better than to interrupt.

On day three Toby came in while we were standing at the coffee machine. Tavi and I were talking through whether or not to hack her supposed boyfriend's Facebook account to enter some pictures of them together. The account had been dead for a while. We could get in to make the changes. Alter the password and email details. He would never be able to get in to see what we'd done. Toby:

-    How's it going?

Tavi gave a response:

-    Good

And I agreed:

-    Yeah, good

We went back to our discussion. Toby persisted:

-    No guys. You need to listen!

We stopped and looked at Toby who was saying:

-    You're working on Alex Harewood right? The guy at Vicarage Crescent has just handed his notice in and I think I've already got a new tenant... Alex Harewood.

Tavi thought about that for a moment. He was impressed:

-    You frigging genius. She can rent it from us so it looks all legal and proper and it's how she knows me.

So Alex Harewood rented one of our properties. She had a place to live. It was a nice flat, too, with a good view of the river. It had the additional advantage of being close to where I lived as James.

After four days we were winding down. We had done just about all that we could. We started shutting stuff down and wiping over the traces. Deleting log file references and copying into backup versions so that no one could ever know. We did the test. There were other tests but this was the one that we liked the best. I logged in to apply for a credit card. Entered all the new details, bank account, address, date of birth etc. Wait...wait...wait... Application approved! Hit! Alex now had better credentials than me and many other members of the human race.

Tavi and I sat back feeling very pleased with ourselves.

Chapter 3
London
April 2014

The Victoria and Albert Museum
Kensington
London

Source: Alex Harewood
Date: Monday 24th April
Time: 19.00
Present: Alex Harewood, Jenny Verdi, Geoff Collins

The Victoria and Albert museum, universally known as the
V and A, was looking for voluntary staff to help with re-
cataloguing part of their collection. In particular they
needed a competent data entry expert. It didn't take them
too long to be convinced that I could handle a keyboard
easily. They discovered my computer skills weren't bad
either. I just had to type what was on the cards they gave
me and enter it into the database. They also had strong
security checks. If Alex could get in here she would pass
just about anywhere. They took Alex Harewood on.

My story was that I had just moved to London from
Canada. Volunteering got me friends and a reference for a
job. I only had to commit to a couple of hours a week and I

could walk away at any time. It was my first attempt to appear as Alex in a fixed setting where I'd have to keep going back. It had been Brian's idea and it was a good one.

The first time I went it took the whole day to get ready and get into girl mode. I was way too nervous to eat dinner beforehand.

We were cataloguing and categorising everything. If I wasn't sure of something I would ask the curator. He was a strange little man. Geoff Collins. He had really thin hair and little eyes that were rarely willing to hold my gaze. He talked quickly as though he was afraid that you would stop listening if he spent too long talking. What he said was usually very interesting though. I tried to encourage him to say more and it was useful for me to practice my feminine conversational techniques. I'd look at him while he was talking and smile and nod and never start talking until he had finished.

The work became more and more enjoyable as I began to relax as Alex. Each week I'd just go in and sit down. I'd log in to their system and start typing in the details from the cards. You could say it was a bit repetitive. That was alright.

There was a woman called Jenny who would sometimes come and talk to me when there was a chance. She talked about the other people around and what she thought about them in a generous and non-judgmental way, giving them reasons for their behaviour and accepting them as they were.

She was a very well-rounded woman with a kind face, cheerful manner and everyone liked her. I asked her about girly things when I wasn't sure. She had been a nurse and her part time day job was working as a counsellor in a school. It seemed like just the right thing for her.

Jenny talked about everything. What she had read, her boyfriends, exactly what she had done with them, what she was wearing and why, the problems she had with her washing machine or what she had eaten for breakfast. All I had to do was not be at all critical and sound like I felt the same way when my tights got laddered or my coffee was too strong. It was like living her life with her. I did the same thing and recounted my latest make up disaster or how I'd lost my keys and nearly missed the bus. I enjoyed talking like this and began to feel more a part of humanity and not the same person that I was when I was James.

She handed me a mug of coffee.
- Geoff seems to like you.
- You mean he fancies me?
- I think that could be right.
My response probably wasn't normal:
- Why?
- Oh Dear. I'm not sure I can answer that one for you. There are hundreds of reasons why he might, but I can't tell you which ones in particular. Perhaps you should ask him.

Jenny came with me on a shopping mission for the flat. It looked very masculine to start with and I wanted some help to feminise it. Walking round furniture stores we found things that seemed right.

We had some fun buying cushions and curtains and smelly stuff. I got some vases and silk flowers. The bathroom filled up with towels and potions. The kitchen gained mugs with hearts and flowers on them. The walls gained some paintings that I really liked. Pictures of domestic scenes by Vermeer and Kroyer and people dancing by Degas as well as some lovely drawings of flowers by Beatrix Potter. We'd helped to catalogue the originals at the V and A. The flat seemed homely and warm. I liked it.

Chapter 4
Russia
May 2014

Straminsky Residence
Rublyovka
Moscow

Source:	Hannah and Eleanor Straminsky
Date:	Monday 3rd May
Time:	11.39
Present:	Eleanor, Sergei and Hannah Straminsky, Genya Pavolika, Doctor Eshtashsky, two paramedics.

Doctor Eshtashsky and the two paramedics ran up the few steps to the front door of the palatial residence. The doctor hadn't been here before. He had attended other homes in the Rublyovka estate. A place where the richest people in Russia lived. Money and absurdity met here.

People here had just too much money. Only twenty years ago the whole of Russia had been owned by the state. Just thirty men now owned eighty per cent of it. They all had houses in Rublyovka along with anyone else who could afford it.

Fashions came and went here. To keep up you had to be seen in the right make and model of car, eating the right kind of cuisine or chumming up to the correct family of Europe's old aristocrats.

The three medical men were entering the home of Sergei Straminsky, one of the richest of the rich, and they were to attend his daughter. This house was one of the more reasonable and practical; it wasn't trying to be an Egyptian pyramid or a French chateau. It looked like a house because it had vertical walls of dark brick with white window frames and a normally sloping slate roof. Much of the bulk of the building was set back and veiled by the many mature trees that had been preserved during its construction. They made the house seem old and established; you could believe that the trees had grown up around the house after it was built.

The comparatively modest looking house sat well with what they knew about its owner. He was understood to be one of the sanest of Russia's outrageously wealthy men. Most of his money was not in Russia. He had bought into communications and electronics elsewhere in the world. It was also part of the reason Eshtashsky and his colleagues were here. The Straminskys had wanted a proper doctor to attend their daughter, not one of the local quacks who spent their time dealing with irrelevant minor ailments, boredom, and giving prescription drugs for recreational use.

The medics were shown into the house and up the broad staircase by an intelligent looking and tidily dressed woman who gave them more information:
- My name is Genya Pavolika. I'm the housekeeper here. I found Eleanor at 11.24. She'd been down for breakfast as normal and left at about 8.20. When I found her I immediately checked that she was breathing, called you and put her in the recovery

position. Her engagement ended recently after her
fiancé was found with another girl.

There was no-one in the sumptuous bedroom the three
men were led into but a voice directed them towards the
en-suite bathroom door.

\-   Over here!

The Russian speaker had an English accent and so the
doctor knew that this was Hannah Straminsky, the wife of
Sergei, who had already been an extraordinarily wealthy
woman when they married. There was no time to look at
her and notice that her skirt was round her waist so her
underwear showed and her hair was going in a variety of
directions. It would have been no concern to her if he had.
She was sitting by her daughter, his patient, who was lying
on the floor of the large marble lined bathroom. Eleanor
was lying on her side, pale and unconscious.

He checked her breathing and her pulse and nodded. She
was not too far gone. He had attended similar cases
before. He knew the options and the possible
complications:

\-   Do you know what she took?

\-   Here.

He was passed one bottle and then another. The first
bottle is Nembutal, a sleeping pill. The second was an
antiemetic. A combination often used by people intent on
suicide.

Doctor Eshtashsky opened up his bag and prepared the
Charcodote with the help of one of the paramedics. They
had worked this procedure together before and few words
were spoken. Hannah Straminsky watched with her pain
and worry evident in every movement. She at least knew
that there was some hope. Eshtashsky inserted the tubes
and raised the bottle:

- The charcoal will bind to the drug in her stomach. She won't absorb any more.

He knew he had to say more:

- She has taken a fair amount. She'll be unconscious for some time. If her brain hasn't received too much she'll regain consciousness, probably in the next twenty-four hours. She's young, she's breathing well on her own, her pulse is depressed but firm. The signs are good.

There was something missing. She had probably taken enough of the drug to make herself unconscious, but perhaps not enough to kill herself. If suicide was the intention here then something else should be here. He looked round the room. Hannah saw him looking and looked too. They both saw it at the same time in a corner by a chair. A plastic bag. It was crumpled, used and inflated; there were signs of condensation on the inside.

It appeared she had taken the drugs to make herself unconscious and then placed the bag over her head and pulled the chord tight. She probably removed the bag herself in the early stages of unconsciousness before her motoric system shut down. It wasn't an uncommon scenario.

There was no doubt now; the last possibility that this had been some sort of accident had gone. Eleanor Straminsky had done everything she could to kill herself.

- It's best if we take her to hospital. Apart from that we can only wait now.

advised Eshtashsky.

Hannah took out her phone and called Sergei to update him on the situation:

- Hello...The doctor has seen her and says she will most likely recover fully... We have to wait... Perhaps twenty four hours...Yes... No, no, no... not a mistake... We are certain... I know... Bye, Darling.

They waited six hours in hospital before Eleanor awoke properly, first drifting in and out of sleep. She saw her mother there and said:

\- I'm sorry, Mum.

Then Eleanor remembered all the other bad things. Her fiancé had left her for a girl that no one liked. A girl with malice who only ever found fault in others. It meant that he had never really valued her for who she was. He had not meant any of the kind, sweet things he had said so often. She had given all that she knew how to give, but it had always been a sham. He had only ever wanted her money.

\- Don't worry, my darling. Good things will come. They will. For today please just be alive.

Her mother held Eleanor's hand and knew the hurt that was in her daughter's mind. There was nothing yet to replace it. Eleanor needed new experiences and friends to fill the gaps. Hannah needed to find people who saw that her daughter's good, tender and affectionate nature was worth far more than any amount of money.

Chapter 5
London
May 2014

Toby's Flat
Paultons Square
Chelsea
London

Source: James Hecketty/Alex Harewood
Date: Saturday 8th May
Time: 18.55
Personnel: Toby Smithson, Tavi Mansur, James Hecketty.

I spent the whole day getting ready. It was the best I thought I could look as Alex with a cocktail dress that had sparkly lace on the shoulders and arms and plain black from the bust down, heels and a wig for long hair.

Tavi called at my flat and seemed quite taken with me. We shared a taxi over to Toby's and he kept saying how good I looked to make me feel more confident, which was nice of him.

We were in good time. Tavi rang the bell and grinned at me. Wondering what Toby's response would be. I greeted the big guy girlishly:

Angelic?

-   Hiya

Tavi introduced us:

-   Hi Toby this is Alex. I don't think you've met before.

Toby looked at me. He said nothing. Just stared. Then:

-   Would you mind just waiting there a moment?

He went back into the kitchen. There was the sound of him clearing things up and putting things away.

-   What's wrong with Toby?
-   Nothing. He just thinks you're a girl.

We went into the kitchen. Toby was still cleaning and tidying. Toby stared again. He was in the middle of putting his breakfast cereal bowl away and looked and sounded more upset than anything.

-   But you're a girl.
-   Yeah. I'm a girl.
-   It's not like you're James as a girl. You're just a girl.
-   Oh.

Tavi came to the rescue:

-   Toby can't believe how well you do it. Neither can I. Can I get you a drink?
-   Thanks, a diet coke, please.

Toby was still staring at me. Tavi handed me my drink. I put my purse down on the table.

I was now contrasting my two friends in their reaction to a woman. Toby couldn't cope. Tavi wanted to look after me. Or were they putting it on? I looked carefully for exchanged glances or exaggeration. There was nothing.

-   What's in the handbag?

asked Tavi. He was eyeing it and wanted to pick it up.

-   Have a look inside if you want to.

Tavi picked up the small bag and started rummaging. I described for Toby's benefit:

-   Make up, phone, money, credit cards. All in the name of Alex Harewood. There's a couple of tampax and a

      personal alarm. You should see my new phone, I got
      this really pink girly thing.

I took out the pink phone and waved it. Tavi asked:

- Do you think you'll need the personal alarm?
- I hope not. But you never know. I've not been out with you before.
- Yeah, I know. Every man is a potential rapist.

He fumbled inside the bag and managed to let several things slip out. He stared at the tampax amid the other items on the floor:

- Sorry.
- Don't worry I won't need it... Will I? ....I shouldn't... I don't know... What day is it?.. Oh!...You're not disappointed are you?

Tavi slowly shook his head in disbelief rather than reply.

- I think I might just cope. You sure do fit the part.

Their reactions gave me a bit of confidence. Still nothing could go wrong here. I was with friends.

Assembly Rooms
Maple Street
London

Source:	James Hecketty/Alex Harewood
Date:	Saturday 8th May
Time:	19.25
Personnel:	Toby Smithson, Tavi Mansur, James Hecketty, numerous others.

We arrived at the top of the steps to the Assembly Rooms and had our invitations checked against the guest list. We went in to a large modern hall. It was well appointed, expensively done, but a bit austere. There was a platform with a lectern and about twenty well laid tables filling the floor space. I ran the calculation. They were taking in about a half a million.

A man asked what we wanted to drink. The lads asked for champagne. I opted for a diet coke again.

I'd almost felt alright before I walked in. Now I just felt wrong. There were some very expensive looking dresses around. The one I was wearing began to feel scratchy and cheap. People seemed to want to look at me. I started to feel vulnerable and well out of my depth; worried that I might give something away or someone notice who I really was. I wanted to leave. Tavi saw the change in my mood:
-    Keep smiling. You look great.
-    I don't feel it.
He put his arm round my waist and pulled me to him,

intending to kiss me on the cheek. I resisted at first and he paused. Then I relaxed, I was supposed to be pretending to be his girlfriend, and his lips just touched my cheek. He was trying to make me feel more confident, but it just felt unusual. I smiled back at him because I knew he was trying to be supportive.

Everyone was invited to take their seats and we found our table. Each table had eight seats so we found ourselves sitting down with five strangers. Toby somehow managed to take charge of the introductions. I smiled my best smile at these people. There was a couple with their teenage son. He had just started engineering at university and said just about as much as I did; which was virtually nothing. Toby did his people thing and kept everyone laughing with amusing tales and jokes between courses.

People started moving round after the meal and a short speech by Sir Someone. Toby left us so he could search for Miss Khrushcheva. We hadn't seen her. I chatted to Tavi about his options for a flat he was thinking of buying. He'd found one that he liked that I had seen with him. We considered the location and the layout. Then we thought about the décor and furnishings. I'd been doing Alex's flat and so had a few ideas to offer that he seemed to appreciate.

Toby returned while we were still talking. He looked despondent after speaking to one of the organisers and delivered his disappointing news. Miss Khrushcheva wasn't there. Apparently she'd bought the tickets to support the cause and then just given apologies. The search for her would have to go on.

Toby was so upset that even he had stopped talking. We left earlier than most because there was no point in staying.

Chapter 6
London
July 2014

Knightsbridge
London

Source: James Hecketty/Alex Harewood
Date: Thursday 17th July
Time: 14.43
Present: Alex Harewood, Tavi Mansur

There was Tavi, just walking along. We hadn't arranged to meet.

- Hi Tavi
- Oh... Hi?...Hi!
- It's good to see you. Have you got much to do?
- No nothing really. Damn, you do this well.

I grinned at him as a thank you for the compliment and tried to flutter my eyelashes a little:

- My friend's busy and I was at a loose end for a while. It would be nice to spend the time with you.

I'd been out with Brian when I spotted my friend. I'd said Tavi was my date and it seemed like a perfect opportunity to practice some feminine charms. I got the result that I wanted when Tavi asked:

- Can I get you a coffee?

- Ooh yes. That's a good idea.

I caught his eye and smiled trying to look just a bit embarrassed and nervous. My hand was twirling the end of my hair. He seemed a bit stuck for what to say next so I helped out:

- Where shall we go?
- Any ideas?
- Montparnasse do great cakes. I like it there and it's only round the corner.

We ordered coffee and a large strawberry flan that we shared. We talked about all sorts of stuff that we hadn't ever before, mainly his family and sisters. I knew a little about them but now he said what they were doing and how excited his mum was at his eldest sister being pregnant. Though it didn't sound as though he liked her husband very much. I asked him more questions about his family; how he got on with his sisters and where he had grown up, did he ever see himself having children and what he had enjoyed doing as a child. I enjoyed hearing him talk and watching the expressions on his face. It was as though I was talking to him about himself rather than about the things around him. He seemed happy to talk and I realised there was a lot that I didn't know about him.

The waitress interrupted us:

- Excuse me!... I'm sorry... We're closed now.

I looked at the waitress and her colleague, then the otherwise empty café. Her colleague, a younger woman who had served us earlier, explained:

- We didn't want to stop you. We've finished clearing up and have to lock up now.

They were both looking at us in a dreamy way I didn't understand. We'd finished our drinks some time before and been talking together for most of the afternoon.

47

Angelic?

Neither of us had mentioned James.

We stood outside to say our goodbye as the waitresses
pulled the fabric blinds down inside the café. The younger
one said something and the older one looked at us, then
smiled and nodded in reply. Tavi was nice to me:
-    Alex?
-    Yes?
-    You're a great girl.
-    You're sweet.
I was hoping to get a parting kiss on the cheek. My luck
was in.

The Story of Sabina Bogomolova

Source:	Alisa and Ulyana
Date:	July
Present:	Dmitri Chazov and Tim Houghton, employees of Freeman and Jacob,
	Sabina Bogomolova, Alisa and Ulyana from Eastern Russia

The firm of Freemen and Jacob had their offices in a large five storey building called Azimuth House. It was on Clapham Road in Clapham and was not easily distinguished from the other similar buildings that lined that road. On the ground floor was a showroom where the firm displayed their legitimate products: chairs, tables, beds and office furniture. Visitors were able to purchase any of the products on display. It was also possible to order from the extensive catalogue by post or online.

Above the showroom was an office which catered for the online and postal orders. The salesmen there also sold in bulk to hotels, restaurants clubs and bars. Above the office were three floors of flats that were available for rent at reasonable rates.

Azimuth House had a large basement below the showroom. It was designed to store furniture. It still was used for that purpose, but only rarely. There was a large central area with a rough concrete floor, a small office with computers, a room that was once used for stripping paint and a washroom. There was also a larger room that had two tables and eight chairs that appeared to have originally been a small canteen where a few people could sit to eat. The easiest access to the basement was via the door at the rear of the building.

A truck stopped outside carrying three tired looking women from Eastern Russia. Sabina, Alisa and Ulyana. They had been travelling in the back of the small truck for seven days with only three short breaks. The only facilities available to them had been a blanket each and a plastic toilet in one corner.

The three girls heard the door roll open and the furniture in the truck pushed aside so they could get out. There were two men, neither looked friendly. The shorter one gave instructions:
- This way. Come inside. Be quiet.
One by one the women got down off the lorry helped by the taller man. They went inside the building and down some stairs into the basement. They were all tired and bleary eyed since they had not slept or eaten properly for days. They stood in the basement where they waited tired, hungry and dishevelled.
- Go through into the canteen. There is a toilet in the back. I'm sure some of you will want to use it. Come out back here once you are all done. There are some sandwiches and some bottled water to drink. Do help yourselves.
The canteen area was clearly visible from the main part of the basement because the double doors were held open. They went into the canteen and Sabina looked round then dashed into the loo. The sandwiches were good. The girls started to relax and took the time to tidy themselves up a bit.

Ulyana had the most beautiful long dark hair and she had been brushing it so that even after the long journey it now shone and bounced. She said something in Russian. She was reprimanded by the shorter tough looking man, Chazov:

-   English! We only speak English here.

She corrected herself:

-   Where are we?
-   You are in London.

Ulyana was pleased at this response:

-   We are?
-   Yes you are in London. You are not far from the hotel where you will start work. You will start there and depending on how well you do you will be moved on to other places where you will make more money.

Sabina was pleased too:

-   You see we'll be fine now. I told you not to worry. I said we'd be OK once we got here.

They were all pleased that the journey was over and felt that things should get better now.

Alisa came out of the washroom. She was the last to use it and had freshened herself at the basin, knowing that no one else was waiting desperately. She was wearing cream trousers and a dark blue jumper. They were never good clothes and they looked a mess now. She joined the others in the main central area. It was a dingy place that hadn't been decorated in years. Chazov sat on a plain wooden chair in front of what looked like an office. Part of the wall and the door was frosted glass so you could make out the shape of a desk. The door had the word "Shipping" painted neatly on to it. Houghton, the taller, friendlier looking man, stood near the door to the canteen.

Alisa was a bit more relaxed now and smiled prettily at Chazov who gave her an instruction:

-   Come over here.

Angelic?

She wandered over.
- You have a pretty smile. Take off your clothes.
- Why?
- So I can see the rest of you. Take them off.
- Why should I?
He took out his gun:
- Take them off.
and he casually pointed the gun at her. Ulyana let out a stifled scream. Sabina's mouth was open though she made no sound. Houghton had taken out his gun out and held it up so every girl could see it.
- Take them off.
repeated Chazov. Alisa looked at the other girls. They all stared back. Ulyana moved towards her but Houghton quickly waved his gun at her and shook his head.

Alisa looked horrified but did as she was told. She took off all her clothes and put them on the floor. She paused occasionally but the gun gestured for her to continue. Now she was naked and trembling. Chazov began to explain to them all:
- Nobody knows where you are. Nobody knows who you are. You have no money. You have entered this country illegally. You will do whatever we tell you to. If you don't there are a range of options. From now on you have only one way to stay alive. We also have some very helpful little details about where your families live. Cause trouble here and we cause more trouble there as well as here. Now is there anyone in any doubt about what you are really here for?
Chazov turned to Alisa who was trembling while standing naked in front of him. He asked her a question:
- So what are you?
She looked puzzled:
- What am I?

- Wrong answer.

He grabbed her by the hand and dragged her into the office. Noises came from inside and movements were visible through the frosted glass. There was no doubt about what was happening. She was being raped. Minutes later she came out in tears and wouldn't look anyone in the eye. She gathered her clothes and tried to put them on but couldn't see through her tears and anger. She got dressed but not with any thought. Her jumper was on backwards, her blouse was hanging out, and her trousers were undone. She went to join the other girls. She cried. Ulyana put an arm around her.

Chazov emerged from the office. He was unruffled. He pointed to Ulyana who was helping the raped Alisa tidy herself up. He asked the same question:

- So what are you?
- I'm a prostitute.
- Yes. We've hit the jackpot.

Sabina was asked the question but she only looked vacant and said nothing.

- Houghton, do you think you could explain to her?
- Yes, I think I can manage that.

Houghton grabbed her arm and dragged her towards the office. Sabina didn't resist much but started to scream and shake her head at the same time. In the office he hit her hard. She stopped screaming and then he raped her.

The door to the office opened and Houghton reappeared. Sabina appeared many seconds later. She was still wearing her hand-knitted red jumper but was naked below the waist. She walked into the middle of the large room. Shock, incomprehension, and a red mark by her eye where Houghton had thumped her were clear to see on her face. She started to scream again. She ran into the canteen and

Angelic?

then out again.

Ulyana grabbed her and held her and hugged her. Sabina was quiet for a moment and then sobbed. Then she pushed Ulyana away and said in Russian:
-    I'm going home now. My Dad will want me to help at home now.
She walked purposefully towards the exit door but was still only half dressed. The two men watched her with resigned expressions. Chazov readied his gun. Alisa and Ulyana could do nothing.

Sabina was hoping that she'd just be allowed to walk out of this. Hoping that this wasn't real. She stopped to pull back the double doors to the basement and looked back as Chazov aimed with his left hand. Bang! The bullet went through the tip of her nose and lodged in the back of her head. She fell back dying and spread-eagled on the floorboards. Sabina's body twitched on the floor as her damaged, disbelieving brain sent out a final set of disorganised nerve impulses.

They say that when you die you first lose your sense of touch, then your sight and smell and taste. Hearing is the last thing to go. Sabina may have heard what Houghton said as she died:
-    Stupid bloody cow. What fucking use is she now?

Team Sport Karting Centre London

Source: James Hecketty/Alex Harewood
Date: Sunday 20th July
Time: 14.05
Personnel: Toby Smithson, Tavi Mansur, James Hecketty.

Toby was putting on his race suit and sounding very fired up and optimistic but not because of the kart race we were just about to compete in.

- She will be there. This is the one. I'm going to get to see her. The summer party at the Mornington Club. The Mornington is the most exclusive of the London Clubs. It's massive money to be a member. Every year for the last thousand years they've put on a do where anyone who is anybody has to be there. She'll be there along with cabinet ministers, billionaires, film stars and every super model who ever refused to get out of bed for less than a million quid. Everyone who anyone else has ever heard about and not met. The entire stock of European nobility and probably God himself. They will all be there. And on this occasion and for one time only: the three of us.

We grabbed our helmets and went out into the briefing room to hear the usual stuff about minimum number of changeovers, breaking and getting flagged. Having heard the informational bit we went to the machine we'd been allocated. Toby got in and asked a question before putting his lid on and buzzing off to do his practice laps in the electric kart:

- The Mornington Club is seriously high-flown shit. It's real top end stuff. They'll give us security scans and all sorts. Does Alex have a secure ID? Will she pass a security check?

Toby had no real idea what we had already done, what was involved or how it was done. He just knew we were damn good at it. We didn't hear about anyone else who had our access levels or our fluency at changing all this stuff. As long as you changed not too much no one was likely to notice. Then if you are good at that kind of thing it's best to keep quiet about it. At least he knew it was important.

Toby returned from his practice laps and Tavi got into the driving seat of the kart while answering Toby's question:

- Alex is pretty much done already. She was good from the start. She'll pass.

We heard the revs go up and the clutch engage. Tavi zipped off for his practice laps and I took my turn when he came back in.

We concentrated on the race for the rest of the hour. Toby was the fastest driver in a real car. Typical rich kid. But in a cart his large frame made his acceleration slow. I was the lightest by a margin but the poorest driver. Our lap times were surprisingly similar. That was an advantage in a team race like this. We were in third and closing in on second when the race finished. We'd lost some time early on when Tavi had spun on a corner. A drop of oil he reckoned later. We let him pretend that might be true.

Toby went up to collect the tiny trophy for third. SafeNet had sponsored the race so he made a little speech to thank the organisers for making it such a great event and thanked everyone for coming along. He hoped they'd all had had a good time.

Later, back at Toby's flat, we were in his sitting room drinking beer. Tavi was curious:
- How do you feel about being Alex?
- It's interesting. You see people differently.
Toby glanced at Tavi and then asked me:
- Don't you mind people seeing you as a woman?
- You know I do.
Tavi:
- Ok but could you get to like it?
- Sod off! I feel very vulnerable and awkward. I feel I'm being looked at all the time and someone is going to see through me at any moment.
There was a look of disgust on Toby's face:
- I know I would fucking hate it.
Tavi knew what that was about:
- That makes sense because you don't get women at all. To you they're just pretty things that turn you on. Jim sees them as functional humans with a different but equally valid set of motivations and priorities.
Toby:
- I guess you're right. I don't get how anyone can like being a woman, even a clever beautiful woman. I'd rather be a complete moron with a dick. That's easy enough because it's close to how I feel most of the bleeding time around you two geeks anyway.
He sipped his beer then complained:
- How did this conversation get to be about me? I'm the normal one here. Jim, you're the one who's crossed the boundary. What's your take?
- With you guys it feels right to be a bloke. When I dress as Alex then it's best to be feminine. I never want to be anywhere in the middle.
Tavi looked thoughtful:
- So you're you for other people? Isn't there a you that

you want to be?

None of this was making me feel good. I hated thinking and talking about myself. I came to a conclusion:

- I just want to feel safe and fit in... I feel alright as James.... Let's just leave it can we?

Toby wasn't happy any more either. He put his beer down on the table as he said:

- OK. The deals off Jim. I don't want to hold you to it anymore. This isn't fun. It's just weird. Do the Mornington party with us, we can't change the tickets now, and then stop if you want to.

Tavi sounded surprised and wasn't happy with Toby. Their argument got to a much higher temperature than our usual knockabout discussions. Tavi was almost shouting:

- When we made up the challenge there was a real reason wasn't there? You're just being bloody selfish.

Toby wasn't very calm either:

- Selfish? I just don't want Jim to do something he doesn't want to do. You're only worried about losing your girlfriend.
- Sod you. That's not fair. Wasn't there a point to the challenge? To let Jim explore dangerous territory and see if it's habitable?
- Look. Jim makes a great girl. Big deal! We know he's well qualified. But if he's not comfortable with it I don't want to make him do it.

I hated seeing my friends argue like this. Particularly as it had to do with me. I got up and went into the kitchen. They both noticed. I heard Toby say in a more thoughtful tone and quietly; I'm not sure I was supposed to hear :

- It's up to him. You know Jim's done it enough already.

Tavi had calmed down too:

- I can't argue with that. I just thought we were trying to move things on.

The conclusion of all this was they decided I didn't have to do the challenge any more. I didn't have to be Alex any longer after the Mornington Party, unless I wanted to. It didn't matter. Nothing we decided then was going to matter after that.

Toby's Flat
London

Source:	James Hecketty/Alex Harewood
Date:	Saturday 30th August 2014
Time:	15:44
Location:	Knightsbridge London

Two whole days I spent finding a dress to wear. The things I liked most seemed to be the most expensive ones and my budget kept escalating. I tried on lots of different stuff and sent selfies to Jenny for approval. It was the longest continuous period of time I'd spent as Alex. Eventually I found one that seemed to work for me and Jenny agreed. I had to get some shoes to match as well, then a small bag and some accessories. My hair had grown out a bit more and I had it done properly, expensively.

The plan was the same as for the charity party. Tavi called round for me and then we went to Toby's. He was far more welcoming than the first time he met Alex. I wasn't sure if that was because he was more accepting of me as Alex or because he'd already tidied his kitchen.

We had plenty of time to spare. Tavi had had done some research on the Khrushchev family. They were rich. Bonkers rich. Billions upon billions of wealth. Her family owned the TPO Oil Company that was run by her elder brother Ivan. None of that worried Toby:

- She's still a girl. I'm still a guy. Normal things can still happen.

Tavi:
- You sound a bit nervous. That's a better start than your usual nonchalance. Perhaps you'll stay with her a bit longer than it takes to get her into bed.

Toby was offended:
- Do you two really think I'm so shallow?

Tavi was blunt:
- Yes.

As I was Alex I tried the less abrupt, more feminine, way of saying yes:
- I'm not sure it's how you feel but you do sound that way sometimes.

Toby looked at me, he'd not had a conversation with Alex before:
- Ok, well... I'll try to be more thoughtful.

I offered a little advice:
- You need to try to get her to say what she likes and enjoys. You need to listen to her and respond to what she says positively, sound interested and get her to say more.
- Ok I have to get her to talk and pretend I'm interested.
- That's good, but, well, it's far better if you really are interested in her and you really do value what she says. She'll notice and like you for it.

He was looking at me oddly still, but was listening too:
- I'll try that. Shouldn't be too hard because I want to find out more about her. And I need her to like me.

Tavi was surprised:
- Jesus, you do want more from this girl; you already care about what she thinks. You're even nervous about meeting her. That's how it should be. She must be quite something.
- Too right she's something! If you'd seen her you'd know.

Angelic?

Tavi couldn't let that go:

- She was beautiful, I get that. She just moves her eyes and you go wow! You get that feeling. Every detail seems so right. You want her to want to touch you and respond to you. It's one of the strongest feelings you can have. But it's really all about sex.
- You see you're just intellectualising. Why make it less than it is? I see Katya and my whole being is aroused. You see your girl and maybe some corner of your brain has an interesting idea.

Tavi didn't know what to say to that, he looked quite off balance. He glanced at me before replying. I thought because he was unsure what words to use in front of a woman. They both used gentler language than James was used to hearing. Tavi asked:

- What form does that arousal take then? You just want to make love to her and that's it?
- Of course I want to make her feel like a woman! I want to share all life's good things with her. I want to be with her, care for her, wake up with her, find out what she likes and help her get what she likes. I feel she can make the whole of my world better. Multiply the good and divide the bad. I don't want her ever to doubt herself and make sure she knows that the world is a far better place with her in it.

Tavi looked a bit surprised, shocked. It made me think I was missing something. But we were both impressed enough with what Toby had said.

He'd assumed a lot about Katya through just seeing her walk into a shop. He saw a lot of women and should be a good judge. I had no idea then that I would soon meet Katya and then trust my life to his assessment.

Mornington Club
London

Source:	James Hecketty/Alex Harewood
Date:	Saturday 30th August
Time:	18.56
Personnel:	Alex Harewood, Tavi Mansur, Toby Smithson, Katya Khrushcheva, Eleanor and Hannah Straminsky, Josephine, numerous others.

As our car came round the corner we spotted the entrance. We saw two young men get out of a Ferrari and casually give their keys to a parking attendant. They went up the stairs into the Mornington Club exuding confidence and wealth. Perfect smiles and immaculate dinner jackets. Women climbed the stairs raising their gowns slightly to climb the steps revealing jewel encrusted shoes that matched the glitzy sparkly affairs around their necks and wrists. One of the staff opened the door of a Rolls Royce and an impossibly elegant girl stepped out followed by a Hollywood star. The car in front was flying the French flag. I recognised the profile of the Vice President through the back window. We hadn't even arrived and we were already so far out of our depth. Tavi was asking:

- Just how did you get these tickets, Toby?

Toby was looking defensive:

- You can just pay for a ticket. They are for sale.
- How much Toby, how much?
- A lot. That's all. A lot. You only live once.

I asked:

Angelic?

- Ten thousand?
- Oh no, not that much.

I knew Toby well enough to know that reply meant only exactly what it said:

- More then.

Our car was waved forward and we got out of the Limo before the exact amount was admitted by Toby. We went up the steps and I held my dress not too high. My shoes weren't so wonderful as the other ones that had been on show. We were trying to look as confident and relaxed as everyone else we had seen. Toby said something like:

- Rhubar unn ruubar!

and made a gesture that signalled he had just made a joke. Tavi and I both pretended to laugh. This was fun anyway. So we relaxed a bit and laughed for real.

We went in to a large hall, it was seriously splendid and busy, with the sounds of expectation and excitement echoing around it. A massive chandelier almost the size of a small house was suspended over the centre of the room. Smaller ones only the size of cars were near the corners. Three huge porticoed doors were along one wall and were matched by the doors at either end of the room. The ceiling was an impressive piece of late 18th century ornate plasterwork.

People were greeting each other and making their way into the main party in other rooms. A smartly dressed tidy looking girl asked what we wanted to drink. No sooner had we given our request than a young man carrying a tray with our drinks on appeared and invited us to follow him.

All parties are pretty much the same. Lots of people in one place. This one was no different. Here, though, everyone looked so expensive. Some of the people looked familiar because I'd seem them on TV. In one pass I picked up a newsreader, a cabinet minister and an actress.

The waiter started telling us that all the main rooms were open that evening. Some rooms had their own atmosphere and purpose. There was a room to talk, a room to dance, a virtual reality room and so on. He handed us our drinks and wished us a good evening after reminding us of the club rule: to abide by the rules. It had been the in joke here for two hundred and fifty years. There were no rules, but you had to behave as though there were.

Toby left us and started looking round for his quarry. The fabulous Miss Khrushcheva.

This was the place to be. If you were exceptionally wealthy or talented or powerful or famous then this was the place to come to feel ordinary. Relationships between people in any of the previous categories would be forged here, deals would be done, romances initiated or pursued. I didn't really have the qualifications to be here. My dress was OK, though every other woman seemed to be wearing exclusive clothes worth thousands. I felt like a fraud.

Tavi noticed the change in my mood:
- Keep smiling. You're here. You look great. Try to relax. You'll be fine. We're going to have a good time.
He took my hand and put my arm around his arm and we started to talk about what we saw as we wandered round surveying the luxurious environment and the tailored, coutured and bejewelled guests. We talked about people and how they behaved. We made assumptions about the character of the people around us just using their clothes, gestures and appearance as clues. We invented names and histories for them and laughed as we embellished these fantasies with extra fanciful details. I enjoyed seeing those other dimensions in Tavi again, the layer of human connections, the family Tavi, possibly the Tavi that his

Angelic?

Mother saw; not the Tavi that his mates saw.

We found our way to the virtual reality room and donned the headsets, entered the sensory zone and became nearly weightless in a fantasy environment where we could effortlessly leap a hundred yards, board rocket ships to orbit the Earth or construct entire landscapes and then walk through them. Tavi had chosen to look very much as he looked in real life. I was an improbably leggy blonde. Reality eventually intervened.

The ladies loos were very plush. A sofa and armchairs, an attendant constantly keeping things clean, tall ceilings, marble counter and basins and enormous mirrors. As I left the cubicle I noticed a girl wash her hands then leave. She was beautiful, immaculately dressed, every stitch and everything just perfect. Miss Yekaterinya Khrushcheva. I had to follow.

I found myself in a distant part of the building. Still crowded, still full of people. All talking. I lost her in the throng. I kept looking round and listening in to conversations for a clue. She was gone.

I started to make my way back but noticed a middle-aged woman who was looking in my direction. Shorter than me she wore a beautiful elegant dress that flowed around her neat and feminine figure. She had dark hair and subtle makeup. I looked away. Had she really been looking at me? I looked back while she was looking at someone else. She nodded her head slightly at the someone else, then looked back at me and smiled, it was a warm and friendly smile. She started to walk towards me. She kept looking at me. I smiled back. What was this all about?
-     Hello, I'm Hannah Straminsky
I wondered if I was supposed to know who that was. She held out a hand. I shook it.

- Hello. I'm Alex Harewood.
- I hope you don't mind me introducing myself. I know it's very forward of me. You were looking a bit lost.

I tried to keep my answer vague:

- Yes I was. I thought I saw someone I knew, but I've lost her now. It doesn't matter though. I'm not even certain it was her.
- You know you look so much like my daughter. Would you like to come and meet her?
- OK. That's a nice idea. I'd be glad to.
- Just over here.

We went into a quiet room with soft chairs and a low ceiling. There was a waitress going round with drinks and taking orders. It was a good place to talk. I saw a young woman about my height and weight stand up as we moved towards her. She had long hair like mine and a similar dress. We grinned at each other spotting that we were alike and liking her meant liking myself and realising the same things at the same time. I offered a hand and we shook hands. Very English I thought. Her mother saw what was happening and let us get on without saying anything. I liked the girl's smile and the glint in her eye. She was looking at me in much the same way. It was a bit like seeing yourself in a mirror. And we both saw that too. I offered a hug. It just seemed the right thing. She hugged me back. We introduced ourselves:

- Alex.
- Eleanor.

We started to talk. It was like the conversations with Jenny, just free open space. No direction. Just sharing life. We talked about our histories and why we were there. Her family had some business dealings with a Russian firm, but they were always there anyway. She had been to school in Brighton and University at Oxford. She mainly lived in

Angelic?

Moscow, or somewhere near it. She was jealous of me for living in London.

I explained that I was there with two man friends, one of whom had had set himself the challenge of meeting a very beautiful girl he'd seen only once. She was amused by this and impressed that we had got onto the guest list for the party just to chase after this girl.

- Who is this gorgeous siren? I may know her.
- We found her name. She's called Yekaterinya Khrushcheva.
- Yekaterinya Khrushcheva? Katya? I do know her! She is around somewhere. I chatted to her earlier. Your friend is quite taken with her is he? She can be rather dazzling.
- I heard Toby got a crush on her after seeing her for a few seconds. He's a real nice guy and doesn't have much luck with finding a girl he seriously likes. He's good looking and good with people.
- So you like him? You sound like you might be a bit jealous.
- I do like him... but not like that. I mean he's not at all my sort of bloke. I came with Tavi.
- So he's your sort of bloke?
- Well... I guess he is. He's thoughtful and kind. He looks after me a bit, makes sure I'm all right.

She looked like she wanted to know lots more:
- So....
- We've only been out twice. This is the second time. I ought to get back to him.

Her Mother was looking at us. She seemed to be following along, but not taking part in the conversation. I saw Eleanor look at her mother in an affectionate way. That was about the same time a large knot hit my stomach. I'd just spent 30 minutes without once thinking about my usual gender. In that time I'd made a new friend. My feminine character had made another small, but vital, alteration to the fabric of reality.

A young woman approached us and was introduced to me as Josephine, an old friend of Eleanor's. She came along with her boyfriend. He didn't say much and I didn't get his name either. Josephine came over as a bit too self-confident and talked incessantly. My conversation with Eleanor had to stop. I needed to find Tavi and Toby. I excused myself and got a that's OK glance from Eleanor. Just before I got to the door she caught up with me:

- Alex?... Could we meet up some time? I mean it would be so good to see you again. If that's alright? I'm in London for a few days.
- You're right. it would be nice. I'd like that, perhaps have lunch somewhere. I'm sorry I didn't suggest it myself.

She took my girly phone and then dialled her number. We waited until her phone responded. I hugged her goodbye and left her behind adding me to her contacts.

It didn't take very long to find Tavi but we couldn't find Toby at all. He wasn't answering his phone. We took that to be a good thing. It wasn't.

I didn't know it then but that evening the world had been pushed onto a very different path by what should have been a simple everyday event. Something that should have been beautiful had been made ugly. That ugliness was about to invade my life. I would find out it had already hit Toby full on and then Tavi would get the very worst of it.

It would take me a long time to find out and understand all that happened that evening at the party. It also took me a long time to find out what I needed to know about Katya

Angelic?

Khrushcheva. It took even longer to find out what I should already have known about my friend Tavi.

Chapter 7
London
August 2014

Tavi's Flat
London

Source:	James Hecketty/Alex Harewood
Date:	Sunday 31st August
Time:	12.17 am
Present:	Tavi Mansur, Alex Harewood

It wasn't late when we got the taxi to take us home from the party. Just after 12. We were expecting to get a success message from Toby and I hung around at Tavi's to celebrate. By the time we knew it wasn't going to happen we were both dozing off so I crashed at Tavi's. Planning to return home first thing in the morning. I had crashed at Tavi's place many times before. I didn't think about the implications of a woman staying overnight with a man.

Sometime very early we got a phone call. There was a woman who explained she was at Chelsea and Westminster Hospital and a few hours ago Tobias Smithson had been brought in. They had been looking for relatives but found that Tavi was listed as next of kin. She wouldn't say how he was. Just that Tavi should come in.

Angelic?

I wanted to go in too. It would take some time to get back to my flat, change back into being James and then go to the hospital. Or I could put a jumper over my dress and go as Alex. That got me to the hospital in minutes. I went as Alex.

Chelsea and Westminster Hospital London

Source:	James Hecketty/Alex Harewood
Date:	Sunday 31st August
Time:	07.23
Present:	Tavi Mansur, Alex Harewood, Toby Smithson (unconscious), policemen and nurses.

We went to reception and said we were there to visit Toby Smithson. Ward 10. A finger was pointed and we followed it and then the signs.

The ward was a collection of individual rooms. I spotted Toby's room. It was the one with the police officer outside. I went in that direction.
- Who were you hoping to see, please?
A woman, not in a nurse's uniform, had appeared.
- Toby Smithson. We're friends of his.
- Would you come this way please?
Tavi and I were directed to separate rooms. They were patient's rooms with a bed and all the normal hospital paraphernalia. I sat down as invited. A man came in and sat on the other side of the bed.
- We'd like to ask you some questions, I know you're concerned about your friend, but would you mind?
- May I ask who you are and see your ID first?
- Detective Sergeant John Woodrow
He passed me an ID card. He asked some questions about the party. There didn't seem anything useful. We hadn't seen Toby all night. I said what had happened to me and

who I had met. I didn't say anything about James. There didn't seem any point.

Tavi and I just stood staring at this body in a bed. There was nothing to do. His head was swathed in bandages. What we could see of his face was puffy and so swollen his eyes appeared shut. Thin lines in a mass of swollen flesh. A nurse reeled off a list of injuries: broken ribs, nose, left eye socket, cheek, jaw, skull, three ribs, punctured lung, ruptured spleen, broken right wrist, bruised left hand and severe bruising over most of his body. All the signs were that he had been kicked repeatedly and with significant force while on the ground. The injuries to his hand and wrist were probably defensive where he had tried to fend off his attacker's blows to his groin where he had severe bruising and some damage. Whether this would be permanent was too soon to say.

We stared at him in silence; there was nothing to say or do. Was he going to recover? What damage there was to his brain could not yet be properly assessed.

I kissed my fingers and touched his cheek. There was no response. I prayed that he would make a full recovery and stepped back from his bed.

We talked as we walked back to Tavi's flat. We were both very shocked and walking seemed to help. He asked:
- What did you say to the police?
- I only said what happened to Alex. There was nothing else to say.
- I told them we slept together.
- Oh... well... oh. ..OK.. Why?
- It felt wrong to say anything else.
I didn't mind. It surprised me that I didn't mind. I put my arm around his waist and he put his arm around my shoulders. It was a small comfort. I would look back on this

moment. Later, when things got even more horrific, the world would see us as lovers and looking at us, just then, that morning, you might have thought we were.

Tavi was wondering about Toby and why and how it had happened. We couldn't think of a reason. The Mornington Club was a sprawling old building with lots of small service entrances and back doors. Toby hadn't been found particularly near any of them. The only thing we could reasonably conclude was that it had taken more than one person. Toby's a big guy.

Just before we got back, as we turned into Wildmore Street, I told Tavi the truth about how we had first seen Katya and what she had said. I had encouraged Toby to chase after her when perhaps I shouldn't have. It felt like I was responsible. Tavi was reassuring:
-    Don't feel that. What you did in no way adds up to what happened.
They were words I would often think of later.

We agreed to do some research. We'd find out what we could about Katya Khrushcheva and her family. Not just the publicly available stuff. We agreed to dig deeper and use our hacking skills to find out more. We didn't know what we might find, or what trouble it would cause.

Angelic?

Toby's Flat

Source:	James Hecketty
Date:	Monday 1st September
Time:	10.47
Personnel:	James Hecketty, Tavi Mansur

There was no change at the hospital although the bruising on Toby appeared worse because it had gone blue and black. He was still unconscious.

Tavi had the key and let us both in to Toby's. We started to clear the place up and empty the fridge before it all went too stale. We wanted to do something to help. This was something. Tavi looked a bit uncomfortable then started a conversation that I didn't want to have:
- I know you don't like talking about yourself but can I ask you about Alex?
- If you must.
- Well... Do you like being her?
- That's all done now.
He looked surprised:
- Why?
- Why? It was you and Toby that said I should stop.
- OK, but we said you should stop if you wanted to. You see one of the reasons that I didn't let on to the police about Alex is that it would have felt like I was letting her down. I like her. I was proud to be with her. She's a good-looking girl with brains. She seems a very different person to James... You don't mind if I talk about her as though she's not here? ... This is a frigging

weird situation.

He was trying to be nice. He was trying to be helpful. We went round putting things where we thought they should go.

- Would you rather I was Alex?
- It's not about me. I want there to be a you that you want to be.
- You don't just want to get laid again then?

Now he looked exasperated:

- Piss off. I am trying to be serious.
- Sorry, sorry... You know there were times when I forgot about being James. It felt alright.
- That's what I see. Toby saw it too. You're so good as Alex. You were stunning at the party. Shit mate, you know we all worked hard to make her as real as possible. Don't give up on her too soon.

I knew what he was saying and I knew why he was saying it, or I thought I did.

- OK, thanks. I'll try.

Then we tried to get back to thinking about Toby's housekeeping and not thinking about Toby or me.

He set the dishwasher going and then we moved on into the sitting room. Picking up car magazines and newspapers. Stowing remote controls in drawers and plumping cushions. I got the vacuum cleaner out.

We hadn't talked much about what had happened at the party before, we'd talked about what had happened to Toby. I found myself wondering about meeting Eleanor and mentioned it to Tavi:

- Alex met a girl at the party.
- Oh yes... This could become complicated.
- A girl called Eleanor. Alex made friends with her. She wants to meet for lunch.

Angelic?

I plugged in the vacuum cleaner and started on the living room carpet. Tavi looked up from wiping down the coffee table when I unplugged to move on:

- So you met this girl as a woman and now you're going out with her as a man? Do you think you'll get laid?

He was grinning at me, so I knew he was joking. I over-reacted a bit anyway:

- What? No. Don't be ridiculous. She's a girlfriend of a girl. I met her as a girl. It's a girl - girl relationship. That's what I'm saying. I thought it was what you were saying. I liked talking to her. We hit it off.

I went through into the kitchen to put the kettle on and got a couple of mugs down. I heard him through the open door:

- OK so who is this new friend of Alex's?
- She's Eleanor ... something Russian sounding ... Straminsky. She's nice

He was leaning on the kitchen doorjamb and looked a bit surprised. I was spooning the coffee into the mugs.

- And how did Alex meet her?
- Her mum introduced them. She's called Hannah.

He stood upright:

- Shit!

I stopped to look at him:

- What?

He started to ask question after question about how I'd met Eleanor. He wanted to know every detail.

- This is like being with the police again.
- Yeah, sorry. Just go with me can you?

The kettle had boiled and I started pouring water into the mugs. He carried on extracting information and he got to hear every detail I could remember. I asked:

- What's the big deal? She's just a woman.
- Oh Jesus. OK. I found out about the Straminskys while

looking up about Katya.

He explained that Hannah Straminsky was worth several billion dollars and was married to a man who was also worth several billions. She was a regular visitor at Downing Street where she advised the PM and sat on cabinet committees.

- She's not just a woman. Her daughter is not *just* a young woman.

I passed the black coffee to him. He went to sip it but it was still too hot while I asked:

- So is all that important? I mean they're still just people.
- We have friends and allegiances; people who might just say a few white lies, do something for us, make a couple of exaggerations to help us out. That much money creates possibilities that didn't previously exist. Any number of people willing to say or do anything.
- Yeah OK. Point taken. What that amount of money can do is unimaginable.
- It's not just what you do, it's what other people around you do.
- So you think Alex meeting Eleanor has to do with Toby getting attacked?
- Hell, I don't know. Probably not. But having a friend like that won't do any harm.

We both sipped at our coffee. I said:

- Eleanor just seemed ordinary though. She didn't seem anything special. Just a bit lonely. Someone looking for a friend. Alex didn't actually arrange to meet her again, though she did ask if they could have lunch together some time.

As I said it I realised how much I was looking forward to meeting her again.

Tavi put his mug down on the kitchen table. I put mine

Angelic?

down next to his and said:
- I'll be at the office tomorrow. Are you there on Wednesday?
- Yeah.
- I'll see if Alex can do lunch with Eleanor on Wednesday and afterwards come to see you at the office.
- Great, that's great.

He grinned then quickly turned away and got back to cleaning the sitting room. I sent a text to Eleanor and started vacuuming the hall.

Monroe's Café
King's Road
Chelsea
London

Source:	James Hecketty/Alex Harewood
Date:	Wednesday 3rd September
Time:	12.20
Present:	Alex Harewood, Eleanor Straminsky

Eleanor was sitting at an outside table, enjoying the warm weather but avoiding the bright sunshine by sitting under one of the café's enormous parasols. She got up from her table and gave me a warm hug in greeting. There was that moment of amusement again as we once more found ourselves in similar clothes, except hers were expensive and mine were cheap. I got the feeling she was hungry:
- Shall we order lunch?
- Yes, let's.
- How have you been?
I explained about Toby and the police. She said
- Oh, that's bad. I'm sorry.
at appropriate moments and held my arm.
- How's Tavi?
- Well we did spend a night together. But only because I couldn't get home.
She raised her eyebrows:
- Oh yes?
- No, we didn't. But he somehow told the police we did.

Angelic?

-   I guess he would like to.

I didn't think that very likely but I couldn't contradict her too directly:

-   Perhaps... I don't know... It feels kind of like he's looking after me. I mean he seems to care. When we're out together he reads what I'm feeling, responds to me and tries to make me feel comfortable.
-   Careful. It sounds now like you're talking yourself into seriously liking him. You've already convinced me that he's a really good guy.

We started to chat more generally. Just that sharing thing. I enjoyed it. I liked being with her. She talked with intelligence and had something good to say about everyone. The meal arrived and we carried on talking between mouthfuls. She also had something to ask me:

-   My family have a party every year. Sometimes parties are for business. This one is for us. It would be lovely if you were able to come. It will be at our Moscow house, most people find it easier to get there. You could come for the party but stay a few days. You could meet my family. If you like you can meet Katya and have a bit of a holiday as well. Does that sound like a good plan?
-   That's really kind, thank you. It does sound like a good plan and yes I'd be thrilled to come.

She looked pleased. Less pleased as I enquired:

-   But can I just ask. There is something I need to say. I looked, actually it was Tavi not me, on the internet. Your family? All that money! I'm not sure that I'd know how to fit in.

I'd hoped for some reassurance. What I got was nearer panic:

-   No, no, please don't. I hate the rich thing. We met. We were friends without all the money. Please, you're so great to be with. The money is an obstacle. It's spoiled loads of friends. People from college. I know. I know it makes things hard. Please say you'll come. Don't give up yet. Please try.

She was almost in tears. People had noticed the change in tone and were looking round. It was odd that her wealth made her the more vulnerable. I put my hand on her arm to reassure her:

- Yes. Of course I will try. You're my friend too! I never even thought of not coming.
- Thanks!

She looked so relieved. I went on:

- But I want to pay my own way. The things I get are valuable to me. They cost me the time to earn the money and the time to think about buying them. I don't want the things around me to lose that value.
- Okaayy... Mum said something a bit like that. She said she was happiest in work when she was still trying to make it. She put in the effort and saw the reward. It was all too easy now, though she still works as hard and earns far more money, there's no connection, it's not as satisfying. Um... that's not quite the same thing is it?
- Your Mum is a thoughtful lady.
- She is. I've talked to her a lot lately. Since I finished university. She's given me a bit more time. She always seemed so busy when I was younger. Now she's a good friend.
- What happened?

She looked at me a bit surprised, but more inquisitive:

- How do you do that?
- Do what?
- You sort of hear things I haven't said. You work things out so quickly.
- Well you said that something had happened. Didn't

you? ... To do with money?
- You see! I don't even have to say anything. I'll just sit here and let you work it all out.
- You do the same thing. You worked things out about Tavi without me saying anything.
- I don't think I'm quite in your league. It's fine. It's clever of you. I had a bad time recently. People from college who were friends stopped being friends. Or stopped being friends in the same way. It would be hard enough anyway with everyone getting jobs and moving to different parts of the world. The money didn't help.

There was a lot more detail here that Eleanor wasn't saying. I was ready to hear it when she was ready to say it. For the moment I just tried to say that I understood:
- I guess when you meet people they want to get to know you. But is that because they like you or want a chance of your money? It must be the same if you're a film star or something. Everybody wants to know you just to say they do. Just to show off about knowing this famous person. It makes it hard to start a relationship of equals.
- Yes that's about it. That's how it feels. Mum's more hard-nosed than me. She kind of controls people in a relationship. Gives people boundaries. When she meets someone she's all charm and friendly. But she's thinking what they can do for her. Like you'll help me achieve this goal and this one. If they can't help she just loses contact. Politely, not so they notice or feel bad. Dad's the same. It's part of their success. I'm not like that. I don't want to manipulate people all the time. Mum says that when I have children they'll misbehave horribly all the time. Great! I'd rather that than have them sit in straight rows and only speak when spoken to. What about you? Do you want to

have kids?

- In time. I like the idea of being a mum. Sleepless nights, sore nipples, dirty nappies and permanent worry. Just what every girl dreams of.

She laughed:

- I know all that but I still want it.
- Yes! Aren't we funny?

We talked about childbirth, losing your figure after childbirth, putting on weight, dieting, eating, things we liked to eat, chocolate, coffee, making coffee and then we ordered coffee.

- Don't you have any security? I mean you're sitting here on your own. Katya has a bodyguard. You don't seem to have anyone.
- I do have security. They're around. I'll show you.

She took out her phone and pressed an icon. Seconds later a young man who appeared to have just been walking by listening to his iPhone came to our table and asked Eleanor:

- Is everything OK, Miss? We're all clear.
- Yes fine thanks. My friend was just getting worried.
- Ok then.

He walked away and scratched his shoulder then became invisible again.

- There's a whole team watching constantly. They're always around. I don't have to think about them at all. But they are always there.
- What if something happens?
- It did once. I just thought it was a little scuffle on the street. Later I was told it was a well-planned kidnap attempt. They check every possible thing they can. Every car going past here will have its plate read. Face recognition software will look at every person and compared to known threats. Any person who

approaches me will be checked without them ever
knowing. If it's not possible then one of the team will
attend closely.
- Every person?
- As far as possible.
- So was I checked before I talked to you?
- Yeah. I guess. Looks like you passed! You're not a
threat!

She laughed. I remembered Hannah looking at someone
before speaking to me at the party. It seemed odd at the
time. She had been checking me with her security people.
What had they found? What had they found since then?
Eleanor went on:
- If there is something that worries me I can check its OK.
I'll see someone give an all clear gesture. I can check an
app on my phone too. There are emergency signals it
can make. You know dramatic stuff like get down or
run. It has a link to Mum's security too and Dad's. They
have a link to mine. I know where they are and that
they are OK all the time. They do the same for me of
course. I can use it to send messages too.
- That is awesome. That's just extraordinary.

Then I remembered Mum and Dad were just about the
richest people in the world. They could afford anything.
She saw what I was thinking:
- You're thinking it must cost a fortune. I suppose it
does. Millions? I don't see the bills. But being safe is
the most important thing.
- So why does Katya have a bodyguard? Because it's
cheaper?
- I don't know. It might be money. Maybe she feels safer
with someone close. You'll have to ask her. She's been
invited to the party. I'm not sure she'll be there though.
She hasn't replied and doesn't have a great reputation

for reliability. I ask her every year. She's been about twice in the last ten years.

- You've known her since you were young then?
- Yeah. I think I've always known her. I'll text her, say you want to meet her and if she can't make the party could we see her another time. OK?

I nodded enthusiastically and her thumbs went to work on her phone. While she did that I texted Tavi to say I was going to see him soon. His reply came back very quickly and I noticed again that he was encouraging me to be Alex:

Looking forward to seeing you soon Alex. T x

No reply came from Katya before I had to leave.

I got a cab back to the SafeNet Office. We tried to make sure there was someone there in the afternoons. We'd look through the logs and feedback on our software and see if there were any updates or revisions needed or any new advice for the help desk.

Tavi wasn't there. I briefly looked round. He still wasn't there. I rang his mobile and it went to answerphone. He should have been there. But he wasn't.

Back in the street I got a Taxi to his flat and knocked. No answer. Where could he be? I went back to Alex' flat. I kept hoping he would turn up. I rang a few more times. Then I changed back to being James, slipped out the back way from Alex' flat and went home.

James' Flat
Sunbury Lane
Battersea
London

Source:	James Hecketty/Alex Harewood
Date:	Wednesday 3rd September
Time:	17.24
Present	James Hecketty, Martin Peters, Tim Houghton

There was a knock on the door. I was expecting Tavi. I was hoping to see him and hear his explanation of where he had been, along with his profuse apologies for Alex. It wasn't Tavi, but two men. Police I thought. They showed me some ID which said they were police officers. There was a middle-aged guy who had a pleasant, friendly looking face. The other fellow seemed, younger, taller, but I didn't get a chance to look at him.

- It's about Mr Smithson, Sir.

That's good. I thought they may have some news about Toby. I was wrong.

The door was open only a little way when these two men pushed against it and burst through. What was this?

The one behind had a gun with a silencer the other had a phone held up in his hand that I was clearly supposed to be looking at. It was playing a video clip. The image was shocking. Tavi, just his shoulders and head, lying on a concrete floor. He had some horrible bruises. Then he moved out of frame. He'd just been kicked. You could hear him scream. Then the phone moved so that he came back into frame. I looked at the progress bar. There were two hours and thirty seven minutes of this. I was feeling ill but I kept on staring and backing away at the same time.

The two men were laughing. I watched Tavi being kicked again and again. I saw the pain on his face and felt the torment in his screams.

- What is this? What happened? Who are you?
- Just so you know that we're not joking. He didn't tell us what we wanted to know. So now we're going to ask you.
- I don't know anything.

He was grinning:

- We're just trying to save you some time and pain. This could be you. He was hurting a lot and he was hurting a lot for a long time.

I went white and started thinking what to do. I was still backing away.

The one with the gun was behind the guy with the phone. If I ran away from the two of them the guy with the gun would shoot his mate not me. Also if I ran the guy with the phone would probably chase. Making it even more likely that his mate would shoot him, not me. Also getting shot in these circumstances was not such a bad option. There weren't any better ones. I turned and ran.

- Hold it!

Somebody behind me shouted. I tried to move quicker.

It's not always easy to see that my flat has a balcony. Some people don't realise that behind the curtain is a door that goes onto it. I usually open the door on warm nights like this but close the curtain because I like my privacy. I ran for the curtain. I flicked it to one side and jumped. There was what sounded like a shot behind me, then there was a second shot like sound. I was in mid-air and hoping to hit the crab apple tree. I did. The branches bent and broke and then I hit the ground on the road side of the fence as I had hoped. It wasn't elegant or remotely acrobatic but I seemed to be on the ground in one piece. I ran for the churchyard over the road.

You wouldn't jump like that unless you had to. If they didn't follow me that way they would have to go a long way round. I was ahead. There were two options at this moment: go left or go right. Straight on was the river. I went to the left of the church and once behind it turned back to go east along the path by the river. I kept running. The rain was pouring down and there was lightning followed immediately by thunder.

Why had they done that to Tavi? Why did they want to do it to me? I didn't know that either but I knew I had to get away to somewhere safe. I kept running.

Part 2
Tavi Mansur

Angelic?

Chapter 8
London
September 2014

Westbridge Road
Battersea
London

Source:	James Hecketty
Date:	Wednesday 3rd September
Time:	18.03
Present:	Alex Harewood, Timms

My mind was still racing, my legs were still running and I was still getting soaked by the pouring rain. I tried to limit my thoughts to the immediate problem of getting away. Battersea Bridge was coming up ahead. I had to decide which way to go. I could go north over the bridge, cross the road to keep going east or turn right and head south. Then I saw a taxi stop by the bridge on my side of the road. I ran up to it and got in. The driver pulled away smartly. He'd got the idea that I was in a rush. We drove over the bridge. It felt like I'd escaped.

- Thanks

I tried to say. But just made a noise.

- I'll just keep driving, Sir, while you catch your breath.

I gave him a thumbs up. He crossed the river and turned

Angelic?

left onto the Kings Road then left again. We stopped there. He turned round and undid the small door in the barrier between us:

-    Are you alright?

Whoever the cab driver was he seemed to be on my side. If he wanted me dead I would be already. If he wanted to take me back to the two guys who were in my flat he could have done. I sat in the back of his cab dripping wet and took deep breaths. I took more deep breaths. I wasn't sure whether to scream or cry. I was trying not to hit the sides of the cab. Then I hit the sides of the cab. Then I was screaming too.

-    Aghhhh! ... Aghhhh!

Then I calmed down a bit. I took some more deep breaths.

-    What happened, Sir?
-    A mate of mine has been hurt. Could you just drive for a bit? I need to think.

This guy was a saint. I'd beaten the sides of his cab and he still just wanted to help. We were moving. I felt safer while we were moving.

-    Your friend was hurt. Are you in any danger sir?
-    Yes, fuck. I'm not sure. I'm not sure what's happening. They really hurt my friend.
-    Can you think of anywhere you might go where you could hide and be safe?
-    Hey? Who are you?
-    My name is Timms. You seem to be in trouble. I'm just trying to help.

I checked his ID at the front of the cab. It said he was Timms. No first name was given.

-    OK thanks, well. There is somewhere. I think I'll be alright there. Can you take me to Vicarage Crescent?
-    That's a good place. Is there someone there that can help?

There was a chance that I could be safe as Alex. No one knew who she was really. If whoever those guys were looking for James they would have a lot trouble finding me as Alex. There was no obvious connection. Alex was just a friend of Tavi's. Right now this was a good option.

- Yes, I know a woman who might help.
- That's good. She can help hide you from trouble can she?
- I think so...
- That could be the right thing to do then.

We drove on and crossed the river again. Wandsworth Bridge. He drove, made a few turns and stopped outside Alex's flat.

- Good luck, Sir. Perhaps you need to be very careful who you talk to about all this. Sometimes you can't even trust the police.
- Yes, yes, you're right. Thanks, Timms.
- Always glad to be of help. If you need me again do call.

He handed me a card through the partition. It had a picture of a cab, a mobile number and just the single name, Timms.

Alex's Flat
Vicarage Crescent
Battersea
London

Source:	James Hecketty/Alex Harewood
Date:	Wednesday 3rd September
Time:	18.31
Present:	Alex Harewood, Timms, Robert Sefton (on phone)

I went round the back of the flats and up the stairs. Then crossed the landing to enter Alex's flat. I went to look out of the window and saw that the cab was still there. Timms was sitting making phone calls. I hadn't paid him! I had been busy thinking other things. He hadn't asked either. He was a good guy it seemed, had spotted that I was in trouble and tried hard to help me. The first of a series of questions occurred to me. Had he been in just that place at just the right time just by accident?

There was a lot to think about and do. I started by changing into Alex's own clothes and doing my make-up. There was still one serious problem with this plan: I now had to pretend to be two people.

First I set up Alex's phone so that it could be used for internet phone calls that couldn't be traced the same way James phone was. It's not that hard to do.

As James I then called the police and told them what had happened to me. They were interested to hear what I had to say and asked many very sensible questions. They said they would send a patrol car round to James' flat as soon as they could.

Alex would want to check up on her boyfriend and she didn't know he'd been beaten up so I phoned Tavi again and left a message.

The police were less dismissive than I had thought they might be when I rang them as Alex. The woman on the other end was sympathetic, took a lot of details and said I should ring back when I found him, which she insisted was the most likely outcome. Now I had to hope they would put the two things together.

The house phone started to ring. I looked at the caller's number. I didn't know it.
- Hello?
- Hello. Is that Alex?
- Yes.
- This is Robert Sefton. We were hoping that you would be able to come in to work tomorrow. Things are very busy at the moment. Would that be OK?
What?
- Err...Yes, yes, that's fine. Umm I'll see you tomorrow.
- OK, see you at 8.30.

I had applied for a job at Robert Sefton's estate agency a couple of weeks before. Employment had been a condition of the challenge. My job had come through just when I really needed to hide as Alex? Could that just be chance? Like the taxi? Robert Sefton had also managed to invite me in to work without saying I was just starting or that I had never been there before. He'd made it sound like I'd worked there for a while. That didn't sound like chance either.

Angelic?

An hour later something else happened. My pink girl phone sprang into life as a whole new conversation dating back weeks started appearing in my messages. They were all from someone called Harbinder, a woman I guessed. I scanned the messages. We exchanged texts a lot it seemed. Work was mentioned a couple of times so I guessed I'd be seeing her tomorrow. Someone was helping me.

I curled up on the sofa and cried. What was happening?

I had the feeling of being a small cog in a very large piece of machinery. I could hear the whirring and clunking of the other cogs around me but had no idea what the purpose of the machine was. Why had someone gone to so much trouble over me? Just about all I knew for sure was that some people were trying to keep me safe as Alex Harewood and some other people wanted to torture me to death as James. The same as they had done to Tavi. Some decisions are easy. It looked like I was going to be Alex, not James, for a while.

I sent a message to Eleanor, saying how good it had been to see her that day and another to Jenny. I mentioned that Tavi had gone missing. I could only say to her the things that Alex knew. I tried to sound optimistic. I got some encouraging replies back:

Oh dear. I'm so sorry. Try to be positive. Eleanor x

That's not so good. I hope things turns out for the best. J xxx

I slowly put myself to bed. There were so many things that I wasn't sure of. There were too many questions in my head and I struggled to control my thoughts. One good friend of mine was dead and another was in a coma. The whole world was just the wrong shape. It didn't feel like I fit into it any more. I tried to relax and almost managed to doze a little. Except that every time I fell asleep I woke up to an image of Tavi screaming.

Robert Sefton Estate Agency
Eland Road
Battersea
London

Source:	James Hecketty/Alex Harewood
Date:	Thursday 4th September
Time:	08.23
Present:	Robert Sefton, Harbinder Patterson, Alex Harewood

The bus stopped at Battersea Arts Centre and I got off. I walked round the corner into Eland Road and into the magazine office space. I waved at security and managed to get past them without being challenged.

I went inside and followed the signs for the Robert Sefton Estate Agency. It was an internet only agency. They had a website, but clients couldn't visit the office. It made the overheads a lot less I guessed.

The door was open and I went in. It wasn't a large room. Each of the three walls without a window had a desk against it and filing cabinets in some of the gaps. There wasn't a lot of space.
- Hello, Alex
- Morning, Al
Two people that I had never met before were greeting me like I saw them every day. The man sat at a desk on the left. I took him to be the owner of the agency, Robert Sefton. The pretty Asian girl at the desk on the right was, I

assumed, Harbinder Patterson who I seemed to keep in touch with by text. Next to her desk was one that said Alex Harewood. Each of the desks had a computer and a phone. Robert's was tidy. Harbinder's was a mess. I spotted a coffee machine in the corner.

- Are you sure you're not late?

grumbled Robert. I could tell that he was about to become one of the great joys of my life. I tried to fit in and sound casual:

- Can I get a coffee for anyone?

Harbinder didn't want one:

- No thanks, I'm good.

But Robert did:

- Yes OK… I've booked for you to show 17 Albert Street at 10.45. The taxi will be here at 10.20. Any problems let me know.

How hard could it be?

- That should be fine. I'll just remind myself of the details.

I sat down at the computer and logged in as aharewood. I entered the password AlexElis, thinking that it would most likely need 8 characters and capitals. I tried another AlexH2208. That worked! These guys most likely had an online database and so I opened Internet Explorer. The home page went to www.RobertSefton.co.uk. I hit log in and entered aharewood and the same password. That got me into the site as an admin so I looked up 17 Albert Street and perused the details of the house: asking price, vendor details, record of previous viewings etc. My appointment for today was entered in already. There was also a showing to the same people that had already taken place; apparently I'd already shown them round once before.

- You didn't say it was the Blackwoods. They looked round last week.

Angelic?

- Oh that's good news. If this is the second visit then maybe you can dig a little deeper into their circumstances. Make sure to keep the notes up to date.

I wanted to say 'I always do, don't I?' but that might have been pushing things just a little too far.

The taxi arrived at 10.20. I got in and did my job. I met the Blackwoods outside the house and showed them round. They didn't seem to remember me, which was the first thing that had made any sense recently. They sounded very positive about the house.

When I got back Robert had something to tell me:
- There was someone in looking for you while you were out. They didn't get past the security desk. I said you weren't available.
- Oh, thanks, any message?
- No they said they'd come back.

Someone had been checking up on me. I wondered who that might be.
- I said you were not to be bothered at work if it was just a social call.

It wasn't the police then. They would have said.
- Was it a tall good-looking guy with dark hair?

Harbinder caught my eye and twinkled. She'd got the tall dark handsome reference. Robert hadn't:
- I didn't see them. I just spoke to security.

Two phones rang at the same time. I jumped towards mine and got back to work telling some woman what we charged and pointing out that we were the cheapest in the area despite the superior service that we offered. Why she couldn't read all this stuff off the website as I was doing I had no idea.

There was a long list of follow up calls that I had to make. I asked people what they had thought when they viewed a property; what they liked and didn't like. I recorded all the answers. Those responses were used to know what they might prefer in another property or as advice to the owners of the visited house to make changes, like tidy up the place, or clean the bathroom. It's astonishing what people don't notice in their own homes.

Just before my lunch break Robert slipped out and I spent a few moments looking up Harbinder on Facebook. After that I asked her:
- How's Hardeep now?
- Oh he's right as rain now, right as rain, thanks for asking. Still a bit stiff and sore, but fixing fast. He's so pleased with that little tent that you got him for his birthday. That was so good of you. He plays in it all the time.
- Does he? That's nice. I'm glad he likes it.

She was shortish - five foot two or three. Her shoulders were a little bit square and awkward as was her rib cage beneath her ample bosom. She had a pleasant honest face and lively black eyes and the small regular features that added up to pretty. Her eyes seemed to want to take everything in. She had her hair back in a bun and wore a black jumper and a black skirt. Clearly this was her work outfit.

I was trying hard to keep a straight face through all this. We were both acting. Pretending to be best mates when I'd never seen her before that morning. How had she been briefed? What about Robert? We had to keep on playing along just in case the office had a listening device somewhere. What did she know? How had she been persuaded to take part in this fantasy? I never really found out and I could never ask. I did find a few clues on the way. It didn't matter now. She was very good at it and was going

Angelic?

to be fun to work with. She'd been a good friend of mine for ages but I hadn't heard of her till yesterday.

Alex' Flat

Source: James Hecketty/Alex Harewood
Date: Friday 5th September
Time: 17.22
Present: Alex Harewood

The 345 bus took me back along Falcon Road. I got off and then walked the rest of the way up Battersea High Street and through the communal gardens. The day had gone well. I was able to just get on with things and there was a steady trickle of straightforward tasks. It was engaging and nothing bad happened. During a couple of spare moments, while Robert was out I phoned Tavi's mobile and his flat. Alex didn't know what James knew. I'd called in at Lavender Hill Police Station on the way home as well, telling them again that my boyfriend was missing.

As soon as I got in I knew there was something wrong in my flat. I didn't know what exactly, but something was not as it had been. Someone had been in my flat, though there was nothing missing and no sign of a forced entry. I started to look around, then stopped, got changed out of my work clothes into some slacks and a t-shirt and jumper and looked around while I was doing it. That told me enough. My flat had been bugged. I made some coffee and curled up in the armchair, just like I had been planning on doing.

Modern surveillance devices are tiny and cheap. They can hear you and track you easily. They can see you too. While getting changed and looking through the clothes in my wardrobe I just felt one tiny bug in the hem of my tweed skirt. It was the size of about four grains of rice bunched together apart from a tiny thin flexible aerial three centimetres long extending from it. There would be others.

Knowing my flat was bugged really was not very much help. If I did something about them then whoever had bugged me would know that I knew about them. And why would I know about them if was really Alex Harewood? Why would I know anything about bugs and surveillance if I was an estate agent's assistant? I just sat in my armchair, sipped my coffee, and tried to get used to the idea that from now on someone would be watching everything that I did and said.

There was nothing I could do in the flat that suggested I wasn't Alex. The only thing I could do was pretend to read or surf at night while actually doing something else. To add to this illusion I could buy eBooks I had read before. That way I could pretend to be reading these while doing anything else that I wanted on my tablet.

It seemed as though I would have to go on being Alex. Being Alex was fine. I could spend the next couple of months living as someone we'd invented, a very acceptable alternative to terminal agony.

I still had no idea what was going on or why all this was happening except that it had something to do with the party. Was this completely unrelated or was this about Eleanor? More likely it was about Katya. They both had reality warping resources available to them. My reality was definitely warped.

Lavender Hill Police Station

Source: James Heckett/Alex Harewood
Date: Saturday 6th September
Time: 09.02
Present: DS Ryan Broadhouse, DI Gemma Black, DC John
             Meehan

- I'm Detective Sergeant Broadhouse. I'd like to talk to you about your missing friend.

I was invited into the soft interview room at Lavender Hill Police Station. I'd been in to see them on Thursday and again on Friday to tell them that Tavi had gone missing. I came in today for the same reason, but the result was different. It was good that they were taking some interest. Talking to a Detective Sergeant suggested that they may have found Tavi. So I asked:

- Have you found him?
- I'm very sorry Alex but we have found a body fitting Tavi's description.

My hands went to my mouth:

- Oh. Oh.
- We've informed his parents and asked them to formally identify him. We've started a murder investigation. We're including the assault on Mr Smithson as part of the investigation.

None of this felt real:

- Tavi's dead?
- I'm sorry, Alex.
- What? How?

Angelic?

- His body was discovered this morning. I can't give you any details but he had some horrible injuries.
- Was he beaten up like Toby?
- He was beaten. Can we ask you some more questions? It would be a help to us to just go over things again. Would you mind if I asked a colleague to join us?
- That's OK. I understand.

A young looking officer came into the room. I was introduced to DC John Meehan. He asked a question. It was the wrong question. There probably wasn't a right one.

- Hello Alex, Is there anything I can get for you?
- My friend. I'd like my friend. I'd like to see him and talk to him. I'd like to touch him and put my arms around him. I want to be able to tell him I really like him, that he's a great guy and that all this hasn't happened. Get him for me. Get my friend.

There were tears on my cheeks and I guess you'd say that I lost it a bit. I sobbed for a while. I'd not been able to before and I just let it all come out. I gave in to the stress and grief. Eventually someone put an arm around me. It was a woman.

- Hello
- Hi, I'm sorry, I'd like to be braver.
- It's OK. You cared for him. That's not a bad thing. It's OK to be upset.

She offered me a tissue from the box on the table. I did a bit of dabbing. Meehan had gone.

- I'm Gemma Black. I'm the inspector in charge of Tavi's case. I'd like to ask you some questions when you're ready.
- OK.
- If you go through that door and across the hall you'll find the ladies loo. You may want to touch up your

make up.
-   Thanks.

I did as instructed. I sorted out my make-up. It took a bit of time.

She sat next to me and asked me all about the last few days. The party. Staying with Tavi. Going to see him on Wednesday. Finding the office unattended. I only did the Alex bits and just pretended I'd been to work on Monday. Of course it was true on Thursday and Friday.

-   When did you last see him?
-   Sunday.
-   And you went back to see him on Wednesday. Why?
-   I wanted to move our relationship on. I wanted to see more of him. We'd been on two dates. The first was a bit weird. It felt like I was just any girl to sort of make up the numbers. When he asked me again I thought: oh great he does like me. I met him in town and enjoyed being with him. At the Mornington party he was lovely. On Sunday it felt like we were an item.
-   So what happened when you got to the SafeNet office?

I told her all the things that Alex had done on Wednesday afternoon. Not finding Tavi, ringing him and reporting him missing. There were more questions:

-   Did Toby have a girlfriend?
-   No, well, I gather he had a lot of girlfriends, but he was looking for a girl called Katya. Why do you ask?
-   There is another body, a young woman.
-   Oh. Oh God, so, so you don't know who it is. Did you find her with Tavi's body?
-   Yes, in the same place.
-   Well, I knew Tavi was missing, obviously, but who that could be I don't know.
-   We think that she was raped and then killed.
-   Oh... how dreadful... Why was she with Tavi?

Angelic?

- Can you think why?
- No, how could I?
- We think that James may have raped and killed the girl.

So the police were also chasing James. The reality of being Alex was, like quicksand, sucking me in. I managed a sane response:

- That can't be right. He's a nice guy.
- They can do it too.
- So Tavi's been killed and this girl's been killed and you're thinking it was all James. That isn't right.
- So what can you tell me that might help us?
- Nothing. There's nothing. Tavi was nice. I liked him. He really liked James. None of this makes any sense.

There was a moment's silence. There was nothing I could say. If they were looking for James they weren't looking for who was really responsible. Gemma asked:

- Can you think of anyone else that they knew?
- I only met Tavi a few times. Why aren't you asking James these questions? He'll know a lot more than I do.
- We can't find him.
- Is he afraid that you'll arrest him for something that he didn't do?
- We can't arrest him without evidence.
- That's not true. Tavi spent three months in jail and everyone admits there was no evidence that he did anything wrong.

She ignored that.

- Can we just go over the timeline again? It's so important for us.
- We went through it all again.

I was on the way out when she handed me a business card.

- This is my mobile number. Call me if you think of anything that might be helpful. Just any small detail

that you might not have mentioned already.
- Ok I'll do that.

The police seemed to be thinking I was responsible for the deaths of Tavi and the raped girl and also beating up Toby. I could easily clear my name. All I had to do was walk in to a police station and reveal that I was Alex as well as James. I had to destroy my cover as Alex to do that and so create a whole new set of problems. If I did that the police wouldn't be after me for killing Tavi. The other lot would come for me instead for the same reason they had come after me in the first place. The same people, I supposed, who were bugging my flat and clothes. I would have to go on the run from them properly and that would be harder than being Alex. I didn't believe that the police would or could protect me.

For the moment I was going to stay away from the police and stay pretending to be Alex.

Mansur Residence
Herne Hill
London

Source:	Alex Harewood
Date:	Sunday 7th September
Time:	15:07
Present:	Tavi's Mother and Father, his sisters, Marven and a Priest

It was a nice house. A large well cared for semi in an affluent and sought after part of Herne Hill. I didn't doubt that Tavi had helped his parents buy this place. He was the only one of us with any real family and was always committed to them. James had met them before. I approached the door with my stomach in a knot because of what had happened to Tavi. I had no idea how I would be received and timidly knocked on the door.

His parents were members of one of the earliest Christian groups in the world and came from a community in Qaraqosh, in northern Iraq, where the Aramaic language spoken was nearest to that of Jesus. An area with a history that included the invention of writing, the wheel, irrigation and the domestication of cattle. Qaraqosh had claim to be one of the oldest continuously inhabited cities in the world. Tavi's grandparents had fled from that part of the world in the late 1980s, when Saddam Hussein's Al-Anfal campaign of genocide was destroying hundreds of Assyrian villages and killing hundreds of thousands with gas attacks on undefended civilian populations.

His grandparents left Iraq with nothing except their two children; Tavi's mother and uncle. It was a journey that required great courage and patience. Their youngest daughter had been killed by a mortar bomb, a device the size of a small coke bottle, while taking water to the family next door. Tavi's family name, one of the oldest in the world was one step nearer being obliterated with his death. There would be no new Mansur from his line.

A woman in her mid-twenties answered the door. She had short black hair and the dusky complexion you would expect from someone whose ancestors were all from northern Iraq. She looked a lot like Tavi and I assumed that she was a sister. She looked like she had been crying. I guessed that I looked that way too.

-   Hello?
-   I'm Alex.
-   Oh hello. It's so good of you to come, Sister. I'm Talitha. She had obviously heard something about me. I was taken through to a large sitting room. His parents were together on the leather sofa. His mother was a large woman. Someone who committed herself to looking after her family and home and worried less about her own appearance. You could see that she was Tavi's mother. Their eyes were so similar. His father was shorter than I had anticipated and had eyes that normally showed his intelligence. Today they showed his sorrow as well. There were a lot of other people in the room whom I took to be relatives and friends and they whispered respectfully all wanting to be there to support his parents. They too had come to commiserate with the family. Talitha introduced me:
-   My mother, my Father, this is Alex.

Angelic?

His father stood up and greeted me grasping both my hands in each of his:

- Thank you for coming to see us, my daughter. Thank you also for getting the police involved as soon as possible. They said that you went to see them as soon as he went missing.
- I only did what I could. I wish it could have been more.

It was an honour to be called daughter and touching too. It wasn't just honorary. It also gave me a place in the structure of this family; my position was daughter. As daughter I would have responsibilities and could be asked to do tasks, answer the door as Talitha had done, or serve a meal, and generally help out in the house. I wouldn't be asked to do this today, but if I stayed for a few days, as I was now entitled to do, I would be asked to start taking on these roles. The whole room had heard me called daughter and understood now how I was to be treated. Had I been a son I would have had the same status, but expected to help out in the family business or provide some income.

I went over and knelt in front of his mother. She held both my hands and looked me in the eye. I bowed my head and she touched me on the forehead:

- Bless you Daughter. Bless you for being his friend and bless you for thinking of us.
- Thank you Mother. Thank you for bringing him to the world. Thank you for making him what he was.

I hadn't anticipated being quite as welcome. She started to explain:

- He talked a lot about you. I never heard him say so much about any girl before. He told me all about you and said you were very special, that you were clever and thoughtful. The world seemed a different and better place when you were with him. I'm glad you've come to see us.

- He was lovely to me. He always made me feel like I could be myself. He gave me a lot of self-confidence.
- He was such a kind boy. It's so horrible that he had to die like that on his own. Nobody with him who knew him and cared for him.

She cried again. I guessed that like a lot of mothers she was always asking Tavi about his girlfriends. I suppose he mentioned Alex. He then found that he had lots to say about her because he helped create her and knew all her background. His Mum would have wanted to hear all this and guessed that all this knowledge was a sign that he got on really well with me.

- Will they find anything out about the people that killed him? .. Those monsters. They are not people. They do not deserve to be treated as people. I want them to burn in Hell.

She said this with venom and conviction. It sounded out of character. I looked for signs of a retraction. A sign that she had gone further than she wanted. She held my gaze because she really did want those men to burn. She had delivered a full blooded old fashioned curse. His Dad nodded and then talked about James:

- I hope James is hiding and hasn't suffered a similar fate. I don't believe it was him that hurt Tavi. Tavi always said how he was a good friend. Not one to mix with people a lot but ready to help when needed. Tavi said if he couldn't find a solution to something then James would. He'd just work it out.

He paused, looked at his wife and held her hand before continuing:

- I'm hoping that James works all this out. I don't really trust the police. They only look for what they can prove and don't care about what is really there. Good and bad are forgotten by the police. The way they treated

Tavi over the hacking showed us that. I don't believe that the police will find the evil men. But James might if he's still alive.

I could only agree:

- I hope he is and I hope you're right and that only James knows where James is. I think that's the safest way for him to be at the moment.
- They were here earlier, the police, asking what we knew. They were polite and one said he was our Family Liaison Officer. We didn't want him to stay. They said we should get in touch if we heard anything from James.

He looked into the distance for a moment:

- It's so odd. They were doing so well. Everything seemed so good.

Tavi's mother started to sob but controlled herself. I put my hand on her forearm. Her husband put his arm around her. I explained:

- I never met James. They say he was the quiet one. I saw Toby in hospital yesterday. He was still unconscious. Perhaps a little less swollen. They don't know when or if he'll get better.

They encouraged me to eat something with them and Talitha took me through to the kitchen. I was introduced to his two other sisters, Martuska and Patsy. We all called each other sister, partly because this was a semi-formal occasion and they were in their parents' house.

- Do you know why? Is there any sense? Why did they have to hurt him so? They beat him for hours. Tortured him. Breaking bones and smashing teeth.

Martuska noticed me turn green. I was close to retching. The reason for the spite in his mother's curse was a little clearer. The image of Tavi screaming was back again. So was the thought of how close I'd come to the same fate.

- Oh! I'm sorry I thought that you knew. Sorry.

I took some deep breaths and seemed to recover a little. She handed me a glass of water.

- I'm OK. I'm OK.

I took a sip of water:

- The police didn't tell me much about how he died. I think they wanted the family to know first.

A young man in his early teens came up to me in the kitchen and said:

- Hello, I'm Marven, Tavi's cousin-brother. You're Alex
- Hello, Marven.
- There is someone here that wants to meet you. Would you come with me please?

He took me to another room. There was a man in black talking to a middle aged couple. He stood up as I came in. He was a priest and had been in the living room when I arrived. I had met his eye then.

He came towards me and I shook his hand. He was an old guy. One of the refugees. One of those people who belong to an intimidatingly long tradition. He had been doing what he did now all his adult life and had learned what he did from people who had done it all their lives for generation upon generation for thousands of years. A man who deserved the greatest respect. He represented a religion, a culture, a people and a history and he had given up everything else that he might have been to represent and protect all those ideas and values. He held onto my hand.

- Who are you, child?
- My name is Alex, Father. I was Tavi's girlfriend.

He still held my hand. I could see that he was thinking. He was reaching back through that ancient oral tradition to remember some piece of knowledge and said:

- Not everyone knows who they are. There are some

among us who have to learn. They go from being one thing to another before they know why they are here, before they realise what they are. Perhaps this event is your awakening. Don't be frightened of yourself. Watch over us.

Something in what he said seemed to fit. He let go of my hand.

- Goodbye, Child
- Goodbye, Father.

I left the room still accompanied by Marven. He asked:

- Did you understand him? Did you get what he said?
- I heard what he said. I don't think I completely understood.
- I've known him all my life. I've never heard him speak that way before. He asked you to watch for us. What did he mean?
- Why don't you go back and ask him?
- I wouldn't know how. I'm a bit frightened of him.
- He would want you to ask. He lives his life to help you. He would not want you to be frightened.

He returned to the priest, who I 'm sure greeted him kindly when he saw that the lad was nervous. Marven returned to me. He looked happier and thoughtful so I said:

- Not so frightening then.
- No, he was nice. He wanted to tell me a story. A story about what he called a Watcher.
- And what did he say a Watcher was?
- I asked if he meant like a spectator. He said no, much more like a guard. The Watchers keep people good. They do good things for good people and help them. They find out the bad ones and punish them. They have enormous power and knowledge.
- So what was the story?
- He will tell it but he asked if you would come and listen

too.

We returned to the priest. He was smiling at me. He had a few other people interested in the story. It took him some time to tell it.

The Story of Methes and Uriel
701 BC

The young scribe called Methes had heard about the battle that was to come. The army of the Assyrian King Sennacherib was advancing to lay siege to Jerusalem. He had heard which way the army was taking and wanted to see this enormous horde of men and their preparations for the siege. The hated Assyrians had the most powerful army in all the world and Methes longed to see it. If he walked all day he could perhaps see the army from the safety of the hills. He hoped to arrive in time.

As he got nearer he saw a few men coming the other way. Their faces were ashen. They only walked forward staring and saying nothing. He asked:
-    Have I missed them? What has happened?
One man spoke without stopping:
-    Go on if you must. You have missed nothing. See God's work and pray.
He said no more and hurried on with the others.

Methes had thought to see a host of organised men camped on the plain readying themselves for the siege. He hoped to see the famous phalanxes of spearmen at the centre of the army. He had heard that there would be chariots, men on horseback. Archers with dazzling armour. He hoped he might see the massive siege engines and battering rams. He saw none of these things.

As he came over the final small hill he saw the plain below

him. He first heard a strange noise drifting up from the plain. An unending sound of sorrow. He saw a few horsemen moving slowly. Their colours and banners suggested that they were scouts from Jerusalem. They moved through the army of Sennacherib whose tents were still standing and banners were still flying. There had been no fight. Almost every man of the Assyrian army, tens of thousands, lay dead on the ground. If there were any survivors they had already retreated.

He saw men canter away to relay news to Jerusalem. Women from the Assyrian camp tended their dead husbands and sons. It was the forlorn wailing of these thousands of mothers and wives that Methes had first heard. He quickly but cautiously moved on to take a closer look.

The bodies on the plain showed no sign of injury. No blood. Yet every face of the thousands of men was contorted by an agonising death. He saw a few others who wandered among the dead as he did. When he asked:
- What happened?
He got similar replies from them all:
- The Judean priests say this is their God's work. He sent an Angel of Death. They say he sent Uriel.

He knew that name. He knew that Uriel was a most powerful and terrible Watcher. He trembled with fear and turned away from the macabre scene of suffering to make his way home. He had seen enough of what God's messenger had done to save Jerusalem.

When he returned to the hills he stooped to drink from a stream. A few yards away he saw a young woman arrive and she drank from the same stream. She was beautiful and moved with exceptional grace. She turned to him and asked:

Angelic?

-   Are you Methes?
He was surprised that this fine-looking young woman knew
him. He replied:
-   I am Methes. Who are you?
She looked baffled by the question and appeared lost in
thought. Then words formed on her lips and she gave her
enigmatic and terrifying response:
-   I have many names. But what I have done they say was
    done by Uriel.
Methes heard this, screamed in terror and turned to run
but she held his sleeve firmly and he could not escape. This
was God's envoy and the deliverer of his justice and
vengeance. If he did wrong she might destroy him and his
family or his whole village. He realised immediately that
this meeting was to be the most important event in his
entire life. Or the end of it.

Yet she held him gently, smiled and spoke reassuringly:
-   Do not be fearful. Today I would have your help. In the
    future you may have mine.
-   What would you have me do?
-   Write down what you saw here today. Then record
    what I say. So that men may know when they are ready
    to know.
She handed him parchment of the finest quality and
writing implements and ink.
-   When you are done hide it in this place that I show you
    now. I will collect it when I can.
She pointed out a small cave. Too small for a full grown
man to enter. Just large enough for him to crawl into.
-   In return for this favour I will guide you through your
    life. You will be not so very wealthy but happy and
    content. You will have many children from a loving wife
    who will care for you and who will show you many
    good things about yourself that you might not

otherwise have known. Will this be payment enough for a day's work? Will you do this thing for me?
- I will do this.
- You will not be aware of me again but I will be among the people that you meet. Sometimes I will appear as a woman. At other times a man. I may seem old or very young. You will not know my real identity. I will appear to you as other people do. You will say saying nothing of our meeting here today. Not ever. Not even to your beautiful wife, your children or any of your myriad grandchildren. God will not be pleased if you break this silence. He will punish me.

The scribe kept his part of the bargain. He wrote down the extraordinary things that he heard that day and hid his writing in the small cave. He told no one. Except that through his life he said things that others thought strange. His priest noticed this and started to piece together his odd pronouncements. As the scribe got older the priest could see that Methes' life was blessed. The priest knew then that the scribe had something to tell and listened more carefully and examined the scribe surreptitiously.

He passed on what was said to other priests and they all learned a little of what Uriel had said. It became a part of what they knew and they passed their knowledge on through the generations. It was never written down and was stronger for that. It could change. The weaker understanding was forgotten and the most useable knowledge was enhanced. It became more than a story, it became a method and a way of understanding the world. The priests knew that this knowledge was supposed to be secret so they did not share it with others but kept it as a hidden part of their tradition. It was recalled and used when they saw a need.

Angelic?

The knowledge was important. It gave them influence in dealing with and helping God's messengers. They knew the beings they called Watchers had hearts and souls. The same beings we now call Angels could appear very human. Even to themselves.

Herne Hill

The story seemed incomplete. I wasn't sure what it was that Uriel had said to Methes. What was it that Methes had written down and hidden? The parchment that Methes wrote was never recovered. Perhaps the Priest knew what was on it.

The bus was crowded on the way home. They weren't very frequent at that time of day. I sat next to a woman who was a little older than me and thought about how well it had gone. The Mansur's had been so good to me. I sat back and relaxed.

The strangest feeling came over me. I looked at the woman next to me. She had changed. The bus had changed. I wasn't on a bus.

> *The office I was in was familiar to me. I knew all the things in there. It was my office. I admired again the wall hangings.*
>
> *Carpenethes knocked politely but didn't wait for my response before coming in. He was looking triumphant and carrying a scroll with the enormous royal seal. He hadn't opened it. We neither of us needed to open it to know what it meant.*
>
> *Yes!*
>
> *He put the scroll on the desk and we embraced in celebration. He was well paid but I still owed him more:*

Angelic?

- *Thanks. Thanks for your help.*
- *You know I wanted this too…There's still a lot to do.*
- *We'll have to get everything organised. The merchants are going to have to come to us.*
- *Once word gets out this place is going to be very busy.*
- *I'll make sure that all the ledgers are ready and get all the scribes briefed.*
- *Ok. I'll send confirmation to the palace and start contacting the warehouses.*

There was a knock at the door. One of the office boys was carrying a tray with two goblets of wine. Carpenethes had been thinking ahead again. He ushered the boy in and we each took a goblet before he left us. I raised my wine in the air:

- *To the Army*
- *The Army*

We both drank. Carpenethes caught my eye over the top of his goblet and I could see the smile in his eyes.

- Are you alright? Are you sure you're alright?

The woman who had been sitting next to me on the bus was worried. I was back in London.

- I'm fine. I'll be okay.
- You were staring at nothing and mumbling. Do you get petit mal? Is that what it was?
- No, no. I'm fine. Thanks.
- Well you do look Ok now.

The hallucination had seemed real. I had been in a far off place. There were no modern materials, no plastic, no metal except for jewellery. There was stone and earthenware pots. So a vision from an ancient time. As I thought I recalled the place. It was a place I knew. I could think what was beyond that office and I knew the streets of the city it was in.

Here I had confusion and doubt. During the hallucination I had felt confident. In control of things around me. I still felt a bit that way. I didn't feel so frightened any more by the events that had engulfed me. Somehow things were going to work out for the best. It was only a feeling. I still had no idea what was going on.

Chapter 9
London
September 2014

Victoria and Albert Museum

Source:	Alex Harewood
Date:	Monday 8th September
Time:	18:47
Present:	Jenny Verdi, Alex Harewood

Monday night was my night at the V and A. I got there in good time having gone straight from work and done a little bit of shopping then grabbing a sandwich to eat on the bus. I got started on the catalogue cards. There was another team working and I had to do their entries as well. Their typing up person had left, but I was fast enough to do the work for both groups.

When there was a break I had a bit of time to talk to Jenny. She was counsellor of young girls and might be able to give me the right kind of advice. If anyone wanted to know about Alex then Jenny was an obvious person to talk to. I wanted to strengthen my feminine credentials while muddying the waters about my Canadian boyfriend, explain why I might appear a bit masculine on occasions as well as need help with things like feminising my flat. There was a magazine article I'd read that I used as inspiration.

She happened to start the conversation off in the right direction anyway:

- Geoff still likes you. You've made a bit of a conquest there.
- Yeah I kind of know but... Well,.. well... Could you help me with something? I'm worried about how I feel.

She was nodding and looking curious, so I continued:

- I've never had a real boyfriend partly because I don't feel very comfortable with the... you know, the physical bit.
- Oh, I see now. Didn't you have a boyfriend in Canada?
- There was a boy called Brad... but not really a boyfriend.

She thought for a moment.

- So when you say the physical bit do you mean having sex, going all the way?
- Yeah that's it, I never have, it's... well it seems odd, sort of wrong. I've been concerned about it for a while... a long while
- I see...

She looked at me briefly, making decisions, then continued:

- Don't worry, lots of girls feel like you to start with. It's a normal feeling, not at all unusual. You could try starting from a different place. Don't think about the physical bit. Think about spending time with someone you like. You know, someone who amuses you, entertains you and values you. Imagine doing things together. Just talk. Or go for a walk, have a picnic, see a film. You can enjoy that can't you?
- Yeah I guess so.
- Stereotypically men get into relationships because they want to have sex and then find other things that are nice about being with a girl. We tend to be more the

other way round - want all the other things and then find sex is a pleasant part of that.

She was looking at me and sipping her coffee. I'd shared a confidence and she was putting it into place, adding it to her picture of me.

- In fact, you don't even need to start out thinking about being with someone. Start by thinking about what you would wear. What will you do with your hair? How would you do your make up if you were going out on a date? Find a dress you want to wear. What shoes will go with it? Can you do that?
- Yeah. That sounds alright.
- OK. When you've done that try to find someone to show it all off to. If you find someone you like you'll probably want to spend more time with them. Then you might find that you want to be more intimate. If you don't want to then don't. You call the tune. Only do what you know you want to do. That's important. Always say no at least once to be sure that you can. Women tend to hold most of the cards in these situations. So relax. Just give it a go. See if you can't enjoy yourself.
- Okay, I'll try. I sort of thought I might be gay.
- Well that's possible, and it's OK if you are, but you won't really know until you try.

She looked at me for a moment:

- This has been a big thing for you hasn't it?
- I suppose. I was a bit of a tomboy for a while.
- Well you certainly appear to be well past that phase.
- Thanks.

Geoff had been missing Jenny from the team and had come to find her. He was kindly rather than sharp. I wondered if that was because I was there and he'd heard about Tavi or because I was there and he wanted to impress me. Then I got back to typing up the cards into the catalogue and thought about what Jenny had said.

Everything was feeling really strange and back at home I wondered for a moment if Toby and Tavi were playing some big prank. That was just wishful thinking. I texted Eleanor and Jenny and even Harbinder just to say hello. They all sent back friendly replies and I felt a bit better. But it didn't feel real because I wasn't really Alex. I wasn't really anyone at the moment.

As long as I was Alex I was probably safe. So doing nothing was an option. It didn't seem like a good one. I wanted to know what it was that Tavi had stolen that was so important. So I started planning other things. It felt better when I did that. I wasn't thinking about my own peculiar circumstances. My mind started to construct ideas and I considered the options and plausible outcomes.

My oldest friend in London was Tommy Dodson, an ex-soldier who now worked as a security guard. He'd helped me a lot in the past and knew all about me so he understood how far off target the police were. He wanted to help again and so we kept up an exchange of emails after that first call. We went over some of my plans to which he offered positive comments and also suggested some improvements.

It was good to talk things through with him and be honest. I didn't have to pretend anything with Tommy. I felt a bit more real.

Lavender Hill Police Station

Source:	Computers at the Lavender Hill Police Station
Date:	Tuesday 9th September
Time:	10.42
Present:	DS Kyriakos Papandreou, DS Ryan Broadhouse, DI Gemma Black, DC John Meehan

One of my internet servers had sent out a text message to Inspector Gemma Black and she received an offer to download a free shopping app on her phone. It was a real app but I'd added just a few lines of code to the package.

On Tuesday she accepted the offer. She wasn't to know. All she had to do now was plug her phone into a USB port on a computer at Lavender Hill. It didn't matter if it was just to get some power for her phone. It would still load the drivers. Later that same day she did and I had access to the police system at Lavender Hill. Information started coming in.

They had set up their incident room on the top floor of the Lavender Hill police station. There was a team of detectives trying to find out who it was that killed Tavi and beat up Toby and I got to know them all.

Detective Inspector Gemma Black, who had interviewed me on Saturday, was in charge of the team. She was the SIO – Senior Investigating Officer. The senior team briefings were very informal and she encouraged members of her team to contribute their thoughts. It was one of her strengths.

The briefings took place in her office. It had one wall that was all glass and looked out over the operations room where most detectives had their desks and computers. Black had a desk near the centre of her office. On one wall was a large display screen. It was the modern equivalent of the notice board. Pictures of the victims, suspects, witnesses, locations and other details are displayed automatically in random order. There was a smaller desk in the corner where DC John Meehan worked. He was on some kind of fast track promotion scheme shadowing Gemma Black. In practice this meant he did the odd jobs and answered the phone.

Detective Sergeants Ryan Broadhouse and Kyriacos Papandreou were sitting in front of the Inspector's desk on office chairs. Meehan was at the side having simply turned round from his own desk.

She went over what I told the police had happened:
- Hecketty says that two men entered his home on Wednesday afternoon They were claiming to be police officers. They showed him a video of Tavi Mansur being kicked to death. They threatened him with the same treatment. He escaped. Yak is there anything to confirm what we're being told?

Kyriakos Papandreou, universally known as Yak, had been supervising the house-to-house enquiries around James flat as well as Toby's and Tavi's. He flicked through pictures of my flat on his tablet computer and they were displayed on the large monitor so everyone could see them.
- There's nothing to contradict what Hecketty told us. The flat was torched on Wednesday night. The firefighters didn't know then that it was a possible murder scene. They made a right mess. The SOCOs will do what they can but getting any useful forensics from

that place might be difficult.

The still photos showed the flat blackened and charred. It was a small flat, two rooms and a bathroom. The smoke had discoloured everything and there was no soft furniture intact.

The pictures on the display changed to the outside of the building and Papandreou described the door-to-door reports from around James flat. They were all very confused. They could tell something was happening in the early evening. They knew that Tavi's phone, the SafeNet van and, according to James' account, two men arrived at his flat around 17.25. Following James' 999 call a police patrol car arrived at 19.59. The fire service were called at 20.03. The police couldn't really make any sense of all the rest of what they had heard from my neighbours. People were clearly coming and going but the accounts of who, how and the timings were confused. Next door might have heard shots, or it could have been thunder from the storm.

Papandreou reported something more:
- There is no useful CCTV from around his flat. Intriguingly there is a camera just opposite. It's never worked properly though. It was installed and stopped working. Whenever it was fixed it broke again. They gave up in the end.

Detective Sergeant Ryan Broadhouse was the second in command of the team, I remembered him from my interview as well. He got the pictures up on his tablet but they didn't show on the main monitor. Yak reached across and tapped twice on Broadhouse's tablet. The room display monitor changed to show a huge hole in the ground full of rubbish. An active landfill site. There were six markers. One of them was next to what looked like a body. The body hadn't been found till Friday evening when the skip was emptied at the dump. There was another body with the rubbish; the headless dismembered corpse of a young woman.

Black showed them some gruesome pictures of Tavi, almost unrecognisable with split bruises, cut lips and missing teeth. She explained what the pathologist thought had happened:

- Tavi Mansur was beaten to death over a long period of time. He was probably conscious throughout. He seems to have been kicked mainly as with Smithson. It takes quite a lot of effort to hurt someone this way. To make it last this long you have either got to like doing it or there needs to be a reason. Like extracting information. Mansur's beating took hours. Smithson's took only minutes. It's possible that they are just supposed to look the same.

The display changed again to show five large white plastic bags tied at the ends. They looked innocent enough but later pictures show their contents to be the arms, legs and torso of the dead girl. Black continued:

- The girl found with Mansur had been frozen then cut up. It's therefore quite impossible to establish a useful time of death. Sometime in the last two months we were told. We found five pieces of her. We can't find her head. We're supposing that is to stop us identifying her. The pathologists are looking closely at her. Preliminary reports say bruising suggests that she was raped shortly before death. We're getting DNA from the semen inside her.

Broadhouse thought he knew what had happened:

- So it could be that James raped the girl and killed her. Then his mates find out about it and he kills them to help cover up the crime.

Angelic?

Black:
- That's a possible initial conclusion.

She delivered some more news:
- James Hecketty went into a branch of Phones4u, just one hour before the chain closed down for good and went into liquidation. He bought two contracts on two phones. He gave the SafeNet Office as his address.

Broadhouse:
- That's good news isn't it? We can trace the phones.

There was another way to look at it. Black nodded but gave the alternative:
- We can and we will. But that has to be why he bought the phones. Wherever and whenever he switches them on we have a record of where he has been. He knows that. He can switch it on and throw it on a truck on its way to Land's End. We have to chase it. Otherwise we look negligent. What he has purchased is a first class way of messing us about. And I'm guessing he knows it. He still doesn't seem to have a phone that connects to the network in a way that we can monitor.

Broadhouse:
- So he can switch his new phones on and tell us where to go!

Black confirmed:
- That's exactly it.
- Sweet.

The Happy Hat Café
Clapham Common
London

Source: James Hecketty /Alex Harewood
Date: Saturday 13th September
Time: 12.21
Present: Mark Troughton, Alex Harewood

There had been some interesting looking young men on the website. I had put in some things about me and my likes and dislikes. I found that difficult. Then I'd searched for someone who looked friendly and intelligent amongst the choices that were offered. This all made me feel very uncomfortable. Nervously I had hit the contact button and found myself with a date to meet a man called Mark Troughton.

I put on a dress that I knew had a listening device in it and added some heels. The dress was a floral print, big flowers splashed over a loose material with a belt at the waist and it didn't go too far down the leg. It looked flirty without being tarty. I thought to let my hair go loose thinking it would be quickest but I was wrong about that; it took ages with curling tongs and a hair dryer to get it looking right.

The 345 bus took me past where I normally got off for work and on to Clapham where I wanted to go that day. I checked my phone and read the good luck text from Jenny. My nerves must have shown because people kept looking at me so I just stared straight ahead. I hoped that I didn't somehow give myself away and that no one would recognise me from before.

We were meeting for lunch, an easy to get away from event, at a café on the edge of Clapham Common, The Happy Hat. In good weather, like today, they put tables outside. I was worried about what could happen even though it was a very public place in the middle of the day. We arrived at the same time from opposite directions and had plenty of time to look each other over and check it was the right person. I smiled at him when we were close enough. He looked nervous and just managed a smile but Hello didn't go so well:

- Helmph
- Hello, you're Mark are you?
- Yeah, yes.
- I'm Alex.
- Hi, ...
- Shall we sit down?
- Yeah. Yeah, sure.

The summer after college Toby, Tavi and I had done some sky-diving. We'd all looked petrified then, this lad looked the same now. But he wasn't about to jump out of an aeroplane.

We sat down at a table in the sun and I tried to give him something easy to talk about:

- Did you have to come far?
- No,.. not far ... just round the corner.

Jenny had said that women had the strongest hand in these situations. I was beginning to see that his usual options of fight or flight weren't going to help him make any progress here.

- Do you enjoy your work?
- Yeah, it's OK.

He gave a couple more short answers and I gave up trying to find out about him and started talking about my work. A waiter arrived and I ordered a tuna salad for lunch. Mark opted for a steak sandwich.

He didn't pause for much conversation while we ate lunch and I talked a bit more about myself, telling him the stuff about my fictitious Canadian background. I kept trying to get him to talk but he now just wanted to eat. He seemed different after lunch, more assertive, maybe satisfying his appetite had lessened his nerves.
-   You're good at talking aren't you?
-   Am I? I was hoping to hear more from you.
-   Well I might have said more but you haven't stopped.
He laughed, but I wasn't sure what was funny so I just grinned back:
-   Sorry, I was trying to help out, you seemed so nervous before we ate.
His face told me that I had made a mistake. He didn't want to admit to needing help, or being nervous:
-   You just started talking.
-   I'm sorry, I did think you were nervous, that's not a bad thing is it? You should be a bit uneasy when you first meet someone.
-   What's all this about me being nervous?
I was beginning to understand him. He'd been too anxious to even contemplate pursuing a relationship with me and take the risk that I might say no, so he'd given up over lunch. I'd given him the excuse that was near enough to the truth for not liking me. I talked too much. Perhaps that was true but he hadn't contributed anything.
-   Shall we get the bill?
-   Ok, I'll pay.
-   Thanks, that would be nice, but I'm happy to go halves.
-   No, I'd like to pay.

Angelic?

He was more relaxed now and not trying to put on a show; it made him easier to like. I shook his hand and we said goodbye and I breathed a sigh of relief that I had not had to deal with anything at all physical.

I wondered what he would tell his mates later. It wouldn't be this story, it would be a tale where I had talked all the time, looked like a bucket of mud – not as good as I had in my photo on the dating site - and he hadn't wanted to see me again. He'd tell that invention a couple of times and then it would be absorbed into his self-history as the truth. In this enormous city we were not likely to meet again so he would never have to confront the falsehood. It was a benefit of urban living. You could create a lot of your own history. I'd created all of mine.

The bus got me back to Battersea as I thought about Tavi. Mark Troughton was already a distant blot. I just hoped this otherwise pointless outing had reinforced my Alex character.

Lavender Hill Police Station

Source: Computers at the Lavender Hill Police Station
Date: Monday 15th September
Time: 12.34
Present: DS Kyriakos Papandreou, DS Ryan Broadhouse, DI
             Gemma Black, DC John Meehan

The detectives were having fun. They were shouting out the names of the famous people that they recognised on pictures from the Mornington Club Party as they appeared on the screen. They argued over the ones that they were not sure of. There were also press shots from the evening with guests arriving, greeting people and drinking champagne.

The team went through what happened at the party. With almost a thousand people there it was hard to pin anything down not least because it was hard to speak to the actual people. Almost every guest there had a secretary, a publicity officer, agent or some kind of security. The police agreed to just speak to the Mornington Club staff to start with and try to build up a picture of what had happened there. They showed pictures of Toby Smithson and Katya to see if any of them remembered anything.

Papandreou reported some positive progress:
-    Eleanor Straminsky was able to give us the private number for Katya Khrushcheva and so we spoke to her. Katya remembers speaking to Eleanor Straminsky but has no idea who Toby Smithson is. She didn't meet

Angelic?

him.
A picture of Katya appeared on the monitor. Broadhouse
stared and breathed in slowly and then out through his
pursed lips:
- Phwewww.
Black responded a little sharply:
- Was that a professional comment, Ryan?
Smiling, Broadhouse attempted a recovery:
- Err, yeah, she looks very intelligent and well informed.
   Probably remember loads of useful information from
   the party. I'm sure she'll make a very reliable witness.
All the team appreciated the humour. But Broadhouse
continued:
- What am I saying? She's a healthy, beautiful, girl. Sorry,
   but I can't ignore that just because I'm a copper. I was
   a bloke first and will be a bloke still when I retire. And
   she is gorgeous.
Gemma saw his meaning and soothed:
- That's alright, Ryan, we're all human.
Papandreou:
- In case it's of any interest I agree with Ryan... I think
   she'll make an excellent witness as well. Which is good
   because she has agreed to come in and talk to us next
   week when she is back in the UK.
The picture of Katya was still on the screen. Broadhouse
was looking at her:
- Obviously, you'll want your best team in for that
   interview.
Black already knew what she wanted:
- I though Yak and me would do it.
Broadhouse was being persistent:
- Well, if you're happy with second best.
Papandreou:
- Thanks for offering your experience, Ryan. I'll ask if

there is any help I need setting up the interview plan.

- I wasn't meaning me. You want Meehan in there. He broke that Harewood woman down in no time. If you have any trouble send him in. We'll have to get him to crack some of the real tough hombrés.

There was some explanation from a defensive Meehan:

- I didn't mean it. I only offered her a drink.

And Gemma supported him:

- Don't worry, John. When you're told your boyfriend has been beaten to death is a very reasonable time to get emotional in my opinion.

Broadhouse had been collating research on Tavi's background, I knew a lot of it already, though I hadn't previously seen the dismal mug shot taken by the police that was on display now. They had looked again at Tavi's conviction for hacking the National Grid. They had found that he didn't do any of it and was only convicted on common purpose after the police got a lot of pressure from above. Ryan explained:

- I spoke to the guys on the case. He helped the police and told them what he knew. He admitted membership of the group but always denied actually doing it. The officers weren't proud of themselves. I got just-doing-my-job responses. Tavi got as long a jail term as any of them though he'd done nothing except help the investigation, apparently having been told that if he helped he'd get off lightly. He was very bitter about it. So was his family. He was locked up for three months. Psychology reports from prison were dreadful. He was on the suicide watch list and was almost sectioned. His family were there in numbers every possible visiting hour. He was a nice guy who wanted to do nothing wrong and the system shafted him.

Papandreou:

Angelic?

- Not the force's finest hour then?

Broadhouse agreed:

- Far from it. When he came out of jail he and James wrote the basis for the SafeNet software and set up the company. He broke up with a girlfriend, Louise Ferryman, when he went to jail. He met Alex Harewood in March. We can't find any reason why anyone would have an issue with him. If he'd started bumping off police officers it would have made some sense. But that isn't what happened.

Meehan asked a question:

- So could Tavi have hacked someone's information like Hecketty claimed? Is that why he got beaten?
- Yeah, it could be. But I've done thirty-one murder cases. Normally it's far less interesting than that. Bet on it being something very mundane here too.

A picture of the SafeNet logo was swiped up by Broadhouse:

- They are still selling about 1000 licenses a week. That's about 100 grand each week. Those guys were making it thick and fast. Apart from the mortgages on investment properties they own there are few overheads.

Then Ryan told them something about my finances:

- We can't find what James does with his money. It all goes offshore. James has access to significant financial resources. He can afford just about anything. He's still keeping the firm running. There was an update that was put out just yesterday. He does everything by email which is what he's always done anyway. Of course he's entitled to go on running his firm as there is no evidence of anything illegal.

None of this was good news for their investigation. Following money is a good way to find people. It wasn't going to work here.

Black wanted to know what her team were thinking:
- Let's just quickly play pin the tail on the donkey and see what ideas everyone has. There is a lot of interest in this case from above. We need to get it right. Broadhouse you first.
- Hecketty all the way. There are always other complications. But this is rape, murder, cover up. It's an old story.
- Yak?
- The party is key. There is more happening than just Hecketty. Somebody upstairs thinks so too, otherwise these cases wouldn't be linked.

Broadhouse just shook his head at that. Meehan agreed with Yak. Black was non-committal.

They were finding out a lot about my friends and me. That wasn't much help. I was no nearer understanding what had happened to Tavi or to Toby. I needed to help the police look in other directions. I had a plan for that.

Internet Café
Battersea Park Road
Battersea
London

Source:	James Hecketty/Alex Harewood and later research.
Date:	Tuesday 16th September
Time:	14.13
Present:	James Hecketty, Jonathan Carlisle (internet café owner), Paul Flowers, Afanasy Shvernik

James was about to make himself obvious. If everything went to plan then the people chasing him were going to be very obvious too.

As Alex I took the taxi to meet the Johnsons; a young couple who wanted to view a house in Warriner Gardens. I already knew they weren't going to be there because I'd invented them and entered the booking onto the system myself. Just round the corner was an internet café which I knew had a door at the side. I knew the owner, Jonathan Carlisle, because I'd been at college with him.

Once I got to the house in Warriner Gardens I got into the James clothes that had been delivered there for me and left by the back door and walked the short distance to the internet café. I was known there so my identity would be confirmed and I made a point of chatting to Jonathan and asking how his wife was.

Of course it's pretty easy to trace anything you do through

an internet café if it has a fixed IP address. I had to assume that these guys were as good as it gets so they would probably have a watch on any account that Tavi had known about. As soon as I accessed any of these accounts that were a possible location for the data they would be automatically informed. They would probably be given the IP address as well and if they wanted to find me then they would have to come straight here.

I set up a portable hard drive to receive my download data. I had played a few tricks with this too.

I logged into every account of mine that I knew Tavi was aware of and every account of Tavi's that I was aware of. Then I watched what was happening out on the street. I was looking for someone in a rush.

There! A car moving just too quickly and stopping suddenly. I left by the side door as a man entered by the front. I walked down the road. Perhaps I should have run. I looked round. There was no one. Then the two men jumped in the car and accelerated towards me. I could see them looking at me. I ran towards the side street.

Just at the corner of the street. I opened a small bag I had with me and emptied it across the road. Then there were fifty razor sharp caltrops all over the road. Just where that car was going to be breaking and turning. Caltrops were originally invented to stop cavalry; four razor sharp points arranged with a tetrahedral angle between each one. They would puncture the tyres of any car.

I ran on. I also took my phone out and started recording what I was seeing on video holding it above my head so that it could record what was happening behind me. The car was rapidly approaching from behind and I heard it brake. Then two dull pops told me two tyres had burst on the caltrops. There was a loud crump and I looked round. The car had crashed. It was stationary with its bonnet squashed against a wall. I thought that was the end of it. Then two guys, one looking young, the other older, got out of the car and started chasing me. Oh shit! That wasn't supposed to happen. I put the phone away. And ran.

They ran. I made it onto the main road. It was busy. That was better. I looked round. One was faster than the other. They were both gaining on me.

There were two buses stopped nose to tail. I headed for the gap of about four feet between them. I knew it took me two steps. Just two steps and I could change from man to woman. I got into the gap. Go! My left hand pulled down the roll of fabric over my chest down to my waist. The reverse side was another colour, so the top went from black to bright blue. The top half had been holding my boobs down. Meanwhile my right hand pulled off the tash and beard from under my chin and then went up and over my head to pull down the hood and release the grip in my hair. Both hands then pulled off the hoodie so that it went inside out and goes from grey to chequered yellow and blue. I wrapped the arms around my waist.

My shoulders were now exposed as was some cleavage. The chequered hoodie was around my waist. My hair had gone shoulder length. There was a little hidden padding in the upper arms of the hoodie that gave me broader shoulders. Around my hips the same padding gave me a more feminine shape. I had taken less than two seconds to go from grey hoodie boy to a girl in bright blue sleeveless top. I changed direction as well and started to walk towards the two men running. I didn't know their names then, but discovered them later.

The older one, Afanasy Shvernik, was behind. He had

darted to the outside of the second bus. The other, Paul Flowers, ran towards the gap I had just left. The first bus pulled away. The second bus followed it.

The two guys were looking round. They had lost me. They were looking for a man. I stopped by a clothes shop window. I looked at their reflection while listening to their conversation. The younger guy, Paul Flowers, was asking:
- So where did he go?
- I thought you had him.
- He went between the buses.
- Which buses?

Flowers pointed at the location:
- The two buses that were just there, idiot.

Shvernik was annoyed at the insult from the younger man, but kept his temper:
- You couldn't have meant those two buses, son. He wasn't between those two. I looked. He didn't come out. So which two did you mean?
- The two that were there.
- But he wasn't there.

Flowers was frustrated and angry. He didn't want to be in the wrong when they reported back:
- He disappeared. You lost him when he came out from between the buses.
- Like fuck I did. He was never between the buses. You lost him and wanted to pass the blame on to me. So you made the shit up about the buses. You must have lost him before that.
- Fuck off. I saw him go between the buses.

Shvernik was still managing to hold his cool:
- Shit. You really are persistent aren't you? So why didn't he come out from between the buses if he went in between the buses. Do you think he jumped on the bus?

Angelic?

- No I'd have seen that.
- You said you saw him go between the buses but he didn't go between the buses. So you must have not seen him do that. Maybe he did get on the bus.

The young guy was shouting now, he'd lost it:

- No fuck that. Fuck you, you TWAT, and fuck this shit. He FUCKING went between the two big red FUCK OFF SIZE FUCKING BUSES.

He stormed off away from the older man. I switched one of my phones on, walked past the elder man and dropped it into his pocket. I'd see where he ended up. So would the police.

This had all worked out OK in the end but they came far too close. Next time I needed something cleverer where I didn't nearly get caught.

The good news was that I had them arguing. They didn't know what had happened and were blaming each other for what had gone wrong. That was my strategy. I was planning for lots to go wrong.

I walked back to the house where Alex was supposed to be, re-entering via the garden. I changed back into Alex's work clothes. I'd left Alex's phone in the house to make an automated call to a mobile while I wasn't there. Both ends of the conversation of me calling Mr Johnson and him giving his apologies were pre-recorded. Alex' location was now in one place while James was elsewhere.

Back at the office I complained about the no show. I said I had rung them and they had apologised. They'd already found somewhere else and forgotten to cancel my viewing. It wasn't an unusual scenario.

The hard drive, which contained a tracking device, sent out a good strong signal all the way back to its destination. The two guys had picked it up from the Internet Café as I had thought they would. I saw its track on the internet site. I could see where it stopped. The place was called Azimuth House and according to the web site the firm there was called Freeman and Jacob. Apparently they sold furniture. I doubted that was all they did.

Then I started getting other alerts. The hard drive was plugged into their network and the software with it had uploaded itself onto their eight machine network. All eight machines were soon sending back data. They were bugged.

Now I had a grandstand view of everything that they did and said within range of those PCs. It wouldn't do as evidence in a court of law, that's not allowed in the UK without a warrant. It gave me plenty of information though about who they were and what they did.

Picking out the interesting bits was hard at first, but I learnt. Eventually I got to the point where I could see what they were talking about just from the attitude of the men. They would adopt different poses when it wasn't furniture on the agenda. I could just fast forward till I spotted the change in attitude. It was even easier with the police. They had organised briefings. Usually at regular times.

There were two more computers in what looked like an office in the basement of Azimuth House. They started out looking very dull. Later they were my window onto the most horrific scenes.

Lavender Hill Police Station

Source:	Computers at the Lavender Hill Police Station
Date:	Wednesday 17th September
Time:	10.42
Present:	DS Kyriakos Papandreou (Yak), DS Ryan Broadhouse, DI Gemma Black, DC John Meehan

Gemma Black was having one of her strategy meetings in her office. She showed the video from my phone of two people chasing me from the internet café. They all watched it. While it was running Black added some additional information

- Straight after this one of Hecketty's phones was switched on. We followed it and found the house of one of the men who were chasing him. He's called Afanasy Shvernik, we visited him at home yesterday which rather surprised his family because we had to go in with the full team, armed officers etc. etc. He has dual British and Russian nationality and is listed as working for a company called Freeman and Jacob. Shvernik says he found the phone in his pocket and took the opportunity to ring his wife, his mother in Russia and his boss at Hecketty's expense.

Papandreou was impressed:

- Clever lad! Hecketty's telling us that there is more than just him involved in this case and making sure that we know exactly who it is.

Broadhouse was shaking his head:

- Muddying the water is all he's doing. These two guys

could be his accomplices. It could be staged to make us think there is someone else involved. Or it may be something else unconnected that he is using to make things look messy. Perhaps these guys were in on the reason why Tavi was killed and the deal they had has gone sour.

Black wanted to know more:

- None of that is impossible. They could be accomplices. But let's find out as much as we can before making too many judgements. The registration plate on the car says it is owned by Freeman and Jacobs, they are a furniture import and export business. They work from Azimuth House on Clapham Road. The boss of that firm is Roman Constantinov the same guy that Shvernik rang with Hecketty's phone. Roman has a bit of old previous but the firm appears to be properly run and legitimate. These two are probably employees.

John Meehan, who I remembered from my interview, explained that Jonathan Carlisle had rung them, as I'd asked him to. Carlisle told them about me going to the internet café, and the two men chasing me and picking up the hard drive.

Black:

- Ryan and Yak can you two go and see Constantinov. Ask him about why his car is being driven around like that. And why he is chasing James Hecketty. Don't expect any sensible answers. Just rattle his cage a little.

After the discussion Meehan and Black talked on their own in the office.

- You look happier today, Boss.
- Do I? It's good when you feel you're making progress at last. There's a lot of pressure on this case. We need to get it right.

Angelic?

She was looking at documents and signing them while he sorted out some of the papers from the briefing. She asked a more personal question:
- How did you get on last night, John?
- OK, but we haven't arranged to meet again.
- Oh, that's a shame. Did you like her?
- Yes, she was confident and clever. She seemed perhaps a bit too confident and perhaps sounded a bit too much like she knew what she was doing all the time.

He didn't sound disappointed. She asked:
- Did she do most of the talking then?
- Well you kind of expect that don't you?
- I like that you talk about her character and haven't said what she looked like. That says a lot about you.
- Looks fade and you get used to them too. Character lasts. I never imagine myself getting into a short term relationship. It's nice to be with a pretty girl, but I always think there is a lot more to people than just looking good.
- I wasn't that wise when I was your age.
- It's not doing me any good. I haven't had a girlfriend in over a year now.
- No? Well young women don't always have good instincts.

John looked a bit confused by that. He was unsure what to say next. He looked away and they both got back to work.

Listening to Gemma and John was interesting. The final outcome of all this might have been very different if their relationship hadn't developed as it did.

Freeman and Jacob
Azimuth House
Clapham Road
London

Source:	Feeds from software on computers using PC microphones and cameras.
Date:	Wednesday 17th September
Time:	11.01
Present:	Roman Constantinov, Afanasy Shvernik, Tim Houghton, Dmitri Chazov, Oleg, Paul Flowers

Roman Constantinov was the head of the Azimuth House group. Also there was Dmitri Chazov, who seemed less affable and who was a short, stocky strong looking fellow in his forties. Afanasy Shvernik was an old stager who talked with the slightest Russian accent. He had the face of someone who had seen it all.

There were also two British men. Houghton in his thirties seemed like a taller, more elegant and less mean version of Chazov. Paul Flowers was a fresh faced lad who had only recently joined the firm. He had started working in the showroom but had now graduated to working upstairs in the office. The questions he asked suggested that he was still finding out what the firm was really about.

The sixth member of the team was Oleg Peruzzi. He was the IT person for the group though he had no particular expertise in the area as far as I could tell, but happened to be better at it than anyone else in the office.

Angelic?

The office was half the first floor of the building. There were desks with phones and computers in one half where Roman's team worked. The other side looked like a furniture showroom, with three sofas, two dining tables, and several armchairs.

I picked up an interesting conversation shortly after they attached my hard drive to their system. Roman was talking. He liked to talk:

- So he may or may not have the data. And we haven't got him. That's not any great success is it? If we suppose that he has got the data then we've got no chance whatsoever of catching him before he goes public with it. Our best hope is that he is a good business man and decides to try to sell it back to us. SHIT! All this because some rich wanker thinks he can't do anything wrong. Which is some fucked up opinion when he is the only one that ever does things that are wrong. FUCK! I'm well tired of clearing up the mess that he makes.

Roman shared another problem with his team:

- To further screw things up. Afanasy got a visit from the police yesterday. SWAT team, flashing lights, the whole works. His wife was just a little upset. Hecketty had dropped a phone into his pocket yesterday. The police followed it and found Mr and Mrs Afanasy at home watching TV with their children. We have to expect a call from these guys today. Everyone on your best behaviour. We do a good job here. Just say what you're job in the furniture business is. Leave out any other irrelevant and unhelpful details. You all know what I mean.

The rich wanker wasn't popular here. This had all been started by Toby chasing Katya. Her half-brother, Ivan, the man who ran TPO Oil, was most likely to also be the wanker that Roman despised. My heart started beating a little faster.

Alex's Flat

Source:	James Hecketty/Alex Harewood
Date:	Thursday 18th September
Time:	Evening
Present:	Alex Harewood

Whenever you switch on a mobile phone it sends out a signal. This identifies the phone on the network. It's not hard to use radio equipment to pick up these signals. The signal changes when a call is made or a text is sent. If you measure the strength of the signal you can say roughly how far away the phone is as well.

I had been recording all these signals from Lavender Hill and Azimuth House and around Alex' flat. There were several thousand devices I had picked up. I had records on a server of when they were switched on, when they were used for texts or calls and what the signal strengths were. The more time I spent recording this information the easier it was to sort out which signals might be useful.

Once you know the signal you can search for people easily. Or at least their phones. Before too long I had a map on my phone showing the location of all the individuals I was interested in so long as they were near enough to a location where I had set up monitoring. The Russians were marked in red, of course, and the police in blue, what else? Each individual had their initial next to them on the map as well as the colour.

All this can be done legally and with publicly available

technology, the police use it too. This is also entirely passive monitoring. It is not possible for anyone to know you are doing it.

The most important data I got from this monitoring was not about the people that I wanted to know about. It was about the people who were interested in me. From the moment I started to get clean data certain signals were regularly with me. My map showed that I was always followed.

The guys in the car outside my flat were a private detective firm employed, I guessed, by whoever was chasing Hecketty. They wanted to be around if he showed up to speak to me or know if I did anything to get in contact with him. They were marked in orange. I worked out their shift patterns and knew when they were likely to knock off early, get a take-away or go to the toilet. I couldn't exploit these loopholes too often or they would realise what I was doing.

It was easy to spot them in real life. Bored looking men in shabby, trying to be smart clothes. They were easy to lose too, but only if I made it obvious that I was trying to lose them. I had to lose them without them knowing I was trying to lose them. It was inevitable that they would underreport the times when they didn't keep up with me because they would want to keep their lucrative contract. They wouldn't be too anxious to disappoint a bunch of Russian thugs either.

Freeman and Jacob

Source:	Alex Harewood
Date:	Thursday 18th September
Time:	15:44
Present:	DS Ryan Broadhouse, DS Kyriakos Papandreou, Roman Constantinov, Afanasy Shvernik, Tim Houghton, Dmitri Chazov, Oleg

DS Broadhouse and DS Papandreou entered the first floor office of Freeman and Jacob at Azimuth House. They were casually dressed and looked a little scruffy compared to the other men in the office who were all wearing smart suits. The others all remained seated when Roman stood up and moved towards the policemen. The visitors introduced themselves and showed their ID cards.

- Hello gentlemen. I'm Detective Sergeant Broadhouse. Am I speaking to Roman Constantinov?
- Yes that's me. How can we help officers. Is this about the crashed car?
- Yes, we thought you might be able to help us understand what happened.

Roman explained that his two employees had taken it. They were looking for an address. He explained that the two employees were Afanasy Shvernik and Paul Flowers who were with him now. They'd phoned him up to say what had happened. Papandreou nodded his head through all this. Broadhouse looked sceptical. He asked Afanasy:

- So who were you two chasing?
- We saw this man throw stuff onto the road. They were

kind of spikes. That's what caused us to crash. We chased after him. Those things were dangerous.
- So why did this man drop a mobile phone into your pocket Afanasy?
- We went through all that last night when you guys visited my home with all lights blazing. My kids were really upset. You guys made out like I was some sort of gangster. I don't know why he put it in my pocket. Though it was nice of him. I enjoyed talking to my Mother.
- What do you do for the firm Afanasy?
- I sell furniture to hotels and restaurants. I help with deliveries. Have you seen our products?

He handed Broadhouse a glossy brochure. It looked very professional. Roman offered more information:
- You can get our stuff online as well. We import from Indonesia, China, Vietnam and we used to get a lot of pine in from eastern Russia; that's how we started. Pine is not so popular these days, though we still get some stuff from there. Everybody wants hardwoods these days. You can see more samples in the showroom downstairs.

Broadhouse ignored this and continued to question Shvernik:
- What's the last sale you clinched, Afanasy?
- The Unicorn Hotel on Bedford Street. They were refitting and wanted some quality modern looking stuff. Everyone wants dark colours and square corners these days. I sold them eight tables and forty chairs from our Burundi range.

Yak asked for more information:
- I know where you mean. Who is it runs that place I've forgotten? The boss's wife was ill wasn't she?
- You mean Terry Stevens. His wife? Do you mean David?

Angelic?

> They're as gay as it gets. We sorted Terry out a few
> years back with some bedroom furniture. We quoted
> him a good price then and we were able to do so again.

Papandreou wasn't fazed; he'd only been trying it on.
Broadhouse started quizzing Shvernik again:

- So why were you chasing James Hecketty?

There was no sign of Shvernik giving up:

- I don't know him. I chased a guy who threw a load of
dangerous shit onto the road that crashed our car.
What would you have done?
- So what was the client that you were visiting doing
when this happened?

Afanasy was sounding entirely reasonable:

- We heard there was a new firm doing imports opening
up on Margaret Street. We were going to pretend to be
clients to get a measure of the competition. I'm not
sure how ethical that is, but I'm sure it's not illegal.
- Yeah, OK, that's great. That all makes sense. Except
that you guys went to an internet café just before this
happened and were asking about a man called James
Hecketty. The same guy you were later chasing down
the road. The proprietor of the internet café says you
took some stuff belonging to James. Can you explain
that to me?
- Yeah we did visit an internet café, just before that guy
trashed our car for us. We weren't sure where this
place was that we were looking for and asked the man
there if he knew it. He said that he didn't. There was an
old hard drive out on the desk and he said we could
have it. It's just over there. He can have it back if he
likes.

Papandreou went over to the drive and picked it up.
Broadhouse continued:

- So why would the proprietor say you were asking after

Hecketty?
- I don't know why he would say that. We just asked for directions. Do you think he confused us with someone else?
- I don't think that he did. There's a lot of odd things happened here. Well thanks for your help, anyway, gentlemen, your responses were all very interesting. We'll be in touch.

The police officers left. Everyone knew it was just an initial call to say that the coppers had noticed the firm who now knew they're being watched. They also knew that all their answers would be checked. Roman was impressed:
- Are you sure I'm paying you enough Afanasy? Beautiful performance. I hope you took all that in everyone. An old master at work. Should be compared to other great performances. Laurence Olivier in Henry the Fifth or Rod Steiger in Heat of the Night.

Shvernik was flattered and looked embarrassed. He sat down at his desk and stared at the computer.

Soft Interview Room
Lavender Hill Police Station

Source:	James Hecketty/Alex Harewood and bugs at Lavender Hill. John Meehan, Police reports.
Date:	Wednesday 17th September
Time:	09.30
Present:	Alex, DI Inspector Gemma Black, DC John Meehan

- Hello Alex. Thanks for coming in again.
- Hello Inspector, what do you need to know?
- There are just a couple of points we need clearing up. Do you mind if DC John Meehan joins us?

He was looking a bit tongue-tied. I spoke first:

- Hello, John, I'm sorry I got so emotional before. It wasn't your fault. You were being thoughtful. It was just a bad time.

I think he had had a whole apology planned and now had no idea what to say. I helped out:

- It would be nice to have a coffee now. Would that be OK?

He was pleased I'd made the suggestion.

- Yes, I'll get you one. Would you like one, Boss?

She nodded and caught my eye. He was a nice, thoughtful, lad. He got up and went to the coffee machine and prepared some coffee for us both. I sat down on one of the soft chairs. Gemma sat just opposite and started asking questions.

She asked me if I'd noticed any thing that suggested a fight or a scuffle at the SafeNet office that Wednesday. I hadn't.

Meehan handed me a coffee and I put it on the table in front of me. I confirmed that the office had shown no signs of a struggle; no chairs overturned or anything obviously broken.

I tried to make some suggestions:
- Who did they upset? James couldn't beat Toby up on his own. Tavi upset someone. Whose information did he hack? That would make sense. If Tavi hacked something important. They would want to know what he had done with it.

She didn't know what to say to that:
- We'll look into everything we can. Were you aware of any arguments going on within SafeNet? James didn't go to the party. Was there a reason? Was he not getting on with Smithson and Mansur?.... Why are you looking worried?
- You're looking for reasons why James did it. It wasn't James.

She looked down at her notes:
- We've got a man who came forward last week. He says that he saw two men arguing in the pub where he is a manager. He saw Tavi's picture in the news and says one of the men was him. He's identified the second as Toby Smithson.
- OK
- He says they were arguing. Can you think what that might have been about?

I could tell she was looking carefully for my reaction:
- No, I've no idea.
- He says that there were two names mentioned. He jumped to a wrong conclusion at first because all the names seemed to be male. Then he spotted that Alex was a she. The other name he heard was James. Apparently it got quite heated. They seemed to reach

an impasse and Tavi left, still angry. Can you think what it may have been about?

- I don't know. You say they used my name. You can't think I was lying to you. I didn't know about this. Why would they argue about me?

The argument was probably a development from the discussion about whether I should continue the challenge or not. It was one of the few times I'd known them argue and the only time that I had been the subject. I couldn't think why that had got so serious, though I had thought there was more to it than either of them would say in front of me. I'd thought for too long. Her reaction told me that I was not quite convincing her. I picked up my coffee and held it in both hands.

- So you're asking us to believe that these two were having an argument about you and you know nothing about it?

She didn't want to let it go. I couldn't tell them the truth and I didn't have time to think up a good lie:

- I'm sorry. I don't know.
- Our witness heard Toby say something about them both loving the same person. Do you know why that might be Alex?
- No. it doesn't fit with anything.
- Is it possible that they were both in love with you?

I put the coffee down and folded my arms:

- What? No. Of course not.
- Why of course not?
- Because they weren't.
- Was Toby in love with you?
- No.
- Was Tavi in love with you?
- No.
- Can I just ask Alex, you're giving very definite answers.

How can you be so sure? You were dating Tavi. Did you get on with him?

- Yeah I liked being with him. How is this helping?
- Love is a very powerful motivation. It creates other powerful emotions like jealousy and hate. It makes people sometimes do things they wouldn't normally do… You're looking very defensive Alex.
- You're asking me these questions that don't make sense.
- Ok. So you didn't know there was an argument between Tavi and Toby.
- I didn't know that.

She was leaning towards me with her elbows on her knees. Pretending to be supportive. I didn't see how this was helping at all. But she had more information that I didn't understand:

- That leaves us with a problem. The man who overheard the argument heard Tavi say to Toby…

She looked down at her notes:

- He said: You know there's no future for James. He's finished.

then she looked at me again:

- What did you think that was about?
- Tavi said that?
- Yes.
- I don't know why he'd say that.
- Ok Alex, we've heard you say that you don't know. What help can you give us?
- I've said all that I can. I don't know why they were arguing.
- Were you in love with Toby?
- No.
- What if Toby and Tavi started this argument again at the party? What if Tavi beat up Toby?

Angelic?

- He didn't
- How do you know? You didn't even know there was an argument a few minutes ago. Were you there?
- No.
- What if James then took revenge on Tavi?
- He didn't. That didn't happen.
- How do you know? Were you there?
- I wasn't there.
- Where?
- I wasn't there when Tavi was beaten.
- Where was that Alex?

This was hard. I had to think before I said:

- I don't know.

She stopped. I was glad to have a break though I would much rather have not been there. She looked towards Meehan. He realised he was supposed to say something. He came out with:

- Have you finished your coffee? Can we get you another?
- No. I'm fine thanks.

Gemma Black turned to a new page of notes and started again:

- OK Alex. Don't worry. You know we have to ask questions. We're just trying to cover all the possibilities. It was very unusual for us to interview a murder victim before he died. What Tavi told us then is now very important. I need to ask you something else. Something quite personal.
- Ok
- Sometimes we come across a contradiction. One person says one thing and another person says a different thing. Finding out why helps us. Tavi said he slept with you. You say he didn't. Why might that be?
- What?

- Why did he say something different from you?
- Oh, we talked about this on the way home... He said he didn't want to let me down.
- Can you help me out a bit more?
- I don't find it very easy ... I mean ... I like men... but ... not sex.
- Oh dear! I'm sorry I had to make you say that. This job is not a good one sometimes... Can we move on? ... Let's move on.

Meehan had blushed wonderfully. He was dark red. I hoped we weren't going to return to this kind of topic. Black kept asking questions:

- Do you know anyone else who knew Toby? Any of his girlfriends?
- No. I only went to his flat twice. I hardly knew him. He spent all his time hunting Miss Khrushcheva.
- Could you have a look round Tavi's flat for us? You were last there on Sunday. Is that correct?
- Yes, Sunday. I'd be happy to have a look round for you. I can't think what there might be to see.
- Thank you.

We got in a police car and I was taken to look at Tavi's flat. There was nothing really to see. Nothing of interest. I thought that some things had been moved. Perhaps. I mentioned it, but it seemed to be ignored.

They gave me a lift home and I was glad to get away. I felt I'd made a mistake in the interview but I wasn't sure where or how.

Angelic?

Freeman and Jacob

Source:	Feeds from software on computers using PC microphones and cameras.
Date:	Friday 19th September
Time:	15:44
Present:	Roman Constantinov, Oleg, Tim Houghton, Afanasy Shvernik, Dmitri Chazov

Roman was talking to his employees. They were all paying a proper amount of attention.

- The man we pay homage to is going to be in town again soon. He'll want to come and visit us and see how we are getting on. He hasn't really come to see us. He has some big important pow wow going on. It's the very one that he has lost all his data for so he's particularly interested to see what's been happening. Have we any happy news for this exalted gentleman?

Only blank faces surrounded him. Roman pushed Oleg for results:

- Oleg, the Russian tech boys are sending you a whole load of stuff. Isn't there anything interesting? Is there anything more that we can do?

Oleg wasn't much help. He had no information about Hecketty at all so he just shrugged his shoulders and said:

- We're covering the girl friend, we've got voice on her permanently, as long as she's in the right clothes, and video from her flat. We're with her all the time. Nothing there. We're following her phone and have heard all that she has had to say to the police. Nothing.

If a fly farts near her we know about it. The men in Russia filter out a lot of the shit, but that leaves nothing. She looks clean. She goes to work, has a date.....

Roman interrupted. He was surprised:

- She's dating blokes already? So much for poor bloody Mansur. He's dead keen on her and a few days after he dies she's dating someone else? So much for all that sloppy stuff women are supposed to love so much... Sorry Oleg, keep going.
- She uses a computer at work. The rest of the time she's also doing nothing interesting. She keeps buying new clothes. The private dicks can't go into her apartment every night. So she can be hard to track. The privates have lost her a few times on visual wearing new stuff and there's no chance of tracking her on the underground anyway. She's always turned up again soon enough.

Roman was disappointed:

- So we have absolutely nothing. The boss is coming and the only thing that we can say to him is that we know nothing. Fuck!
- He gave some advice:
- When this Ivan tit from the motherland comes in would you do me the favour of not mentioning the bad bits, like when the privates lose her? Keep it positive. If things go a little bit wrong then we don't need you to tell him. I think that this is the healthiest approach. The one most likely to lead to a happy and long life. If you see what I mean.

There was information here to help me. I now knew for certain who it was that was chasing me. Ivan Khrushchev, Katya's half-brother, head of the TPO oil empire. He was at the centre of all this. He had enough money to do anything

Angelic?

he wanted.

Roman also mentioned a meeting. An important meeting for which he had lost his data. That could only be the data that Tavi had died for. I was getting closer.

I wondered what sort of character Ivan was. He certainly wasn't impressing these people. He had been running the oil firm for only four years. I couldn't find any reference to him being involved in the firm before that. His father, Yevgeny had created the firm from nothing. Yevgeny had become ill and given up running the firm to Ivan.

There was no mention of Katya on the company website. If she was working for them then it was recent or unofficial.

The Barceloneta
Clapham High Street
Clapham
London

Source:	James Hecketty / Alex Harewood
Date:	Friday 19th September
Time:	18.32
Present:	Alex Harewood, Callum Creighton

I met Callum at a small cafe bar where they would serve you just a drink or a full meal. We'd start with the drink and have a meal if we wanted to continue the conversation and the relationship. Callum looked better in reality than he had in the photo. Friendlier and less self-assured. He met me with a handshake which he then extended to a kiss on the cheek.

We sat at a table while he talked about his work as a teacher. He made big gestures while telling stories about how he had been so right in a situation or brilliantly amusing with a class of his or outsmarted someone else. I wondered how true all this could be.

He clearly liked himself but I couldn't hear anything else in what he was saying. I couldn't hear that he cared for his students or his colleagues. He didn't show any doubt or sign of awareness that he could be wrong. No thought of other possibilities. He seemed to think that the idea of our meeting was to impress me with what he could do. I had said almost nothing since the original hello, but had been

Angelic?

nodding and listening.

I'd heard enough and didn't want to eat a meal with him. I
made an apology, stood up and he came outside with me.
-    Alex, can I have just one kiss?
I hoped he wanted a kiss goodbye
-    Just one.
I walked up close and offered a cheek. I could smell him
and feel his warmth. He kissed my cheek briefly. Then he
put a hand behind my back and pulled me in towards him.
He kissed me full on the mouth and ran his tongue along
my teeth. A hand started to caress my breast I tried to pull
away. He didn't let me go. There was a leg between my
legs and I could feel his excitement against my side. I was
still pulling away. His hand grasped my bum and pulled me
in.

There was a loud noise, someone screaming. I realised it
was me. He stopped and let me go.
-    What's wrong with you?...Why are we here if you don't
     want this?... You've been leading me on all night and
     then you don't want it?
There was no logic in those words. No point in arguing. He
couldn't judge my reactions any better than anyone else's.
There was something in him that told him he was fantastic
and he created a reality around him to fit that feeling.
-    I want to go home now. On my own.
-    Women are so odd. Do you call your behaviour
     reasonable?
-    I'm sorry things have turned out this way. I'm leaving
     now.
I turned away and saw a taxi. The taxi stopped as I
gestured and I got in. There was another one pulling up at
the same time. Was that Timms driving? I couldn't be sure.

In the taxi I tried to control my thoughts and stifle the

memories. Callum hadn't been a good experience. I had only met conceit and lust. Why would any woman want that man to touch her?

I let Eleanor and Jenny know how badly it had gone. Jenny was very reassuring when I spoke to her. I shouldn't feel that I was odd, he was just not someone that I liked. She said it would feel different with someone I liked.

At home I had a shower and thought through again why I'd been forced into this corner. I still had only the very beginnings of an explanation.

Chapter 10
London
September 2014

Lavender Hill Police Station

Source:	Computers at the Lavender Hill Police Station
Date:	Monday 22nd September
Time:	10.52
Present:	DI Inspector Gemma Black, DC John Meehan, DS Kyriakos Papandreou, DS Ryan Broadhouse

The Lavender Hill detectives had done some delving around my James Hecketty background from college. Yak had found that some people at college suspected I was an online gamer called Anirnisiack, but they weren't very sure.
Meehan:

- Yeah that fits. The SafeNet guys were a three man paintball team. Hecketty was brilliant. Super quick and an outstanding shot. He would hit whatever he aimed at. Someone would pop out from a hiding place and James was already aiming at that exact spot. Splat. The team started winning stuff and getting their pictures in the press. Then they stopped. The rumour was that James didn't like the publicity.

Black asked:

- Girl friends?

Papandreou:
- None that anyone knows about. He didn't go to parties either.

Broadhouse:
- A week ago this guy looked ordinary. That's apparently what he wanted the world to see. Far from being ordinary he's about the weirdest thing since people started eating snails. Seriously geeky and no parties? No girlfriends? Did he do something kinky in virtual reality?

Meehan:
- Not having a girlfriend doesn't rate as criminal does it?

Broadhouse:
- Are you not getting much either then?

Meehan looked embarrassed but said nothing. Papandreou got back to business:
- People we talked to liked Hecketty, but no one saw much of him. He was very personable and helpful according to his neighbours. He rarely went into college and avoided people he didn't know. The only people he knew well were Smithson and Mansur.

Nodding slowly, Broadhouse said:
- Like I said. Seriously peculiar. Shall we put his picture out in the red light districts? We may be able to find someone who had him for a client.

Black:
- Yes to that. Good idea Ryan. After the news we heard about the argument between Mansur and Smithson and the second interview with Harewood we have a sniff that there may be something that happened at SafeNet. James won't come in to talk to us. And we think there is a possibility Harewood knows something she's not saying.

They were still looking in the wrong direction. I'd failed to

Angelic?

convince them that the argument between Tavi and Toby was irrelevant. It might have helped if I knew why it had got so heated.

Freeman and Jacob

Source: Eavesdropping computers at the Location. Later
             examination of the scene. Some eyewitness
             testimony.
Date: Thursday 25th September
Time: 11.20
Present: Ivan and Katya Khrushcheva, Roman Constantinov
             and his team.

The feeds from Freeman and Jacob got very interesting.
There was a bit of a commotion. Someone was arriving.
Ivan and Katya Khrushcheva. He was a good looking guy
and appeared like he had some intelligence, immaculately
dressed in a well fitted grey suit. Katya was looking as
stunning as ever. Her hair was half up and half down and
absolutely perfect. She was wearing a dress that was a
little too colourful for her to be a secretary, but still wasn't
casual. It had a high collar and long sleeves, a wide belt
that matched her shoes and fitted closely. It reeked of
money and said to 99.99% of the male population that
they were well below her league. The guys there still
stared at her. They didn't seem to know her though.

Roman greeted Ivan with a proper Russian embrace. Katya
just shook hands. The other guys were still at their desks.
Two of them were on the phone still. There was some
small talk.

Then Ivan got down to the reason for their visit; he wanted
to know if Hecketty had been found yet. Roman didn't
have any good news for him. Ivan did not look impressed

and asked:

- What's the coverage on the girlfriend looking like? I've checked myself a couple of times but you may know more.

Roman points Ivan towards the computer that Oleg is sitting at and does his best to answer the question and make his team appear to be doing a great job:

- We can't see anything that helps. Oleg's getting real bored watching her. Apart from when she flashes her boobies in the morning. We've listened in to just about every conversation she has had. Your tech guys are sending us all the data from her phone. We know where she is all the time. We've got her covered at work, at home. It's incredibly uninteresting. Weeks of tedium. She's just skirt. She only met Tavi on three occasions. You can kill her, fuck her or whatever you want. It won't get your data back.

Ivan grunted an acknowledgement. Katya wanted to know more:

- Has your coverage been permanent? Have there been any breaks?

Romans tries to make it sound good:

- They've done pretty well. It hasn't all been plain sailing though. We thought we'd lost her once at the cinema. Turns out she had to go home early via the chemists because her monthly thing had started early. The private dicks lost the visuals on her for a while.

She kept digging:

- There must be something about her. We saw the recording with Mansur. He bleated about her a lot. He seemed really keen on her.
- That may be so but she's seen other guys since then. Maybe she wasn't quite as keen on him as he was on her. The only thing that is remotely interesting about

her is that she made friends with Eleanor Straminsky at the party.

Katya was not impressed:

- Did she? I know Eleanor. She wants everybody to be nice all the time. Just doesn't get that the world isn't like that. She's been suffering from depression since her fiancé failed to meet her ideals. She doesn't get that self-interest sometimes outweighs being polite. She's one of life's weak and unfortunate innocents. She's wouldn't be involved in anything that should concern us.

Ivan had heard enough of that and asked Roman again about me:

- If Hecketty can't get the data, and we do know he's looking now, he may want to start asking this Harewood girl for clues. So she may be a way to find Hecketty that doesn't involve the police. But you say there's nothing to her at all?

Roman:

- Not a thing except that she somehow tripped up in an interview and managed to get the police looking at SafeNet again. She's off to Russia soon. Should we follow her there?
- Why's she going to Russia?
- She's going to a party at the Straminsky's and hoping to meet Katya.

Katya didn't look impressed:

- She'll be lucky. What would we talk about? Isn't she an estate agent? I'm supposed to be going to the Straminsky party. I'm not sure I want to have to pretend to be nice to people all evening.

Roman raised another issue:

- This shit-storm is exposing us too much. We had a visit from the police. The first we have ever had. Afanasy showed just how good he can be, but they are watching us now. It's risky. We're getting far more exposure than we need because of a mess that you started.

Ivan didn't see it that way:

- This shit storm started around here. You guys can help pay for it. If your clowns hadn't lost Hecketty in the first place, or the second place, we'd all be happy wouldn't we. Sort it out. He's only one guy.

Roman doesn't' look happy with what he is being told:

- I'm not sure I'm quite getting this, Ivan. Why do I send you so much money? You're supposed to be a help. In fact you just cause problems. I've got my team running all over London for you. I'm losing heavily there, just to clear up a fucking mess that you made. Please explain to me why it is that we are doing this. Why don't I just stop sending you money and tell you to piss off?

Ivan wasn't looking too happy either and the argument could have gone on but Katya came in to try to break the deadlock:

- This isn't the best situation for any of us. We all could have done better. What you really need is to stop getting attention from the police. We just need to make sure that the things we have in place go ahead as planned.

She talked directly to her brother:

- Ivan, if anything crops up while we're in town why don't we deal with it? Let these guys have a break, at least until after the meeting. Your mates would appreciate a chance to have a go at Hecketty, wouldn't they?

Ivan gives a reluctant nod. Then Katya turns to Roman:

- Would that be a compromise, Roman? We don't want this nonsense to be the end of a relationship that has been productive for all of us.

Roman is nodding his head:

- Yes I guess that would do for now. I'll talk to your friends and tell them whatever they need to know. I'll throw in some hospitality as well. I'll come round Wednesday evening with some very willing female company. There'll be plenty to go round. Get you guys some proper relaxation before the meeting. Sorry, Katya, I just don't deal with your end of the market.

Katya displayed an appropriate middle finger and gave him an unfriendly grin.

So the meeting was most likely on Thursday. There was only one hotel mentioned in their email system: the Chelsea Imperial. I knew it had a conference suite, so I guessed that was the venue. The meeting had something to do with what Tavi had unearthed. I had about a week to get things set up properly.

The time out at the cinema had proved to be just enough time to buy a car. There were other times when they had lost me from their surveillance but they weren't admitting to these in front of their boss. The period problem both got me away from the surveillance and strengthened my femininity. It made a bigger gap between James and Alex in case anyone started to make the connection.

Katya on this performance was not likeable. She was different from the person we had seen in Harvey Nichols. They looked the same but the characters were different. Toby would have an interesting time if he ever met this version of her.

From another perspective this was all looking positive. They were no nearer finding me whereas I was getting a lot of information about them. I checked through my options again. The big meeting was in a week. It would prove to be

Angelic?

a very interesting week.

Robert Sefton Estate Agents, London and a House for Sale

Source: Alex Harewood
Date: Friday 26th September
Time: 12.30
Present: Alex Harewood, Harbinder Patterson, Richie
           Richardson, Robert Sefton

I showed a young man around a flat, not an expensive one. He seemed to like the place and I felt I was doing a great job selling it. Or maybe I wasn't. You find out quite a lot about someone showing them round a house. It's part of checking them out to see how serious they are. Why are they looking to buy? What job do they do? What are they selling? How far has their sale gone? After an hour with this guy and just before we parted. He said:

- I'm going to see Dawn of the Planet of the Apes tomorrow. I had thought to go on my own, but it's nice to have company sometimes.

This was a nice way to be asked out. I didn't have to say yes, or no. I could just continue a conversation, which is what I did:

- Are you a fan of the Planet of the Apes series?
- I'm ashamed to say that I am though I rarely admit to it. Rather embarrassing don't you think?
- It is rather. I suppose you have a whole array of embarrassing habits, just like the rest of us.

He looked amused:

- Of course. You can tell me all yours, if you like. Which

end of the alphabet shall we start at?
-   Alpha or Omega?
I said with the cheekiest grin I could muster. He didn't get it at first and only replied:
-   Huh?
Then he worked out the Planet of the Ape's reference and his face lit up. I said:
-   Where tomorrow? What time?
He was still grinning:
-   Umm... the Odeon, Kensington, 7 o'clock
I kissed the end of my finger and planted it on his cheek. He looked awestruck.
-   See you there.
-   See you tomorrow.
he said as I walked away.

That was fun, I thought as I got into the taxi that had just arrived on time to take me back to the office.

Harbinder asked:
-   How was Mr Richardson?
-   He was alright.
She picked up that it wasn't my usual response:
-   Oh was he now? And was there an... offer? And have you planned another... viewing? And does he want to... move in... soon?
-   Stop it! You're naughty.
but I was laughing at her clever innuendo. She exaggerated peering at me and said:
-   So...?
-   Seven tomorrow.
She rolled her eyes at me and nodded her head slowly, knowingly:
-   Hmmm.. Well, have fun and go prepared. Make sure you take everything you might need. Spare knickers. A

toothbrush perhaps.

She was grinning suggestively. I sounded shocked:

-    We're only going to see a film!

She raised her eyebrows, dropped her chin, looked very sceptical, turned round and went back to work.

Lavender Hill Police Station

Source: Computers at the Lavender Hill Police Station
Date: Friday 26th September
Time: 09.48
Present: DI Inspector Gemma Black, DC John Meehan, DS
             Kyriakos Papandreou, DS Ryan Broadhouse

A picture of Katya appeared on the screen. Everyone looked at her. Broadhouse loosened his collar and Black gave the information about her interview:

- She is one cool character. She came in with her solicitor, a man called Flyorov. She says she knows nothing of any use to us whatsoever. She didn't recognise Smithson, or Mansur, or Harewood, or Hecketty. Her brother owns Freeman and Jacobs and she's met all the employees there, but doesn't know them well. What did you think Yak?
- She showed us a blank screen. She may know nothing or everything.

Broadhouse:

- Not like the Harewood girl then. She gets emotional and curls up in her chair when you start asking her difficult questions.

Meehan didn't quite agree:

- No, she just gets defensive when you ask her questions about herself.

Broadhouse:

- You two ought to get on fine then.

Which produced a quick grin on Papandreou's face but

Black didn't approve and wanted to move past this:
-   Yak you have something else, don't you?

The picture on the screen changed as Yak swiped his
tablet. It showed a small white van parked in an uncared
for courtyard at the back of a brick built building. Just
visible on the door of the van was the SafeNet logo. They
had found a lot of Tavi's blood inside it. In the back of the
van was also a sealed decorator's bucket. Inside that was a
sort of sludge, the remains of the headless girl's head
dissolved in sodium hydroxide solution. There was enough
bone left for DNA testing but no soft tissue. Papandreou
briefly displayed a picture from the pathologist's lab. There
was one large piece of bone that used to be the crown of
the girls head sitting in a stainless steel tray along with
smaller pieces of bone and some sludgy bits. There was no
known cause of death except that it had to do with her
head.
Meehan:
-   Someone will be missing her. Someone will want to
    know where she is.
Papandreou reported the news about James' flat from
forensics. They had found Tavi's blood spattered on the
walls, a tooth of his and blood from the dead girl in the
freezer. They also managed to find some hair in the u-bend
of the sink that had some DNA in it. The DNA there
matched that of the semen in the dead girl. They thought
this all proved I had beaten up Tavi in my flat after raping
the dead girl, possibly because he found the girls' body in
my freezer. The fire and the fire brigade may have ruined a
lot of possible evidence.
Broadhouse looked satisfied:
-   So it was Hecketty.
Papandreou:
-   It is looking that way. This new info from the flat seems

conclusive. It doesn't come close to explaining why the beating of Mansur was so prolonged. Or how or where or when Hecketty raped and killed the girl, or who the girl is.

Meehan:

-   There was an argument. I get that. Tavi may have beaten up Smithson at the party because of it. But what then? Why did Tavi Mansur stand his girlfriend up to go and look in James Hecketty's freezer? And why did James ring us straight after doing it and before dumping the bodies next day? I thought we had him down as clever.

Black, Broadhouse, Papandreou and Meehan talked it all through again. The conclusion that they came to was that with the argument, the evidence from the flat, the tooth and the blood, but mainly the DNA, was that I was definitely guilty of raping the girl and killing my friend in my flat. They thought they had enough evidence for a conviction. They saw the stuff with Roman from Freeman and Jacob as an irrelevant sideshow. They were going to get an arrest warrant for me.

What happened later between Black and Meehan told me a little more.

-   Boss?... You don't look happy.

Gemma looked caught out, as though Meehan wasn't supposed to have noticed.

-   No? Well take it from me. I am. I'll be happier still when we find our killer. But I would like to understand a lot more.
-   We're after James but we can't work out what really happened. It just doesn't make any sense if it's James. Why are we doing this?

She tried to sound authoritative:

-   It's always like this. It's always a mess with things you don't quite get. Young men straight out of college want it to be neat and everything tied up. I've read books like that but real cases always have untidy endings and lingering questions. That's life. It's never perfect. You just do what you can.

- Ok. OK. I am still new at this and I know you know what you're doing.

Black still looked a little upset; she wasn't comfortable. Meehan saw this and moved the conversation on:

- Are you going away for the weekend?
- Yeah we're just going to spend Saturday night with Carl's mother.
- Is that a good thing?
- Yes. I like his Mum. She's a really good lady and part of the reason I married him I suppose. She seems to understand the world and how things fit together. Wise, I suppose you might call her.
- Is Carl like that too?
- No he's not really. He's more the alpha male type. He seems to think that if he does what I want then he's less of a man.
- Not quite what you signed up for?
- Oh no nothing like that. We're fine. We've got three beautiful children and I wouldn't change a single thing about any one of them.

So the police knew I was guilty. They had evidence to prove it.

How had they worked the DNA? They only had a few hairs and it would be easy to prove they weren't mine. So that person had to be in my flat. Could the hairs be from one of the people who'd visited me? Had one of them raped the headless girl?

My two personalities were becoming more distinct. Alex

was now a much loved girlfriend who Tavi had dated and perhaps slept with. James was a shadowy character who raped women and killed his associates. Being Alex was becoming so easy. I felt safer now when I was her and could pretend that I was an ordinary person, which I may have been once but I clearly was not now.

I knew that Ivan had beaten up Toby apparently because Toby was chasing his sister, which was some way from normal. Tavi had stolen his data but Tavi was dead. The police had me in their sights. They were looking everywhere for James Hecketty. But they weren't helping me find out anything about what exactly had happened at the party to start all this off. Neither was I any nearer to discovering what it was that Tavi had found to get himself kicked slowly to death.

Odeon Cinema
Kensington
London

Source: James Hecketty/Alex Harewood
Date: Saturday 27th September
Time: 19.11
Present: Richard Richardson, Alex Harewood, girl selling popcorn.

- Popcorn?

He asked after kissing me on the cheek and saying hello. I answered with another question:

- Is it possible to see a film without eating popcorn?
- I don't think so, I don't know, you know I don't think I've ever tried it. Sweet?

I nodded. He gave the order to the girl behind the counter.

- Extra-large sweet to share

The price was extortionate and the popcorn was a little stale.

- Where shall we sit?

There was an almost empty row near the back:

- Will this do?

I shuffled in first and Richard followed me.

- So it's Richard Richardson?
- Dreadful what your parents do to you isn't it? But I'm afraid it's even worse than that. My Dad was also Richard Richardson and his dad and his dad. Once the rot set in it was impossible to stop.
- It's no more than you'd expect.

Angelic?

I sat down in a seat. He sat down too:
-   Oh I know what's coming here. You can't think that you're the first to have thought that line up.
-   What line?
-   It's no more than you'd expect from a complete bunch of dicks.
-   Oh, OK. Yes, I was just putting that together.
-   Sorry, I should have let you say it. Then I could have laughed and told you how clever and funny you are. As it is I've only managed to indicate that you're unoriginal. Foot in mouth again. I'll try to be more flattering in future.
-   I'm happy being flattered but keep putting the honesty first. It's a good thing.
-   I think I can manage both at once.
-   That's good to hear. Please go ahead.
He looked at me, studying my face for a few seconds. Then he grinned cheekily and said:
-   You're gorgeous.
I started to laugh and so did he. He was clever. I liked that. The film started. His arm went around my shoulders. I grabbed his hand to make sure that he knew it was meant to stay there, but not stray anywhere else. That felt OK.

The film ended. I offered the first comment as the credits were still rolling and we were queuing to get out:
-   Just an action movie then.
-   Yes it lacks any underlying philosophy that most of the others have.
-   No, no serious discussion of time travel or man's capacity for self-destruction
-   There's nothing about the rights of other species. The baddy was an ape. That's a bit unfair really.
-   With that material they could have made some play with both sides being in the wrong.

- He had another view on it:
- It's not really a girl movie is it?
- Neither were the others.

There was something else I wanted to talk about. After my last date, with Callum, I wanted to make sure things stayed at a distance:

- Would you mind if we went back to the embarrassing things about ourselves conversation?
- You want to hear more? I do have a very large repertoire.
- No. No...Well I wouldn't mind hearing more. But I need to say something.
- Oh, OK...

Then he looked worried and added:

- My list of embarrassing things hasn't put you off has it?
- No, don't worry. I just don't want to get too physical at the moment.
- So... Keep off the grass?
- Yeah well... not the grass.
- Hills then.
- Yeah, keep of the hills, maybe ... and the valleys!
- Okay, that's OK. That's nice.
- That's nice?
- Yes it is, I haven't suggested any intimacy and you're telling me no. So you must have thought of it and, if I'm right, that means you'd like to and this is a real reason, not an excuse. There are some obstacles but this beautiful, clever girl wants to be intimate with me. That's nice.

We stood on the pavement outside and I stared at this thoughtful, likeable bloke and knew exactly now what Jenny had meant. Being with Richie was fun. He wanted me to be with him, but only if I wanted that too. I got close, touched his arm and let him kiss me. I couldn't relax

Angelic?

but it felt like an enquiry, not a certainty, an insistence, or a dominance.

- That's not a hill or a valley is it?
- No, not a hill, not a valley.
- Just let me know when the roads are open again. In case I should be lucky enough to be invited to navigate in that direction.
- OK. I'll do that

We got a taxi and it took me home first. He waited in the taxi until I'd got through the ground floor door.

As I tried to sleep a whole mix of feelings were washing through my head and churning through my stomach. I had dismissed Mark and Callum immediately. It was harder to not think about Richie.

Lavender Hill Police station

Source: Computers at the Lavender Hill Police Station
Date: Monday 29th September
Time: 10.52
Present: DI Inspector Gemma Black, DC John Meehan, DS
            Kyriakos Papandreou, DS Ryan Broadhouse, DC
            Janet Turner

Black and her team were looking at pictures of the men who worked for Freeman and Jacob at Azimuth House. Broadhouse managed to get a picture of each of them to appear on the screen as he mentioned their names:

- These are Roman Constantinov, Tim Houghton, Afanasy Shvernik, Paul Flowers, Oleg Peruzzi, Dmitri Chazov. There are no convictions of any significance on their records. Nothing or only minor stuff from years ago.

That raised a query from Papandreou:

- What was that name again? Chazov?

Broadhouse reviews his list:

- Dmitri Chazov.
- Yeah, there was a Dmitri Chazov involved in the Sun House Case.

Meehan:

- What is the Sun House Case?

Papandreou:

- A trafficked prostitute, called Angelina, got hold of a gun and killed every man in the brothel. Most of them were armed but she was exceptionally good with a gun. Every bullet hit its target.

Yak touched the spot between his eyes and continued:

- It's not like they were standing still in front of her. They were shooting back! She got away. She just disappeared. Nobody knows where. The case was archived a while ago.

Meehan was full of wonder and kept on wanting answers from Papandreou:

- And we don't know who she was?

Yak replied, it was an usual case and easily remembered:

- We couldn't get a very good description of her because every one of the girls at the brothel told us something different. We're not even sure her name was Angelina. They didn't want her caught by us and even managed to mess up the forensics. The last guy she killed was the brothel boss. She shot him so that he died slowly and painfully. The traffickers weren't coming forward, neither were the punters or the girls. We had eight dead men, no willing witnesses and hundreds of man hours leading to nothing.

Meehan:

- Jesus. So what did Chazov do there?
- He wasn't there when it happened. He was only an occasional visitor. A couple of the girls we spoke to came up with his name, but there was nothing we could get him on. He was a real hard ass. Said nothing in the interview room. Nothing. It didn't help that a lot of the girls were very frightened of Chazov. No one was willing to say anything against him and we suspect, only from that, that he was a wrangler. A guy who breaks in new girls.

The policemen briefly considered the possibility that Freeman and Jacob could be the front for a trafficking operation. It was exactly the right kind of business. They couldn't see any relevance to their case and Black wanted to pass the information on to another department and move on to other business.

A firm of solicitors called Witter and Proctor solicitors had been in touch. Meehan had taken the call:

-   They say they have been instructed by James Hecketty to act on his behalf. The brief said that their client was innocent until a court of law said otherwise and as such had a right to defend himself. He pointed out that there were clearly people chasing James and that he was entitled to respond with proportionate force if he was in danger. Any actions he takes in future should be seen in that light.

Broadhouse wanted to know more:

-   So is he threatening the guys who are chasing him?

Meehan:

-   I asked the same question. He wasn't threatening anything. Just pointing out a right to self-defence. If people were chasing him with intent to cause him harm, and we had evidence that they were, then he could respond appropriately, he could take action to preserve his life.

Broadhouse:

-   So this business with the Russians is going to get more serious.

Black:

-   It certainly does carry that implication. I'm going to brief SCO19 so that they already have the background and can respond more effectively if something does happen. Keep everyone tight on this. Stay on top of all the paperwork. There's plenty of opportunity for something to go awry with this case and we don't want to be left with egg on our faces.

Angelic?

When the others had gone Meehan and Black talked on their own. Black sounded like she was not looking forward to going home and a bit regretful:

- Things could have turned out differently for me. I knew a lad at college. Perhaps I should have taken the initiative. But Carl was so forward and things were so passionate from the very start. Now I feel I could have handled a little less passion and a bit more consideration.

Meehan looked embarrassed and could only provide a neutral response:

- I guess that marriage is always some kind of compromise.
- Sorry John, I shouldn't be saying all this to you. I'll see you tomorrow.

Witter and Proctor? I hadn't ever heard of them. I was being helped again.

There was a new officer on the team, working in the operations room. She was not high up enough to be involved in these discussions. Janet Turner was very slim and had long hair. Not many people would call her pretty but she moved beautifully. Every time she did something it seemed to say something about her character. It said I like people and care for them. She was attractive. All the more so because she didn't look like she would get a lot of attention from men; while the opposite was probably true.

I thought she had caught John Meehan's eye. So did Gemma Black.

Basement
Azimuth House

Source:	Eavesdropping computers at the Location.
	Later examination of the scene.
	Eyewitness testimony.
Date:	Monday 29th September
Time:	19.12
Present:	Dmitri Chazov, Tim Houghton, three young women from Eastern Russia

Later that day I got confirmation of what really happened at Freemen and Jacob. My information came from the two computers in the basement office. It was very hard to see what was happening at the time. I filled in some of the gaps in my knowledge later.

It was late in the evening when three young women got down from a truck and are invited down in to the basement of Azimuth House. They went into the large central area through the double doors and were told to only speak English. They eagerly accepted the offer of something to eat.

Houghton and Chazov introduced them to the idea of why they were really there and the fact that it has nothing to do with waiting tables or servicing hotel rooms. They show their guns and Chazov grabbed a girl with dark hair and black eyes. He raped her in the office. Chazov then asked Houghton:
- Which one do you want?

Angelic?

- I'll take the fair hair.

The girl with fair hair had no idea what to do. She started walking towards the door.

- Hold it!

said Houghton, which sounded familiar to me. There was some exasperation in his voice. He ran after her. She stopped. He said:

- It's not much to me, love. You can be screwed by me or shot by him. I know which I prefer. You make your own mind up

She turned round and started walking back towards the other girls. Houghton stood in her way:

- Me first.

She looked utterly lost. Hopeless. The other girls were staring. Trying to assimilate what was happening. He coaxed:

- I'll be gentle

Her eyes were wide with horror. She trembled but submitted and went quietly with him to be raped. Minutes later they both emerged from the room. The girl was quiet but distraught.

Chazov didn't seem to do compassion:

- Have you all got a complete picture of what is happening to you and where you stand now?

The girls were huddled in a corner. They nodded while weeping.

- That is one good result. Boy, do I like this job.

They were told to go back into the canteen. They did so without complaint, pleased to be leaving the men and Houghton shut the door behind them. I heard the women talking and whimpering inside the canteen.

I trembled and shook when I saw this. I gulped in air as I tried to settle my stomach down and get my brain to stop replaying scenes of rape and abuse as I imagined what these girl's daily lives were to become.

They would learn how to please men; what lines to say to get men relaxed, what actions to take to get them going, where to press to hurry those few cubic centimetres of fluid out of him and into themselves and how to keep him happy afterwards and wanting to come back another day for more.

The 21st century had just disappeared for these women. They shared a lifestyle now that would be familiar to many slave women from any place and many cultures and any time.

The dead girl found with Tavi was most likely a girl like these; trafficked from Russia. Now she was a nameless headless dismembered corpse. It mattered that I might be able to find her name somehow. It mattered beyond it helping me find the killers of Tavi. She would want to be a person, not a body.

When I calmed down I realised I also had some very useful information. "Hold it!" was what Houghton said when the girl moved towards the door before he raped her. I had heard that said that way in that voice before. In James' flat. Houghton was the man with the gun in my flat the day Tavi was killed. He may well also have been the man that had raped the headless girl. Perhaps they then planted Houghton's hair in my flat to make it look like me.

They didn't want me in jail. These depraved people only wanted the police to find me. As long as I was wanted for rape and murder, any data I found that Tavi had stolen would be immediately discredited. If I walked into a police station to give a DNA sample I wouldn't survive long after I walked out. I was not going to give a DNA sample though.

Angelic?

Neither was I going to walk into a police station.

I had made some progress. The police had me down as guilty of murder and rape because they knew so little. It was even clearer now that they were the least of my worries.

Alex's Flat

Source: James Hecketty/Alex Jones
Date: Tuesday 30th September
Time: 09.01
Present: Alex Harewood

There was something extra in the post amongst the usual collection of catalogues and bills when I got in from work. There was a small envelope, just big enough for a passport. I had applied for one only the previous week. The story was that Alex had got back into the country from Canada on a temporary passport. I needed a real one to get to Russia. She had been born in Kendal, Cumbria, to British parents so she had every right to be in the UK. I had expected the application to be returned, asking for more documentation, the way they would do it if they wanted to turn the application down. They did a lot of checks and I hadn't expected to be successful. Fooling financial institutions is not the same as fooling the UK government.

The package was soon open and I stared in wonder at a small booklet. A British passport. There I was on the second page:

> *Harewood*
> *Alexandra Elisabeth*
> *British Citizen*
> *22 Aug 92*
> *F Kendal*

I'd never had a passport at all before. James had always

Angelic?

stayed in the UK. This was special. It felt real, solid. Alex felt real. I had a passport to prove it. I looked at the picture of the woman in the photograph. Officially, this was me?

The Duke of Cumberland
Hanson Street
London

Source:	James Hecketty
Date:	Tuesday 30th September
Time:	10.35
Present:	James Hecketty, Leonid Erdeli and Nikolay Yurlov, the Landlord

I went out a lot as Alex. I'd go shopping, to the cinema, the theatre or maybe an art gallery. On Monday night I'd go to the V and A. Harbinder welcomed me at her home as did Jenny. There were several times when I visited Toby in hospital and I saw Tavi's parents a couple of times. I tried to keep all this as irregular and unpredictable as possible. All so that it made it easier to escape the people watching me when I wanted to. I couldn't have them lose me every time I went out, so had to go out a lot. This also increased the character distance between James and Alex. I tried to make it just once a week that I escaped, depending on need. On Sunday, Monday, Thursday and Friday I'd work at the Estate Agents, that was very regular and I only rarely used the client no shows to escape the orange dots of the private firm watching me.

Today I left my flat heading for the underground which was the easiest place to lose them. A lot of planning had gone into this escape and I'd arranged things with Dodson already. He'd put everything in place. There was a phone hidden in the ladies loo at a Coffee House on Polland Street. I'd make it send text messages from it to Eleanor, Jenny and Harbinder at a time when I was returning from the main event. This would make the time gap between their missing me and James appearance elsewhere smaller. I was wearing my quick switch kit in case it all went wrong.

I went in to the Duke of Cumberland.
- What will you have Sir?
The man behind the bar was the archetypal pub landlord; greying hair, portly and with a luxurious handlebar moustache. He was in the right place. It was the archetypal pub. Panelled wooden bar, dark carpet, leather seating.
- A pint of Gold please.
The head on the beer stuck to my moustache and I enjoyed wiping it off with the back of my hand. It was exceptionally good beer and the landlord thanked me for saying so. I went to sit outside at the tables on the pavement. I switched on the second of the phones that were registered to me, the first one had gone into Afanasy Shvernik's pocket. I dialled. There was an answer:
- Roman Constantinov.
- Hello Roman. This is James Hecketty.
- James! I was hoping to get in touch with you. There's a number of things that we can discuss. How are you?
Roman was pretending to be my best friend.
- I'm doing fine thanks, Roman, remind me, how is it that you know me?
- I thought we'd discussed a furniture deal at the SafeNet Office. Wasn't that it?
It was a good answer. There were things I didn't want to admit to either, so I did a bit of invention.
- No I don't think it was that. I got someone to chase a car number plate for me. A plate on a car that was chasing me. You sent two men after me. I've been

talking to Afanasy Shvernik's mother. She's a nice lady. Does she know what her son does for a living?

- Afanasy is a top ranked furniture salesman. She certainly knows that.
- Why don't we talk in person, Roman, I'm at the Duke of Cumberland on Hanson Street. We could talk about the headless girl, or how it is that you really make money.
- I'm not sure what you mean by that. But, yeah, let's meet. Good idea. Get a pint in for me would you?
- Sure Roman. See you soon.

I closed the connection and then dialled 999 but didn't press the call button. I sipped my beer and waited a few minutes. I drank some more. It tasted good and settled my nerves a little. I could easily be dead in the time it might take me to finish that pint.

Ivan's goons arrived. A car too expensive, driven too fast, too badly parked with two men who were moving too quickly. I pressed the call button on the phone and got through to the emergency services:

- Police please…. There is a gun battle going on in Hanson Street. Shots are being fired. My name is James Hecketty.

I stood up and let them see me. Then started running. They followed. So far this plan was working beautifully.

Chapter 11
London
October 2014

Lavender Hill Police Station

Source: Computers at the Lavender Hill Police Station
Date: Wednesday 1st October
Time: 11.47
Present: DI Inspector Gemma Black, DC John Meehan, DS
                Kyriakos Papandreou, DS Ryan Broadhouse
In the Video: James Hecketty, Leonid Erdeli and Nikolay Yurlov

The police at Lavender Hill were watching footage from CCTV on the screen in Black's office. The recording has been edited between five different cameras. I had picked a location where I knew there was a lot of coverage.

They saw James sitting at the tables outside the Duke of Cumberland. He stood up and looked across the road at two men who had just arrived in a car. The men spotted James and started to run after him. James ran down a narrow street with tall buildings on either side that were set close to the pavement.

The two men followed. Just before they passed the only parked car on the street shots were fired at them from above. The two men looked up at the buildings where the sound was coming from. They saw the rounds hit the ground at their feet so they ducked behind the car for protection. They could see two men on the rooftop and returned fire. One of the men on the roof slowly collapsed. The gun battle continued.

People on the adjoining road were panicking at the sound of the shots. There were screams as people realised what was happening. Some peered round the corner to see what was going on. Then they ducked back as they heard the gunshots and saw the men shooting at the roof.

The two men shooting and sheltering behind the vehicle cover their eyes as the car windows shatter, blown out by the shots from the roof. The car rocked as the shots hit it. For over a minute the gun battle continued. The two men by the car both took shelter and reloaded their weapons on two occasions.

A police patrol car stopped suddenly and its occupants tried to keep people away. Moments later SCO 19, the firearms team, arrived. Quickly they set up at the end of the street. The two men in the street had no idea what to do. They had SCO 19 one side of them and the shooters above them. They thought they were going to die. SCO fired warning shots over their heads but that just added to the confusion. The sound of shooting from above did not stop.

Then they started to realise it was just the noise. There were no longer bullets hitting the ground or the car. The noise of shooting then stopped. There were only two men in the road. They put down their guns while nervously looking up at the roof.

SCO 19 reinforcements arrived at about the same time as the helicopter. They prepared to storm the building where the gunshots had come from but eventually took a more relaxed approach and went up to the roof calmly.

Gemma Black stopped the video. She pressed the remote control and the screen showed a still from the beginning of the video of me as James calling the police. She started to explain to her team:

- This was the scene on Hanson Street yesterday. We were alerted about the gunfight 20 seconds before it started. The caller was James Hecketty. He gave his name. You can see him in the street just before the shooting starts. These two men started chasing him.

Black continued after retaking her seat.

- The gunshots from the building were all blanks fired from four remotely operated starting pistols like you get at a running track. There were also two rubber blow up men who were inflated when the shooting started and just visible from the street.

She pressed the remote again and the screen showed the rooftop the men were shooting at, apparently taken from the helicopter. There were two deflated rubber blow up men and four starting pistols all connected to a box with lots of wires.

Tommy Dodson had dressed like James while setting this up. Similar hoodie and baseball cap. He was about the same height, though stockier. Anyone looking at any security camera shots of it being put in place would have assumed that it was James.

Alex had made a point of putting the rubbish out at her flat at the same time. She was very definitely at her flat at the time all this was put in place.

The detectives continued listening to Black's explanation of what had happened:

- There were theatrical caps on the ground in the street

that were activated remotely and look like bullets hitting the ground. If you do not stop to look you don't see them and assume that real rounds are hitting the ground. The car had been left there by Hecketty. It contained some small explosive charges on the windows so it seemed as though shots were smashing the windows. Other devices inside the car moved the vehicle to make it seem it was being hit by bullets. These two fell for a well-planned prank.

The picture on the screen changed to a still of the car with the two men sheltering behind it and shooting upwards. Yak was still not sure:

- I saw this on the news last night. There were no real shots fired at them? They were never in any danger?

Gemma confirmed:

- That's right.
- Why didn't he just blow up the car and kill them?

Meehan answered that:

- He could have. I guess he either didn't think of it, which you will agree does not sound probable. Alternatively, he was being nice and did not want to kill anyone. If he has already killed his best mate, why would he not want to kill these two clowns?

Yak added the two main options:

- He may just want us to think that. We knew he was clever. Is he clever guilty and throwing us off the scent somehow? On the other hand, is he clever innocent, forcing us to look at who is responsible?

Gemma passed on information that the two men were Leonid Erdeli and Nikolay Yurlov. They were in police custody but claiming diplomatic immunity from prosecution. They arrived on a plane from Russia on Tuesday. When interviewed they didn't say who they were working with or why they were chasing Hecketty.

Angelic?

Papandreou was swiping through pages on his tablet while Black was talking. Then said:
- Hold on to your hat.

He hit a button on his tablet and the screen changed to show a list of names. Two were highlighted. Yak continued:
- The two shooters, Leonid Erdeli and Nikolay Yurlov; they are both on the guest list for the Mornington Party.
- Broadhouse:
- What?

Papandreou flicked through some more pages on his tablet:
- They were at the Mornington party and... they are down as working for TPO Oil.

The detectives all paused while they took in this new information. Black was still looking thoughtful when she said:
- Well, well, so what was it that happened at the party that kicked all this off? Smithson's beating is the first event on our radar. Why did that happen? So now we know this is not just about SafeNet and the Azimuth House team. The only thing we do know about the Mornington Party is that Toby Smithson was chasing Yekaterinya Khrushcheva. We know her brother runs the TPO Oil Company as well as being involved with Roman Constantinov. We need to start looking seriously at what is going on there.

Gemma Black had some other news to share with her team. Witter and Procter had been in touch again to remind them of James Hecketty's right to self-defence. He had the right to respond with violence in the face of clear threats to his life.

My plan had worked out perfectly. I was beginning to find

out what was happening now and what had happened at the Mornington Party. Perhaps more importantly so were the police. I would be a lot happier if they were on my side.

Angelic?

Chelsea and Westminster Hospital

Source: James Hecketty/Alex Harewood
Date: Wednesday 1st October
Time: 09.30
Present: Alex Harewood, a nurse, a doctor

The nurse at the hospital stopped me as I was about to go into the room that Toby was usually in.
- Oh, Hello. Hasn't anyone told you?
- I don't think I've been told anything.
He gave me some useful information:
- Mr Smithson has been moved.
- OK. So what room is he in now?
- Room? No, he's been transferred to another hospital.
- Where? Can you tell me why?
- Well, I will see if I can find a doctor to talk to you.
- Ok, I'll wait.
I sat down in the chair that I was offered. Then I waited for someone to give me some bad news.

A man arrived who was not wearing a white coat. His sleeves were rolled up. He told me that Toby had been moved to a hospital in Cape Town, South Africa, because they have a team that specialise in dealing with his particular injuries.
- Is he still in a coma?
- I think it's now been reclassified as a static vegetative state. That's normal after four weeks.
He looked at the notes in the file he was holding and told me Toby had developed an infection in his urethra. It was

hard to treat because of his injuries in that area.

There was something rather odd going on here. I wasn't too sure whether it was good odd or bad odd. Was this someone taking Toby away to keep him safe? If he had started getting better he might have been able to talk about his attackers. Or had Ivan's mob arranged for him to be taken away for the same reason?

I rang the number I had been given and a pleasant sounding woman told me he had arrived yesterday and should begin his treatment soon. But it was just a voice on the end of a phone. She could have been anybody anywhere. I did some checks on the number and the hospital and they did indeed have a specialist who was doing pioneering work with that type of complication. Everything I could check came up as bona-fide. I was still suspicious but there was nothing I could do.

Chelsea Imperial Hotel
King's Road
Chelsea
London

Source:	James Hecketty/Alex Harewood
Date:	Wednesday 1st October
Time:	17.25
Present:	Alex Harewood/Elisabeth Greyling

The Chelsea Imperial is one of London's most expensive hotels. I did some research online to find out who owned it. I got the name of one company then found that company was owned by another and that one by another. I was not willing to play this Russian doll game for too long; I didn't have much time. I knew the owners didn't want me to know who they were.

Getting into a Hotel couldn't be easier. Book a room. I needed two.

One of my rooms was booked in the name of Elisabeth Greyling. The other James Hecketty. James got the cheapest room for Friday and Saturday. Elisabeth got an expensive suite. It was going to help the camouflage if she had some company. I rang an escort agency who were more than happy to provide a good-looking guy for two nights. There was some written information and pictures. I looked for someone who was not too much taller than me, had a bit of maturity and appeared to have some brains which wasn't all that easy.

James room needed only a few things in it, including a hidden camera and a microphone. Playing the part of Elisabeth Greyling I arrived with two large suitcases and expected plenty of help getting them to her room. She looked about forty. Not many women put make up on to look older but you don't have to try for very long to find that it's easy. Just darken a few lines. There was a bit of grey in her wig too. She dressed expensively with high heels by Jimmy Choo, fitted skirt and jacket. The jacket had class and colour. Very obvious and erring towards casual. She made sure her suite was adequate and booked a table for two for dinner.

The exclusive lift was empty when I got in to go down to the restaurant. It stopped on the next floor down. The doors opened and Katya Khrushcheva got in. She didn't know me but getting this close was a bad idea. She was in a grey dress with a gold and pearl choker, bracelet, watch and handbag to match. She may have counted these as her work clothes but it was a very sexy outfit and a powerful business tool. Most men would find a woman looking as alluring as Katya very distracting. Any sort of attention from her and their brains would become even less functional.

I hadn't wanted this meeting in a lift and was determined to say nothing but Katya started a conversation.
- I like your jacket.
- Thank you. I find everything rather plain and angular at the moment. I wanted something colourful and not too formal. They did this for me.
- It's nice. You did well. The current fashion is a bit drab. Browns and beiges everywhere. Warm but not exciting.

We both got off on the busy ground floor. She disappeared. I was pleased to see her go.

Angelic?

I arrived for dinner at the restaurant. There was a group having dinner together at a table set away from the rest. Five men, one woman. The woman was Katya. Ivan was there too.

- Ms Greyling … your party is waiting.

The maître d' took me to the table and the young man who I had paid to date me gave me a three-cheek kiss. Perfect. He was the right height too and had a nice beard. He smiled well and talked politely. Contrary to popular belief, his is a difficult job. He has to read what I want and why he is there without me saying anything. He did very well asking if I'd had a good journey and pretending he knew me well.

The waiter arrived and I asked him a question:

- Who are the people on that table? Are they the Khrushchevs?
- Yes ma'am they own the hotel. They are not often in. So it's a good night to be here. All the best chefs are in for this weekend.
- So what do you recommend from the menu?

my escort sensibly enquired. We followed the waiter's suggestions.

There was a character reference there on the Khrushchevs. One of their employees had gone to a lot of trouble to hide who owned the hotel, although they were happy to make it obvious to anyone who asked. It smelt of arrogance and suggested the slack security that had let Tavi at their data. They probably had a fabulously secure system, but were too careless to create a good password for it.

This did not say much about the way their company was run at all. The worker tries his best and the boss undoes it all. Perhaps Ivan had taken over the company too soon, before he had any useful experience of dealing with people. Roman Constantinov seemed to have a similar opinion.

Lavender Hill Police Station

Source: Computers at the Lavender Hill Police Station
Date: Thursday 2nd October
Time: 15.24
Present: DI Inspector Gemma Black, DC John Meehan, DS
              Kyriakos Papandreou, DS Ryan Broadhouse.
              Toni Pasternak and Vladislav Pajari (on the video)

The police received an email from me that contained a link
to a video. Gemma Black showed it to her team.

Two men went into James Hecketty's hotel room, Toni
Pasternak and Vladislav Pajari. The camera was in a corner
and you saw the whole room. It was one of the smallest in
the hotel. Just enough room for a bed and a wardrobe.
There was a sound from the en-suite bathroom and both
thugs drew weapons and pointed them at the door. One
screwed a silencer onto his gun and then the other. There
was another sound from inside.

They looked at each other. One kicked at the door and
then stood back. They cautiously peered inside but the
bathroom had no one in it. Vladislav was standing just
inside the door, Tony just outside. They looked down to
see what was happening at their feet and turned to run out
of the room, but it was already too late.

The bathroom contained a weak container arranged to
rupture when the door was forced open. The fluid in the
container had gushed out over the bathroom floor and into
the bedroom. It was a clear liquid but they could tell it was

not water because there was a horrid acidic smell in the room. The liquid was methyl cyanoacrylate. Superglue.

Superglue has some interesting properties. It bonds rapidly in thin layers. Both men had it on the soles of their shoes. It was not actually strong enough to stick their shoes securely to the floor yet, but the bonds that have formed made it hard for them to move their feet. Tony stayed put but when Vladislav turned to leave the bathroom his feet stuck a little and he tripped and fell.

He fell onto his hands and knees on the cyanoacrylate soggy carpet. So far this was just a comedy routine. It got much worse.

There are some natural materials that cyanoacrylate does not bond well with. Wool and cotton are good examples. It doesn't bond well but it has a strong exothermic reaction with these materials that creates a lot of heat. Both these men are very well paid, they don't wear polyester suits and someone else does their ironing. They do wear the finest woollen suits and fitted cotton shirts.

The chemical reaction started on Vladislav's superglue wet suit trousers and his skin burnt. He moved away from the intense pain and other parts of his garments got wet with superglue and started to react. The glue stuck to his skin, which then stuck to the synthetic carpet. When he moved because of the pain from the burns he ripped skin off, causing more pain and so more movement and more agonised screams. Tony could do nothing for him and became stuck to the spot.

After about fifty seconds the glue has mainly set and they were both stuck to the carpet. There were patches of red raw flesh on Vladislav's legs, buttocks, thighs, back and shoulders. He was motionless and moaning sitting on his buttocks with his hands stuck to the floor. Tony had worked out what was happening and simply stood where he was trying to console his friend and stop him from moving and at the same time keeping his balance. He took out his phone and called for help.

Black stopped the playback and started to explain what had happened since. The police had spoken to both of these men. Vladislav would be out of hospital in a few days. Both of them worked for TPO and were on the guest list for the Mornington Club Party where they could have helped beat up Toby. They had also found that there were no possible charges that could be brought against me for what had happened at the hotel.

Black was looking a little weary:
- His lawyer is probably on his way up the stairs now about to tell us how restrained his client is being in the face of these very significant threats to his life.
A long list of names appears on the screen displayed by Papandreou:
- We've already spoken to over a hundred people who were at the party. Shall we start asking if anyone saw these two and the others from the gun incident?
- Yes, do that and keep working on the party. It's most likely where all this started.
Broadhouse's brow was furrowed and he sounded angry:
- This is all just pissing about. We have enough evidence to get a conviction. Hecketty raped and killed the girl, then killed Mansur. The rest is just a smokescreen.
Black spoke slowly:
- Maybe. We do need to find Hecketty. He should have some answers. We also have to show the upstairs people how hard we are trying.
Papandreou:

- We've had his picture out there for weeks now. Every officer in the Met knows his face. We're monitoring every account we know he has. Every hotel, hostel and guesthouse and food store has been given his photograph. The Crimewatch TV appeal came up with nothing useful for three weeks in a row.

Black's team believed they were already doing all they could to find me.

Freeman and Jacob

Source: Alex Harewood
Date: Thursday 2nd October
Time: 15.53
Present: Ivan and Katya Khrushchev and her bodyguard.
              Houghton, Chazov, Flowers, Oleg and Roman

The double doors at the office entrance to Freeman and
Jacobs flew open. Ivan, Flyorov, Pasternak, Katya and her
bodyguard all marched in looking purposeful. Ivan was
shouting:
-    Which one of you twats is Houghton?
Roman and the members of his team were all got to their
feet. Houghton looked at Roman who nodded. Houghton
then reluctantly stepped forward:
-    I'm Houghton.
Ivan waved a document in the air:
-    Did you make up this report? This one that says about
     all the things we've done to find Hecketty. The trouble
     we're having finding Hecketty and makes me look like
     an idiot.
Houghton was confused:
-    Yeah..No.. I mean it's what we were asked for. It took
     me and Oleg ages to write up that report.
-    So why did you send it?
-    Roman asked me to.
Roman:
-    Tim, I didn't do that.
-    Yeah in your email.

- What fucking email?

Houghton turned to a computer and looked at his email inbox but couldn't find any email from Roman that said anything about a report. I'd known he wouldn't be able to find it. I had deleted it. I'd also sent it.

Houghton had no doubts:
- It was there. You sent it. Oh shit. Where is it? I thought I'd done alright. I did what you asked me to do. What have I done wrong? ... Oh shit.

Roman tried to reassure him:
- You didn't do anything wrong. You did what you thought you should.

Roman knew Houghton and you could see he was puzzled by what had happened, but had no good explanation for Ivan who could only see simple explanations today:
- One of you is leaking information to Hecketty. How else would he know where my meeting was and when it was? My bet is on this Houghton prick in front of me now. You fuckers are really pissing me off. Have you any idea how much money I could have lost today? This guy sends an email asking for this report to be included in the notes for my meeting. It was on the table ready for the buyers to see when Katya spotted it and they would have thought I was a right tit.

Katya seemed pleased with herself:
- If you guys wanted to mess us around then you failed. Everything is still right on schedule.

This was not going a good way for Roman who was looking anxious:
- There's more going on here, Ivan. It's Hecketty. Can't you see it's him? He's got us bugged or something.

Ivan was getting angry:
- I don't believe this Hecketty exists. Your men lose him to start with. Then somehow his phone turns up in one

of your guy's pockets. Then this donkey brain sends
this report to a meeting to screw me over. I almost lose
a half-billion dollar deal and Vladislav ends up in
hospital. Shit! All you guys can complain about is a visit
from the police!

Ivan took out a hand gun, a small weapon and easily
concealed. It had a silencer attached. Katya saw what was
about to happen:

- Ivan don't!

Roman also saw that Houghton was about to get shot and
shouted:

- NO!

Ivan paused. He didn't shoot. In that same moment Chazov
had drawn his gun and pointed it very definitely at Ivan.

The bodyguard, Flyorov and Pasternak all moved to grab
their weapons but, hampered by outdoor clothing, were
slower. Neither had they anticipated this situation as well
as Chazov who said:

- Any of those shits move and you die first Ivan. Anything
  happens I don't like and you die. Stay still.

While saying this he moved around behind Houghton so
that he was partly shielded by Houghton from Ivan and by
Ivan from the other three men. Chazov:

- Drop the weapon Ivan.

Ivan paused.

- Drop it now.

Ivan dropped the gun. Houghton and Flowers took out
their own guns at the same time. Roman's men were in
charge.

Houghton moved forward to Ivan and hit the muzzle of his
gun against Ivan's lips. Ivan involuntarily opened his mouth
to gasp at the pain and found the barrel of Houghton's gun
inside his mouth. Houghton grabbed Ivan's shoulder with

his free left hand and continued to press his gun into Ivan's mouth. Ivan started to step backwards while Houghton pushed Ivan to the right so that he fell backwards into a sofa. There was a sharp crack as the metal gun hits against Ivan's teeth and one of them broke. Ivan's head was against the back of the sofa and Houghton's trigger guard was against Ivan's bottom lip.

For those few seconds everyone was watching what was happening to Ivan. Except Chazov who was watching Flyorov, Pasternak and Vladimir the bodyguard. Pasternak moved suddenly. Bang! Chazov shot him in the shoulder.

Everyone was shocked by the violence from Houghton and Chazov.

Chazov went to Pasternak and took out his concealed gun. Bang! He immediately shot Vladimir the bodyguard in the shoulder with Pasternak's weapon and then took the bodyguard's gun as well. Chazov relieved Flyorov of his gun while saying to him:
- Get these two to hospital before they start bleeding too badly on the carpet. You can say they shot each other when the police start to ask questions. You go too Katya.

Roman contradicted:
- I think Katya should stay here.

The uninjured Flyorov along with Pasternak and Vladimir all did as suggested. They understood that Chazov really did not mind using a gun and the two injured men needed medical attention. He escorted them downstairs and put them into their car.

When Chazov returned Ivan and Katya were sitting next to each other on the two-seater couch. Houghton was watching both of them, gun drawn. Things had calmed down a little. Ivan's lip was beginning to swell.

Roman started talking. He had a lot to say:

- Ivan you behave as though you know nothing about this business. Let me explain some realities to you.

Houghton took the gun out of Ivan's mouth but still pointed the gun at Ivan and Katya. Roman continued:

- I just don't care if you two get shot right now. It won't worry me at all. You know we can get rid of the evidence easily. Now I'm not bothered either way but you two have a decision to make. Listen, live and carry on making money or alternatively you can opt to not listen and die. My business is suffering right now because of you Ivan. If you decide to die, that's fine, but something here has to change.

Ivan and Katya were both sitting still looking very shocked. Roman kept on talking:

- Now it's looking like you two are going to listen. Great. Good decision. There are some things about my business that I want to make absolutely clear to you.

Ivan was seething. Katya was looking thoughtful. Roman went on:

- The problem is that you have such amateurish ideas about how all this works. You think that hurting people and making threats is all it's about. It's actually about being generous and leaving enough space for people to make mistakes. Loyalty and trust. That's how you stay in this business for a long time. These people here have families. They want to be able to see a future. That's why I was put in here. I've kept things running well and paying for your Lamborghini for a fair few years now. I don't carry a gun because if I do my job right I shouldn't have to. If the police turn up it's not a problem. My books look legitimate. In fact in the three years I've been running this we've tripled the profits

and not had one single visit from the police. This is a
real furniture business. The only thing that doesn't
really exist is the quantity of wood that we move. All
these guys can bore your pants off talking about
wardrobes. They are professional. Part of their job is to
make this look like a real business. They actually do sell
furniture. Chazov was a carpenter, OK he was shit at it,
but he's ace at breaking in whores.

Chazov grinned. He loved doing that. Roman briefly looked
at Chazov then explained further:

- Why do we do this? Because it turns about 50 times as
  much profit. Mainly because there's limitless demand.
  You buy a table once every few years but we have
  some customers who fuck two or three times a week.
  We keep the shithead customers away and make sure
  that the girls are safe. That keeps them happy so
  they're a lot less of a problem. We also say we'll be
  nasty to their families back home. We've never actually
  had to do it. We make up the odd rumour that we have
  done it occasionally. That's enough. Chazov puts the
  fear of God into them when they arrive and they're
  meek after that. It costs us a girl sometimes but it gets
  things off to a nice quiet start. Turns out they'll put up
  with getting fucked ten times a day as long as it's the
  best deal on the table and the alternatives include
  being dead. We offer them rewards if things go well.
  They get better, cleaner customers and guys that don't
  like it rough. They get free healthcare and dental work.
  They want to be clean and healthy. We want them to
  be clean and healthy. They eat well. We take them out
  and let them choose good clothes for themselves.
  There are rules, we make them, explain them and they
  follow them. They get sort of used to the deal. It looks
  fair. After a couple of years they go off so we sell them

on to places that don't mind that they can't smile and
fuck like zombies.

Ivan had calmed down a bit. How much he was taking in
was unclear. Roman wasn't going to stop anyway:

- We run five establishments from this office. They have
their own staff; men who look after the girls. They keep
our customers happy by matching them up with girls
they like. We have reward schemes for regular
customers and make sure that they always leave
happy. This is a business, same as any other business.
The only difference is that it's not fucking legal to keep
girls as sex slaves. The catch to that is that we have to
be more careful - not less. Sure we are the Russian
Mafia as far as the rest of the world is concerned. To
our customers we are providing a very useful and
discreet social service. They like us. We make arriving
at one of our places real easy. You feel welcome and
relaxed. A pretty girl smiles at you and takes your coat
off when you arrive. We offer food and drink. We take
credit cards. You leave feeling like you're an attractive
and successful bloke who doesn't have to bother with
all that wooing women shit, which is slow, uncertain
and expensive. You can afford to pay and it's worth it.

Roman sighed and paused for breath. Then he carried on:

- Then when you're in London you want to make fucky-
fucky with some girl that doesn't. We clear up the
mess. Smooth it all over. It happens more than once.
You like it that way. We help sort it all out. It's a favour
for our boss, so we do it.

Ivan started to say something. Houghton shoved the gun
onto the end of Ivan's nose and pushed Ivan back into the
sofa so that Roman wasn't interrupted:

- We're right in the police eye now. We need you to stop
pointing them in our direction. Stop screwing us over.

And I seriously hope that I'm saying this in a language that you understand. This Hecketty bloke is your problem. I don't care about whatever it was that his mate did. I care about my business. You're so fucking rich that you can afford to lose a few million here and there. To you we're just a sideshow, but it's our lives. So bring some more of your mates over and sort this fucking problem out yourself. Or make more use of those private firms. It'll be far cheaper in the long run. We're not helping out any more. So you can piss off. Don't worry we'll carry on sending you millions each year. Which we can't do if we're all in jail.

Roman gestured at the computer while saying:

- And another point. I didn't send any fucking email to Houghton. Get your computer guy to confirm that spoofing email isn't that hard. Houghton here really stuck his neck out for you over the Hecketty thing. You've left me with few options here. The only other option I have left now is to kill you. If Katya wasn't here I think I would have.

Houghton stepped back. Roman was winding down:

- With luck your pride will recover in time and I'm gambling that your business sense is strong enough to help you see the reason in what I'm saying. Katya I'm relying on you to help him a bit here. You show good judgement. I think you get all this. It's a shame you're not running things instead of him. You two can go now. Thanks for stopping by. Go and help clear up the mess your mates are in.

Ivan and Katya both left with impassive faces and saying nothing.

Chapter 12
Russia
October 2014

Straminsky Residence

Source:	James Hecketty/Alex Harewood
Date:	Friday 3rd October
Time:	18.23 (local)
Present:	Eleanor, Hannah, Boris and Sergei Straminsky, Alex Harewood

I stepped out of the plane and into a superb black BMW driven by a friendly, polite chauffeur who knew my name. I texted Eleanor to say I had landed safely and was on my way. The car took me through some built up areas, then after some minutes, entered a sparse forest. We passed through a massive security gate that opened automatically and allowed us onto a wide well-maintained road.

Rublyovka. This was the place where the Russian mega-rich set up their homes. There were enormous residences, all different, set back from the road, well-tended grounds with beautiful trees and very few people to be seen. We turned off up one of the side roads. It led to a complex of buildings. Most were discreetly hidden by trees. A central building stood out and the drive led to the steps and a front door. It was grand while still being human in scale with a short set of steps up to the front door where we stopped and I was invited to get out.

Eleanor was coming down the steps. She hugged me then looked back at the house:
- It's a bit too much isn't it?
- It would be in London, but round here it's almost subdued.
- I grew up here. We have other houses. This one is home.

We started going up the steps. I looked back for my bag. Eleanor touched my arm and said:
- Don't worry it'll be taken care of.

I was led into the enormous hall and up the central stairs and I was briefly shown around the family rooms on the first floor.

Eleanor showed me the room that was to be mine for the stay. It wasn't too big. There was a painting I recognized on the wall. A picture by Vermeer that is called Mistress and Maid. The maid is bringing a letter to her mistress. They both know it is from a suitor, but neither is sure what news it might contain. I'd always liked it. Looking closely I realized this was most probably the original. A priceless work of art.
- Dad likes Vermeer.
- I like Vermeer too. This is one of my favourites. I used to have a print of it.
- That's good. We specially chose it for your visit. We have quite a varied collection of artwork. When someone stays we talk about which picture they might like best. It gets us talking about our guest. What they like and don't like. What they are like. We got it right for you then. Dad's really good at it. You just talk about someone and he goes "Nothing modern then" or

"something impressionist". Then we start narrowing it down. Once we bought a picture just because it seemed right for a guest.
- What a nice habit. It's a way of introducing someone. What if it's someone you don't like?
- Well we only put people we like in this room. But it's interesting you should ask. It's kind of a test too. If we get it wrong it seems to mean that we've misjudged them in something else as well. It's like a bad omen.
- Oh I passed then.
- Mmm... I suppose you did.. But it feels more like we have.

She caught my eye for a moment then looked away:
- I've brought friends here before. Some don't cope. All the money spoils the relationship. It stops them staying friends for the friendship. They stop seeing the person and stay friends for the money and status. You can see them change. They don't want to change and often don't see that they have. I've seen it a lot.

She sounded quite sad:
- I know we're not ordinary. Mum tries hard to make us normal and Dad's great but the money becomes a barrier. I have friends around here but the things we have in common are just massive money.
- So you get lonely sometimes.

She stared at me with those lovely round eyes. They had gone a bit glassy. I grabbed her hand and squeezed a little:
- Will you tell me about it all when you're ready?

She nodded slowly. Hannah came in and Eleanor enthused:
- Alex is here Mum!
- So I see. And very welcome she is too. Did you have a good journey, Alex?

I got a very welcoming hug.
- I did, thanks.

- I try to keep things fairly normal around here. We have people who help but they stay very much in the background. We all cook occasionally, when it's just family, which includes you of course, Alex. We look after things like serving meals, laying the table and clearing up ourselves. It keeps us intimate. I'm cooking tonight. I was hoping that you two would do something for us on Sunday, if that's OK.

I exchanged a glance with Eleanor. We both looked back at Hannah.

- Great

said Eleanor

- That'd be nice

I said at the same time.

- Nothing too fancy. Just keep it really simple. We have a lot of fancy meals and prefer simple everyday things while we're on our own. A stir-fry or a pasta salad kind of thing would be fine. I'll leave you to settle in Alex.

Eleanor helped me unpack my things and put them away in the wardrobe and drawers. She commented on a few of them saying what she liked and maybe holding it up against herself. I'd not included my original party dress. Eleanor had said we would sort something out for the do.

- Come and see my room

she urged once my things were sorted.

We went into her room, which was about the same size as mine. There were four paintings by 19th century artists. I opened the double doors and walked into her wardrobe. It was large and well organised with an island of cleverly organised drawers in the middle.

- You can borrow anything you like... Just give me a couple of minutes would you?

She disappeared and I had a look round the wardrobe and

had started to look at her shoe rack when Eleanor returned wearing the world's most expensive evening gown.

It reached to the floor and was an inch or so too long. She had to lift it up to stop it from dragging. It fitted closely round the waist and covered a minimum of breast and back. It was made of two white materials of differing textures so that there were subtle stripes running vertically up and down. The narrowest parts were at the waist and knees and it flared after the knees. It was very elegant, very sexy and very expensive.

- Oh that is just awesome. It's fabulous. Subtle and eye catching all at once.
- You're not just saying that? You know... to be nice.
- No it's gorgeous. Truly beautiful. You look so good in it.
- This isn't my dress

She had a funny expression on her face:

- I'm glad you like it though. Try it on. It's for you.

I tried hard to say something but couldn't quite manage it.

- I thought you liked it.
- It's just that I've never worn anything quite so beautiful. It doesn't feel like me.
- Don't be silly. Put it on.

She took it off while I shed a few garments. She handed it to me. It felt beautiful. I spent a few moments admiring how well made it was. Just its fabric, its sound, its feel, its weight dripped with class. I pulled it up over my legs and then put my arms in the short sleeves. Eleanor clipped the back and smoothed the dress down over my waist and hips.

- Alex, please look at yourself.

The elegantly dressed woman in the mirror looked back at me. I was more relaxed than I had ever been in London. Nobody here was likely to recognise me. At least for now this was me. I felt very confused and for a moment I wanted to run away. Eleanor didn't notice. She let my hair out and started trying it in different ways.

- You do fit it well. You look fabulous. We'll get you some sparkly things for your neck. And your hair we can work on too! Are you OK? Why are you crying?

I was.

- I've never thought of myself like this.
- I don't always get you. Don't you like looking so good?

She turned me round and held my shoulders. I answered:

- I love it. I just wasn't expecting it. I've never even considered wearing something so beautiful. Thank you. Can I see yours?
- You can, that will be fun. If you don't start crying. But I think it's time for dinner now.

I put my normal clothes back on and we went downstairs.

Eleanor's father, Sergei, was a big man with a tidy beard, large hands and a large chest. He grasped my shoulders and kissed my cheeks. He spoke with a slight Russian accent

- Hello Alex. Welcome to our home. Did you like the painting in your room?
- She did Dad. It's one of her favourites. She used to have a print.
- I'll enjoy looking at it every day. I gather you like Vermeer too.
- Yes he's caught my interest more than once. How does this compare to the print?

He'd managed to say it was the original without boasting that it was.

- Well you can see the expressions on the faces more clearly. The hope and expectation is more obvious. There are details in the dress that are easier to see. The print is like a synopsis of the story. This feels more like the complete text. You've got some others then?

Angelic?

- Oh you really are interested? I'd like to show you, perhaps on Sunday afternoon.

I'd got into art a bit at the V and A and visited a few other galleries while getting out as Alex.

- I would love that.
- Has Eleanor shown you round yet?
- She hasn't yet. I know she meant to. I think she was showing me a dress instead.
- Of course! How foolish of me to think that seeing your surroundings would come before a gown.
- She looks stunning in it, Daddy, I'm afraid that no-one will notice me if I stand next to her.

Sergei agreed:

- I can see how this might be possible. Though I will certainly notice you, Eleanor, however many heads are turned by your beautiful friend.

My cheeks started burning and I could feel the blush spreading down my neck.

A young man had arrived behind us. He appeared to be in his early thirties, clean shaven, handsome and with a mass of unruly fair hair. He was about the same height as me. This had to be Boris, Eleanor's brother.

- Boris, come here and meet Alex. Eleanor's good friend about whom we have heard so much.

Sergei clearly enjoyed seeing me blush and I glanced at Eleanor in the hope of some sort of rescue. Then I wondered at how much she might have said about me to her family. Sergei introduced me to his son. I was kissed twice again.

- Pleased to meet you.

He didn't smile as much as he might have and I sensed more reserve and less charm than in any other member of the family. There was plenty to go round though.

Hannah had cooked us all a chicken dish with rice. It was lovely. Then we just had a fruit salad with ice cream. Half way through the meal I started to relax. This was nice. They were thoughtful kind people. Not at all frightening. I didn't have to worry about using the wrong fork or eating my soup the wrong way or any other silly nonsense. If any problems did arise they would help me sort them out. I was with friends.

- Thank you. This is well... Thank you.

Hannah touched my arm. She somehow caught my meaning.

- You thought we'd would be all posh and pompous.
- Yes! I'm really sorry, but I did!
- Shh don't tell anyone.
- Oh, don't worry your secret's safe with me. I won't tell anyone what thoughtful, unpretentious people you are. Not a single soul.

There was a glimmer of humour from Boris:

- Our reputation as vampiric baby eating monsters is safe then?
- Yes I'll be happy to keep that rumour alive. It's so much more believable.

Hannah:

- Our wealth is all that some people see.
- That's sad. They're missing out.

I saw Hannah catch Sergei's eye. She asked:

- Did you like your dress? I'm sorry there wasn't time for you to choose it yourself.
- She did like it. She cried, Mum

I thought of myself again in that gown:

- I couldn't believe it was really me.

Hannah lightly pinched me:

- Hmm I think it probably was you. It certainly wasn't anyone else.

Angelic?

I realised that even the meal was a test of sorts. Some people arriving there would be hoping for golden goblets, servants and seven courses on a long table with candelabra. I'd been pleased that it wasn't. So I guessed I had passed that test too.

We did look round the well-designed gardens. From the house you saw a large broad shape and it seemed simple. Once you were there you saw it as smaller areas with ponds and statues separated by a hedge or a low wall. Near the house was an area with a few seats and broken up with archways and trellises. It was a good party area perfect for small groups to collect and talk. There was a broad central pathway. At the end of the path was a small lake.

Hannah clearly wanted to talk to me and Eleanor knew it, so we were given some space. It was a glorious evening and we walked down the garden. The sun was settling behind some clouds but it was still warm enough to be pleasant. Hannah took out her phone and spoke into it.
-      Two G and Ts by the small pool. Thanks Genya.
This was to be a long conversation. As I thought there was a plan:
-      How are Tavi's parents?
-      They're doing OK. As well as they could I suppose. They are very welcoming and seem to have assumed there was more to our relationship than there was. But there seemed little point in saying we only went out twice. I don't know what he'd told his mum. He told the police we'd slept together. He may have told her the same thing. I'm not sure why he said that. We did spend a night in his flat but we didn't sleep together.
We sat down on the stone bench seat by a lily pond. She sat close by me, almost touching.

- Yes I see. Did you like him?
- I did like him. He was a lovely, thoughtful, special guy. He looked after me really well when we went out and he took the trouble to find out how I felt. He helped me to see myself differently and seemed to know how to make me smile and feel comfortable. He wanted me to be me.
- That is the thing that I wanted to talk about. Some people I know were able to tell me a fair bit about you. They were able to tell me that there is danger for you in London and that you are a lot more than you seem. I know you're in trouble and I know that isn't fair.

This wasn't good. How much more did she know? She told me:

- I'm also aware that you knew Tavi as James as well as Alex.

She must have seen the shock on my face:

- You do?... Oh God. I'm so sorry. Oh... It's bad isn't it? It looks really creepy and weird. When I think about it I feel like I'm lying to everyone. Oh God. Do you want me to leave? I really like Eleanor. I don't mean any harm. She's so lovely. I love being her friend and seeing the world as she sees it... Oh dear... I feel horrible. I'll leave.

She put her arm round me:

- Hush now. You won't leave. I knew before you came and I didn't mean to make you feel bad. I don't want to add to your worries. You're a lovely girl. You get on so well with Eleanor. Only I know. I chose you, remember? I would still choose you. I wouldn't have brought the subject up except to ask your opinion.
- You want my opinion?
- I do. What should we do if Eleanor finds out? Or should we tell her before she finds out? Before we talk about

that I want to let you know that Eleanor had some
problems recently.
- I sort of guessed that.
- I'll let her tell you the full story. Just be aware that
people may make comments tomorrow, or ask the
how-is-she-now kind of question.
- I'm guessing that she tried to do something very bad to
herself.
- Yes, she did.

Hannah told me that she had discussed this meeting with
Eleanor and she knew that we would be having this
conversation.
- You must have been so upset. What an awful thing. I'm
sure Eleanor still feels bad for the pain she will have
caused you.
- I know she does. In some ways I'd much rather she felt
badly about hurting herself.
- She always feels for other people. I think it's one of the
things that's so wonderful about her. I try to be more
like her but I can be nasty sometimes. She never is. She
doesn't judge people and only ever really wants to
make them feel better.
- You're right she's always been thoughtful and
generous... So should we tell her about you?
- I'll try to find a way to tell her. So she knows what she
needs to know. Meanwhile if you feel you should then
please just tell her yourself. If she starts to suspect
then let her know. Or if she asks. That way you don't
need to be in a position of having to lie.
She took my hand and held it between two of hers:
- Thank you. I will do that. How do you feel about you,
Alex?
- I feel better that you know. In some ways. Less of a liar.
But I still feel like I've cheated you.

- You don't need to feel that. You're an extraordinary person and a lovely girl. It's impossible to think of you as anything else.
- Tavi said something like that. He wanted to be good to me and was always so considerate.
- He liked you as Alex?
- He boasted about his relationship with me to the police and to his family so he must have done.
- It's very easy to believe that.
- Thank you. I'm glad you're happy to see me that way.

She pressed my hand a little more firmly and then let it go and picked up her gin. But she stayed sitting very close:

- At the party tomorrow. Just be yourself. Have confidence in yourself. Almost everyone there will be a proper friend of the family who has shown support for Eleanor.
- Ok, I'll try to be confident, but I feel uncertain about how I should behave sometimes.
- Really? That doesn't show at all. Very few people surprise me. You've surprised me a lot.

I took a sip of my gin. It had a good taste. Hannah sipped at hers:

- There's something else that I need to tell you. You should have been told before about Toby.
- What about Toby?
- I know you can keep things to yourself. This is one of those things. Not even Eleanor can know.

She knew something about Toby? I didn't see how it could be bad news so I eagerly said:

- Is he getting better?

She grinned:

- Yes, he is, slowly. Tell no one. No one.

Toby was safe. He was being looked after. I smiled and clinked my glass with hers:

Angelic?

- Toby

We drank and I started to say how beautiful their garden looked. We must have reached the end of her agenda.

That evening I checked all my inboxes for interesting messages. There was one from my escort for dinner at the Chelsea Imperial. It did the formal thank you bit then said that he had met a woman called Katya Khrushcheva the next day. She had said she was a friend of Elisabeth Grayling and seemed to be fishing for information. He didn't think he had given anything away. But who knows what she had noticed. She'd found something of interest from our meeting in the lift and was following it up. It shouldn't matter because I wasn't planning on being Elisabeth again. But it was an additional worry. I now knew that Katya was cleverly and actively seeking possible holes in their security.

Straminsky Residence

Source:	James Hecketty/Alex Harewood
Date:	Saturday 4th October
Time:	17.32
Present:	Alex Harewood, The Straminsky Family, Steven Sarren, Imogen Khrushcheva, Katya Khrushcheva, The Norwegian Royal Family, several others.

Eleanor helped me get ready, and I helped her. We talked all the time about what looked best from the jewellery box, what makeup to wear, about my work or which of her houses she liked best. There was a pleasant relaxed feel to it. Perhaps the most relaxed I'd been for months.

We went down to the party together and sipped our drinks talking to Boris and his girlfriend before joining in properly.

I gave her the I'm-going-to-mingle-now shuffle and she gave me the OK-have-fun look. I had my glass in one hand and was holding my dress off the floor with the other. I caught the eye of a middle-aged man in a small group. He beckoned me over. He looked at me just a little the wrong way, but it was too late to back out without appearing rude. I knew he thought of me as a minor character here. He was doing me a favour talking to me. I turned off my beam and gave him a flat smile instead. It made no difference. I was a young woman and he was very rich so I should be grateful for his attention. He may also have known that I was not the daughter of anyone important and too young to be anything else. I was just a courtesan as far as he was concerned.

Angelic?

-    So how did you come to be here today?

He was asking what my connections were. I wasn't
answering that:
-    By plane and then by car. How did you get here?
-    I flew in from New York yesterday. Can I get you a
     drink?
-    Thanks a diet coke please.

I saw him have a quiet word with a waiter. I didn't hear the
words diet coke as I should have done. I took two steps
after the waiter, tapped his elbow and said:
-    I'm sorry did I just order a double vodka and coke.
-    Yes Miss.
-    Could I just have a diet coke instead?
-    On its way Miss.
-    Thanks, that was silly of me.
-    I didn't quite see it that way Miss.

He seemed to have understood the situation. I turned back
to the guest:
-    He somehow seemed to get the wrong order for me. I
     can't think how that happened.
-    What's your name dear?
-    I'm Alex. I'm sorry I don't know your name either.
-    Stephen Sarren. I'm the CEO of TPO Petrochemical.

This could be interesting then. This was the man who ran
the Khrushchev's oil firm. We shook hands.
-    Wow, that sounds really important. Do you make a lot
     of money?
-    They pay me well. I was headhunted last year after
     turning round the Desmos group and putting them
     back above where they had been before.

I wanted to say how amazing that was considering you
can't get a drinks order correct. But didn't.

- They were in bit of bother were they?
- I don't suppose you follow these things. Business is a bit boring for a girl. Yes, their shares were down by 27 points. I put them up by 40 points from 56 to 72.
- Is a point the same as a percentage point?
- Yes. Well done. That's right.
- 56 to 72 is 29 per cent isn't it?.. Yeah it's 28.6 per cent.
- Oh... These things are complicated. Even I find them hard to understand sometimes.
- Sorry, I'm just using the numbers you gave me. Have you got a calculator? Perhaps we could check it? And if they came down by 27 per cent and then up by 29 per cent weren't they still below their original value? It would be great if you could explain it all to me.

He was looking annoyed. He thought that I just didn't understand and was being awkward. I should just accept what he said without question and not make him explain. I noticed Eleanor had arrived and was watching and listening. She looked rather amused:

- Hello Stephen.
- Oh hello Eleanor. It's good to see you. Are you well? I've been talking to this self-assured young lady.
- I'm really well, thanks, I'm pleased you two have met.
- She's asking me about money, she seems a bit confused.
- That's a first then. I don't think I've ever seen Alex confused. Normally it's the people around her that can't keep up. Though I'm sure you feel you're doing fine. Can you excuse us? There's someone else I want Alex to meet and she's already met you now.
- That's OK. Perhaps we'll do some more maths later.

We turned and walked away. She was grinning at me. I was apologising:

Angelic?

- Sorry. I should have been more patient.
- He behaved himself better once I was there and he started to see that you were so far ahead of him. He realised you were not a girl on the make who'd sleep with him if he promised you some nice pretty thing that you couldn't afford.
- Wow. I've never heard you be so definite about anyone before.
- He went off with a friend of mine once.
- I guess that kind of explains it. But I think you're hiding something. You like him really. You have a secret crush on him.
- He's just so sexy and so charming. I dream of him all the time.

We both laughed. I didn't think very much of any company that could employ him as a CEO. He couldn't do maths and didn't admit to mistakes. TPO was the Khrushchev's company. How could they do so well?

Eleanor pulled me away:
- Alex, there's someone here that would very much like to talk to you. She's nervous though and wanted me to introduce you. It's Katya. I know you want to meet her too.

I breathed in quickly. I was about to introduced to the girl of Toby's dreams. Eleanor noticed me pause and must have wondered why I would be apprehensive. She took me to the other side of the party area. There, waiting and looking very gorgeous, was Katya Khrushcheva.
- Katya, this is Alex.

She looked anxious. Was she worried about meeting me? Why would that be? We shook hands, a gesture that is supposed to indicate friendship. Was that the case here? She was smiling at me. A beautiful smile:

- Hello Alex.
- Hello Katya.

Eleanor had other people to see:
- I'll leave you two to talk.

Katya didn't know how much I knew. Did she want to kill my friends and then be friendly with me? I couldn't let her know how much I knew though. Perhaps she was checking me out again, intending to report back to her brother. I had to play along with whatever game it was that she was playing. She said:
- I like your dress. It really suits you.
- Thank you, Eleanor got it for me.
She was surprised:
- You must really trust her to let her get you a dress.
- We do seem to like the same things and end up wearing similar things and I wouldn't have dared spend as much as this cost.
I thought I'd push her a little:
- I had to go to a funeral. A friend. There wasn't any time to get it with her.
She seemed upset and looked away. Those feelings didn't quite come out in her words:
- I heard. I'm so sorry. Still it's nice that you can trust Eleanor so much.

We sat down on the cushioned wall that was there for that very purpose while she asked:
- You work don't you? I rather envy you that.
- I do work. I don't have a lot of money. I thought you worked with your brother?
- Yes I do when I can. It's interesting.

She managed to say this with so little conviction and said some more the same way:
- It would be nice to get some real responsibility. Do

something more.

The words didn't match her expressions. She didn't seem to mean what she said and looked uncomfortable saying it. She looked better as she asked:

- Have you always lived in London?
- Only the last few months. I was in Canada for a few years. I gave up university in Edmonton and came to London.
- Didn't your parents mind you dropping out?
- My parents died a few years ago. When I was sixteen.
- Sorry, I didn't know.
- That's OK. It's a long while ago now.
- So why did you leave university?
- I was really quiet as a child. Even quieter after my parents died. I was just doing what I was expected to do. I wanted to make my own decisions. University may have been the right thing but it wasn't my choice. I wanted my life to be my own.

She looked distant and almost upset. She didn't respond at all for a few seconds, though she was still focused on me. She touched my arm and gave me her best smile:

- Sorry, I was well away there.

Toby had been right. There was a sadness in her. She even tried to cover it up. I touched her arm back:

- What is it?

She looked unnerved by the question. I wasn't supposed to have noticed.

- I was worrying about my Dad. He's not well.

This didn't feel like the source of the reactions I'd just seen. The waitress arrived with some drinks. She offered us both champagne and there was a moment of confusion as we both went for the same glass and we ended up with our heads side by side reaching for the same thing. I was laughing as she picked up the glass. She laughed too. Katya looked me full in the eye as she took it from the tray. An expression crossed her face. I couldn't read it.

- My Dad forgets new things. He knows he does and that upsets him and you can tell he feels sad, though he tries to hide it. He's not so very old. I was a late child. He was 52 when I was born. He gets by, but he knows he is no longer a strong purposeful man. Now he lacks confidence and is reluctant to meet people.
- Was he good to you when you were younger?
- He was good when he was home. I have good memories of him when he was well. He made me feel very special and cared for. He'd bring me little presents all the time. It wasn't the present that was important. I had lots of things that I wanted anyway. It was that he brought them and he had thought about what he gave me. He got me a dress for my favourite doll and a pretty blanket for my pony. He started getting ill when I was a teenager and things weren't so good after that.

There were so many contradictions in her. She liked her father but seemingly not her mother. I moved the conversation on and searched for some history:

- Eleanor says you've known each other for a very long time.
- Do you think she's all right now? I wanted to be in touch more but you get busy don't you?
- She'd like you to be in touch more.

She caught my eye then looked away:

- I do when I can.

Then she was more thoughtful:

- We used to be together a lot when we were little. We were good together. We had fun. We'd play all sorts of games, dress up and pretend. They seem like magical times now. We were little princesses. It's different when you grow up. Things change.

I was surprised how warmly she remembered being with Eleanor. There was more:

- Things are so different when you're older. She went off to school and I stayed here. She always thinks the best of people, even when there are all sorts of reasons not to.
- I know. I love that about her. It's great that she can always be so generous.
- Don't you think her view of the world is a bit too generous? A bit too forgiving?
- It is. But that's so much better than being the other way round. She get hurts because of it. Is your experience so very different?

She was looking into the distance again. So I added:

- Maybe things can change.

She was still thinking about something else. Then she had an idea:

- You live in London?
- Yes I like it. There is always something happening.
- I love London. I get there as often as I can. It has an extra spark somehow. I am more relaxed there than most places. I always see a show. Sometimes two. Sometimes the same one twice!
- So what have you seen? Who do you go with?
- Let It Be was the last one. The group were just so good. They encourage the audience to join in and you can really forget yourself. It was as though they were the Beatles. They seemed like nice guys too. I liked John. Not for me though perhaps.

I'm with this most beautiful woman and she's talking about men as though they are not available. She was astute enough to pick up my thoughts:

- I can like a guy, can't I?

- You can. Guys can be nice.

Then I got something else. She looked away, thinking, making connections and then gave me a glance:

- Will you come with me? Will you see a show with me? When I'm next in London. I often go on my own. But you live in London. You're right there. Will you?

I heard her excitement, which I took to be genuine. She normally went on her own? I remembered what Eleanor had said about wealth being a lonely place. But there was a conspiracy here too.

- Of course I'd love to. It's a great idea.
- Don't worry about the tickets. I'll get them.

She was being thoughtful. She wanted me to think she was on my side. And she'd just set up a private meeting with me in London. This could be dangerous. I couldn't say no and maintain the friendly pretence.

She hugged me tightly with genuine warmth when we parted.

Katya was two different people. Today with me she had been considerate and vulnerable, but trying to be friendly. The sadness was there too. This was a sensitive and thoughtful soul: more the victim, not so much the instigator. She had wanted to see me and seemed so positive about Eleanor.

When I observed her with Ivan, Roman and his crew she fitted in very well; she was hard and unforgiving. Here with me she seemed so different. Not the same person I knew from my Azimuth House surveillance.

Either way she was adept enough to make both characters appear to work. I wondered which was the real Katya. Was she trying to win my confidence? Was there a plan she was working to? She couldn't know I'd been watching her. As far as she was aware this was the first time I'd seen her.

Angelic?

Playing two different people was something I knew about. Katya's motivation could be similar to mine. Self-preservation. Though I couldn't see how that might be. For the moment she remained an enigma.

Eleanor introduced me to someone else. A woman in her thirties with shortish wavy dark hair and a sharpish nose that gave her beautifully symmetric face more character and intelligence. She was English and had the round voweled accent of the British aristocracy. It made her seem haughtier than she was. The more we talked the more she relaxed and the accent faded. This was Imogen, Ivan's wife.

We talked for a little while. It was a good conversation, but what she didn't say was far more interesting than what she put into words.

She volunteered nothing about her husband. She never said "we" in the way that most couples do. There were no positives about him and no negatives. Whether she intended it or not she gave the impression of a cold marriage where she played the honourable wife. There were no children and no mention of why not. She didn't mention joint holidays. I mentioned Katya's name and that was not welcomed. I thought of her as a bird locked in a cage in Ivan's castle. Unable to escape because of her marriage vows, her old fashioned family's ideas of proper behaviour and her access to wealth, which her family probably had less of but more need than ever before. I wanted to see the cage opened and the beautiful bird fly out.

A couple that I didn't know, but seemed to know Imogen well joined us. I had spotted something that I wanted to investigate on the other side of the formal garden and so made my excuses.

There was a young girl playing hopscotch on her own next to a small pond. There didn't seem to be anyone else around of her age.

- Hello.
- Hello.
- I'm Alex who are you?

She looked at me oddly. Perhaps she didn't have good English. I tried again.

- My name is Alex.

She looked. She got that. I got a bit of a grin.

- What is your name?
- My name is Ingrid.

Her English wasn't great. I tried to keep it simple.

- Hello Ingrid.
- Hello Alex.
- How old are you?

She counted up on her fingers, translating into English.

- Ten.

She smiled. It was a good smile. I took the stone and gestured is this OK? She nodded and I threw. My shoes came off easily and I pulled my dress up over my knees. I took the first turn. We got through a couple of rounds before I realised we were being watched. We finished the game before I looked round. I pointed the man out to Ingrid. She ran towards him. I put my shoes back on and shook my hips so my gown settled back down around my ankles. I wondered if I was supposed to behave with a bit more grace.

- Hello Papa.

Said Ingrid to a man in his seventies.

- Hello Ingrid.

When Ingrid replied to him it sounded a bit like

- Hennes num ad Alex.

I was being introduced.

Angelic?

- Oh, he said, you're Alex. Of course you are. Hannah was talking about you.

He had a slight accent, a pleasant smile and seemed very amiable.

- I'm sorry I don't know your name. I could call you Papa.
- Call me Papa if you wish.

he said with good humour.

- I could but it seems to me that it is a title and not a name. Though it is one of the most important titles.
- That's a nice thought. I think you may be right. It is an important title and one that gives me a lot of pleasure. I certainly am most proud of it. I'm Harald. I've been friends with Hannah for a while.

He offered a hand and I shook it.

- Are you two here on your own?
- No my wife's over there.

He nodded towards the most elegant woman with dazzling eyes and deep smile lines. Even in a glance you could see his admiration for her.

- Can I be a little daring and ask you to do me a favour?

He looked a little puzzled.

- I will. If I can.
- Would you please look at your wife again, but for just a little longer.

He did as I asked and I again saw the admiration and he really didn't mind looking. As I hoped his wife noticed, looked up and smiled at him. She loved him right back. It was a lovely moment. His wife noticed me, nodded and smiled, clearly amused. I returned her warm smile. Now Harald was looking at me. I said:

- You two are beautiful together. Thank you for the favour.

He laughed.

- It's a favour I would be pleased to repeat at any time.

> You're right of course. We are lucky. And you are remarkable. Here you can meet Sonja.

His wife was walking towards us. She was smiling at me. I offered a hand. She gave me a hug.

- You just have to be Alex, Hannah said that you really see people. She wasn't wrong.
- I'm a little embarrassed. There seem to be all sorts of really important people here, with big jobs and long titles and enormous wealth, but I find that I've been very well announced.
- That's Hannah, she's like you, she sees people. It's why she's so successful. We've been friends with her for some time. Hannah was so pleased when you came along and made friends with Eleanor.
- It didn't take very long. We seem so similar in some ways. She's funnier than I am, and more generous with people. If I'm honest I think she's a little prettier too. But don't tell her I said that.
- Well I think you're the prettier, but I'd be happy if you didn't tell her I said that either. In any case there are far more important qualities.
- I agree. But they're harder to spot.
- Not always. You spotted our relationship in moments.
- That is true. But I spotted you were pretty first. Wow. This is a lot more fun than small talk. I think we all know what the weather's doing really.
- Yes but don't rush conversations. Some people need to be given time. Not everyone is as quick as you. The weather can be a useful neutral opening. While you're hoping to find other directions to go in.
- I guess so. What language was it you were speaking to Ingrid?
- Norwegian.

There was a look in her eye. I'd missed something. It didn't seem to matter though.

- We're trying to arrange for Eleanor to come and visit us in Oslo. Would you like to come with her?

I was a bit shocked:

- Yes.. Of course. Thank you. Thank you.

She grinned at me:

- We'll set it up through Hannah. Would that be alright?

Perhaps it was all Hannah's idea but I couldn't find fault with it.

After leaving them I met up with Eleanor again and she asked:

- How's it going? Are you coping?
- Oh yes. I just met two friends of your Mum's - Sonja and Harald. They seemed approachable and willing to engage in a proper conversation. They are so much in love. Enchanting.
- Harald and Sonja? Alex, they are the King and Queen of Norway.
- Oh? Oh, OK. Anyway they have invited us to go and stay with them. She gave me a hug. Should I have curtsied or bowed or something? I didn't spot any expectation or notice any pause for...

She was laughing:

- No, No that's fine. Don't worry you would have been charming and you obviously have charmed them. They are good friends.

She finished chuckling and then took on a different tone:

- There's something else that I wanted to tell you and I think you'll be pleased. We've been invited to dine with the Khrushchevs while you're here. Katya wanted us to go and seems to have arranged it. Is that OK?

Why had she done that? What was the game here? Was I supposed to be getting to trust her? I tried to sound enthusiastic rather than befuddled:

- Yes, great! That should be interesting.
- It'll give you a chance to get to know her better.
- I do hope so.

Eleanor moved on:

- There's someone else that I want you to meet. Mercedes Sarren. Stephen's wife. She's the reason that we keep inviting them. She's a bit of an event all on her own. She's clever, knowledgeable and doesn't suffer fools.
- Amazing that she's married to him then.

She laughed:

- Yes it is. It is. They are pretty much apart. He goes off with other women sometimes, as you know, but they stay together.

We spent a little time together with Mercedes. She was fun. The time came for people to start leaving and we said goodbyes. Eleanor and I went up to our rooms.

I slept well, but I still meddled. I had set a very nasty trap in London, a sort of interactive trap. A well-meaning policeman walking in would probably walk out mildly annoyed. Anybody with real evil on their minds might not walk out at all.

Chapter 13
London
October 2014

Florists
Battersea High Street
London

Source:	Bugs set in shop. Conversations with Louise Ferryman
Date:	Saturday 4th October
Time:	10.32 am
Present:	DS Ryan Broadhouse, DS Kyriakos Papandreou, Florist Louise Ferryman

Broadhouse and Papandreou were at the florists on Battersea High Street. James Hecketty had sent a wreath to Tavi's funeral and it had come from this florist. They were here to see if there were any clues to help them find James. There was a pretty black girl arranging a bunch of flowers on the counter. She smiled briefly at them when they arrived. Broadhouse was just looking at her. Papandreou started asking the questions:

- Did James Hecketty place an order here for a wreath for the Mansur funeral?
- Yes I spoke to him.
- You know him?

Louise looked up from arranging her flowers:
- Don't you people talk to each other?
- Sorry?
- I spoke to two policemen who came to my home a couple of weeks ago. They wanted to know about Tavi. My name is Louise Ferryman.

Papandreou looked like he just remembered the reports:
- Of course. Sorry Miss. We didn't know it would be you here. Go on please. You were Tavi's girlfriend for a while weren't you?
- We went out for eight months. We stopped when he went to prison. I didn't support Tavi and I should have. I'll always regret that. You guys didn't come out very well either. You should have done better. He did nothing wrong and you locked him up. Do you like your jobs? Do you enjoy that kind of thing? Persecuting good decent people? I tried to get back with him afterwards, when I realised the truth.
- Hold on Miss. That wasn't us.

Louise was looking straight at Yak:
- No? So why are you here looking for James? It wasn't him that killed Tavi. James is a really decent guy too.
- So you do know him.
- Of course I know James! I went out with Tavi. They were good friends. James was a quiet, really likeable guy. He liked to chat. He was also very thoughtful. Like now. He wanted to send some flowers to the family home as well as the wreath. So he asked if it was OK to order them from me, knowing that it would give me an excuse to see Tavi's parents. I was glad of the chance. They were good to me. They didn't make me feel bad for dropping him. You guys can take all the blame for that.
- OK, OK, we're getting the picture. Did James give you

an address or anything?
- Yeah. He said you might want it.
- Did he?
- Isn't that what you came for?

She hands over a piece of paper with an address in Camberwell on it:
- You know the one good thing to have come out of this? I trust myself more now. I trust my judgement more now. I thought Tavi was good. I believed you guys though. You were wrong.
- OK, Miss, I think you've made your point clear now.
- Not if you're still after James I haven't.
- So when did you last speak to James?
- Four days ago when he ordered the flowers.
- And he rang in the order?
- Yes.
- And you haven't seen him apart from that?
- Yes.

There is surprise on Yak's face:
- Yes?
- Yes.

The policemen learned that James called on Louise ten nights ago and stayed long enough to drink a leisurely cup of coffee. Papandreou continued the questioning:
- Can you tell us what you talked about, Louise?

She looked amused:
- Excuse me?
- What was it that you talked about?
- No wonder you detectives are doing so badly. You can't work out the most basic things about people.
- Miss?
- He has two good friends. One is dead. The other is in a coma. You guys want him, laughably, for the murder of his friend and raping some poor girl. What do you think

we talked about? We discussed what a bunch of plonkers there are in the police force these days. At some length actually. There's a lot to say on that subject.

The detectives eventually retreated and talked to each other on the way out. Broadhouse:

-   Do you think Hecketty sent those flowers from here just so we could hear all that?

Papandreou couldn't disagree:

-   Probably. But don't expect that to be all.

Angelic?

Wadkins Factory Security Office
Urwin Road
Camberwell
London

Source: Bugs in the security office. Later conversations
             with Tommy Dodson
Date: Saturday 4th October
Time: 12.05 pm
Present: DS Ryan Broadhouse, DS Kyriakos Papandreou,
             Tommy Dodson

Detective Sergeants Broadhouse and Papandreou drove to the address in Camberwell. It wasn't very far. They found the place they were looking for. It was a large terraced house opposite a factory. The factory was HR Wadkins, they made small plastic car components. The security camera looking at the factory gates also had a view of the door to the house because from where the camera is the door was beyond the gates.

The house was a Victorian double fronted mid-terrace and had four floors including the basement. There were steps up at the front to a new looking front door. There were also steps down to the basement level and another door. The windows looked new too, but they were in keeping with the house. It was a tidy looking property.

The two detectives went into the factory and asked for the security office at reception. They were directed up some stairs on the outside of the old building. It didn't look well cared for. They knocked on the door and were invited in. They produced their ID and the security guard welcomed them:

- Good morning can I help you officers?
- May we see the security tapes for the front gate?
- Sure you can.

They watched the tapes back a week or so. They could see someone arriving and leaving. The times are irregular. The shot was too indistinct and it was too far away to see exactly who it was. It could be James, the clothes were similar. If it was then he clearly has been living at this address.

They fast forwarded the tapes and found that he should still be in there. There was a recent shot of him going in at 9.37 today. There was no more recent shot of him leaving. The security guard started to take an interest in what they were doing:

- Are you looking for James?
- Yes we're looking for James Hecketty. The man whose house it is.
- Nice guy. Helped us out with the computers.
- You met him?
- Yeah I was just coming through the gate one day and we started talking. I mentioned that we had a problem with the computers. Our IT guys don't fix anything. Just a useless bunch of stuck up tits. To them I'm just the security guard. Why should they have to help me? James said he'd have a look for us. It's been fine since.
- So he was in this office?
- Yeah sat right there.

The guard indicated the only chair in the cramped office.
- When was this?
- Last week. Tuesday? Yeah Tuesday. A week ago. It was a hot day and I'd just been watering the plants at the

allotment.
- We'll have to get this place dusted for prints. And get the forensics team in at the house.
- What? This place? You want this place dusted for prints? I'm not supposed to let anyone in here. I'll lose my job.

Broadhouse was not sympathetic:
- Sorry, mate, that's your problem.
- But I was being helpful. I didn't have to say any of that stuff.
- You let him up here. That's the problem.
- Fuck that! He helped me. I help you and you screw me over. You're supposed to be the good guys. Can't you keep it quiet?
- Sorry. We have to be formal about it or the evidence won't be admissible.
- So for helping you guys I get to lose my job?
- No for letting James Hecketty up here you get to lose your job. You shouldn't have had him in here.
- James seemed a decent guy. I'm not so sure about you two.
- Well thanks a lot anyway, Pal. Don't touch anything.

Broadhouse got a call. He answered. Meehan was talking to him from Lavender Hill.
- ...that house is owned by SafeNet...It's been done up to his own specification....Shit. It looks like he's been living here....What specification? ... Anything dangerous? ... Bullet proof glass and armour? It's a fortress! We think he's in there now.... Yeah we'll wait for the bomb squad and SCO19.

Broadhouse ended the phone call and then looked at the live camera feed. A people carrier had drawn up outside the house. Three men exited the sliding side door in a hurry. Papandreou ran out of the security office towards the house. Broadhouse followed shouting into his phone about what was happening. The security guard looked very amused.

The House Owned by SafeNet

Source:	Cameras inside and outside the house. Later conversations with Tommy Dodson and others.
Date:	Saturday 4th October
Time:	12.22 pm
Present:	DS Ryan Broadhouse, DS Kyriakos Papandreou, The Mandelstam Brothers, a man with a shotgun, a man driving a people carrier. Numerous other police officers etc.

One man was standing watch outside the house. The driver was still in the car. The other two men went up the stairs and into the house. The door opened easily and then shut behind them. The web cameras inside went live and an email with the link was sent to Lavender Hill. There were four cameras. One in the hall, one outside the house and two more in rooms of the house. The email marked from James Hecketty got immediate attention and the detectives at Lavender Hill saw what was happening in and around the house.

Moshe and Nachum Mandelstam were contract killers. It was a good guess that they had been engaged by Ivan. Once inside the house they opened the door on their left. It opened but with difficulty. The self-closing spring was very strong. Too strong for a door of this size. Moshe put his modest weight against the door and pushed hard. It opened and Moshe kept his back against the door as his brother peered round the door into the room. It seemed almost empty. Nachum flicked the light switch and nothing happened for four seconds. The room had wallpaper but no furniture apart from a single swivel armchair. Moshe still stood with his back against the door so it wouldn't close.

They were both carrying the same weapon, the Uzi-Pro automatic handgun, lightweight and easily concealed. The magazine holds 25 rounds, which at its maximum rate of fire can all be delivered to the target in less than a second. They have been well briefed before today and were aware of the self-defence issue raised. If they were shot it would be taken as self-defence, particularly as they were in Hecketty's house. They have discussed their solution to this. If he was dead then he wouldn't be shooting back. They planned to fire first.

After four seconds the arm chair spun around and they saw what looked like muzzle flashes and heard shots. Bullets seemed to hit the wall behind them. Nachum started shooting while Moshe spun round letting the door shut and fired his gun in the same direction. They both emptied their magazines in the direction they believed the shots to be coming from which was the armchair. They were both experienced with firearms and hit the target with accuracy. They would have started to reload.

Outside Papandreou ran through the factory gates towards the house. He shouted warnings to the man outside. He knew the house was probably booby trapped. He had a duty of care and he knew what happened at the hotel. He also knew what Hecketty's solicitor said about self-defence. He considered the men who went inside to be in great danger. His shouts were misinterpreted by the man outside the house who took out a pump action shotgun from the open door of the people carrier and fired it into the air as a warning. Both the driver and he had pulled ski masks down over their faces.

The Mandelstam brothers inside the house were being hit by bullets. Their own bullets. There are some materials that absorb bullets; human flesh for example. There are others that they bounce off, sheet steel works reasonably well. This room was lined with an arrangement of Hard Faced Composite armour. Bullets bounce easily off it because that is what it is made for. The armchair was made from the same HFC material and is such a shape that bullets hitting it are most likely to return in the direction they have come from. Both men had emptied their magazines before realising what was happening. Additional confusion was caused by the bright muzzle flash from their own weapons in the darkened room. Fifty bullets started bouncing round the room creating sparks, noise and confusion. Two bullets struck Moshe. Nachum was hit by three.

The door was hard to open before they were injured. Now it seemed impossible. They had to pull, not push which meant gripping the handle. Moshe had a chest wound that was bleeding badly. Nachum had leg wounds and could not stand properly. They struggled to open the door and lost blood doing so, the exertion raised their heart rate and blood pumped out from their wounds even faster. The blood also made it hard to get purchase on the floor. They stopped trying when they realised they could not open the door. Blood loss was now substantial.

Nachum Mandelstam called the man outside on his mobile to come and assist. He went into the house through the front door, still waving his shotgun in the direction of the police. He managed to push open the inside door and wedged it open with his shotgun. He helped first Moshe then Nachum to the front door. Then he tried to open it.

He couldn't. It was locked.

Outside Papandreou and Broadhouse have sheltered behind the factory wall. The driver of the people carrier looked at his watch. It had been four minutes. He'd heard the gunfire and saw a patrol car arrive at one end of the street, lights flashing. He put his foot down and his vehicle accelerated away.

Minutes later the firearms squad arrived at the front of the building. Then other officers at the rear. Megaphones were used but the men inside would not come out. The only uninjured man inside was shouting, but he could not be heard above the noise of the helicopter overhead. No one realised that they could not get out. Eventually the uninjured man used his mobile to call the police and explain. The firearms team cautiously approached the building and one man tentatively tried the door. It opened easily from the outside.

The uninjured man was desperately trying to slow the blood loss from Moshe Mandelstam's messy chest wound. The bullets had been sharpened and shattered by their impact with the armour. Their slow speed had caused them to lodge in the body rather than pass through and their sharp edges have caused further internal injuries while the injured men struggled to open the door. An artery in Nachum's leg had been just slightly cut causing his blood pressure to decrease rapidly. He had slowly lost consciousness and was now dead.

Moshe was attended by some paramedics who put him into an ambulance and drove him away with a police escort. Papandreou and Broadhouse had a good look round the house, still thinking they might find James Hecketty. The basement was inaccessible from the upper part of the house which was empty. Someone had been

Angelic?

living in the basement.

Lavender Hill Police Station

Source:	Computers at the Lavender Hill Police Station
Date:	Sunday 5th October
Time:	10.52
Present:	DI Inspector Gemma Black, DC John Meehan, DS Kyriakos Papandreou, DS Ryan Broadhouse

The coppers were discussing what happened at the house. Meehan was looking surprised:

- So James Hecketty's killed Nachum Mandelstam, but he's done nothing wrong.

Papandreou answered:

- Nothing at all. It's unusual to put the lock of your front door on backwards so that you need a key to get out and it's easy to get in. But it's not illegal. Even if they hadn't shot themselves they wouldn't have got out. It's not illegal either to have an art installation made of HFC armour or lining a room with it. Of course if you're expecting heavily armed assassins to come calling it looks like a great idea. He set this up six weeks ago. He knew. He's been planning everything. We're so far behind it's just not believable.

Broadhouse:

- He killed the headless girl before that. He was expecting a showdown. Isn't he on the CCTV?

Papandreou points out that the recording has clearly been altered in some way. The tech team are trying to find out how. It could not be used as evidence.

Yak had been doing some other research and has found

that there are very few good photos of Hecketty. There are some apparently good pictures for SafeNet publicity but they had been digitally altered. Papandreou adds something else:

- We went back through the camera data for the area around SafeNet. We wanted to see if there was anything odd that we could see. Then we realised that the odd thing was what we couldn't see. James Hecketty avoids cameras. He knows where they are and avoids them. We get a glimpse here and there, but he's very good at it.

The whole team looks surprised and Broadhouse asks the question:

- This was before we were looking for him?

Yak:

- Yes, that's the point. He's very secretive, hates publicity and won't do parties. We don't have a good picture of him. If he walked in here now without his signature beard, hoodie and baseball cap we'd have trouble recognizing him. He doesn't have a proper bank account and his phone can't be traced. We can't find a convincing history for him. He appears at college in September 2011, before that we can't confirm anything. He...

Papandreou stopped. His jaw dropped a little as he stared into the distance for a moment. Black enquired:

- What is it, Yak?

He recovered:

- Nothing, .. sorry. Err.. I suddenly thought I'd missed our wedding anniversary. It's ok though. Not till next week.

Black didn't look convinced by that response. She continued the police work:

- So, Hecketty, was he hiding from someone or something already?

- That's possible. The SOCOs got nothing from the SafeNet office. It was extraordinarily clean. A firm was contracted to go in each day and wipe everything down. They had already been in before we knew anything about all this. Every mug was put in the dishwasher every day. The keyboards were replaced every week. The carpet was replaced every month. Either one of them had a compulsive disorder or they were trying to keep it forensically sterile.

Black:

- So is Hecketty guilty of another crime? Is that part of the reason he won't come in and talk to us? The two people who might have known are either dead or in a coma. Has anyone any idea about all this? Does anyone know where we might look next?

They all looked blank. Broadhouse started to say something then stopped. Their chances of finding Hecketty were diminishing and their problems multiplying. Black moved on to some other news:

- The solicitor has been in again. He wants us to confirm that there will be no charges against his client. They want to know what charges will be brought against the surviving gunman. Clearly the firearms are illegal and there was an attempt to endanger his client's life. The solicitor talks about self-defence again. If his client comes in to talk to us then how can we guarantee his safety? I'm abbreviating. Witter and Proctor had another umpteen clauses.

Meehan made a comment to Gemma Black later that I found interesting:

- Are you OK? You seem a bit stressed. Not quite relaxed. Is there something going on at home?
- No nothing at home. Just a bit overworked I suppose.

Angelic?

Meehan had a very good point. Gemma Black had been looking increasingly stressed. There had to be a reason for that beyond what she normally did.

Chapter 14
Russia
October 2014

Alex's Room
Straminsky Residence

Source:	James Hecketty/Alex Harewood
Date:	Sunday 5th October
Time:	05.22 (local)
Present:	Alex

The police had arrived at the house opposite the Wadkins factory and then waited for the bomb squad. While they waited the Mandelstam brothers arrived with the two local thugs. How had they known to be there?

There was a leak within the police. I had thought so earlier and the conversations at Freeman and Jacob had suggested police collusion. Meehan had given me the clue to look for Gemma Black being the leak. There was a way I could check. It was time consuming and I couldn't do it for everyone, but I could check one person. I could check to see if there was any evidence that Gemma Black was leaking information.

I looked at the data I had collected of all the mobile phone signals from Lavender Hill and Azimuth House. I looked back through my records to see if I could coordinate any calls made from the station with ones at Azimuth House. I filtered for all the calls that Roman had received and tried to find any calls made from Lavender Hill on Gemma Black's phone that were made at the same time. That gave me nothing.

What if Gemma had a phone that I didn't know about? I looked at all the signals that were always in the building at the same time as Gemma's other phone. That gave me just one extra phone. It wasn't always on. I tried to see if calls from that number coincided with calls made to Roman's phone. They didn't coincide. There was a time lag. That phone made a call and a few minutes later there was a call to Roman. This is what happened before the incident outside the Wadkins factory.

Gemma was calling someone who was immediately then passing on the information to Roman. This wasn't quite proof but it was highly indicative. Gemma Black had been working for Roman. There was probably pressure on her to keep the investigation looking in my direction and when the police found me the information was to be passed on to Roman. The police were going to find me then the Russians were going to kill me. I hadn't actually been at the house opposite the Wadkins factory of course, but they had firmly believed that I was in there when that call took place.

Knowing that information was being leaked by Gemma was very different from doing something about it. I already had far too much to do. I'd need some help.

Straminsky Residence

Source: James Hecketty/Alex Harewood
Date: Sunday 5th October
Time: 17.07 (local)
Present: Alex Harewood, The Straminsky family

We were playing a game. It was one of those old parlour games that were invented when people didn't have televisions or radios. The teams were Hannah, Eleanor and me playing Sergei, Boris and Yelena. They were winning. My phone started ringing. It was only set to ring if the call was from very few people. People I would need to talk to straight away. It was Gemma Black.

-   I'm sorry. Can you excuse me?

I got up from the game and answered the call as I left the room and went into the hall.

-   Hello, Gemma,
-   Hello Alex. We've just found something out that I thought you should know. The last call that we know Tavi made was to the V and A. He left a message for you. A girl there has it for you. She's called Sarah Ross. I think you should speak to her.
-   Thanks. Why didn't I know about this before?
-   Well, the message was somehow deleted from the V and A system. Sarah remembered and didn't realise its significance until recently when she connected the call to Tavi's death. I think you should call her and get the message. I know she's there now.
-   Thank you Gemma.

Angelic?

I tried to say good bye calmly as I finished the call.

My heart raced and my breathing became shallow as my adrenalin levels increased. My brain went into overdrive. This could be what I needed. This message could get me access to the data that Tavi had found. I didn't know yet what it was but Ivan Khrushchev thought it was worth half a billion. Tavi had died to protect it.

I rang the V and A:
- Could I speak to Sarah Ross please? I think she is in today….
- I'll get her for you. Who is it please?
- Alex Harewood.
- Oh!... Oh, OK….just a moment.
There was a pause.
- Hello, this is Sarah.
- Hello Sarah, this is Alex Harewood. Do you have a message for me please?
- Oh yes, yes, I do. Tavi says he loves you... I'm sorry. I heard. You must feel so awful.
- Sarah, what exactly did he say? Exactly
She may have thought me cold, but this was important.
- Yes, funny, he was particular about that too. He said the message was "Tell Alex I love her".
- So the message is "Tell Alex: ILoveHer".
- Yes, that's exactly it. That's how he said it.
- Thank you Sarah you've been really helpful.
- Ok bye, good luck.

I had it. I had the password. A password Tavi could possibly have given to anyone, even under duress, and they would think he was just obsessing about his girl.

I sat down on the stairs in their impressive hallway and started typing in web addresses. I tried Drop Box first. That wasn't right. Then I tried OneDrive. Not that either. Then

Google Drive:
user name: AlexHarewood2208@gmail.com
password: ILoveHer

….and...Yes!!

It's all so easy when you know. I was in the account and finding the information that Tavi had uploaded when he knew they were coming for him. I started looking through it as quickly as I could. There were word files with the minutes of meetings, notes on selling something, the route it was to take and the weight of the cargo. There was only one reference to what the cargo was amongst some technical details:

Novichok

I went cold and shuddered as I put together all the information I was seeing. Ivan Khrushchev was selling deadly nerve gas to ISIS terrorists.

Novichok is the most horrific nerve agent. It was developed by the soviets as an undetectable form of nerve gas. It is actually a fine powder rather than a gas. This makes it easier to handle as well as harder to detect. Contact with it would cause your muscles to contract involuntarily. If those muscles were in your heart or your lungs you would die. Untreated, even in microscopic quantities, it could lead to permanent disability. One hundredth of a gram on the skin could be absorbed and kill a person. Theoretically a kilogram could kill a hundred thousand people and ten kilograms could kill a million.

The quantities mentioned in the notes was 100kg. The weight of a largish person. That was only a small truckload if you include the transport and containment vessels. But that was enough nerve agent to kill millions. ISIS were the worst people in the world to have such a weapon. They were very likely to use it.

Three days ago Katya had said it was on schedule. I looked at the route plan. It should be at a place called Hadrut in Southern Azerbaijan by now.

I went back to the sitting room. I was still white and trembling.
-    I'm sorry, could I have a word with Hannah please?
Sergei didn't look up and said:
-    Nothing too serious I hope?
Eleanor did look up and said:
-    What's wrong?
Hannah saw me and stood up immediately:
-    Come with me.
We went into her study. A room I had not been in before but I didn't look round. I looked at Hannah, she said:
-    You can talk freely here.
I showed her the documents. She looked at them. She didn't get it. I showed her the pages about Novichok on Wikipedia. Then she looked horrified. I could see her eyes widen, her mouth open and her breathing quicken. She now understood the full meaning of what she saw.
-    I just got the information about it just now. Tavi told me where it was.
-    But he's dead.
-    He was very clever and brave. Can you get this information to some people that can make best use of it? I don't know anyone, but you might.
-    Are you sure that this is all correct? All true?
-    Tavi died for this. He knew he was going to die. He died horribly so that I could find this information and pass it on. Please! It may already be too late.
She looked humbled:
-    Oh God, I'm so sorry. That wasn't a very sensitive

question.

She reached across to her phone, picked it up, and looked up a number on the display. She pressed a button.

- This is Hannah Straminsky for Arthur Boswell-Clerkson.

There was a pause and some clicks. I realised that a scrambler had just kicked in. I recognised the name. She was on a secure line to Boswell-Clerkson, the permanent secretary to the Home Secretary:

- I have information of a highly time sensitive nature that needs an immediate decision and action.

She gave the grid reference that I showed her on my tablet and said:

- There are 100kg of Novichok nerve agent destined for ISIS. Schedule and route to follow. Certainly on time 72 hours ago at most. This information is 100% certain.

I attached my phone to her computer and downloaded the data. She entered a messaging system and sent it. She looked at me and said:

- Let's hope it's still on schedule.
- I hope so too. It should be. Thanks for your help.
- Oh No. Oh No. How can you thank me? You do all that on your own and you thank me? I really don't understand how you can do what you do.

She looked at me. It was a look that I remembered. The priest had looked at me the same way. I began to feel very strange again.

Hannah was still talking but I couldn't hear her. Then I couldn't see her either.

> *The warehouse was busy. Men carried sacks from the stores. Then took them up steps onto platforms. Wagons drawn by oxen drew up at the platforms where they were loaded with the sacks of grain. The drovers then moved them on their way.*

A scribe was keeping a ledger. Recording how many wagons and how many sacks. His assistants did the counting moving a thumb along a marked stick and shouting as each score was reached. The scribe checked occasionally and then made the marks to record the total number of sacks of grain in multiples of twenty. I shouted at the scribe:

- *How many?*
- *Getting there, sir. Seventeen score and eight.*
- *Good work*

I watched the line of wagons reaching out into the distance as far as could be seen. They made their way slowly and certainly towards the distant depot.

Then I saw Eleanor. Just Eleanor. Those lovely eyes, that kindly face. She was talking to me:
- Alex, you fainted or something. Stay lying down. Stay where you are.

I stayed where I was. She touched my cheek and then kissed my forehead.
- Please be all right.
- I'll be fine.
- Oh good. Thank heaven. That's good.

I slept really well that night. In the morning the BBC news was on when I went down for breakfast. The headline was about ISIS destroying ancient monuments in northern Iraq. Some of them looked familiar.

Sergei was eating his cereal and reading the paper with half an eye on the news. He looked up at me. His eyes followed me across the room, sizing me up trying to see me in a new light. Hannah had told him about the Novichock. I wasn't just a friend of his daughters any more. I was looking back at him when I said:
- I still love my ball gown!

He grinned, shook his head and went back to reading his paper.

Tavi had had to do many things in a short time. He knew that he was taking a risk, but he could not possibly have expected that they would find him so quickly. He must have set up a tortuous route across the internet to get at that data. Soon after he had found the information he probably saw them coming for him on the security cameras at the SafeNet office. Men he didn't know coming up the stairs. He had to rush. He could have just had time to set up an account, confirm the email and upload the data. Our internet was blisteringly quick. Nevertheless the data was probably still uploading as they came through the door. He was probably on the phone at the same time.

He then had to endure hours of pain while they tried to get him to tell them where he had uploaded the data. He would have started saying nothing and then perhaps given out the names of every account that he could think of and their passwords. I guessed that they checked them as he did so. Possibly they stopped while they checked, each account and password. Maybe he kept shouting out "I love her" all the way through. Fixing on that one thing. He could then give away the password as often as he wanted without them realising what it was.

He'd left a message for me at the V and A without realising how long it would take to arrive. His message strengthened Alex' identity and, at the same time, gave me the password. Genius. He had to send a message in code; and that is what he did.

Tavi knew why he was hurting. He knew what his agony might hinder. His family had left northern Iraq to escape the Sadam Hussein regime that was gassing civilians in the Al-Anfal offensive. He had some idea what a gas attack on civilian populations entailed. His family would have relatives and friends who were injured or died in those attacks.

He had told the police and his family that he had been keen on me and had sex with me. He had persuaded me to go back to being Alex. My cover was good because he had made it good. Tavi had a real girlfriend so I had to be a real girl.

They came after James too, of course, thinking that I might have access to the data. It was possible that Tavi had told me where it was. He hadn't but they couldn't know that. All this only made sense if he had downloaded the data that Wednesday lunchtime. Tavi knew how to stay hidden on the net. So how had they been able to find him so quickly? That still didn't make any sense.

Red Square
Moscow

Source: Alex Harewood
Date: Monday 6th October
Time: 2.14 pm
Present: Alex Harewood, Eleanor Straminsky

We wandered around the boutiques and shops at GUM and I enjoyed admiring some of the things that were for sale. Everyone comes to GUM. It's popular with locals and a must-go-to tourist destination. The prices seemed to reflect its popularity. Eleanor wanted to pay.

- Eleanor, I know you can afford it and it's great that you want to get it for me, but I want the things I buy to be my things. That I earned money to buy.
- That's OK. I get it. I wanted you to say that, but I had to offer didn't I? TSUM is down the road and we pass some nice shops on the way. I go there sometimes. It has some good things.

I had to ask:

- And it's less expensive?

She grinned:

- Yeah. A lot less.
- That's good I'd like to get something for you. I'd like to get something for your parents too. To say thank you for having me to stay. You might be able to help me find something they would like.
- You don't have to get us anything.
- It's a better gift then.

Angelic?

- I guess so.

We walked out and down the road. On the way Eleanor started to talk about Katya. She said how good Katya was at buying presents for people. Getting something that the recipient appreciated. That was hard to do with people so wealthy, so I said:

- You have to be thoughtful to do that. You have to care too. It's a bit like fitting the picture to the person.
- Yeah. I suppose it is... When I started buying clothes she was great too. She always seems to like the more dressy formal modern stuff but she could see what I liked and what would suit me wasn't the same as what she liked. She'd get me to try things I wouldn't have considered. She'd be right. It would work well.
- That sounds clever.
- She always seemed clever but she didn't do well at school. She tried hard and got lots of help. Studying didn't seem to suit her.
- I guess intelligence comes in many different flavours. Hers is one of the more unusual ones.

We went in through the double doors and I found that TSUM was a lot quieter and a lot more to my liking, though nothing like as impressive as a building. I could look around the shops and actually consider buying things. Eleanor helped me pick out a tiny pretty brooch for Hannah, a colourful tie for Sergei and a pair of socks for Boris. The socks were a joke really; they had bats on them to remind him of the remark he had made on the first evening.

- What shall I get for you?

Eleanor didn't answer. She was thinking about something else. Then she started talking. We pretended to be looking at clothes while she told me what had happened when her engagement had broken down.

He had chased her, bought her flowers and little surprises, wooed her and said how very much in love he was. She had responded and for a while she had thought they shared something very special. He had proposed to her on top of an ancient pyramid in Guatemala and they were planning an extraordinary wedding by Lake Como. She loved him. Then someone sent her a photo of him with another girl. Not a girl anyone liked. She didn't understand and asked him to explain but he said nothing that was worth hearing. He left her with a shattered heart and her faith in people permanently degraded. I wanted to say something supportive:

- I'm so sorry. One day the world will look better.

She grinned at me:

- It already does.

We left TSUM and started back towards Red Square, re-visiting one of the small shops we had browsed on the way. I got a little make-up bag for her in one of the shops, but didn't let her see. We had about done with shopping for the day. She phoned for her car to come and pick us up and we returned to the absurd suburb in the forest.

Khrushchev Residence
Rublyovka
Moscow

Source:	Alex Harewood
Date:	Wednesday 8th October
Time:	14.03
Present:	Eleanor Straminsky, Alex Harewood, Hannah Straminsky
	Klarra, Yevgeny, Asya and Gleb Khrushchev

The Khrushchev residence was one of the more traditional ones. Built in the 90s and followed the tradition then of not appearing modern. I guessed that the architect had fancied himself as copying Lutyens design for Nashdom in Buckinghamshire. It was an elegant building. We were to arrive there in the early afternoon and spend the rest of the day there, having a meal in the evening and leaving for home soon after that. There were supposed to be seven of us there and it seemed like a good plan for a day.

Everybody was very pleasant during the introductions and we got the Russian kiss from everyone. Katya was not there which felt really odd. Apparently there was important business to complete in London and she sent the most ardent apologies but had insisted that the event went ahead. So there was just Eleanor, Klarra, Yevgeny and me. The younger children, Asya and Gleb, would get in from school later.

We were in a large drawing room. With three tables four

sofas and several armchairs. It was a bit too big for only four of us. There were several paintings and one photograph. I looked at the paintings but studied the photograph. It was fascinating. An old photograph showing a line of people, a family, that I assumed had been taken around 1940. There was a man on the end in Red Army uniform. At the other end was a woman in her best clothes. In between were five children. Two boys and three girls. The soldier looked a little like Yevgeny. I guessed that this was his father and that the tiny boy who stood next to him was Yevgeny. The woman on the end was his mother. The oldest girl, next to her mother, had dark hair, but otherwise the resemblance to Katya was immediate and so I asked:

- Who is she?

He answered in a slow, measured, respectful way:

- She is Yekaterinya.
- And the others. Who are they?

He pointed to them each in turn:

- Alexandra, Yevgeny, Anna, Sergei.
- This Yekaterinya looks very much like Katya. Your own daughter. They share the same name. Is there a reason for that?
- Many things happened in the war. It doesn't always help to talk about them.

He wasn't saying, but I still wanted to know and asked again in a different way. He still wasn't saying. Yevgeny continued to talk to me. He'd been in his early fifties when Katya was born. He was in his seventies now and not doing well on it. His eyes were a little glazed and there were clear signs of dementia. He knew that the sharp mind that had helped him become one of the world's richest men as the Soviet Union collapsed was lost to him. When he forgot things he would ask Klarra. She responded with patience and care. She told him how much he could drink and had already drunk. It was a little sad to see but so charming too. The nature of their relationship was changing. She was a little more the nurse and less the wife. They still very much loved each other and it was heart-warming to see his utmost trust and her care.

I got him to talk a little more about his family. He grew up on the steppes West of Kiev near the banks of the great river Dnieper in what would now be Ukraine. He had lived in a traditional home with little space and no privacy. One of five children. There would have been more but for the Great Patriotic War. His father, Katya's grandfather, went off to serve in the army and was not seen again. There was never leave from the army at that time. The only way to get home was serious injury or desertion; both were rare. They eventually received word that he died in January 1944 at the Battle of Korsun Pocket, a battle fought not far from the banks of the Dnieper, where the Russians had first proved that they could take enormous chunks out of the German Army at will. They used their abundant manpower and American vehicles to effectively implement the kind of mobile warfare that military planners had dreamed of for half a century.

He told me his mother had died in the fifties, permanently harmed by the starvation she had inflicted upon herself in order to give every chance of survival to her children. Yevgeny had never forgotten her sacrifices and it was in part in her memory that he had strived to amass as much wealth and security as possible. He portrayed it as an act of necessity. It had been essential to take control of the countries assets before left wing elements reorganised. No one, he felt, wanted a return to communism.

He got tired and started to doze. It was lovely watching

him drift away still talking and thinking of the old days. One day, not so very far away, he would drift off like that and not wake up. I gently got up from my seat next to him and left quietly so as not to disturb him.

Klarra seemed pleased that I had spent time with Yevgeny.
- You were talking to Yevgeny for hours.
- Hours? Was it? He's so fascinating. All the things he has done. He called me Alexandra. I didn't say I was her, but I let him think that I was.
- Alexandra was one of his sisters. He looks the most content that I have seen him for a long while.

Klarra was a thoughtful careful woman but she had never taken any interest in the business. She bustled around like there was only her to look after her guests. She was sweet, but I couldn't see any of Katya in her, neither in character nor countenance. She was several years younger than her husband, his second wife and Katya's mother. His first wife, Ivan's mother, he had divorced in the eighties.

Around 4 o'clock two children appeared, still in their school uniforms. We were introduced, Asya and Gleb. They both greeted Eleanor warmly. Gleb wandered off to do his own thing in typical boy style, probably to get involved in some project. Asya talked to Klarra and the conversation was clearly the how-did-it go-at-school-today chat. The same one that happened all over the world at that time of day. I watched the expressions and listened to the words. There was something worrying Asya something that she couldn't do. She showed her mum a book. I recognised what it was. Quadratic equations. Klarra was shaking her head but I knew I could do that.
- I'd love to help. May I?
They looked a bit surprised. I'm not sure they knew I had been listening and I didn't speak Russian, but algebra is

pretty much the same in every language. I glanced at Eleanor for reassurance that it was an OK thing to do. She grinned. It was fine.

We sat next to each other on the sofa while Klarra talked with Eleanor. I gave Asya a couple of easy ones. She had to do the hard ones with non-unitary coefficients of X squared. I got Asya to show me the steps she took to get started. We only used one pen and Asya handed it to me if she was stuck and I'd give it back to her if it was time for her to have a go. I showed her the bits she was having trouble with and pretty soon she was doing them very efficiently. She was keen to learn and I teased her by getting some simple things wrong. She pretended to be hopelessly stuck when it was easy. I watched her finish off the set of twenty she had to complete and checked them for her. It had been fun. Asya got up to show her Mother and her mother praised her thoroughly.

Asya came back to me with a kiss and a question. I was taken by the hand and led away to see her room. I looked back at Eleanor with a what-choice-do-I-have shrug. She gave me the go on you're doing fine grin and then the expression changed to a mockingly conspiratorial one. They would be talking about me while I was gone. I figured I was doing OK though.

I knew what to expect in Asya's room. A mixture of little girl and teenager. It was tidy, but the maid probably saw to that. There was a bit of make-up and some jewellery, lots of girly pinks and fluffy things. Cushions with hearts on them and a couple of magazines that probably had stories about first dates and falling out with friends. I picked out a few things and said how lovely they were. I gestured a question about looking in her wardrobe, which was the size of a small room. I got a nod in reply. It was full of brands. Expensive brands. She could afford them. There were a couple of pretty gowns. They were too flouncy and small to be current. But one was new. I took it out, held it up to her, and made some approving noises. She was a bit embarrassed but loved the dress. I mentioned the b word and got a scowl back. She didn't yet have a boyfriend. Nor had anyone caught her eye.

We went back out into the corridor and as I had hoped she gave me a quick look at the other rooms. Gleb was in his room killing some rather stupid aliens by the dozen. She showed me Katya's room. I tried not to look too interested.

The room I saw wasn't austere and functional as I had expected. It wasn't very different from Asya's, though the things in it were more feminine and less fluffy; there was less pink and more subtle tones. One thing stood out for me. The woman who sold nerve gas to terrorists had a teddy bear on her bed. The small, serious looking, care worn bear didn't look at all out of place in that room.

It was possible that this room was not much used now and it was a remnant of what she had been. I managed to ask if Katya was often there. Yes she was often there. She said that Katya was sad. She drew a finger down her cheek to show that she cried in her room.

Katya was unfathomable. None of the ordinary measures fitted. I had hoped that meeting Klarra would help me understand Katya better. It hadn't so far. Their characters seemed too dissimilar. Was it also possible Katya had asked Asya to show me her room? Was Katya trying to paint a picture of herself for me that was different from what I had already seen? How could she even know what I had seen?

We returned to the others. Her mother was pleased to see her daughter looking so happy and thanked me for helping with the homework. She had lapsed into Russian but I knew what she meant.

- She did ever so well. I just pointed her in the right direction and she got it. She's clever.

This confused Klarra. Because I understood her she thought I should speak Russian. Eleanor helped me out by explaining that I couldn't speak Russian but usually understood what people were talking about when it was obvious from the context anyway.

- I will speak English with you.
- Thanks. I'll try to make it easy.

She smiled back at me. She was a beautiful woman. Asya's features were a lot like hers.

With a little prompting from me she started to tell how she had met Sergei. Klarra had been a first class skier and had medals for slalom and giant slalom. Yevgeny had sponsored an event and had presented her with a medal. He had been charming. What had started as a relationship of the wealthy man beds beautiful athlete kind turned into something far more substantial.

Klarra talked just a little too much. She appeared nervous and fussed over her children. She wasn't the first woman to find that having children completely changes the way you look at the world. She could see that she was now just as her mother had been, and understood now why mothers worried so much.

It had been a good day. A pleasant occasion. I wondered how different the atmosphere would have been if Katya had been there. Not very different I thought, depending on which Katya lived in that house.

Why had Katya invited us? Had it been so that I could see something? Was I supposed to see her room or her family circumstances? Was I supposed to have noticed her Teddy

Bear?

The thing that had most captured my attention though was that old photograph. I was curious about the things Yevgeny wouldn't say about the past. There was something about the old Yekaterinya that was too important and painful to talk about. I didn't know what that was. I started to think how I might find out.

Straminsky Residence

Source:	Alex Harewood
Date:	Thursday 9th October
Time:	10.03
Present:	Eleanor Straminsky, Alex Harewood, Klarra, Yevgeny, Asya and Gleb Khrushchev

Hannah had a word with me before I returned to London. She called me in to her office to talk. She sounded critical:

- I've heard that two men went in to a house that you own and one of them died. The other is seriously injured in hospital.
- The Mandelstam brothers. They were horrid, violent people, well known contract killers.
- Did you have to kill him?
- He killed himself with his own weapon, or his brother did. They were in James' house. They had gone there to kill James. That's quite clear. What do you do to people that come to kill you?

Now she looked shocked. I don't think she had thought about it that way and could only say:

- I don't know.
- He tried to be gentle at first. James played a joke with starting pistols and blow up men. They didn't get the message. Then he hurt the friends of Ivan in the hotel. They still came after him. Then he arranged for this man to kill himself. They kill and torture and rape people casually every day without a second thought. They beat my friend to death. Should I be nice to

them?

I paused. She was listening. She was taking it in. I had more to say:

- I don't like that these people are so terrible that all that has to happen. I hate having to be all this mixed up and confused about who I am. I like helping people. I want to be good. I want to be like Eleanor. She can't be bad. She can't be nasty like me and I can't be bad when I'm with her. I think about doing good things when I'm with her.

She looked like she was beginning to understand me better. She gave an explanation:

- It's so hard to think that anyone would want to hurt you. You poor girl. You do remarkable things. You are remarkably good.

Her expression had changed. She was not critical any more. She was seeing the world a little more as I saw it. She moved the conversation on:

- I wanted to give you some news. Some news of good you have done.
- That would be very welcome.
- Arthur Boswell-Clerkson got back to me. The SAS have destroyed the Novichok. It was at the location you gave. I don't know the details. They're keeping the whole thing as quiet as they can.
- Thank you for telling me.

She was looking at me, thinking about me while saying:

- You should feel good about yourself. None of this is your fault. I know you're in trouble in London. Don't worry. I've made some calls.
- Thanks, thanks for your help. Can you do something for me?

There was a moments thought before she responded:

- Anything, anything I can.

Angelic?

Oh wow! I drew in my breath and touched her arm. I had her complete support. She could see she had made an impact. She held my arm too. I didn't need much from her though:

- Try to keep Gemma Black and her family safe. Let her know that they have the best possible protection. It's important that she knows. If James escapes she may find herself in trouble. Make sure she knows you're the good people.
- Is she one of the good people?
- I don't know yet, I think so, but the protection works both ways. If she's good she will appreciate the help. If she's bad then she knows we're watching her. So will the people who may be threatening her.
- I'll see what can be done.
- Thanks, that'll stop me having to worry about her. Hopefully it will save her from having to worry so much as well.
- That's another good thing then.
- I hope so.

There were a lot of things that I had kept hidden even from her and just about everyone else. I had helped her believe something about me that wasn't true and I knew she didn't know too much about my past.

Hannah had been desperate to find a friend for her daughter. She'd arranged my protection team, my cover and probably my passport. Despite my extraordinary circumstances.

On my way home I thought through my time in Russia. It had been a good time. Actually I'd had the best time. Everyone had been so kind. None of the things that had worried me before had happened. I had to be so different from how I was as James, but it had all worked out. People seemed to like Alex and I liked that. Where would I be if I hadn't met Eleanor at the party? Would I be tortured and dead or would I be on the run and sleeping rough?

The balance had changed now in London. Perhaps I wouldn't be watched so carefully. The only reason to be after James now was revenge, although that was a potent motivation. James had made a powerful enemy. Ivan Khrushchev would not forget what had happened. If he had employed the Mandelstam brothers I could expect there would be others and if I appeared as James for too long or too often I could reasonably expect to die. I would always have to be careful that no one found the connection between James and Alex.

There were still things that I couldn't yet judge. Katya was one of them. Her character was the largest variable left whose value was not known. There was one thing that I hoped would give me a better idea. I was en-route from Moscow to London. Perhaps to find out what I wanted to know I would have to return to Russia, visit the Steppe and go back seventy years. Possibly there I would find a clue that would finally help me understand better why Toby was in a coma, Tavi was dead and what it was that happened at the Mornington Club Party.

Angelic?

Part 3
Katya Khrushcheva

Angelic?

Chapter 15
London
October 2014

The British Press

Source: The Press
Date: Friday 10th October

The Press had been awakened by two major firearms incidents within a fortnight. They had found out that the case involved a headless, naked, raped young woman; perfect material for selling newspapers. They started trying to put things together. They easily found that a character called James Hecketty was involved and their investigation followed very much the same lines as the police investigation.

The basic outline they wanted to present was clear. David versus Goliath. Hecketty was being hunted by Ivan Khrushchev who represented the Russian Mafia and the TPO oil giant. The police were nowhere. Ivan was, inevitably, dubbed Ivan the Terrible. His image appeared on the front of newspapers. They had found a picture of him that made him look sly and unlikable to confirm their supposition that you can tell people's character from their appearance. This ran alongside pictures of a helmeted James in action man poses from his paint balling tournaments. They loved the tale of one British man taking on this powerful Russian Bear.

All sorts of stories appeared about me as James Hecketty. People who knew me at college recounted tales of how I had solved all sorts of impossible problems. Some claimed that I was a famous anonymous online gamer called Anirnisiack. Women claimed to have dated me and said how they had always known there was something special about me. One girl even claimed to have slept with me. College tutors had always been so impressed with my brilliance. I actually did recognise a couple of the names and just one of the large number of incidents mentioned did sound familiar. The rest was nonsense.

None of this could have happened without some financial consequences. The price of TPO Oil on stock exchanges around the world began to fall. Nobody wanted to be associated with Ivan Khrushchev. The list of places where he was welcome became small. Within the Oil Business he was a pariah. Within the Arbat group he was a bungler. Sales in SafeNet security software doubled. And then tripled. SafeNet also made a profit from buying short on TPO stocks.

Azimuth House

Source:	Emma Wilkinson/James Hecketty
Date:	Saturday 11th October
Time:	11.24
Present:	Emma Wilkinson, Azimuth House Caretaker

Azimuth House had flats for rent above the showroom and offices of Freeman and Jacob. I had applied for one using the name Emma Wilkinson. I needed a new character to do this because it couldn't be James; the police wanted him. It couldn't be Alex and it couldn't be Elisabeth Greyling.

Emma Wilkinson got her flat. She dressed in a kind of Goth style and had thick black hair and metal rings in her nose and eyebrows. Of course she always wore black and make up that made her look like she was recently deceased. I collected the keys for her flat from a tiny office at the entrance. Her bags went upstairs easily in the lift. There was a staircase as well.

The flat was furnished and decorated, though not so anyone could possibly like it. This was not the expensive end of the market. All the furniture looked like it would break within the month. I pointed out all the faults to the man from the little office who showed me round and made sure he was aware of all the scratches, stains, frayed carpets, chipped mugs and dirt on the walls that I could catalogue. He started to get annoyed as I continued to add to the list. That was fine with me. Alex would have tried chatting him up a bit, but Emma was a grump and I absolutely definitely wanted to make sure that he remembered her. To anyone who asked him about Emma it would appear he knew her well. Eventually I was willing to sign the document that said I would take responsibility for everything in the flat apart from the following long list of exceptions. I went back down to the small office to make sure that I had a copy of the document before I finally put pen to paper. Then I signed both copies.

I went back upstairs and set up my kit. There were some speakers to play loud music when I wasn't there, I'd also recorded some domestic noises and set up all these to play at appropriately random intervals to convince people I was at home even when I wasn't. There were two cameras that looked outside and recorded arrivals and departures at the back door to the flats. One was a thermal imager that would let me see things that were not in the normal spectrum. I guessed the furniture store was a legitimate business operation. I wanted to build up a picture of the other things that were happening in this place that were far from legitimate. I hid the cameras so that the flat looked normal. The fridge was stocked with ready meals and I put other appropriate stuff in the cupboards so that the place looked lived in.

There were some cars parked outside. I needed to know which ones were part of the business. But I could track them anyway. I placed trackers on them and could then watch where they went and record conversations going on inside the vehicles.

I also put in place the devices I needed so that I could get back to knowing what Roman and his team were doing in their office and the basement. This was slower than the previous method. It would be a while before I had any useful information. It had the advantage of being almost untraceable. I had small crawler robots that I operated remotely and gradually and carefully worked their way through the roof spaces and ventilation system and down the lift shafts. At night they would cross floors and scout out locations. They trailed wires for communication and unless seen were undetectable. Data came back through wires to a server and then combined with the normal internet traffic from Emma's flat. This would give me quality data, good enough to be evidence.

Lavender Hill Police Station

Source:	Computers at the Lavender Hill Police Station
Date:	Monday 13th October
Time:	15.24
Present:	DI Inspector Gemma Black, DC John Meehan, DS Kyriakos Papandreou, DS Ryan Broadhouse

Broadhouse reported to the briefing. He'd managed to get a picture of the Wadkins factory showing on the screen and swiped through pictures as he talked. He'd found that the person on the security tape coming and going from the house where Nachum Mandelstam died was Thomas Dodson who was also the security guard from the Wadkins factory.

- Capita Investments purchased the property for a client. That client is SafeNet. James Hecketty effectively is SafeNet and James has lent his house to Dodson. Dodson has done nothing wrong. He was given somewhere to live for nothing and took the chance. He didn't tell us before because we didn't ask.

Yak wanted to know:

- So the stuff on camera, showing Hecketty coming and going?

Broadhouse answered:

- We're guessing it's been doctored to show the wrong times of arrival and departure. We're having it examined. Dodson used the basement door not the main one. He claims to have had no idea what was in the two front rooms.

There was something else that Broadhouse thought worth mentioning:

- I looked up this Tommy Dodson. His name cropped up in the Sun House case. He was a guard at a Language college close to where she was last seen. Somebody helped Angelina escape. He was one of the possibles. Nothing concrete though.

Meehan perked up:

- So we have another link to Sun House?

Yak was not so keen:

- Not really. It's more a coincidence. Security guards tend to move around a lot.

Black seemed to agree:

- We don't need to look at that. Sun House has been dead for a long while.

Meehan looked disgruntled. He clearly thought they were missing something.

Meehan and Black got personal again once the others have left. They were just tidying up at the end of the day.

- Do you like her John?
- Who?
- You know who I mean. Janet. The new constable on the team.
- I don't really know her. I like to see her move. You feel that she understands people. When I talk to her it's like she values you and wants to be involved with you. I find it hard to talk. She seems to find it so easy.
- So you have noticed her. You're looking.
- Yeah, I guess that I have been.
- I think she likes you a little bit as well.
- She's older than me.

Gemma smiled knowingly:

- You can't think that that might stop her from falling for you.

Angelic?

- Why do you say she likes me?
- Everyone else already knows. Does she sit near you? Doesn't she always walk past you and not take a shorter route? Don't you see her looking at you?
- I don't know. I see those things but don't believe they are to do with her liking me that way.
- You really do like her then.

Black stopped what she was doing for a moment and turned to face Meehan:

- There are some men think that believe every woman fancies them. Do you find it so hard to believe that someone could like you? Talk to her. See if she doesn't listen. See if she doesn't want you to talk more.
- OK

He looked a little uncomfortable at being offered such direct advice. They said nothing more on that subject.

Emma Wilkinson's Flat
Azimuth House
Clapham Road
London

Source:	Listening Devices and Cameras in Emma Wilkinson's Flat
Date:	Wednesday 15th October
Time:	10:37
Present:	Katya Khrushchev and her bodyguard.

My phone got an alert. It was in the form of a text message asking if I had suffered any industrial injuries. What it meant was that someone was in Emma's flat.

When I got a chance I looked at the recorded feed from the camera in the flat. It was Katya. She was looking around it. I guessed that she wanted to know what Azimuth House's latest resident was like, looking for more holes in their security. I knew all my tricks were well hidden. She'd have to get into the roof spaces to find anything. She was with her bodyguard.

They looked round and found nothing that they shouldn't. Everything seemed normal. Katya looked in the wardrobe and then in the chest of drawers. There was not a lot there, Emma wasn't wealthy, but it all looked normal. There were a few letters and papers, mail order catalogues and magazines. Katya took a few photographs with her phone and then left. She looked pleased. In fact she looked like she had found what she was looking for. I spent an

Angelic?

hour thinking through what was in the flat and what it might mean to Katya. There was nothing. I checked the recording again. There was something that she had found, and she was pleased she had found it. I didn't know what it was.

Lavender Hill Police Station

Source:	Computers at the Lavender Hill Police Station
Date:	Thursday 16th October
Time:	15.24
Present:	DI Inspector Gemma Black, DC John Meehan, DS Kyriakos Papandreou, DS Ryan Broadhouse, David Evans

- Jesus Christ!

Meehan was staring across the operations room from Black's office. In his sight was an enormous, fat, bald and ugly man.

- What in God's name is he doing here?

Yak followed his gaze:

- Shit!

David Evans had arrived with two acolytes in tow. He took large strides and his assistants appeared to have to run to keep up. It looked as though the floor might shake with each footfall. Evans was the head of the British Secret Intelligence Service and had a reputation for being clever, decisive and severe. Gemma had frozen in the middle of sipping her coffee as he arrived at her door. She mouthed an expletive and then looked embarrassed and flustered.

- Are you Gemma Black?

Gemma nodded. Evans looked at Papandreou and Meehan:

- I'm going to talk to this lady. You two piss off for a while.

They both got up and left. One of his men swept the office

for bugs. The man nodded at Evans and then left to join his colleague standing guard at the door.

- Are you listening good, Lady?
- I am, Mr Evans.

He grunted at the title:

- Hnhh. Good, I won't keep you long. I'm here on behalf of an associate of mine. He's indirectly asked me to do him a favour. I owe him one. I've been asked to make sure that you and your family are safe from any one that might have been threatening them. As of about ten minutes ago, you, your husband and your children are all covered by the same level of protection as the Queen herself. It's a big favour that I owe you see.

She looked blank. Shocked. He clarified:

- Do you understand me? If anyone pops a balloon near any of you or yours they get immediate attention from everything that I have at my disposal. There is only one thing that you have to do. Follow every clue you can that leads to the killers of Tavi Mansur and the woman.
- Smithson?
- Yeah, him too. That's all. Can you do that? Are you happy?
- I am. So I just have to do my job?
- Yes that's it. But let's be clear Lady, *only* your job.

She looked a bit thoughtful at that, but gave nothing else away:

- OK... and you guys will make sure that I don't have to worry about my family.
- I said that already. We need to keep this brief. It's hard for me not to swear all the bleeding time... Oops.
- Alright, err thank you. One more question?
- Shoot
- Who's your associate? The one who asked you to do this?

He looked at her for a moment. Deciding whether to tell her or not:

- James Hecketty is the fellow...

Evans got up to go:

- OK, we're done. Good luck, Lady.

She was shocked, her mouth was open, and then she blurted out:

- I'm looking for him!
- Ha! Good luck with that!

She was too surprised to say anything. Then she relaxed a little. He had brought good news, a weight had gone. Evans knew about her lapses and the world hadn't collapsed. The anti-corruption team weren't on her case. He then said in a more conversational tone:

- Jim's quite a character, hey?
- He certainly is.
- You don't know the bloody half of it.

He left. All eyes followed him back across the operations room. His two subordinates struggled to keep up.

That was a bit more than I'd had in mind. But it made the point in every way possible. Thanks Hannah.

Basement
Azimuth House

Source:	Cameras set by Emma Wilkinson
Date:	Friday 17th October
Time:	16.23
Present:	Paul Flowers, Dmitri Chazov, Five young women from Russia, Martin Peters

There was another furniture delivery. It started out looking similar to before except that Flowers had taken the place of Houghton. It was obvious that Flowers was new at this and he kept looking to Chazov for an idea as to what to do. He struck the right kind of poses and made the right kind of noises. There were five girls this time. Chazov took a girl with short dark hair called Vladlena into the office. Flowers declined the offer of raping any of them.

There was still a problem for them.
- Why did we get five? We have room for two, maybe three.
- Isn't there a guy called Peters who takes them from you? See if he'll take a couple.
- The guy's a twat. I hate dealing with him. He thinks he's so fucking clever. But he's too stupid to know how stupid he is.
- Yeah sure, if he was a genius he'd work out in no time that he was stupid. But as he's got the intellect of a potato he'll never work it out.
Chazov picked up the phone and dialled:
- Peters... We've got some real comfy armchairs you

might want to take off our hands…yes top
quality….yeah, yeah, yeah, straight legs and plump
cushions of course…quality fabric. Yeah really
comfortable to lie on, just your style. They'll look great
in your house. Yeah…in the bedroom too ha ha ha……

He ends the call and puts the phone on the table.

- What else am I going to say on the fucking phone? That
  they're ugly bitches with saggy tits? He'll be round in
  thirty minutes, he says. Fuck its painful hearing his cogs
  turn. There's this sort of grinding sound as it happens.
- I guess that's the sound of him feeling pleased with
  how clever he is.

An hour later the girls were told to come out again and
they stood in a line. They saw that another man had
arrived and he glanced over the five girls. He was a very
ordinary looking man. Brown hair, average height, average
weight, pleasant, friendly looking face.

I knew him. This was the man who had shown me a
recording of Tavi being kicked to death at my flat and was
probably the man who killed him. Martin Peters. I was
getting closer.

Peters walked down the line eyeing each of the girls. They
looked away. He pointed out some of the girls and
commented:

- This is a sorry collection. I'm not sure I can use any of
  them. She's got a massive nose, this one looks like a
  boy, and this one's got something funny with her eyes.

The girls knew better than to say anything. Chazov
responded:

- It takes all sorts. I thought you might have figured that
  out by now. So which ones do you want?
- The red hair and the blonde with big knockers on the
  end.

Angelic?

- They're the best ones. Thirty thousand.
- Twenty. They aren't worth more.
- Not enough.

Peters started to walk out. Chazov didn't look impressed:

- You pull that shit every time. Walk out if you want to.

It seemed that he didn't want to, because he stopped and turned round.

- Twenty-five thousand.
- Twenty-eight or go.
- Ok twenty eight thousand it is.

The girls were looking at each other. They saw what was happening, but couldn't believe it.

- You two come with me. Yeah. You and you.

Chazov confirmed:

- Yes you two are his now. Behave very well. He's not as nice as we are.

Peters went out with Flowers. They were each escorting a girl. Chazov gave an order:

- The rest of you go back to the canteen.

Flowers returned on his own a few minutes later and spoke to Chazov:

- What happens to the girls that he takes from us?
- If they're dead he freezes them for us till we have enough lye for the stripping room.
- What if they're not dead, like those two?
- He sells them. Or keeps them for himself.
- Who buys them?
- There's quite a trade in people. Young women get the best prices. You can make thousands a month from a girl.
- So who's Peters?
- He used to work with me. He liked to hurt them though. You can go too far and then they go off. They won't be reasonable. Peters went too far too often.

Roman found a use for him in getting rid of spare girls.
- He sounds really sick.
- He is. There are a few people like Peters. They just enjoy hurting people. It's what Peters lives for. That's why we bring him in to do gritty stuff, like with Mansur.

Now I knew exactly what it was that had happened and where the dead girl found with Tavi had come from. I knew who had tortured him and killed him. I had a good idea where to find the evidence as well.

This was the time for putting some plans into action.

You can find many things on the dark web. There are people on there who advertise anything. You can buy anything. Some people's desires take them in unconventional directions; perhaps drugs, or guns, or bombs. Let your imagination run further and you come across people like Peters. My mind had gone in a different direction altogether.

I needed some time out. I needed time when no one at all was going to see what I was doing, not even those who were on my side. This was a time to play one of my wilder cards. So far people had been coming to me. Now I was going to go to them. This particular little trick had cost me a lot of money. I wasn't even going to see much of it but I'd see it next day on TV the same as everyone else. I sent an email and at the agreed time the motors started, the gears engaged. Two enormous 40 tonne juggernauts rolled out of a garage. The weather was perfect.

Battersea Park
London

Source:	James Hecketty/Alex Harewood
Date:	Sunday 19th October
Time:	18.23
Present:	Alex Harewood, a taxi driver.

One thousand zombie twitter accounts had started to give out the news. Then it hit Facebook. Local radio stations carried word of the event in prepared adverts. There was to be a world record flash mob attempt in London. Now. The previous record was for fifty thousand people dancing in sync set in the United States in 2012. The instructions were to wear green or brown clothes and a red wig if possible, but come whatever.

The two juggernauts set up in Battersea Park disgorging people and equipment. Massive fold out stages with video screens, speakers and a laser light show appeared from inside the trucks. There were also crowd control barriers and a very professional team who knew just what they were doing. They had documents giving them permission to do all this that looked exactly like the real thing. The massive speakers started to pound out music at 19.30. The video screens showed a team doing a version of the Groot Dance to the Jackson Five's "I Want You Back". People started arriving in small groups and joined in. The team on stage instructed the crowds and praised them for doing so well. The video screens picked out members of the public doing the dance with particular enthusiasm or skill. The main man on stage called himself Mr Marvel and kept everyone entertained with jokes and news of how many people there are estimated to be in the dancing crowd. He made the dance look good too.

I joined the throng on Battersea Park and became very hard to track in the enormous crowd of people also wearing green clothes and red wigs. Then I took two steps amid the tightly packed people and flashing lights. Alex Harewood disappeared.

This was something that I would do best as Emma Wilkinson. She had no history and could not be found. I wore her long black skirt and face piercings. I walked for a bit and then flagged down a cab. The driver seemed like an obliging sort. It wasn't Timms. I had to ask:
- Have you got any bookings later tonight?
- No, Love, will you need me later?
- I'll need you for the next couple of hours. It's mainly waiting time. Is that OK?
- Fine by me. It'll cost you a fair bit. Have you got cash?
I flashed five twenty pound notes.
- Down payment?
- Pay me when we're done, love.
I put the cash away. He asked:
- You're not wanting to get anywhere quickly are you? The traffic's thick tonight because of this flash mob thing that's on. That side of the river is a real mess.
- Don't worry, I have the time.
He took me to Emma's flat at Azimuth House where I collected the things that I needed. I met Dodson there.
- Hi, Tom, I'm Emma, James sent me. Is everything ready?
- Pleased to meet you, Emma. Yes it's all ready. You look good today.

Angelic?

Was the only comment he made to Emma's all black outfit, body piercing and undead make-up. Tommy Dodson wasn't confused about my identity. He knew exactly who I was.

-    Thanks

He gave me a hug then helped me downstairs with all the things from my flat but didn't come out to the taxi. We didn't want the cabby seeing him. The last item to go in was a heavy box about a metre long.

-    What's in there? A machine gun?

joked the taxi driver.

-    Yes, it's a machine gun.

He looked worried for a moment and then laughed.

Peters' Arch
Lendal Terrace
Clapham
London

Source:	James Hecketty/Emma Wilkinson
Date:	Sunday 19th October
Time:	20.32
Present:	Emma Wilkinson, Marin Peters, Stanislava Popovera, Alyona Kotova

We arrived at Lendal Terrace and I told him to stop when my phone said we had reached the right spot. I knew where it was because I had been tracking all the Azimuth House vehicles. I got out and looked at the archway lockup. It was the traditional kind. A big arch under a railway viaduct. This was Martin Peters' arch.

There was no sound from inside when I put my ear to the door. I got out the first few items from the back of the taxi. There were sandwiches, cans of drink, towels, clean clothes and underwear, hair brushes, stuff to wash with and cash. Then I got the box. I put it all on the ground outside, then asked the cabby to wait just round the corner, easily accessible but out of sight.

I opened the box and assembled the gun. It was like an old fashioned tommy gun. There were two circular magazines of ammunition and I slammed one of them into the breach and released the safety. I covered the gun with the box. I opened the wooden door to the arch and shouted

327

through it:

- Hello?... Hi?... Is there anyone here?

I picked up the blanket, clothes and sandwiches in both arms and went through the door. It was just like a garage inside with oil stains on the floor and tyres and car parts around the walls. There was a partition at the back and two doors, suggesting two rooms. The door on the left opened. A man came out. I had seen him before. I'm sure now. He was at my flat showing me a video of my friend dying. I greeted him cheerfully while putting the blankets and things down on the floor:

- Hi! Are you Peters?
- Who are you? What's that stuff?
- I'm Emma. These things should come in handy. There's more. I'll get them.

I went out and picked up the gun. By which time Peters was nearly at the door. I poked the gun through the door and let him have the first round in the right shoulder.

The weapon was an FN 930. It fires gas propelled non-lethal ammunition. A magazine held fifteen impact rounds that are each capable of delivering enough force to incapacitate and bruise severely. Hit the wrong part of the body and they could just kill. At this range they would probably break a bone or two wherever they struck.

Peters reeled away from the shot and moved rapidly backwards to keep his balance. He was shocked that he had been hit and surprised that he wasn't dead. He grasped his shoulder and I hoped that a bone was broken. This was a man who took pleasure from inflicting agonies on others. His victims included a friend of mine and I fully intended that his evening was not going to get any better.

I pulled the trigger again and the second round disintegrated on his stomach. He was winded, gasped for breath, doubled up and collapsed on the floor. I watched him carefully. He would have been reaching for a weapon if he had one by now. I went to the back of the arch and opened the left hand door. It looked like a sort of bedsit with a small bed, a desk and a washroom at the back and a huge freezer.

I opened the door to the right hand room. There was an immediate stench and I looked in to see the prison room of Martin Peters. There were two girls in cages. They were both OK, terrorised, filthy, but OK. I went to them.

- My name is Emma. I'm here to help you. Where are the keys?

The redhead pointed to the other side of the room where they were hanging. I looked outside where Peters was recovering. Round number three struck his left knee cap. His reaction told me there was some damage. The keys opened the padlocks to the cages and the girls were free.

- Come with me.

I took them next door and got them both to sit on the bed.

- Stay here.

The pile of towels and clothes were still by the door and I delivered them to the two girls. I pointed out the washroom and offered the towels and shampoo and clean clothes. They were still trying to assimilate what had happened and not quite getting it. It had been a horrific day for them.

- Who are you?

asked the redhead.

- I'm Emma. Do you want a shower? What's your name?
- Stanislava.
- Hi Stanislava, will you help your friend? She needs some waking up. Please help her.

Stanislava turned to the girl by her side who was just staring and becoming distant. She hugged her and rubbed

her and talked to her.
- Alyona. It's OK. This woman will help us. We're going to be alright.

Alyona started to look a little more alert.

Peters needed my attention. He was still writhing on the floor. I grabbed his right arm attached to his damaged right shoulder and he screamed. I pulled him slowly towards the prison room and he slowly came with me, hopping on one leg. I pointed to the cages and he placed himself in one of them. I snapped the padlock shut and left him.

Alyona was looking more alert.
- Hello Alyona
- Hello

At last I had a response. Stanislava got undressed and showered. She came out and encouraged Alyona to do the same. They got dressed in the clean clothes and I handed them something to drink. They both looked brighter. I started to explain:
- There is a cab waiting for you outside. It will take you anywhere you want to go. There is a place that you can go where someone is waiting for you. He's a nice man. He'll help you and give you anything that you need. Does that sound OK?
- Yes...OK.
- I have to stay here for a little while, but I'll be along later to make sure you're alright.
- OK
- He runs a hotel. He has a room for you.

I handed them each a prepaid mobile phone:
- Ring your families. Tell them you're OK. Not now, when you are on the way. Tell them you've got a job at the hotel. You have if you want it.

They took the drinks and the sandwiches and I showed

them the way to the taxi. They both got in. I gave the address to the driver and handed him a wad of cash:
- Give the change to the girls.
- OK Love.

Then I spoke to Alyona and Stanislava:
- Are you both going to be OK?
- Yes, thank you.

said Stanislava. I looked at Alyona and she said:
- Yes, thanks.

The cab left with them in and I went back to clean up and have a conversation with Peters. I needed information from him and I had twelve rounds left in one magazine and fifteen in another.

When I'd finished with Peters and had the information I needed I left him in the cage. He would suffer. Exactly how was up to him. I had that satisfying and complete feeling that I remembered from before.

I walked away from the arches and got another taxi to see the girls at Dodson's hotel. They were sitting in a bedroom, having had something to eat and were looking comfortable. I talked to them for a while about how they got there and what had happened during the day. I made it clear to them that they were free to go wherever they liked but they were also free to stay for as long as they liked. They should go out soon to do some shopping and buy whatever they wanted. If they needed more money they should ask Dodson. He was here to help.

They were worried about the threats made against their families in Russia. I explained that they didn't need to worry. The people who had the details of their families didn't know they'd gone and were not interested in them anymore because they were passed on to Peters. No one was looking for them now.

Angelic?

Then I chatted to Tommy for a while. He gave me a hug before I left and said something nice about me being a girl:
- You have a glow. You seem so much more alive than James. I'm looking forward to meeting Alex.

I smiled at him. I owed this man my whole life:
- I think I'm going to have to be her. You should get your chance.

We embraced again as he said:
- Well I hope so. Good luck You.
- Thanks Tommy

There was a another cab waiting for me outside. My third that evening. I'd been expecting to see this one. This was the one I had taken only once before. The one I didn't have to pay for or flag down and whose driver seemed to look after me. I got in:
- Hello Timms.
- Hello Miss. Have you had a good evening?
- Yes. A good evening. I did all that I had to. You know where we're going?

Timms' taxi stopped on the edge of Battersea Park and I re-joined the crowds. Things were breaking up now. People were going home. After two steps behind a tree I returned to being Alex. I checked my phone for the location of the private guys who were supposed to follow me. There were six of them. It looked like they panicked when they lost me and called in reinforcements. I saw a nice looking guy in his forties on his own and chatted to him about the flash mob, finding out how it had gone. We walked past one of the private security guys and I saw the relief on his face when he indiscreetly spotted me. He made a call to say he'd found me. His firm would be pleased to be able to report that I was there and in sight the whole time.

Alex' Flat then Chesterton Theatre London

Source:	Alex Harewood
Date:	Friday 24th October
Time:	17.17
Present:	Alex Harewood, Katya Khrushcheva.

It had been a pretty dull day at work. There was not much to do. One viewing in the morning. I was looking forward to putting my feet up for the evening and getting to bed early. Then doing some meddling during the night.

The doorbell rang. I looked through the spy hole. It was Katya! Oh God! What was this? What was about to happen? I opened the door and said:
- Hello.
- Hello Alex. How have you been?
- Just fine.
She looked deflated at my unsupportive response and I immediately regretted it. This was the Katya I liked. I stood back to let her in:
- Sorry. Long day. It's good to see you.
She brightened up again:
- That's OK. I have an idea.
She came in giving a very definite gesture to her bodyguard that he should place her shopping bags inside and leave himself outside. You didn't get the impression that she liked him.

She was different. Lighter, more relaxed, not serious. Why

was that? Was it me? Was it London? She was so beautiful in this mood. The weight had gone from her. This was the Katya I wanted to be real. She waved two tickets at me and I glimpsed the Wicked logo.

-   Can you come? I've only got tonight. I just came on the off chance. Say no only if you really have to.
-   When does it start? I've only just got in.
-   7.30. There's plenty of time. We can eat first.
-   What are you wearing?

She pulled back her coat to show off the most expensive cocktail dress I could imagine. It wasn't quite my style, but just perfect for her. I pulled a face. I couldn't match that. She grinned a cheeky grin while opening one of the bags that she had with her and pulled out a similarly expensive garment and put it against me, it was absolutely my style. Then she showed me the label. It was Versace. She smiled and shrugged her shoulders. I dropped my dowdy work clothes on the floor and slid into the dress. It felt great and fitted well. I looked at my unshod feet. She was still grinning while she opened another bag. Out came a lovely pair of shoes. Jimmy Choo. They were a reasonable fit.

Versace could have been accidental. Versace and Jimmy Choo was not. She was saying that I was the same woman she'd met in the lift. She knew I'd been Elisabeth Greyling. How did she know? The good news was that I wasn't dead. She saw the worry cross my face. She touched my cheek and shook her head; I mustn't worry. We weren't to talk about it either. She started to say how good the show was just to keep talking. Then:

-   Can I help you sort your hair; something a bit more relaxed?

We went through to the bedroom. She pulled out the tidy work bun and started brushing. She made it look a bit like hers. All loose and fluffy. She was good at it. I tidied up my

make-up a bit.
- Ready?
- We should have time for dinner. I know a place that's very good to me.

We went into the restaurant. Her bodyguard was around somewhere. Katya clearly hadn't booked and as soon as she was seen a table was moved so that we could sit at it and we were ushered towards it.

We sat down and looked at the menu. I hardly dared look at the prices but they were outrageous. We ordered just a single course and made it clear that we needed to be out in time for the show. I found myself chatting to Katya about how her dad was, how Eleanor was and how she loved being in London. She seemed relaxed and happy to be with me.

She had a word with the manager before we left; they seemed to be talking about me. The theatre was just round the corner. We had a pleasant walk and she talked:
- I've arranged for you and anyone you want to take with you to eat there whenever you like. Just go in and ask for a table, say it's on my account. There won't be any problems. I told them to make sure that they recognised you and be sure to know that I would be paying.
- Thank you. That's not really.....
She put a hand on my arm to stop me from saying more.
- I know you don't want me to do that. I wouldn't do it if you did! I know you won't abuse it. You probably won't even use it. But I want you to. It's not even my money. It's the firms. Spending gives me not so very much pleasure as it did once. But you can enjoy spending some of it. Have some fun. I'd be very happy if you did.
I wanted this to be the real girl. This lovely, thoughtful,

cheerful, character, not the one who'd allowed my friend to be tortured and killed, not the one who arranged for terrorists to have weapons of mass destruction.

We checked our coats in at the theatre cloakroom and then went to the box office. She swapped the tickets she held for different ones in the stalls. Then we went to our seats. Her bodyguard had to go to the security office where he could watch things on the cameras. Once sitting down she relaxed even more. She had things that she wanted to say.

- I know I'm not clever, Alex, no, you don't have to be nice. Well, I just don't get *organized* stuff. I've stopped trying now. I tried at school, so did my teachers. They were nice. But it's like someone always asking you to run fast. You keep trying and you keep trying and you get tired, but you know you'll never be able to go as fast as they want you to. I'm tired of trying now.

I started to say something. She took my arm and pressed a thumb into my wrist. It was a way of asking me to be quiet without letting anyone else see. It was as though she had a confidence to share. Her eyes pleaded. So I said nothing. She spoke quickly and quietly.

- My brother, the firm, I know what they do. They think I don't get all the business stuff and sometimes they're right. I don't understand... but I know what they *do*. I get that it's *wrong*.
- Okay...okay...
- It would be good if someone stopped the wrong. If it could happen I'd like it to happen. It doesn't matter about all the money. Someone needs to stop the bad things.

She squeezed my arm again while saying quietly and clearly:

- Ivan Khrushchev likes Lamborghinis. I think the

Hurucan is his favourite at the moment. It's a funny spelling. I had to look it up.

Why had she told me this? Why his full name? A login and password? She had given me a password? The music started and the curtain rose. Clever comes in many flavours.

I kept on thinking throughout the rest of the performance.

She was wearing a brand new dress, so was I. She'd checked my hair. Checked our handbags in. Had she just cleared out any bugs? We were in a public place in a seat she had booked that day and changed only that hour. Her bodyguard was a long way off. What she had just said was enough to get her into a lot of trouble.

In any case one thing was clear. Katya had just given me the green light to go ahead and destroy her family's business. In the end it was going to come to a lot more than that. Did she know what I was planning? Did her brother know? Did she know or was she just working on the possibility that I might be able to help?

Was it a test? Was it a trap? If I accepted the offer I would be admitting something. If I asked for help I would be admitting something. If I stopped to think about it too long I would be admitting something.

Wicked was a great show. I clapped when everyone else clapped and laughed and oohed and ahhed the same as everyone else. My brain was working on a lot of other things. As the final riotous applause broke out I heard her in my ear. The rest of the auditorium would have assumed it was a comment on the performance.
-   There's something extra in you, Alex, and I hope I'm right. Let me know. Let me know if I can   help you again.

Angelic?

Again? When did she mean? Had I missed something else? Then I thought. At Freeman and Jacob before Ivan drew his gun and Roman made his speech, it had been her that had said the Novichok was on schedule. Had that been because she thought that someone was listening? Or had it been a mistake that she was now covering up and using as a way to gain my trust?

There was another additional possibility. Ivan said she had alerted him to Houghton's report on me. Had she then promoted the discord between her brother and Roman? It was possible.

I still didn't know; was she good or was she bad? Was this all a trap set for me to expose my identity? I knew she'd been looking for holes in their security. Was that to try to plug the holes or was it to find a way to get help as it seemed now?

Was this a genuine plea for help, from a girl who wanted to be good, but was forced to go along with her brother? There was no way to know. This could all be a sham and everything I saw could be part of that illusion. Even the teddy bear in the room and her little sister's comments.

I had arranged to go to Russia next week and I would make up my mind then. That, after all, was why I was going.

Chapter 16
Russia
October 2014

Voronezh District
Russia

Source: Alex Harewood
Date: Tuesday 28th October
Time: 13.10
Present: Eleanor Straminsky, Alex Harewood

It is a global geographic feature. Across the continents of Asia and America are flat plains that have low rainfall and continue for thousands of miles. In the US they use a local word taken from the peoples who first lived in North America. They call it prairie. In Asia and Europe it is called steppe.

Steppe is dry and harsh. Temperatures alternate between forty degrees in summer and minus forty degrees in winter. Within twenty-four hours the temperature regularly varies by thirty degrees or more; heatstroke in the day, frostbite at night. Variations can be greater in one day than over a whole year in Britain.

Grass is the dominant natural vegetation because it optimises the use of the available resources: sunlight and water. Forests cannot grow; it is too dry. When the wind blows there are no hills and few trees to hinder its progress and it will blow for days carrying dust and debris. At other times it is still. Still for days so that in towns the smell of habitation lingers and amplifies until taken away by a welcome breeze, or a fearsome gale.

Across these massive plains huge rivers make sedate progress. Wide and shallow, they hide in low sided valleys in the flat terrain and are given away from a distance only by the trees that hug their banks.

Eleanor and I were driven across this landscape under a grey sky. Grey skies mean it won't be too hot in the day or too cold at night. The colour matches the concrete that dominates all construction. Eleanor asked the driver to stop at one point, a place where there is nothing except a straight road, bare freshly harrowed earth and that huge sky. We stepped out, breathed in the dry air and earthy smell and felt tiny in that enormity under that edgeless, featureless sky.

We got back into the car and continued south. We were heading for Liski, a town on the river Don. Apart from that and its name it is almost indistinguishable from the other poor utilitarian towns we had passed through. All the buildings had been constructed in the last sixty years. This part of the Don River marked the furthest advance of the Nazi invasion in 1943. Every structure had been destroyed in the fighting.

Flat 24
Beronski Building
Tsar Road
Liski
Voronezh District
Russia.

Source:	Alex Harewood
Date:	Tuesday 28th October
Time:	15.30
Present	Alex Harewood, Eleanor Straminsky, Anna Khrushchev

We turned into the road that had been our destination. There was a lady of advanced years making her way along the road with her shopping in bags. She heard the car and stopped, put down her bags, and turned towards us. Cars were rare. Cars as healthy as the one we are in were even rarer. She knew from the sound alone that we were her visitors.

We got out of the car and walked towards her. She looked at us through keen eyes as we introduced ourselves. She was 74 years older, but almost still recognisable as the same person as in the photo at the Khrushchev's house where she had been five years old. Anna. Yevgeny Khrushchev's sister and Katya's aunt.

We picked up her shopping for her and carried it into her grey and impersonal block of flats, up the two flights of stairs and right to her door. She looked us over again before inviting us in. She asked us to sit down in her tiny room and went to make tea. We sat in the small armchairs with wooden arms. She had hardly said a word.

She came in from the kitchen carrying two mugs of tea and handed one to each of us. She brought in a high backed dining chair, then some tea for herself. She sat down with us, peered at us some more and sipped her tea.

- What can I help you with?
- Thank you for inviting us in. Thank you for speaking with us.

Eleanor put what I was saying into Russian.

- We hope that you will be able to help us with something. Something that may be important and that could be forgotten soon. I asked your brother about it. He either didn't know or wouldn't tell. I was hoping that you would tell us.

I showed her the family picture. The one from the family room at the Khrushchev's. The same picture was on her bookcase. I pointed out the people in the picture. I pointed out the older girl; the one who looked so much like Katya.

- When Yevgeny had a daughter he named her after this girl. Why did he do that? None of the others were picked out in this way. What did she do?

Anna looked carefully at the familiar photograph I had handed her. Then she looked at me:

- What will you do when you know?

I took a short, sharp breath of anticipation. There was no doubt there. She was going to tell us. I answered her question:

- I think her niece, your niece, may be in a lot of trouble. I want to know what kind of person she is. You only really know people when they are in the most extreme situations; when they are threatened the most. That's when you see what people are really like. I think Katya may be in that kind of situation now. Knowing what her aunt did may help me understand her better.

I stared out through the window and drank my tea as Eleanor translated. The landscape was still flat but from here, in the distance, I could see some trees. They marked out the edge of the massive Don River.

- You think that she will react the same way as her aunt? You think the same genes will behave in a similar way?
- I don't know. I might know if I hear, or I might have another clue, or a bigger mystery.
- I will tell you this family history. It is many people's family history. Those of us women who were in the west of the country and survived the war all have similar tales. You are right, you do see people as they truly are when things are at their worst. Sometimes they do good. Sometimes not. Often the same person does both. I think this is what you should hear...

The Russian Steppes
West of the river Dniepr
1945

Source:	Anna Khrushchev
Date:	January 1945. Until recently the winter of 1945 was the coldest on record.
Time:	08:23
Present	The Khrushchev family: Genya, Yekaterinya (13), Anna (10), Yevgeny (5)

Genya, their mother, had been out looking for food. She hadn't found any.

They had arrived in this town yesterday. Continuing their journey east. They never had enough to eat and finding food was a constant battle. In winter they froze. In summer they were hot or soaked and shivering. She had started the war with five children. Two were dead already.

She knew in a strange way that she was doing well. To be alive at all in this environment was an achievement. There were more dead people than living. She saw death often and knew that it almost always came when interacting with people. She tried to stay away from people. Especially soldiers.

She hid now as three trucks came down the road. She was almost back at the shelter and crouched behind a wall to hide while they passed by. She had been out in the night to look for food and wood. It was safer than being out in the day, and she could see clearly by the full moon.

344

Their mother saw the grenade being thrown. Watched with horror as it arced towards the shelter. The wind in the night had blown the fresh snow from the shelter and made it visible to the passing trucks. The soldier had thrown the grenade absent-mindedly, as though he was throwing a stone into a pond. Why it happened was not important. Why? had stopped being a reasonable question years ago.

There was a pause and then the muffled crump of the explosion. Her children were in that shelter. Some of them would be hurt. They could all be dead. There were no screams no shouts. That meant nothing; her children knew not to make a noise even if they were hurt. That might bring the soldiers.

She hoped for a terrible thing. She hoped for the least worst outcome of that grenade detonating where her three surviving children were hiding.

She and Yekaterinya, her eldest, had seen a small bunker once where just one soldier lay dead in the middle. He had thrown himself on a grenade before it went off. Killing himself but saving his comrades. They had talked about it. It seemed so sensible. She always thought that it would be her on top of the grenade.

Once the trucks had passed she ran to the shelter. The soldiers would have shot her if they had seen her. She had seen this happen many times before. Soldiers had no reason to be kind. Dead people were never a danger. The soldiers were more important. They had the food and the weapons. Winning the war was, to them and everyone else, more important than her survival.

She dived through the entrance to the shelter. Possibilities were running through her mind. Who was dead? Who was injured? Injury was a very uncertain outcome. An age ago her youngest, Sergei, had a piece of shrapnel cut through his clothes. At first she thought he had escaped injury, then discovered a deep gash in his upper arm. Cleaning it and dressing it hadn't helped. The infection had still set in and become gangrenous. When the infection had gone too far she did what any brave mother would have done.

She entered the shelter and saw immediately what had happened. The least worst outcome. The younger ones, Anna and Yevgeny stared at her, blood spattered, but healthy, uninjured. They looked away from their sister whose body was a horrific bloody mess. Genya gathered up the two little ones and held them to her. She cried silently but wanted to wail, wanted to let the whole world know how she felt. Her bravest and eldest, her greatest ally, lay dead. She had not died cleanly.

Yekaterinya had seen the grenade thrown. She had tried to hit it away, but had missed. It had landed on the rough floor, bounced onto the wall by Anna, and then come to rest near the middle. If this hadn't happened she might still have had time to throw it out. Instead she threw herself on top of the grenade.

She had been right about the timing. It exploded immediately sending jagged metal through her stomach and her chest. She couldn't breathe but she could still feel and think. She felt agony and writhed on the floor spilling out her guts which became tied in knots around herself. She thought to keep her teeth clenched and make no sound until the pain left along with every other feeling, thought and memory.

Their mother stared at her dead daughter and prayed for her while she silently wailed and despaired. Then she prayed for the living. Then she prayed that no one in her family would ever have the opportunity to show such courage again. She knelt by the body, put her hand on her daughter's cheek and kissed her forehead. She closed her eyes and rubbed her face to make the muscles relax so she could once again look like the beautiful, lively, intelligent girl she had been just four minutes before.

They took her boots and socks from her and her hat. They were valuable. The other clothes were now useless. From around her head they took the simple necklace that she had always worn and stowed it away safely under many layers of clothing. The ground was too hard to bury her body. They knew how it would age. They had seen many like it. It would freeze now. In the spring it would thaw and rot and become a stinking mound of putrefaction in the middle of which would be the signature bones of dead humanity.

It was 1945 and someone had said something about the war being over soon. Eventually they heard news that it was over. It was still a long time before it made any difference. A long time before there was enough food or anyone who could help them feel warm or welcome.

Flat 24, Beronski Building

Source:	James Hecketty/Alex Harewood
Date:	Tuesday 28th October
Time:	17.12
Present	Alex Harewood, Eleanor Straminsky, Anna Khrushchev

On the bookshelf next to the photo of the family in 1940 was a small cardboard box. I got up and asked with a gesture if I might look at it while Anna was talking and Eleanor was translating. Anna nodded. It was OK for me to look. Then she asked:

- So what do you know now?
- I know that Katya, our friend, your niece, is in a lot of trouble, and I know that she has asked me for help... Will you tell Katya this story? I don't think she knows it.
- I haven't spoken to Yevgeny in a long time. We have had political differences.
- Yevgeny is not well. He may have forgotten. He may remember more important things than politics. Katya, I think, has a right to hear about her aunt and she has a right to meet you.

She nodded to say she had heard my request, but was still unsure of me:

- I could have told many stories. How do you know that this one will give a picture of who my niece is now?

Eleanor was struggling to keep up with the translation. I paused and opened the box. As I suspected the box contained a simple wooden necklace that I supposed

Yekaterinya had been wearing when she died. The only reason it had survived was because it had almost no worth. Jewellery would have been sold for food or fuel.

- I don't but I know that this is the story that you chose to tell. That tells me that this story is the one that you think tells me most about your sister.

She was curious and asked me more

- How do you know I didn't just make all this up? To impress you. To help my niece.
- Doesn't it still tell me your hopes for how people will behave when things are at their very worst.

She was still looking interested, then I saw a moment's realisation as she listened to Eleanor repeating what I had said. She started again:

- You came here to find out about me as much as my sister.

There was some truth in that:

- I apologise. I have tricked you a little. What is important is what you chose to tell. I didn't ask for any story in particular. Yet you chose this one of death and self-sacrifice. There must, as you say, be many others, in that long war period, of survival, of courage where others met their end. You are as much Katya's aunt as Yekaterinya and you chose this one. This is your ideal of courage.

Eleanor was looking a bit worried. Perhaps I was sounding too self-assured. I was:

- You sound very sure of yourself for one so young. How do you know that I hold my ideals so close to my heart?

I tried to sound less certain, but I didn't really know how:

- I'm sorry, I don't think that I am wrong to believe what you have told me. I am certain that you are a woman of principle and that your ideals are most important to you.

Angelic?

- How can you know this?
- Because you live here, in poverty, because of an argument over politics when a simple phone call could reconcile you with your brother, who is one of the richest men in the world, and you could then live in comfort. So why should I disbelieve the story of your sister when I see you making a sacrifice every day for your ideals?

Anna was in some part annoyed with me. In another she was pleased. I had come asking about her sister. She knew now that I had also come to find out about her. She looked at me not knowing quite what to think. She asked:

- Do you always see people so clearly?
- I don't mean to show any disrespect. There are things that may help Katya. She has asked me for help.
- You show no disrespect, child. Quite the opposite in fact. If my niece is in trouble then please help if you can. She did well to ask you.
- I don't know yet how to help her. I think she may need your help soon, she may need your support.

As we drove away from Liski Eleanor asked me how I could tell so much from what was said:

- It was the necklace, too.
- The necklace?
- It held a dream. The dream of a young girl. The same dream you have.
- How can a necklace hold a dream?

I started to explain. Then the odd feelings started again. I was shaking as I fought against it but the world of now still became a different world.

I was in a camp. The overnight camp of a massive army on the march. It was quiet for something so huge. There was a continual hum as two hundred thousand people slept, breathed, ate, talked and carried out all the other normal processes of being alive. Above this background murmur could be heard the occasional order cracked out or the movement of feet in unison as a guard was changed. Sometimes you heard raised angry voices but most often it was laughter that punctuated the nocturnal sounds. I wandered around the camp as I had done many times before. I had no military rank but had sufficient status and position as a civilian to only rarely be challenged. There were guards back at my tent who were supposed to come with me. But it was easier for them and more comfortable for me if they pretend they hadn't notice me slip out.

There were many men. There were tall proud men who sat sharpening their spears and daggers. They were resting at the end of another long day's march. A few of them had taken off their high leather boots and massaged their feet. There were others who tended to horses or restrung bows. Towards the rear was a whole section of craftsmen who could fix broken chariot wheels, cut and sew new boots or planish and burnish armour.

At the back of the army was the supply train where drovers and slaves worked to keep the army supplied. Here there were also many women who tried to avoid authority. Officially they were not supposed to be there. Unofficially they were an asset and provided useful services. Companionship, sex, entertainment. After a battle they would give solace and medical care to the injured and dying.

Soldiers talk a lot when they do little. When we had first left the capital you could hear men talking of their families or the women and sport they had left behind. Now as we neared our destination there were more of other kinds of stories as the soldiers readied themselves in mind as well as body for what lay ahead.

They talked about the siege that was to come and the work that would be needed to prepare for it. The city would fall to the same tactics that were always used. The veterans explained to the newcomers that they would build a battering ram and an earthen ramp. Many, many lesser cities had already succumbed to these well tried methods. Nobody doubted that Jerusalem would fall and they would plunder the city. It did not seem likely that the proud and misguided Hezekiah would bend to the will of their ruler, Sennacherib.

There was talk of other defeated cities and what happened when they got inside the streets. They recounted tales of women they had raped and men whose heads they had smashed. They laughed at the telling of tales about maiming women or the unusual and apparently funny screams one victim had made as he was mutilated. Terror was as much a part of this empire's war method as their standing army, iron weaponry and battering rams.

Some men plotted and planned the depravities they would inflict on the inhabitants of Jerusalem when they broke through its walls. They would do these things to a man. Women would suffer in this way and children would be persuaded to perform these deeds before all these unfortunates met revolting and bloody ends. No one cared about the poorest inhabitants of any sacked city.

There were similar conversations going on in other

parts of the camp. I had heard these same kinds of things said in the capital about the razing of Elam. A country where no man now lived. I had heard enough and was pleased that what was to happen was now inevitable. We would reach the depot soon.

I heard, then saw Eleanor and I felt human again. I grabbed hold of her. I wanted to be with her not in that other place where I knew now what horrors were certain to come. She was screaming:

- Alex! Alex!

I found that I was gripping her arm. My fingers were digging into her wrist. I let go and I saw the dark marks on her wrist. I wept. The thing that I feared doing was the thing that I had done. I had hurt Eleanor.

- I'm sorry! I'm sorry, I didn't want to hurt you.
- It's OK. It's OK. You didn't mean it.
- I held on to you because I wanted to be with you. Not in the other place. I'm sorry.
- It's OK. I forgive you. I'm not worried about my wrist. It'll get a bruise and it will get better. I'm worried about you. Are you alright now? Just relax. Be calm.
- You don't mind? I don't mind hurting bad people. I mind hurting you.

She was a bit puzzled by that. She didn't know what I had done. Or what I was going to do in that other place.

- Just relax. Don't worry. Go to sleep. It will be OK.

I did as she said and followed her guidance. She was holding me round the shoulders and I let her pull me over so I lay down on the back seat with my head on her thigh. Her goodness seeped back into me as I fell asleep. I slept well and didn't remember getting back on the plane.

Eleanor woke me.

- Alex...

Angelic?

There was a man on Hannah's plane with us.
-    Alex, this is Doctor Eshtashsky. He's here to help.
He looked me over and asked all sorts of questions about
what had happened and when it had happened before. He
thought I was OK now for now but I needed to see my own
doctor when I got home. Eleanor made me promise that I
would.

He asked Eleanor questions as well about how she was.
The questions told me that this was the doctor who had
attended Eleanor immediately after her suicide attempt. I
was pleased to hear her assure him how well she was. He
wished us both well and left the plane. We took off
immediately for London.

Chapter 17
London
October 2014

Alex's Flat

Source: James Hecketty/Alex Harewood
Date: Thursday 30th October
Time: 01.22
Present: Alex Harewood.

The password that Katya had given me was on my internet server: Hurucan. There too was the login: IvanKhrushchev. I had already identified the TPO Oil Company site but my server was set up to search for any other sites where these credentials would gain me access. It would automatically download any data it could find. All I had to do was press the *commit* button. My pointer hovered over it as I pondered whether I should press it or not.

There were two possibilities. Katya was good and her brother had a hold over her somehow. Part of me felt that I should know what this was; that somewhere in the things I had found out about Katya was a clue to why she had to cooperate with her brother. In which case she had given me the password so that I could stop the corrupt things that her brother's firm did with their Mafia connections.

Angelic?

Her brother was a whole collection of nastiness. He had Toby beaten for chasing after Katya. That fact alone suggested an unusual relationship with his sister. Then there were all the other things. Selling Novichok. Sending killers after me. Torturing Tavi.

It could be Katya was evil like Ivan, and this was a trap. She wanted to find out if I was an estate agent's assistant or someone investigating and disrupting them. This login and password might have been given only to me. Log in with it and they would know it was me, Alex Harewood, logging in and hoping to steal their secrets whereas I would in fact just be giving myself away.

My remote observations at Azimuth house had given the impression of a hard-nosed and cunning woman who helped her brother's plans along. Everything at her house, at Eleanor's and what she said in the theatre could have been part of that deception.

There was no more information for me to collect. I'd seen Katya first in Harvey Nichols. Toby had made an assessment of her immediately and that could hardly have been more positive. It was hard for me to think that he could have been so very wrong. I pictured her kindly bending down to speak to that young boy. There had been no reason for her to put on an act there of any kind but she had looked like a person who cared. She had looked like a person who felt for others.

What I had seen of her personally at Eleanor's suggested a distracted and anxious young woman. Her aunt Anna had said enough to suggest that Katya could be capable of great self-sacrifice. Most of what I knew pointed the way I wanted it to point, towards Katya being good. I couldn't think of any way in which she could be both good and bad.

If this was a trap I might not know it until I died. My protection was who I was pretending to be. Get this wrong and they know Alex Harewood is a threat to them. No one could protect me from a sniper at the top of a building or a bomb in a litter bin.

She was the good Katya. She had to be the good Katya. I had already pressed the *commit* button.

Chapter 18
London
November 2014

Lavender Hill Police Station

Source: Computers at the Lavender Hill Police Station
Date: Wednesday 5th November
Time: 10.31
Present: DS Kyriakos Papandreou, DS Ryan Broadhouse, DI Gemma Black, DC John Meehan

Gemma Black described a body that had been found in the river the previous day. She didn't show any pictures. She said the man had been horribly burnt on the front and hardly at all on the back. The speculation was that the live man was tied to something, perhaps a car, which was then set alight. He escaped to drown in the river where he was found. It was not clear and probably never would be if he intended to drown or was escaping the heat of his burns. His DNA matched what was found in my flat and the headless girl and identified as me. Broadhouse was unsure:
-    So Hecketty is dead?
Black puts up a picture of James' burnt out flat.
-    Not if the hair that we got from his flat is not his hair. He always said it wasn't. And this man seems too tall for Hecketty. So who do we think is the dead guy?

There was more information that Papandreou could add:

- Tim Houghton, one of Roman Constantinov's employees has been reported missing. So he could be one of the men that Hecketty says was in his flat. The DNA says this dead guy, even if it isn't Houghton, raped the headless girl. What do you say to that Ryan?
- Evans is screwing with us.

Meehan couldn't let that go:

- That doesn't work. It's what Hecketty said from day one.

The police were now almost convinced of my innocence and they were getting nearer and nearer to the truth. There was no cause or time for celebration. What I found when I got in to work next day was the thing that would eventually put a bullet in me.

Robert Sefton Estate Agents

Source:	Alex Harewood
Date:	Thursday 6th November
Time:	08:29
Present:	Alex Harewood, Robert Sefton, Harbinder Patterson

I could see Harbinder glaring at me before I had even stepped through the door. She had those raised eyebrows and the expression on her face that told me that there was something I had done that I was going to be grilled about. I felt her eyes follow me across the room to my desk. There was a copy of "Hello" magazine on her desk. Open at the society pages.

I got down to work and kept my head down. Robert went out on a key exchange. I tried not to look in Harbinder's direction. Eventually a cup of coffee landed on my desk and then the pages of "Hello". At the bottom of the page was a pair of photos of two women. Harbinder's finger was on the article. One photo was of two young women having a meal at a restaurant looking happy and talking to each other. The other was of the same two young women talking animatedly going into a theatre with a Wicked poster in the background. The caption read:

> *Yekaterinya Khrushcheva daughter of the Russian oil multi billionaire and her best friend Alex Harewood enjoy a night out in London and eat at the Sentinel.*

Having my name and picture published in the press was

not good at all. It would be on the internet too. I tried not to show how concerned I was:

- Oh. My hair's a bit of a mess isn't it?
- Your hair? Your hair's a mess?
- A bit of a mess I said.

She was pretending to be annoyed with me and every phrase was tainted with sarcasm:

- A bit of a mess? Well that's fine. That's just fine. What are you doing tonight? I ask my friend. Oh I think I'll stay in and watch the television. She says all innocent. Not only does she go to the theatre. She goes to the theatre with this incredibly rich and gorgeous girl wearing this amazing dress and then has a meal in the most exclusive restaurant in the capital. Do I get to hear about this? What else are you holding out from me?
- I'm not really her best friend?
- Any other errors or omissions? Like maybe it's not really you?
- We had the meal before the theatre?
- I think you owe me lunch.

She prodded a finger at the restaurant in the picture.

- I can't afford that place! Will the coffee shop round the corner do? If I promise to confess all?
- All?
- Every last drop of information.
- I suppose that will have to do.

Then she whispered, as though keeping a secret:

- What's she like?

I whispered back:

- She's very mysterious. Very hard to fathom.
- Oh this sounds interesting. Very interesting. An enigmatic Russian heiress. And I work with her best friend. Hmmm. Lunchtime is far too far away.

Angelic?

Robert arrived back in the office:
- I hope you two haven't spent all your time gossiping. Anything new?

He asked. Harbinder replied in a bored voice:
- Nothing of interest

I asked Robert:
- There's not much on. Is it OK if we take lunch together today?
- Yes fine. Unless something turns up. It might stop you two wanting to gossip all the time here.

I picked up the phone and dialled our regular taxi firm:
- Taxi to the Sentinel at 12.00 please.

Harbinder quickly turned round. I had no idea how much our lunch was going to cost Katya. I would have paid every penny of it myself to see the look on Harbinder's face. I gave her a grin and a properly excited gesture. Robert had no idea what was going on behind his back.

Dip and Strip Room
Basement
Azimuth House

Source:	Microphones in Main Area. Observations at other times of equipment and room. Forensic data later collected by police.
Date:	Thursday 6th November
Time:	15:45
Present:	Paul Flowers, Dmitri Chazov, Roman Constantinov (dead)

There is a room in the basement of Azimuth house that was first used to dip and strip furniture. The equipment in there was an old design, looking like it was originally built in the thirties and had been adapted many times since then. Stripping paint from furniture had once been a popular process, but it was not used today for that. There were two large tanks that originally held the methylene chloride that was used to strip paint. They now held lye, sodium hydroxide, which is very effective at dissolving all sorts of things, including people. From what I heard very many bodies were disposed of here. There was a flat deep cuboidal bath that was big enough to contain a door. There were safety screens and a hoist so that furniture, or anything else, could be lowered into the bath.

The lye had been delivered to Azimuth House. Chazov and Flowers were moving the five gallon containers to the dipping and stripping room where they intended to carefully empty the containers into the main holding tank.

Angelic?

They opened the door to the room. Chazov saw Roman first:
- Oh shit
Flowers just stared, mouth open.

Roman was suspended above the empty lye bath, hanging by his hands. He was dead, but it had taken him some time to die. He had four wounds in him, suggesting four bullets. There was a wound in his right shoulder, two in his stomach and one in his left knee. He had died from blood loss. Dried, congealed blood, mainly from his stomach wounds, caked his legs. There was a pool of dried blood under him in the bath.

Chazov grabbed the hoist control and pressed the up button, lifting Roman out. Chazov opened the water tap and flushed the bath with water; clearing away some of the blood in the bottom. He got into the empty bath and dampened his handkerchief with a little water from the tap. Flowers was still standing motionless, shocked.

Romans face was contorted and covered with salt from dried sweat produced in his dying hours. He hadn't been dead for very long. Carefully, gently Chazov wiped Romans face, like a mother wiping the face of her child. He wiped around the nose, wetted the hanky again, and moistened Roman's lips. He squeezed the cloth over Roman's head and the moisture dripped down over the man's face as though he might have been alive still to appreciate the care and the pleasant cooling flow of the liquid. Chazov appeared upset:
- Fuck mate you're in a bad way. You sure, sure don't deserve this. You're the best boss I ever had. You kept it all quiet and well oiled.
Chazov's mood changed a little. He was thinking of vengeance:

- I'm wondering who the bastard is that did this to you. There are three possibilities. Ivan, or someone doing it for Ivan. Peters, who always hated you. There's one more option that is the least palatable. Killing someone like this takes confidence, accuracy and hatred. The first shot goes to the shoulder, just here severs the nerve, so you can't fire a weapon. The next shot goes to the stomach so you feel awful and know you're in trouble. Then one to the knee. You won't move far after that. Then another to the stomach if necessary because it means you're more likely to die before help arrives.

Flowers has recovered a little ands says shakily:

- You know one shit of a lot about killing people.
- Yeah I learned it all the hard way. I've got scars and dead friends.
- So who kills like that?
- Angelina, she was cruel and efficient. She killed like this.
- Sun House? Fuck I heard that story, but not that bit. How do you know?
- I was on my way there when it happened.
- You were at Sun House? When she shot everyone?
- I got there when it was all over, but before the police arrived. I saw the boss, Bronislav Adaksin. Good bloke. I spoke to him as he was dying. She looked ordinary. She was from the far east of Russia. Good English. She killed every man. A whole fucking string of them. The other girls were running around like headless chickens but she'd already gone.
- It could be her that killed Roman?
- Same way as Adaksin. Could be her. Could be Ivan. Could be Peters.

Chazov was thinking what to do.

Angelic?

- We'll go and see Peters. We'll know from the reception that we get whether it was him that did this or not. We'll finish this job first.
- They carefully emptied the twenty five litre cans of lye into the main tank. Chazov took from Roman his wallet, phone and keys. He stepped out of the bath and opened the tap to allow the lye to flow in. It filled up. Then he lowered Roman's body into the lye. They left it there to dissolve and locked the dipping room door behind them. Flowers:
- Hasn't he got family?
- Yeah, Sandra and three kids.

Peters Arch

Source:	Bugs and cameras placed by Emma Wilkinson after rescuing Alyona and Stanislava.
Date:	Thursday 6th November
Time:	17.34
Present:	Dmitri Chazov, Paul Flowers, Martin Peters

Chazov and Flowers arrived at Peters' archway garage. They were wary going in, but there was no sign of life, no sign that he was alive. They found him in the room at the back locked into one of the coffin shaped cages. He looked thin, haggard, grey and lifeless.
- What the fuck has been done to him?
- I don't know. Perhaps he was just left here to starve.
There was a tube connected to an inverted water bottle so Peters could drink if he wanted to, except that the bottle was empty. He was motionless. His eyes were staring. Starving to death is not a comfortable process. Peters couldn't move either in the cage. He will have had cramps and his body would have started to painfully digest its own muscles to produce the energy it needed to survive. Flowers had a question:
- So where are the two girls that he took from us? They're not here.
- Either he had already got rid of them or the sick git that did this let them go. Or kept them for himself. Or herself.
- They seemed like nice girls.
- Fuck! Are you in the wrong job or what?

Angelic?

- I came here to sell furniture.
- Don't make me cry.

Eeeeksssssshhhhgh. Peters' body makes a noise. Flowers:

- Fuck! Shit! What was that?
- He's not dead. That's fucking what.

Flowers went white and vomited on the floor before blurting:

- Fuck. Fuck. Ohh Fuck.. I don't want to do this.. I don't want to do this.

His nerve had gone. Chazov took him out of the room and got him to sit down on a pile of old tyres, then sat next to him.

- It's not your fault, mate, it's that shithead Ivan Khrushchev. He knows how to fuck people around but doesn't actually care for anyone. He can't even see it in other people as a strength, only a weakness. Even in this line of work you have to look after people. I learned the hard way when I was younger, I was only ever looking for an angle to get one over on people. I got seriously shafted. I learnt.

Flowers isn't listening to Chazov. His mind is far away. Chazov just talked:

- This twat Khrushchev always got away with it because he's had so much fucking money. It'll catch up with him in the end. Someone close will do for him, one of his mates or that fucking sister of his. Someone who he really should be looking after and caring for. Everything is going screwy. We've lost Roman, Houghton and Peters, plus the Ivan thing. That's too much. The police will be everywhere now. It's all going to break up. This is Angelina's killing style again. She likes hurting people. She's probably getting help from Hecketty. Did they set all this up from the start? I don't know and it doesn't matter. This is all over now.

Chazov went back to Peters in the back room, took out a knife and slit Peters' throat with a single decisive flick. Peters just slumped, blood dripping down his chest. Chazov returned to Flowers who was still sitting on the tyres. He thought for a moment then asked a question. He still had his knife in his hand.

- Have you got a girlfriend?

Flowers shook his head. Chazov carried on talking. He seemed to be including Flowers but talking mainly to himself:

- OK Pal. You remind me of some of our clients in the brothels who see the girls not really to fuck, but to have a girl be nice to them. Technically the girl's getting raped, no question, because she knows she'll be butchered if she doesn't. But the guy wants to feel he's getting something gentler, warmer. It's part of the oddness. The same physical thing, a fuck, can be the most violent act, a rape, or a tender sharing act of love. I've done it both ways. It satisfies different parts of me. This situation is so screwed up anyway that I've got two choices now with you. Pretty much the same two: violence or tenderness. Which part of my soul do you want to satisfy? The violent or the tender? The knife or the heart? The tender I guess.

He turned so he was facing Flowers, sheathed his knife and grabbed Flowers head with two hands so he looked at him square in the face to be sure that he was being listened to.

- Listen to me. Do what I say now. Forget about all this. The police will talk to you. Deny everything. Whatever they say you were never involved in any of this you only worked in the showroom. Got that. Deny it all. Say nothing. Know nothing. Get a lawyer. If you have to say something because you can't hold back say it to him. Got that?

Angelic?

Flowers nodded.

- Now here's the slushy bit. You know some of the girls, right? Can you think of one that might like you? One that looks to you for help or said something half way nice? Not one you like, one that might like you. Got a girl in mind?

Flowers nodded again.

- Get her from the brothel. Tell the boss you're getting her for me. Take her home. Like her. See if you can get her to like you. Be tender. See if you can't make this love thing real. You're the type. I always thought it was shit but recently I saw a man get kicked to death who was still, all the time, only thinking about a woman he loved. I'm not the type. But you might be.

He paused again thinking about what he had said:

- There you go. My one chance in life to play fairy godmother. I've done enough bad shit. Piss off now. Go grab a girl. Go rescue a damsel in distress. See if you can't make a fairy tale come true. Before I start crying like a girl or change my bloody mind. I'm never going to be like you are, but I don't want to be too much like that fuck-head Ivan either.

Chazov pushed Flowers away. Flowers was staring at Chazov. Then he realised that he was free to go. He could escape. He nodded, grinned and slapped Chazov affectionately on the shoulder

- I'll see you later.

He said and left. Chazov was left sitting there shaking his head:

- That little twat would do anything for me right now.

He got up and went to the door. He shouted at Flowers who eagerly returned:

- We can leave this all here. We can leave together.
- Ok.

They left together. It was the last I saw of Chazov. Though the world would hear soon enough that he and James Hecketty had killed each other in a gunfight.

Odeon Cinema

Source: Alex Harewood
Date: Friday 7th November
Time: 19.01
Present: Richie Richardson, Alex Harewood.

-    Hi Richie!

I was pleased to see him and I hoped it would go well again. We walked in to the cinema and talked while we bought the tickets and the popcorn. I let him make all the running.

-    Hi Alex, did you have a good time in Russia?
-    Russia was fascinating. I met lots of people.
-    And were you able to share embarrassing stories about yourself with them.
-    Well for some reason I didn't, though I could have done if I had wanted to.
-    Oh so they were proper people then. Not the sort you have to put on a show with. You could be honest and admit to faults.
-    Yeah most of them. Pretty much like that.
-    And were there any who were horribly famous or extraordinarily wealthy.
-    Yeah, well, I suppose all of them.

He sounded surprised:

-    All of them? What? Famous or wealthy?
-    Wealthy. Obscenely so I'm afraid. They really should be embarrassed about it. My friend is, which is nice.
-    So you flew there in the private jet and got chauffeur

driven everywhere?
- Yeah, of course.
- For real?
- Yeah. For real.
- Your friend has her own jet?
- No it's her mother's.
- And does Daddy have one as well?
- Yeah, I think so.
- I can't tell if you're serious or not.
- Does it matter? I mean is it important that it's true? Do you want me to be friends with rich people?
- I don't care. But I'm certain that I want to be friends with you.
- That was a good answer. I like that. You're making good progress there.

There was something so easy about being with Richie. Everything seemed OK. He put an arm around me when we sat down at our seats. There was no hint of any sexual intimacy. I didn't need to worry about that. So I just let myself dissolve into his warmth.

We watched a movie called Pride. It was brilliant. A real story about human beings doing their best to do what they believed would make the world a better place.

After the movie we sat in the cinema café and talked about the film. When we had finished talking about that, which was a while, Richie started on something else:
- So tell me about the friends you made in Russia. Who are they?
- I met all of Eleanor's family and a lot of Katya's.
- OK so who's Katya?
- She's an interesting character who is an old friend of Eleanor.
- Is that Eleanor with the jet?

Angelic?

- Yeah that Eleanor.
- Is that Eleanor Straminsky? I looked her up on the internet.
- Yes, why did you do that?

He'd been asking me questions earlier about Eleanor. I couldn't think of a reason why he would do that if he already knew, unless he hadn't found out what he wanted to know.

- I was interested. I found out some other things too. Did you know the guy who was killed at SafeNet? That sounded bad.
- It was.

He was asking these questions but he didn't feel relaxed. It sounded forced. Not at all conversational.

- Tavi Mansur, he was killed. Were you close?

This didn't feel right at all.

- Yes... Why are you asking?
- It sounds so bad, I just wanted to ... you know.
- What?

It felt forced because it was. They had put pressure on Richie, or that was why he was here in the first place.

- It must have been bad for you. It's been in the press and everything. Did you know what was happening?

Perhaps it was a journalist, not Ivan's mob, but it didn't matter who or why. Things were difficult enough without having to analyse the motivations of a boyfriend. If he could help me relax that was good but his questions meant that I'd now always have to include him in my calculation. Or I could just remove him from the reckoning altogether:

- I don't want to do this anymore, Richie.
- What? What do you mean?
- Us, I don't want to do us anymore.
- Oh no! I didn't want that to happen. I'm sorry. Jeez, just a few questions.

- Sorry, I want to go home now.
- We're so good together. Why?

I went for a gentler approach:

- Let me go home now. Ring me in a week or so. Give me time to think.
- OK. I'm sorry Alex. I just wanted to help. It felt wrong to say nothing.

He was sounding upset and close to tears. I kissed my fingers and touched his cheek.

- I have to go. I have to.
- Oh God. Oh God. Please. I never felt as good with anyone else. I hoped we'd go on forever.
- Sorry, Richie.

He said something that surprised and frightened me as I got up to leave:

- You've been really hurt haven't you? I thought so last time. Someone really hurt you.

I shook my head and rushed away. He watched me go. I'm sure he found it hard to see through tear-filled eyes. So did I.

I phoned Jenny and blurted out what had happened but I couldn't explain my suspicions to her. Eleanor was lovely when I spoke to her. Somehow she made me think again. Had Richie been prying or was he just trying to help?

The pressure on me to prove my identity had gone. Tavi had already done such a good job. I didn't have to date anyone. My brain was busy anyway with all the other things that I had to do and watch. I knew now what I wanted to have happen in London and the necessary pieces were being moved into place. Some were already in place.

Lavender Hill Police Station

Source:	Computers at the Lavender Hill Police Station
Date:	Monday 10th November
Time:	10.31
Present:	DS Kyriakos Papandreou, DS Ryan Broadhouse, DI Gemma Black, DC John Meehan

Papandreou clearly had some new information. He flicked up a picture of a large, four storey Victorian building. It could be several flats, or a massive house or a hotel. There was scaffolding on the outside. He explained that the building was owned by SafeNet and the man who was in charge was Thomas Dodson, the security guard who was living in the SafeNet house where Mandelstam was killed.

- The hotel will be a really smart place. Due to open sometime in the New Year. I talked to him for a while. He seemed open and friendly, but still volunteered nothing. The picture is this. It's a small hotel but too much for just one man on his own. He says this to Hecketty. Hecketty says not to worry. Help will be along soon. Just keep setting things up and keep the works schedule on track. Sunday 19th these two Russian girls turn up sent by someone called Emma. Dodson looks after them. The woman Emma comes in to chat with them. Now they're helping him set up the hotel. One of them seemed to be getting on with Dodson really well.

Broadhouse:
- So Hecketty is being nice to women now? What do you

suppose he wants with these two? Are they in danger?

Black:

-   Sunday 19th? Wasn't that the night of the flash mob on Battersea Park? Green shirts and long red wigs?

Yak:

-   You're kidding. The girl with Dodson had long red hair.

Meehan shouted excitedly:

-   What!? …

Then more calmly:

-   OK… hang on … hang on.

He tapped on the window of the office. Janet looked up from her desk in the operations room and saw it was Meehan. She gave a jubilant grin and a double thumbs up. Broadhouse commented:

-   I see your luck's improved Meehan.
-   Meehan brushed aside the jibe and started to look very animated:
-   Not just mine. We've got something.

Black:

-   Ok John can you tell us what's going on?
-   I asked Janet to check some stuff on trafficking. We'd put the issue to one side but I kept looking at what information was coming in. The other night there was an anonymous tip off that a van was on its way out of the country via Harwich. The Border Agency stopped it. They interviewed the driver but he was saying nothing and they had to let him go. They found an excuse to impound the truck though.

Meehan hit a key on his computer and a picture of a roll back seven and a half ton truck appeared on the screen. The next shot showed the cargo space. It looked mucky and used. There were some blankets on the floor and a plastic portable toilet in the corner at the back.

-   The timing is interesting. This is also the night of the flash mob. The van looked like it had been used to bring people into the country and was now on its way out. They did a full forensics sweep inside the truck. They had trouble isolating individuals from all the muck. It wasn't cleaned well. There are some long red hairs, clearly from a woman.

Yak sounded curious:

- So Dodson's girl may have been on there?

An enthusiastic Meehan explained further:

- Yes. But it gets better. I got them to check the DNA from the truck to see if there was anything there from the headless girl. There's a match. That's what Janet was telling me. The headless girl was on that truck.

Black:

- Where is it now? We need that truck here.
- Janet's already arranging it.
- Good police work John.

Gemma looks ecstatic:

- Oh Fuuuuck!

she says in celebration.

- Boss, you don't swear.
- Today is different. We have a lead! We have to talk to this Dodson girl. There is certainly some connection with Hecketty, possibly linking back to Roman Constantinov.

Broadhouse:

- So supposing that the hair in the truck is from the woman with Dodson, what are we thinking happened?

Meehan explained:

- The girls were brought into London on the truck. Someone rescued the girls and tipped off the Border Agency. The two girls are sent off to Dodson, who seems to be doing a good job of looking after them.

Yak looked puzzled still:

- And the flash mob is just a coincidence? In Battersea? On the same night? With long red hair?

Black:

- Well we don't know. We are going to run with this anyway. We have to talk to this redhead. Broadhouse draw up the best interview plan I've ever seen. We'll talk to her in soft interview. She's a victim not a suspect. And...

The office phone rang. Meehan answered. He talked quietly. Nodded. Black was still talking:

- .. Papandreou go and collect this girl. You be really nice to her. Offer her sweets and candy or anything else but get her in here by being nice. If you can, get the...

Meehan put the phone down:

- Boss? Boss?

Black snapped back at him:

- Yes, Yes, Meehan, Meehan. Why are you interrupting? We have to get this right.

He looked abashed, but muttered:

- They're downstairs in reception.

She was still annoyed:

- Who?

- Two young women. One of them with long red hair.

Gemma's eyes went wide.

Angelic?

Soft Interview Room

Source:	Bugs in soft interview room placed by Alex Harewood, operating through wireless link to Local Area Network then out as normal Internet traffic.
Date:	Monday 10th November
Time:	10:47
Present:	DS Kyriakos Papandreou, DI Gemma Black, Alyona Kotova, Stanislava Popovera, and a translator.

The soft interview room at Lavender Hill was looking more crowded than usual. Gemma Black and Papandreou were interviewing the two young women. There was also a translator to help out if needed. Black started by introducing Papandreou and the translator to the two young women and then asks:

- What are your names please?
- I'm Alyona Kotova.
- I'm Stanislava Popovera.

said the redhead who did most of the talking. They both accepted the offer of a drink.

- Can you tell me why you came in today?
- We have a friend who asked us to be here. She asked us not to before. Today she got in touch and said come over here to tell you everything and not to be frightened. You would be good to us.
- Who was this, your friend? What is she called?
- Emma.

Alyona nudges Stanislava who then adds:

- She said that wasn't her real name. We don't have a second name for her.

- What did she look like?

They described a kind of Goth character, with long hair, white skin and black everything else. They went on to describe what happened when she rescued them from Peters Arch.

Emma told them after letting them go they could go anywhere they wanted, but suggested that they go to Dodson's hotel. She said he was a nice guy who understood the situation and would give them anything they needed. They would be safe there. She also mentioned that he needed some help running the hotel. Emma had asked them not to go to the police. She said the time for that was soon and that Dodson would let them know when.

Papandreou asks:

- Can you tell us anything else about Emma?
- She's been to see us a couple of times to make sure we're OK at the hotel.
- Do you know James Hecketty?
- Yes. Dodson works for James. It's his hotel.
- So have you met James?
- No, but Emma says he's nice and we'd like him if we did meet him.

Black pointed at the two empty mugs, silently asking if they want more. She got a negative response from both girls. She then said:

- So Hecketty has never been to the hotel?
- We've not seen him. Dodson goes out to see him and does jobs for him sometimes.
- What kind of jobs?
- We don't know. He just goes out.
- When?

Alyona elbowed Stanislava and the girls talked in Russian

Angelic?

for a moment.
- Sorry we'd rather not say.
- That's OK. Have you met anyone else there?
- A black girl. Louise.

The detectives all took notice and Yak showed the girls a picture of Louise Ferryman:
- This woman?
- Yes that's her. She talks to us as well. Just about what has happened and do we need anything. She brought us flowers on the first day.
- Ok, thanks. Do you know where it was that you were kept? Can you describe it to us?

Alyona looked in her purse. She took out a piece of paper. Checked what was written on it and handed it over to Black:
- Emma said to give you this. It is the address for where we were kept.

Black took the paper
- Ok thank you.

She looked at it and added it to her file.

She then asked about what happened before they were rescued from Peters' Arch. They said how they were duped with job promises into paying money to come to Britain. They thought they would work in the hotel trade once they arrived and had been expecting to serve drinks, wait at tables, make beds and clean rooms. They had heard rumours of young women being trafficked but had discounted these rumours because the firm they paid money to recruits openly in Eastern Russia. The two girls described the events that took place when they were in the basement of the furniture store.
- Helena was raped. We thought we'd come to Britain for something better. We were sold. That man bought us. How can that happen here?

- It shouldn't happen. We have very strong laws against it. Those people are criminals. We're hoping that talking to you now is going to help us stop them.

Papandreou went through a selection of photographs one by one. The reaction to the image of Chazov left no doubt who had raped Helena. They also recognise Flowers. They described the inside of the basement but couldn't give any further clue to where it might have been. The police had a good idea anyway.

Alyona started another conversation in Russian. The translator looked intrigued. Stanislava explained:
- Emma said that she would invite you round for tea soon.
- Do you know where she lives?
- No, but she said just two people should go. Pretend you're looking for her.

The girls paused again. They were worried about something:
- Will we be sent back to Russia?
- I don't know. That's a very different thing. It's not for the police to decide. But go home now. Can we come and see you if we have some more questions?
- Yes you can.
- Do you need a lift?

Both girls smiled and nodded gratefully.

Peters Arch

Source: Bugs and cameras placed by Emma Wilkinson.
Date: Monday 10th November
Time: 15.05
Present: DI Black, DS Papandreou, DC John Meehan, Scene
             of Crime Officers.

Black, Papandreou and Meehan looked around Peters'
Arch where the two girls had been held. There were Scene
of Crime Officers coming and going. All wearing face masks
and white polyester overalls. At the front of the arch was a
large open area behind large wooden garage style doors.
The rear portion was walled off and there were two doors.

They opened the left hand door. It was an office, a
bedroom, and a kitchen. It was clean and tidy. Another
door led to a tiny bathroom with a shower and toilet.
There was a fridge that was well stocked. Nothing very
recent. Nothing very out of date.

There was also a large freezer. Much larger than it would
normally need to be. They opened it. Empty. But it was
probably the place where the headless girl was frozen.

One of the SOCOs came into the room and spoke to Black:
-    Inspector we have a body in the next room.
They went out and looked into the right hand room.

Peters' body was inside a cage. It was in much the same
state as when Chazov and Flowers had left. Except the
blood from his throat wound had dried on his chest. The
detectives said nothing. They started to look around the

rest of the room.

There were two coffin shaped cages on one wall, one of which contained the body of Peters. There was a drain in the middle of the floor and the place looked reasonably clean, apart from the filth around Peters' body, perhaps because the hosepipe fixed to the wall was regularly used. They left the room before starting to talk.

The SOCO explained that Peters had been left to starve for days. But he did have a way out. There were three fully charged mobile phones with him, but they had no credit on them. He could easily have phoned for the emergency services, not anyone else. He was killed by having his throat cut. Meehan asked the obvious question:
- So an innocent person would have escaped in minutes?
The SOCO agreed:
- Yeah they would have. He chose to starve rather than call for help. He had some water that he could suck through a tube. The phones would probably have run out of charge in a couple of days.
The detectives started to look round, noticing the cages where the girls were held and then the source of the foul smell. Black told the SOCO to check the drains thoroughly for human remains.

Meehan thought out loud:
- So Emma Wilkinson found the two girls here. How does she fit in with Tommy Dodson and Louise Ferryman? We're missing a connection here. We know that Louise is an ex-girlfriend of Tavi Mansur. Hecketty is involved too. What about Angelina? She's here somewhere.
Black:
- Angelina? The Sun House case? There is enough happening without worrying about all that.
- I can't help it. It just keeps rattling around in my head.

Angelic?

- That's how I felt when I first started. I wanted to work it all out and understand everything about a case. Now I know you just need to chase the evidence.

Meehan didn't look happy with that. Papandreou added his thoughts:

- You're going to get nowhere looking for a Sun House connection.

John looked rebuked while Yak wandered off back in to the office to look around. Meehan stayed with Black in the large main area. He was still asking questions:

- Boss?
- Yes, John.

Gemma sounded a little weary but Meehan's brain had moved on:

- Two women trapped in awful circumstances. Could that rescue have been handled any better?
- I was thinking that. We would have had to have lots of noise and flashing lights, tens of people, medical checks, translators and white coveralls. This was personal and well prepared.
- This case gets more and more extreme. People are beaten to death. Then acts like this. So thoughtful. Rescuing those girls and getting Dodson and Ferryman to look after them. I hope I could be that thoughtful.

Black looked pensively at Meehan. She hadn't known any man before who could respond like that.

- Meehan?
- Yes, Boss
- Someday, somewhere, sometime a young woman will fall very much in love with a man like you and they'll live happily ever after.
- Really?
- Yes, really.

Meehan looked absurdly happy.

Victoria and Albert Museum

Source: Alex Harewood
Date: Monday 13th November
Time: 18:56
Present: Jenny Verdi, Alex Harewood

Jenny spoke to me about my latest failed date:
- I thought he might be the one Alex. You seemed to like him.
- I didn't feel like I could trust him.
- That's a shame. Don't worry. Give it time, there's no rush is there? You don't have to have a boyfriend. Just relax, maybe you'll start to feel differently.

She paused and was looking at me again. She knew all about Tavi, but sensed something else and supposed it to be in my invented past:
- Alex, I need to ask this. Did something happen? Did something bad happen in Canada? Is that why you left?
- No, nothing in Canada.
- But something bad did happen?

There wasn't an answer I could give her. I didn't want to lie that way to Jenny. She would have seen through it anyway. I couldn't tell the truth, but I had paused for too long. She looked puzzled:
- So...?

Then she asked urgently:
- It's not still happening now is it?

I had to answer:
- No, not now.

Angelic?

She looked at me thoughtfully and I looked back at her.
She was weighing up my responses with her questions, my
reactions with what she knew about me, working it all
through that powerfully empathic brain. She knew there
was something missing, something that I wasn't saying, but
she only said:
-    Some things are hard to deal with aren't they?
There was nothing more that I wanted to say. She
understood that and just put a hand on my arm:
-    You'll get there. You will get over it. Talk about it if you
     want to. I'm here, you know that.
We heard Geoff coming along the corridor, so she started
to talk about something else.

Jenny was beginning to see through my present and into
my past.

There was someone that I needed to see through. Katya
Khrushcheva. I thought I now knew an awful truth about
her. I needed an opportunity to confront her directly.

Lavender Hill Police Station

Source:	Computers at the Lavender Hill Police Station
Date:	Friday 17th November
Time:	10.09
Present:	DS Kyriakos Papandreou, DS Ryan Broadhouse, DI Gemma Black, DC John Meehan

The police had been collecting together the forensics and other information they found at Peters Arch. They have found the DNA from seven people so far. This included Tavi. They had also found one of his teeth. They were certain now that Peter's Arch is where he was beaten and killed. There was blood from the headless girl in the freezer. They have also realised that Houghton and Peters placed all the evidence in my flat deliberately.

Papandreou showed part of a video recording from Peters' phone. The same phone and recording I'd been shown in my flat when they came for me. It showed Tavi being beaten. The background was clearly that of the room at Peters Arch. You could hear Peters and Houghton asking him questions and Tavi screaming. Papandreou stopped the playback. He had more to say:

- This video is appalling, extraordinarily awful, though it's also in some way uplifting. The only thing Tavi would talk about was his girlfriend. He filled his head with her and nothing else. He must have known he was going to die but in the end he just keeps saying, Tell Alex I love her. Houghton and Peters seemed to have gained some respect for Tavi before they finished him off.

The detectives took that in. Then Black announced that she had cancelled the arrest warrant on James Hecketty:

- Everything he told us was true. The beating of Smithson now looks unconnected. We know what happened to Tavi Mansur. It looks like the headless girl was trafficked from Russia, killed for not cooperating and then put into cold storage. She's taken out of the freezer and her blood put in Hecketty's freezer to make us think that there was a reason for Hecketty to kill his friend. Crude, but it kept us off the real scent for some while.

Meehan flicked up a picture onto the screen of a family sitting on a sofa. It was a staged shot taken in a photographer's studio. The wife and husband were in the middle, one child either side of their parents and a third, a young girl with a charming smile, at their feet. They all looked happy. The father looked approachable and fun. He had one arm round his wife and another round the child at his side. Yak asked:

- Is that Roman Constantinov?

Meehan answered:

- It is. Sandra Constantinov contacted the police yesterday. She's not sure where her husband is. She went into Freeman and Jacob and asked about him. They had no idea either. I did some checking up. Roman Constantinov has disappeared. So have Dmitri Chazov and Paul Flowers. The body in the river has been confirmed as being that of Tim Houghton.

Broadhouse looked stunned:

- Jesus Christ! This can't be just James Hecketty picking them apart. It has to be Evans and the SIS. I count three dead, two deported, two hospitalised and three disappeared. Those guys have been seriously mauled.

Hecketty was probably never real. Just a ghost that
Evans set up.

Meehan:

- How can that be?

Broadhouse's answer was more puzzling than Meehan
anticipated:

- It's a lot easier to disappear if you didn't exist in the
first place.

- Huh?

The meeting was terminated by Gemma with Meehan still
deep in thought.

Chapter 19
Norway
November 2014

The Royal Palace
Oslo
Norway

Source:	Alex Harewood
Date:	Friday 21st November
Time:	17.24 (local)
Present:	Alex Harewood, King Harald, Queen Sonja, Eleanor Straminsky

The drive up to the front of the Royal Palace in Oslo was extraordinary. The imposing building dominated the skyline. I was pleased when, Joseph, the Royal chauffeur, took me round to a more intimate entrance at the back rather than the massive front portico.

The Queen greeted me just as warmly as she had the first time we met. We talked about the journey and what I'd been doing since we last met though there were, of course, some significant details that I had to miss out.

The Royal apartments weren't quite as homely as I had hoped for but certainly nothing on the scale threatened by the front of the building. My room had a ceiling that was a bit too high but had the most cosy looking four-poster bed that I could have imagined, chairs, a wardrobe and a dressing table that were beautiful, well-coordinated and functional. I saw the Queen's hand in this. She couldn't change the dimensions of the room, but the furniture reflected her sense and thoughtfulness.

Eleanor arrived and the Queen greeted her very warmly too. I held Eleanor for just a little too long. She felt like a refuge from my troubles. She held me at arm's length and she saw the tear in my eye:
- What's wrong?
- No nothing wrong. I'm sorry. Just pleased to be with you again.
- I can't work you out Alex and I really hope I never do. Sonja watched our greeting and wore her mother-like expression of approval.

I helped Eleanor settle in and then returned to the Queen. I was looking forward to the promised tour of the Palace. Harald had spent a great deal of money renovating it when he came to the throne.

The King returned from some official engagement that he pretended had been very tiresome and got changed into his being at home clothes. Part of me wished that this could be an old torn pair of trousers and a jumper with drips of emulsion on it. I didn't get the rips or the paint stains. The jumper was made a little more formal by a collared shirt underneath. His greeting was as warm as the Queen's though I got kisses rather than the hug. We settled down to eat almost immediately and were served a simple two-course meal. The wine was exceptionally good.

He was pleased that we had looked round the Palace. He asked which bits had pleased us most. It had been his project for a number of years, even though he had to apply to parliament for the money. I said my favourites were the front staircase and the Family Dining Room. He was flattered and pleased because he claimed these as his favourites as well. I got the how-do-you-do-that look from Eleanor. The Queen noticed. Harald was too busy telling us how difficult it had been to do the staircase.

We had a plan for tomorrow. Eleanor and I could see the famous Christmas market in the afternoon and we'd get to meet Haakon and his family in the evening. Sonja managed to answer my question before I asked it. Of course I could spend some time with Ingrid if I wanted; apparently she was looking forward to seeing me again too.

Eleanor got a buzz from her phone. Sonja noticed it:
-    Go on see who it is.
Eleanor took out her phone. Her eyes were wide with surprise:
-    It's Katya. She's going to be at the market tomorrow. Can we meet up?
She was looking to Sonja for approval. News of Ivan's troubles had reached Oslo. Katya was tainted too. She worked with him as well as being his half-sister and it was reasonable to assume she knew something of what he did. The Queen did not want the association. This was a meeting outside the palace in a public place. She wasn't planning to be there. Nevertheless we were her guests. We wanted her approval. Sonja looked at me. I gave a pleading look and nodding head. The queen was intrigued:
-    Do you know Katya?
-    I've met her only twice. But I know her well. She's been in some trouble. It's not her fault. It's very much not her fault. Please be generous.
There were three pairs of eyes looking at me. Eleanor asked first:

- Is this because of what Anna said?
- Yes.

The queen raised her eyebrows:

- Who's Anna?

Eleanor and I went into a double act as we explained about visiting Anna and the story she had told. We remembered all that we could which we thought was all of it. The Queen and King listened. They were fascinated and horrified. They had both lived through the war and knew its terrors.

- Do you know more?
- Yes, but I can't say. You'll see. Soon probably.

Sonja was a good friend of Hannah's. It was likely that Hannah had talked about me. Whatever she had said it probably helped. The queen knew that her reputation was at stake. That of her whole country too. She gave her judgement:

- There is a lot I don't know of what has happened recently, but I will take some guidance from history and a little more from my perspicacious young friend. Please tell Katya we'd be delighted if she would join us here for tea here after meeting you tomorrow.

It was a brave decision. I beamed at her I wanted to clap and shout Bravo! I made do by putting my hands together and saying:

- Thank you, thank you, thank you, that will help her a lot.

There couldn't have been of a better way to send a signal of hope to Katya. With luck she would understand that I had a hand in this invitation. There was another reason to meet her, to tell her that I understood her situation. I wanted her to know that I knew she was in the darkest place. Eleanor's face was all questions. I had a stab at assuaging them:

- You'll all see soon. It won't be very long.

Angelic?

Eleanor came to my room that night and we talked in bed. She wanted to know what was happening:

- My mum says things about you. Like you're in trouble. Like there's lots going on between you and her. It never makes sense. Just half pieces of information. She's worried about you. Or there's things to be sorted out. Then she says you're remarkable, exceptional. She said that you were dumbfounding. What is it all about? Is it that business with Ivan in London? You were close to those people.
- Please don't ask. Please. It really hurts not to say to you. It's easier with other people. It's hard to keep a secret from you. Please don't ask.
- Ok, OK, I'm not asking. But can I help?
- You are. I know you're on my side. That's important. More important than you know. I think there will be a time to help. A time to help your old friend.
- My old friend? Katya? I'd like to help her. She used to be such a good friend.

If we were to see Katya the next day this could be the opportunity I had been looking for:

- I think that she will be again. I need to talk to her tomorrow on her own. Without her bodyguard. Will you give us some time?
- Of course. How?
- You'll know. You'll find a way.

Oslo Christmas Market

Source:	James Hecketty/Alex Harewood
Date:	Saturday 22nd November
Time:	14.21
Present:	Eleanor Straminsky, Katya Khrushcheva. Katya's bodyguard, Alex Harewood

Katya was looking strained. But was clearly pleased to see us both.

- Was the Queen OK about you meeting up with me? I'd understand if she wasn't.

We'd agreed that Eleanor would deliver the invitation:

- She was very welcoming. She would like you to come for tea afterwards.
- She would?... Well.. That is unexpected. That is so kind of her. Well...

She had no idea what to say next. There were all sorts of thoughts and questions. She looked at me, at Eleanor and back to me:

- I'm very lucky to have such good friends.

Eleanor still had a little old hurt:

- I've always been your friend.
- I know! I do know...things can't always be how you want them to be.

I added:

- Sometimes you can't even be who you want to be.

Katya looked at me and shook her head slightly. This conversation had to stop. I moved things on:

- How are things at home? How are your parents?

Angelic?

- They're fine. Dad's doing OK. Mother's fine. She sends her love.
- And how is Asya? And Gleb?

Her expression changed. She was delighted that I had asked the question:

- She's good. She's such a happy little girl. Gleb's fine too.

We wandered round the busy market place. I wasn't looking to buy anything, though it might well have appeared that way. I was looking for an opportunity to get Katya on her own and give her a message. I saw my chance.

We were next to an accessory and make up stall. There was a small lipstick section. The colours were trying to be Christmassy. There were deep berry reds and even some holly greens, chocolate browns, as well as glosses with big sparkly bits in the shape of trees or Santa. There was no point trying to be coy if what I was thinking was true. I picked up some sample lipstick and some tissue. There was a small mirror so you could try the products out. I saw the bodyguard coming towards us. Perhaps this wasn't the moment. Then Eleanor intercepted him and engaged him in conversation.

I scrawled on the mirror:

> *I know*

She looked at me quizzically. I wiped it off quickly then continued to write:

> *your brother*

She was looking worried. I wiped it off again. Then wrote:

> *rapes you*

Again I wiped it away.

She looked at me. Her mouth was open. Her eyes were wide. Her face contorted not knowing what to do, say or how to react. There were a lot of emotions there. Mainly it was anger and shame that I knew. She started to walk away. This reaction was confirmation enough. No argument. No don't-be-silly or disbelief. After several steps she stopped and started to look at a jewellery stand. She was at the display and fingering the items but not thinking about them. She was thinking about what I had said. Then she returned to me.

We had been too long there so I took her arm and we moved on to the next stall, away from the bodyguard and Eleanor. I felt the neckline of her dress. I could just feel the tiny bug and it's long aerial in the seam. I was making sure she knew I knew and she nodded, confirming. I gripped her arm and squeezed in some sympathy. We carried on looking round the stalls.

Katya could not accept the Queen's invitation. I wasn't certain why this was. I suspected that she was worried about the security or she may also have been concerned that the Queen had been over generous. Katya's reputation had followed her brother's and she was possibly unwilling to taint her too. The message had in any case been in the invitation, not in the visit.

I was so unwilling to part with Katya and see her go back to her brother. I hugged her tightly. She read my thoughts, saying:
-    It's OK. It'll be OK.
-    Come and stay with me in London. Stay for a while.
She shook her head. She reassuringly touched my cheek and took my hand. I then watched her walk away and return to her dreadful life. A life where she had to be touched and penetrated as often as someone else wanted

her to be. It's hard to imagine what that must be like, but not everyone has to imagine. I chased after her and she heard me behind her and turned round. I silently mouthed:
- Stay.
- My eyes were full of tears and I could hardly see her, but I could tell she was shaking her head. I mouthed:
- Please.

She was anxious. She had to leave. I wiped my eyes. She just shook her head and walked back towards her guard.

Ivan controlled everything that she did. There were bugs and tracking devices in all her clothes. Everything that she did and said was monitored. She could only pretend to have private conversations. Her bodyguard was there not so much to protect her as to keep her under control and ready to be taken back to Ivan whenever he had need of her. In private he took all that he could from her. I knew what he could do; he liked to hurt people.

A few months previously I had wondered what it would be like to be Katya. Ironically, now I knew, her life horrified me. I tried again to think of ways in which I could help her that didn't involve lots of variables and serious personal risk. I still couldn't come up with any.

My thoughts kept sticking on something else. Something that stood out. When we'd met I had asked her about her family. The answer about Asya had been different from the other answers. That should tell me something. It did.

Asya was what I was supposed to have seen when we visited her house in Moscow. The reason for our invitation hadn't been to see her room or her Teddy Bear. It was to see Asya.

It was all about Asya. Katya gave herself to Ivan to keep him away from her sister. Klarra hadn't been able to save

Katya and there was no reason to think that she would be able to protect Asya from Ivan's rapistic, incestuous attention. Katya had put herself in harm's way to save her little sister from the same fate that she endured. The details were very different but in some way a seventy-year-old history was being repeated. She gave herself to shield the child.

There were two good things. The password that I had worried over for so long was good. I didn't have to worry about it anymore. And it was far better Katya was aware now that I knew the situation she was in. That had to give her some hope, a thing without measurable value.

Eleanor and I started walking back to the palace as we had planned but the weather had turned foul; an unexpected storm. Sludgy, sleety, freezing rain descended upon us and we huddled together as we walked back. I spotted the royal flags and the car with Joseph driving that had come to collect us. The Queen had been thinking of us. We clambered into the back and I held Eleanor close to me. She could tell how upset I was and understood that I couldn't say exactly why. She knew it was about Katya's troubles and pressed her forehead against mine:
- When?
- Soon.

Chapter 20 London November 2014

Lavender Hill Police Station

Source: Computers at the Lavender Hill Police Station
Date: Tuesday 25th November
Time: 17.32
Present: DS Kyriakos Papandreou, DS Ryan Broadhouse, DI
             Gemma Black, DC John Meehan

Gemma stood upright and clearly had something important to say to her team. They were being reassigned to follow up on the trafficking and the dead girl. Toby Smithson was a separate case.

She paused for a moment, then:

- Before we get on with that and wrap up the case so far has anyone got any questions?

There was one big question. Papandreou asked it first:

- We know Roman and Ivan wanted information from Mansur and didn't get it. We have no idea what that was but assume it's big because David Evans walked in here once. What did he say Gemma? Or did he ask you not to talk about it?
- He said we had to do everything that we could to catch the killers of Mansur and the headless girl.
- Was that all?
- He also said he owed a favour to James Hecketty.

Broadhouse:

- I told you, I told you all along that he's altered the evidence to get Hecketty off the hook.

Meehan:

- That doesn't scan at all.

Broadhouse:

- Hecketty did him a favour. Evans wants us to think Hecketty is the good guy.

Papandreou:

- You'll screw your head off if you keep twisting it round like that, Ryan...So what do we think was the favour that Hecketty did for Evans?

Broadhouse shrugged his shoulders. Meehan had the ideas:

- If we ignore Smithson and the headless girl it gets a lot easier to see what's going on. It was information. That's what Hecketty said they wanted. Tavi died protecting it but Hecketty found it and passed it on to Evans. That was the favour. That information was big enough to get these Russian goons tearing up half of London to find Hecketty. It was so important Mansur refused to reveal its location under torture. Hecketty found it and passed it on to Evans. That's the favour and all the motivations we need for everything that has happened.

Nodding, Broadhouse relented:

- Shit, Kid, even I have to admit that does make a lot of sense. You really can make it all hang together can't you?

Black:

- So we really were the bad guys there for a while. If we'd caught Hecketty then Evans wouldn't have got his information. Small wonder James wouldn't come in to talk to us.

Angelic?

There was a buzz from Black's phone on her desk:
- Sorry I thought I'd switched that off.
She picked it up and looked at the email she had received.
She looked twice then held up a finger for them all to wait:
- From Hecketty
is all she said. She turned to her desktop computer and
accessed the same email. She turned the sound up and
played the video on the room monitor.

They all watched and listened. It was Roman's speech to
Ivan and Katya at Freeman and Jacob. The whole team got
to see Roman describe how his business worked. All the
officers were shocked at the lack of humanity. It was
Meehan who said:
- Oh Jesus. He thinks that's OK. The women aren't
  people They're just livestock.
The email also contained a link to all the other recordings
from Azimuth House. The coppers skimmed through the
data. Papandreou:
- It'll take days to go through all this stuff!
Black:
- There's one more thing in the email. Hold on a
  moment.
A video showed a young woman in a house, dancing round
the room at the same time as moving the vacuum cleaner
to and fro and grinning at the camera. The clip finished
with a freeze frame of her looking into the camera and
smiling. She looked sweet, innocent. Black paused and bit
her lip. Her eyes were glistening:
- This is Sabina Bogomolova. Hecketty says she's the
  headless corpse we found with Tavi Mansur.
She picked up a tissue and wiped her nose:
- I guess we have plenty of reason and information to
  start investigating our new case. But we'd best finish
  the last one first.

Meehan:

- What have we got left to do?

Papandreou:

- Informal debrief. Don't they teach you anything useful at college these days?

Meehan:

- Hey? Yeah we learn lots. Where's the debrief? When?

Black and Papandreou exchanged isn't-he-innocent glances. Broadhouse said:

- Now, kid, at the pub. And the Boss is buying.

Alex' Flat

Source:	James Hecketty/Alex Harewood
Date:	Thursday 4th December
Time:	Evening
Present:	Alex Harewood

The password that Katya had given me was opening a lot of doors. The remote servers had been churning away downloading documents, spreadsheets, lists and logs. I started by piecing together what had already happened from the numerous documents I could now access. There were a few assumptions that I had to make but the overall conclusions were probably sound enough.

Ivan had taken over the running of TPO when only thirty-one when his father had become ill. Despite its wealth it had always been a family firm. Before that Ivan had just been a playboy. He spent money and lived the lavish lifestyle of the absurdly wealthy. He had enjoyed running the firm at first. He enjoyed the power and making deals. But he made poor decisions. Particularly in appointing people and managing people. If this had been his only fault he might have still done well.

He had a character flaw that was not forgivable; he loved to be cruel. He liked to hurt people and he liked it most when they couldn't hurt him back. It confirmed his unchecked feeling of supremacy.

Numerous key personnel at TPO left because they did not want to work with him. The company started to lose money. This didn't sit well with Ivan; it was a challenge to his ego. He started down the road of falsifying the company's accounts. He found some people very willing to help him do this: the Arbat Mafia Group.

Once they were in the door they were not going to leave. Ivan didn't mind. It suited his personality. He had power over people beyond his firm and found that he could get away with the most outrageous acts because neither policemen, judges nor juries were willing to confront him. His firm still produced oil but a huge proportion of its turnover was Mafia money made to look legitimate by passing through TPO's books.

Steven Sarren, nominally the CEO whom I had met at the Straminsky's and found lacking, probably had no idea what was really happening in the company he was supposed to be running. Either that or he was very good at pretending to be a buffoon.

I found numerous falsified reports and suggestions of creative accounting that kept the firm looking better than it was. This was where I would start. I'd release data and information that they would rather was kept secret. TPO Petroleum was going to crash. Then if everything went to plan it could be built up again.

Chapter 21
Russia
November 2014

Ski Slopes
Sochi
Russia

Source:	Alex Harewood
Date:	Saturday 29th November
Time:	15.17
Present:	Alex Harewood, Thierry

Klosters had no snow. We might have gone to one of the exclusive US resorts but it wasn't worth doing the time difference for just the weekend. So I was in Sochi along with Eleanor, her parents, Boris and his girlfriend and a lot of other very wealthy people all of whom could ski downhill on prepared pistes at great speed

I'd done some downhill skiing with Toby and Tavi in the Cairngorms. This was not the same. Here there were wide open runs across pristine snow with clear skies and views that went on for ever of sharp picturesque scenery instead of narrow fenced runs with mist and occasional glimpses of lonely northern heather and rounded ancient mountains. I wasn't that bad a skier, but far better at going cross-country with familiar equipment. I was nowhere near the standard of the others going downhill. They'd all had private tutors since the age of nothing and spent weekends in every part of the world. They were all on the black runs enjoying the ear popping descents available at Sochi. I'd skied with Eleanor on Friday afternoon but I could see that I was holding her back.

Today I was on my own with Thierry, my very own guide, tutor and possibly bodyguard for the day. Eleanor had said that he would look after me, so I wasn't too sure exactly how far that went. There were not many other people around this early in the season and it was easy to pick your own line. I thought I was doing OK.

The Khrushchevs were supposed to be there. Klarra was an ex-champion and had made sure that all her children were also given the chance to be ace skiers. Though I wasn't aware that we had any plans to meet. There was a big reception planned for the evening, all posh frocks and glitz because a watch company wanted to have its products seen amongst the super-rich and glamorous. We would probably see the Khrushchevs there along with everyone else.

This early in the season the snow was not very deep and going off-piste was riskier than later, when the snow has greater depth. I made a slight mistake and caught a rough patch just off the edge. I thought I was going to be OK but found myself falling and came down heavily on my wrist. It hurt and didn't feel very useful. Thierry was at my side immediately. He looked and thought it best to have it checked out at the clinic. Then we examined the skis and saw what had gone wrong. One of my bindings has failed, my ski had come away from my boot and that was why I'd fallen. He had some tools for just such an event but still couldn't fix the problem. He made a call and a snow cat appeared from the trees a few minutes later. I got a lift down with my broken kit. Thierry skied down and met me again at the clinic.

The clinic pronounced me OK, nothing broken, having been X-rayed about three minutes after walking in, though it might be best to rest it a little. It seemed a bit pointless going back to the slopes. I'd have to buy or hire some functional skis anyway and it would be getting dark soon. I returned to the hotel instead. Thierry had done his bit and I said I could manage without him for the rest of the day.

As I returned to the hotel, I noticed a girl on her way up to the slopes. She was dressed in the same clothes as me, even down to the hat and ski googles. They were all the same brand and so an obvious combination, but it still felt odd. She looked a lot like me. I looked at her and she looked at me. I smiled. She didn't.

There were about three hours to spare before the reception. Time to do a little meddling. I got in the lift to return to my room on the sixth floor and thought to text Eleanor and say what had happened. But where was my phone? Did I lose it when I fell? Or in the snow cat? Or at the clinic? I looked again through the pockets of my ski suit.

Ding! The lift had arrived at my floor. I went along to my room and used the room phone to ring Eleanor to tell her I was OK. I got through eventually and she said she'd come to my room before the reception so we could go down together. I looked round for my phone. Everything had moved a little because the housekeeper had been in. I couldn't find it. I knew I'd taken it out with me in the morning; still I had to look anyway. I saw my stunning gown on the rack and found myself slipping into it.

The door burst open and two big men rushed in. There was nowhere to run to. I hit one with the bedside lamp. He brushed the blow aside and they both grabbed me.

Room 513
Arcturus Hotel
Sochi
Russia

Source:	Alex Harewood
Date:	Saturday 29th November
Time:	16.08
Present	As text.

The two men easily dragged me out of my room and across the corridor. The room looked like it had been in the process of being decorated. There was plastic sheeting everywhere. There was no bed and no other furniture, except for a table in the middle of the room and an office chair with arms. They placed me in the chair and taped my arms and legs to it. Then the two men gagged me and left. I was on my own, tied down, waiting for something to happen. Nothing happened. I started to think.

How could anyone find me? My phone was a good way to trace me. I'd lost that. I was only wearing my gown. Any trackers in that could have been removed. The broken binding on my ski was looking very non-accidental. So was the girl who looked like me. This whole thing, whatever it was, had been very well planned. And the plan was not to kill me immediately or I would be dead already. The plastic sheeting around the room was another clue. The intent was to kill me slowly. My stomach was churning. This was Ivan's doing and I was expecting him to arrive soon.

The alarm wouldn't be raised until Eleanor came for me. I first assumed I was still on the same floor. They couldn't search the whole hotel, but surely this floor. Ding! It came back to me. There was a reason I'd been surprised by the lift bell. It was too soon. I wasn't on the same floor.

Had they switched the labels on the lift buttons so that I pressed the button for the wrong floor? My things could have been moved to a room on a lower floor, it only looked the same. I thought the housekeeper had moved them. Had they changed the room numbers too? Had they swapped the feed from the security cameras in the corridor? Had they then put my things back in my room, so that anyone looking would find my things in the right room? I'd confirmed with Eleanor I was there, the security camera would show the same thing. I was untraceable.

There were lots of variables, far too many to work out exactly what might be going to happen next, and I was at very serious personal risk.

The door opened. Ivan walked in. He was casual, relaxed and started talking as though we were on a date.
-    Hello Alex, I've been so looking forward to this. I've had a great afternoon skiing knowing you would be here for me afterwards.
He was grinning and his tone entirely conversational:
-    You must have thought me very stupid. You must have thought I hardly had a thought in my head. This girl, Alex Harewood, appears and at just that same time my business starts to crumble. Things go wrong. Things that should be secret are not. I don't know all the details. I don't need to know. But I do know that you're somehow involved in all that. Even on the bare surface you were dating the man who hacked our systems. Then you start appearing around here. Just a friend.

> Just a friend I keep being told. I've been told too many
> times.

I was not wondering who might have said that. It must
have been Katya.

- It doesn't matter if I'm wrong. We'll still have a good
  time together. This one's going to be expensive. I
  estimate the cost at a million or so. To keep everyone
  quiet about what we're going to do in the next couple
  of hours or so. It'll be worth it. That's a compliment.

He undid the tape on my legs and arms. I tried to kick out
but it only amused him. He pulled me upright and then
simply pushed me back towards the table. He was twice
my weight and probably three times my strength.

He pushed me back till I fell over the table behind me. As I
fell he placed a leg between mine.

- Don't worry. It'll be fine. We'll just take this slowly and
  you can enjoy it, like me. It's good that no-one knows
  we are here. We can take a little longer. There's some
  stuff that I had been wanting to try out. This baseball
  bat should help. I wanted to see how it all worked out.
  Really old things that they used to do to people. It'll be
  interesting. There shouldn't be any blood either. I know
  that will please you as well.

I writhed and twisted in an attempt to get away.

- Hey! Stop fussing. This is going to be good.

He pushed my hair back over my forehead in a gentle way,
as though he cared for me. It may have been the same
gesture but it wasn't care. Something more like a collector
admiring a butterfly before he kills it, sticks a pin through it
and mounts it for display to add to his collection.

I tried to get up again but couldn't. His other leg came
between mine and my knees were roughly forced apart.
His left hand across my mouth and shoulder pinning me to

the table. My free left arm hit him ineffectually; there was too little space between him and the table. I tried to find an eye to gouge but he protected himself by pushing his face into mine. He was in no rush and my struggles simply exhausted me. He let me squirm till I was short of air and had too little energy to fight.

-   That's better. I can see that you're beginning to enjoy it now. You should. Not many girls are this lucky.

He could take it easy now that I was too tired to do him any harm.

-   Don't worry I'm really enjoying this. You could enjoy it more if you relaxed a little.

He took out a cord and tied my hands together above my head fastening one end of the chord to a leg of the table. Then he separated my hands and attached my right hand to another table leg.

There was a scream. His face became distorted and moved rapidly to the right. There was a crunch and snap noise as of bone breaking. He had been hit very hard on the side of the head.

He collapsed onto the floor. Blood was oozing quickly from the base of his skull; a huge dent behind his ear.

The baseball bat hit him again and again. Blood and bits of bone were flying everywhere. His face disintegrated. His head lost its shape. Brain tissue was splattered around. I watched in horror.

-   Katya! Katya! Stop! Stop!

She stopped. The baseball bat fell to the floor. That wasn't about me. That venom wasn't even for her. She was still protecting Asya.

She turned to me. Held my head gently and said:

-   It's OK. All OK now.

She freed my hands and then just sat down on the floor

next to her dead brother. I sat in the blood, flesh, and bone next to her. I put my arm round her:

-    Don't worry. She's safe now. You're safe now.

She was crying. I hugged her and started to think ahead:

-    What will happen about him?

She shrugged:

-    He was raping my friend. No one will miss him. Mother hates him and father will hardly notice. The police will ask what happened. You'll tell. I'll tell.

A man poked his head into the room and then another. Security people. Moments later Eleanor arrived. She saw Ivan and the two of us on the floor in a messy pool of gore and blood. She was sick in the corner and then came over.

-    Are you both alright?

I nodded. Eleanor was concerned that some of the blood was mine or Katya's.

-    Police?

I nodded again.

She took out her phone and made the call. Then she came to sit down next to me. I motioned that she should sit next to Katya. She sat down in the blood without hesitation. She touched me and hugged Katya. She made an enquiry with her eyes. I just said:

-    Katya rescued me from Ivan.

-    Oh God.

She looked shocked and still a little puzzled.

Katya started to rock slowly back and forth. She sobbed and sobbed. We held her.

Other people started to arrive. Boris came in:

-    What do you need? The police are on their way.

-    Nothing. Nothing for now.

No one bothered us till the police arrived. Though there was a small number of people by the door. I could tell they were there but had my back to them.

I tried to get up but Ivan's blood was congealing around us. It was hanging off me in disgusting sheets and ribbons as I rose. I sat down again. A female policeman found us some bathrobes and the room emptied. We left our gowns in the bloody sticky offal and put the robes on. We were ushered into the room next door.

A policeman came to speak with us. I think he thought Katya had been raped. He wasn't so very wrong. He asked questions and I gradually put him on the right track.

Somebody suggested that we be split up. Katya got very distressed at this and started mumbling and shouting. We stayed together. She calmed down. I could feel her breathing settle. Normal breathing. Eventually we got Katya to take a bath. After the adrenaline had stopped flowing she said nothing and just stared.

Klarra and Hannah arrived. Eleanor spoke with Hannah while I stayed with Katya who seemed wary of her mother. Hannah was organising everything outside our room. I could only imagine what instructions she gave to the police about how to handle things.

There was some need to leave the hotel. The security people thought we were very vulnerable to reprisals from Ivan's mob. We would be better off in a less public place than a hotel. We went straight to the airport, boarded one of the Straminsky jets and flew back to Moscow.

Angelic?

Straminsky Residence

Source:	Alex Harewood
Date:	Sunday 30th November
Present:	Eleanor Straminsky, Katya Khrushcheva, Alex Harewood, Asya Khrushcheva, Klarra Khrushcheva,

The three of us were not much apart over the next few days. The police talked to us and we made formal statements. Sergei took charge of them but there was not a lot more that could be done.

Klarra and Hannah discussed how best to help, they sought some professional advice, thinking then that I would need help more than Katya. I already knew better and tried to make it clear that it was Katya who needed most support. Klarra must have seen the truth in this but had trouble admitting it to Hannah. They got help for all of us and we talked to the counsellors and took the medical tests. What seemed to help most was talking to each other.

We took Katya to the only place she knew well and could think of as safe and untainted; the room in Eleanor's Moscow house where she had sleepovers when they were young; the room where I had stayed. I wondered what picture was on the wall. Had anyone thought to change it? It was still the Vermeer. Still the picture of love, hope and trepidation. I had no idea at the time how appropriate this was for Katya.

At my request there was a beautiful, but not too large, bouquet of flowers in the room. Katya silently admired them when she arrived.

There was a knock on the door on the same afternoon. It was Klarra. I'd asked Katya's mother if she could deliver something that might just help and was very unlikely to do any harm. She had come with Asya which was a bonus. Asya walked forward and handed a small item wrapped in cloth to Katya who took it and smiled at her sister who then left quickly with her mother.

Katya unwrapped the package to find her teddy bear. She smiled at him a little, sat him on her knee, asked him how he was and hugged him. He had been her only confidante for many years. I asked:
-    What's he called?
and she responded:
-    Flipp.
-    Does he know everything?
She nodded.
-    Do you think he would mind hearing it all again?
She shook her head and looked up. Aware of what a silly question it was and gave a little smile. He got to hear it all again. Eleanor and I listened in.

Katya was first raped by her brother when she was 14. He'd told her it was a good thing to do. She should be happy but it was best kept a secret. Many more rapes followed. Eventually Katya spoke up and told her parents, but her father, Yevgeny, was already too ill to deal properly with his son. Wanting to avoid a family scandal Klarra simply spoke to Ivan, only a few years younger than herself. Ivan said it was Katya, she had been provocative, that she was odd and should be watched. He managed in part to convince Klarra that this was true.

Klarra told Katya it was wrong to behave this way with her brother! Katya was always thought a little strange by her family after that. Ivan caused Katya a lot of pain to punish her for telling anyone about what they did. Saying she had broken a confidence. Isolated, ashamed and full of self-doubt, she failed to engage properly with people and did badly at school. She pushed her best friend, Eleanor, away.

Katya would have left home and could easily have done so. Except her brother had threatened to chase after and punish her if she did and he clearly had the resources to do so. He told her that their's was a normal arrangement. Her mother seemed to be saying the same kind of thing:

- Oh lots of families are like this.

or:

- Most women end up in situations where they have sex when they don't want to at some time in their lives.

Which wouldn't make it right even if it had been true. Katya knew this. She knew it was wrong. She knew it was grotesque.

Katya saw her brother looking at Asya and knew what was going to happen. She pleaded with her Mother to send Asya away to school but Klarra wouldn't. So Katya made her own decision.

She made a bargain with her brother. She would do anything he wanted to stop him doing the same things to her sister. What he asked for he got from her. He even started passing her round his friends, not in a very overt way but the friend would say to Ivan that he liked Katya. She would then pretend to like the friend who believed she was willing and think of her as a proper girlfriend. To her mother this made Katya appear as Ivan had portrayed her.

Katya's strategy worked and Asya was not touched. Katya now still had to cope with her sister loving her brother more than her. How and when and if it could ever be explained to Asya what Katya had done for her it was too soon to say. Asya needed to be older to even begin to understand.

She had persuaded her brother to let her work with him and become part of the business. She hadn't realised that most of what he did had little to do with oil. She tried to fit in. She had to try to think like them. A mind-set where everything is a deal and relationships are only there for what money you can get out of them.

- I said horrible things about people, things I didn't believe, just to try to fit in.

Then she said despondently:

- It won't go away ever will it? All of that. It will always have happened to me.

I tried to give reassurance:

- It's not you, Katya. It's not what you are. You are the kindest and bravest soul. You will get better. I know. Life will be good. You will like yourself again. Believe me. I know.

She'd done everything she could for everyone else while getting no help for herself. I wondered if it was often this way. Men could be brave in dashing and dare, women in quiet and unassuming ways. She'd got nothing out of her situation; no glory. Asya, the person she'd given most for, would probably hate Katya for killing her beloved brother.

We found out that she had tried hard to keep Ivan and me apart because she thought that I was in danger from him. She had been watching out for me. That's how she came to be there when he attacked me. She knew I was around, as did he, and stayed with him to keep me safe. When he sent her on an errand and then disappeared, she had chased him down, bullying hotel staff to say what they knew. She had already overheard mention of room 513, the room where she found Ivan tying me down before inflicting all that violence on him. It still looked like I had been very lucky.

Eventually we started to chat about other things, everyday things. Normality would return slowly to her brain and her body so she slept better and she looked better. She started to become the person that she wanted to be. She had a future now and started to ask Eleanor and me about university. There was little wonder she hadn't done well at school. Perhaps her intelligence could start to become a more ordinary kind now.

The Garden Lake
Straminsky Residence

Source:	Alex Harewood
Date:	Sunday 30th November
Present:	Katya Khrushcheva, Alex Harewood

It was a beautiful morning, a last wave of mild weather before the winter freeze. Katya and I strolled around the impressive Straminsky gardens. We were admiring the immaculately kept grounds when we were surprised to find we had arrived at the lake. It wasn't enormous. Almost the size of a football pitch with a small island covered in small trees. There was a pier and a small rowing boat. We both had the same idea and shared a grin. The water was near freezing and we looked at each other wondering if we should. Then we helped each other into the wobbly craft and cast off. I found myself facing backwards and doing the rowing.

Katya was looking thoughtful. Then she asked something in a way that didn't quite fit with what I knew:
- How is Toby? Is he alright?
I wasn't supposed to know so I avoided the question:
- Hannah may know. You should ask her.
- But... aren't you with the British Secret Service. Isn't that why you're here?
- No...
- How can you not be? You played all those parts. Elisabeth Greyling, Emma Wilkinson. Are there others?

Angelic?

- Why did you think they were all the same person?
- I got suspicious of Elisabeth Greyling. She was older from the front. From the back she looked young. Then I started checking every woman. I noticed that Elisabeth and Emma and you were all the same size and shape. I'm good at judging people's size. I rarely get a dress, bra or shoe size wrong, as you know.

I did know and I realised that was why she looked happy after looking round Emma Wilkinson's flat. She saw Emma as being there to help her. She guessed it was me. I still hadn't answered her question and she persisted:

- You're not the SIS? So how were you involved? It doesn't make any sense if you're not.
- Can you be patient? I want you to know. I want Eleanor to know too. But it's not over yet.
- It's not over? What's not over?
- There are things that still need to happen.

She looked a little worried at that but didn't ask any of the questions that seemed to pass across her face. I rowed on for a few more strokes before a thought hit me. My stomach knotted, I stopped rowing, the boat drifted, and I had to ask:

- Katya.. Why were you asking about Toby?
- I really liked him.
- You liked him?... Katya please explain... So you met him?... You talked to him?

She nodded.

Katya had met Toby! Somewhere in the universe a sun was exploding. It felt quite close. Its brilliance revealed a whole new set of possibilities. Initially I was lost for words as I realised I was about to find out exactly what took place at the Mornington Club Party. I didn't have to ask anything. Katya could see I was full of questions so she just started talking:

- I met him at that party, where you met Eleanor. We spent some time together. We talked and laughed. He was great. Well, you knew him. You know what he was like. He was so easy to be with. I think about him a lot. I couldn't say before or Ivan would have hurt me. He would have hurt me bad.

The shockwaves from that supernova were still hitting me. Things were beginning to make sense though. Toby had succeeded. He'd found her. He'd met his princess and I felt so pleased for him. That lovely guy had met this gorgeous girl. He'd set the challenge and won. He must have been ecstatic. I imagined his smile of satisfaction. That broad beam of happiness that he would have had on his face brightening up the world with his success. What's more she had liked him. He didn't know all the consequences, the series of events that would follow. Even Toby would have thought the outcome in some way fitting. In his philosophy it would be better to die pursuing a dream than to just die. He'd found his dream. He'd met her, won her, and then suffered for it.

Katya kept talking:
- Toby was so great, he was what I have always hoped for. A man who can love and care. He was funny and confident and listened to me too. I really fell for him. I didn't want to leave him ever but I had to go to the ladies. I couldn't not. So silly, but I just had to go.

I'd seen her in the ladies and followed her that day. That was when and why I met Eleanor. Katya paused and sighed:
- My brother could tell that I was keen on him. That is why he was so hard on Toby. He wasn't just punishing Toby. He was punishing me. He said I was disloyal. I was breaking the rules. When I got back I saw Ivan

sitting where Toby had been. I had to watch while they beat him up. It was horrific. Toby on the ground. Ivan and his mates just kicking him. Hard. So hard. I tried to stop them. I did eventually. Then Ivan kicked him hard in a bad place. There, said Ivan, I don't think he'll be chasing you again.

Katya had been hurt so much, but she was confused about something:

- I didn't think he liked me so very much. If he liked me why didn't he touch me? I guess I'm not much of a looker.

She looked at me with the morning sun catching her hair as if to contradict what she had just said. I gave her what I thought was the most important piece of information:

- He thought you were stunning.
- No.. I'm not stunning. I look odd. People stare at me because I look odd. Ivan said I was bit weird looking and so I should always dress well to make up for it... I know my hair's alright.

I wasn't surprised that Ivan had taken this from her too. I tried to correct the wrong:

- Katya, people stare at you because you are very beautiful. Toby called you the most beautiful girl in the world, Miss Russia and the only girl he'd ever dream of. He said you were perfect.
- He did? He did? So why didn't he touch me?

She'd never had a real boyfriend and didn't know what to expect in a proper relationship. I also recalled Tavi and me advising him to not be too forward.

- Men who respect you will look to you for a sign that it's OK to touch you. You give them permission. Normally just by touching them first. I'm certain Toby will have wanted to.
- I know it's supposed to be that way.

- He would have wanted your permission to go further. He wouldn't want to touch a single square centimetre, not a hair on your head, your knee or the hem of your skirt unless it was OK with you. He was a real old-fashioned guy.

She seemed satisfied with that.

There was one last blinding flash of light from the supernova as she said:

- Toby had said how good his guys were. When someone hacked the site and Ivan's notes were stolen he knew who it had to be.

I had never before thought that Toby might have talked to Katya at the party, but he had. He had talked to Katya about his business. What else does a man do? He boasted about how good his partners were. He said they were brilliant hackers. Toby didn't know the listening devices on Katya picked up every word and passed it all on to her brother. When his site was hacked Ivan had only one place to look. That's how they had found Tavi so quickly. They went straight to the SafeNet office and found Tavi. Then they came for me.

Katya looked at me:

- I think about him all the time. I often cry about him and that awful evening when Ivan hurt him. It hurts to think about him, but he's always there, in my mind. Can you…

She stared solemnly at the water. Then she turned back to me:

- Can you fall in love in an hour?

After all that had taken place since the party her thoughts and hopes were still for Toby so I replied:

- I wasn't sure before. But now I know. Yes, you can. You can fall in love in an hour.

Angelic?

Tavi had been beaten to death, the Novichok destroyed, Ivan killed, TPO Oil stock sent into freefall, Katya had been liberated and I'd become Alex for months. None of this would have happened if Toby hadn't been beaten up. And he was beaten up not because he'd looked for Katya, not because he'd met her and not because he'd talked to her. It had happened, it had all happened, because in that hour, on that summer evening, the most beautiful and selfless girl, Miss Katya Khrushcheva, had given her heart to Toby Smithson.

The boat softly bumped into the island on the lake and I remembered where we were. Katya was looking at me imploringly:
-    Is he alright?.. Is he OK?.. You must know.
Katya had been through so much.

She smiled. She grinned from ear to ear, splashed the water, rocked the boat and let out a little scream. Then she leaned forward and hugged me. She could not have looked any happier. The only thing I'd done to get this reaction was smile at her and wink.

Lavender Hill Police Station

Source:	Computers at the Lavender Hill Police Station
Date:	Monday 1st December
Time:	17.09
Present:	DI Gemma Black, DC John Meehan

The police team have had a dull day looking through phone records. They have found nothing of any interest to help with the case. Meehan pushed his chair back and turned round to face Black:

- Boss. Can I talk to you? There's something on my mind.
- I thought there might be. You've been quiet all day.
- Well.. There's.. There's something I don't quite get. Or rather I'm worried about what I think I do get.

She looked back at him. He avoided her eyes while she said:

- I'll help if I can.
- There have been times when the things we have done appear to have been known to other people. There was a leak. One of our team was giving away information to Ivan's mob.

Gemma looked concerned as she said:

- Why do you say that?
- Well there were a few times where they seemed to be ahead of us. Or at least catch up very quickly. The most obvious was at the Wadkins factory. Someone told them that Hecketty was there. They knew as soon as we knew.
- I do see what you mean.

Angelic?

He looked nervous and downcast. This was not something that he wanted to be saying:
- I thought you would. You see I looked into it some more. I found some phone records. I think I know what was happening...

Gemma was beginning to see that Meehan knew what she had done. He looked at her. Now she looked away. He confirmed:
- The records show where the calls came from.
- John...
- How could you?

She wanted to defend herself. She tried to find a way to make him understand. But she sounded desperate:
- They threatened me. They threatened my family. They're not nice people. I was frightened. There was no choice for me. You know what those people are like. You know what they did to Tavi Mansur!
- Yes! But we're supposed to be the good guys. Aren't we here to do good? Aren't we hear to stop the bad guys. You helped them!
- You're young. You think everything is black and white. It's not. Life is complicated. Everything is grey. My priority is not my job. It's my family.

That wasn't
not quite enough for Meehan:
- What about everyone else's family? If we don't stop it then it just carries on and on. More and more people get hurt.

He paused for a moment. Another thought:
- Hang on. Hang on. The calls stop. Why did they stop?
- Evans.
- Evans? Is that what he talked to you about?
- Yes he told me to stop.
- So.. Is that all he said?

- It's why he came in.
- He knew what was happening?
- He didn't say it that way. He said he would protect me and my family.

Meehan does not know how to respond to this new information. He's trying to work out what it might mean. She can't let it rest. She needs to know:

- You're not going to do anything are you? You're not going to tell anyone.
- I don't know. I really don't.
- Please John.
- I need to think.

He turned round and sat down at his desk. He sat with his hands in his lap and stared at the computer. He didn't look round to see the tears welling in Gemma's eyes.

Straminsky Residence

Source:	Alex Harewood
Date:	Tuesday 2nd November
Present:	Eleanor Straminsky, Katya Khrushcheva, Alex Harewood, Asya Khrushcheva, Klarra Khrushcheva,

We were eating breakfast when Genya came in to whisper something to Hannah, who then looked at Katya:

- Anna Khrushcheva is here. She has asked to see you. Do you want to see your aunt Katya?

Katya nodded eagerly:

- Yes, very much.

We finished eating and went through to the sitting room. Anna was already there looking as sharp as ever and taking us all in with just one glance. She greeted everyone and seemed pleased to see Eleanor and me again. She handed a box to Katya. I knew what it was. It was the necklace that Yekaterinya had worn in the war.

- This is for you. I heard what happened and I heard what you have done. Open this when I have told you the story that goes with it. A friend of ours said that you had a right to hear the story. She was right. I think now you have a right to own this as well.

Anna told Katya the story of Yekaterinya in the war. We all listened.

Katya heard the story and made the connection. She looked round at Anna, Eleanor, Hannah and me. She saw herself a little differently; more as we saw her. She sat a little more upright then glanced briefly at her aunt who nodded back. Then she opened the box.

The necklace had started life as a simple one: round balls of wood with a hole drilled through them and threaded together with a string. There was no fancy clasp. Just one smaller bead and a loop on the other end to pass it through. The beads had been decorated over time. Different patterns carved into them to make concentric hoops or simple dimples in the surface. One of the wooden balls had zig-zag rather than straight lines. The skill of the carver appeared to have increased over time. And while some of the carving appeared crude, some of the beads showed some skill. A few of the wooden balls had even been transformed into a head of a person. With a nose, a mouth, ears, hair and eyes. Some of the balls had been painted with whatever colouring came to hand.

Her father had presented it to Yekaterinya, Katya's aunt, on her 10th birthday before he went to war. She had sat through days in summer and in winter when her hands were not too cold working on the necklace. Doing a little more during the long dull periods when there were so few things to help her forget the hunger and the discomfort and the despair. She may have dreamed of better times. When she could be warm and dry and not hungry. She may have wondered if she would ever have a husband and children of her own. Perhaps she wondered what her own children might be like.

The dreams had ended along with her life when that grenade had been thrown with so little consideration and so much accuracy.

Carved onto one ball of the necklace was a young man. Another ball clearly showed a young woman. They were next to each other on the string. This was the dream I had seen at Anna's house. The dream of romance. Yekaterinya had carved it into her necklace as soon as she was old enough to have such dreams. It's hard to imagine how those thoughts might have started in that harsh time. Perhaps she had met a boy who was kind to her and he had kindled that flame. We would never know. But we know she wanted to find someone to love her.

Katya took the necklace from the box. She examined and felt each bead. Anna, her aunt, was next to her:

- She sat just like that. She held it just like that. You two are so much alike.

Then, in the formal way that is still used in Russia, she said:

- Keep this. Love it for who wore it. Honour it for the hopes and dreams that it holds. May the hopes and dreams that you share come true.

There was only one proper response to that:

- Amen.

I found I wasn't the only one saying it.

Eleanor was giving me a funny look. Katya looked up too. I'd given something away.

At that very moment in Melbourne, Australia, on the other side of our globe, an envelope was opened. It contained a single plane ticket to London and an instruction to be at SIS HQ on Thursday 18th December.

Chapter 22
London
December 2014

Emma's Flat
Azimuth House

Source:	James Hecketty/Alex Harewood and cameras and devices hidden in the flat
Date:	Tuesday 9th December
Time:	2.15 pm
Present:	James Hecketty, Gemma Black, John Meehan

Meehan and Black arrived at Azimuth House and found the entrance to the flats. Meehan was not quite sure why they were there:
- So Emma Wilkinson sent you a text inviting you round for tea?
- Yes. She says she has some things for us.

They went up the stairs and knocked on her door but there was no reply. Emma was not at home although the door was unlocked. They went in and found a kettle boiling in the kitchen, two mugs and tea bags. A note, signed Emma, said they should help themselves. Gemma poured. Then they started to look round.

The flat was full of documents and photographs. They detailed all the members of the Russian mafia gang in

Angelic?

London. All the names were there and their addresses. There was camera data from each of their five brothels, the men who ran them and how they ran them. All the details of the killing of girls and the rapes. All the bank accounts. More than enough information to help prosecute everyone involved.

Gemma was working out what to do with all this information. There would have to be a lot of very detailed and secretive planning, simultaneous dawn raids on all five locations, enough care for sixty traumatised and trafficked women. There was a lot to do and many people that she would have to contact. Gemma was curious:

- It must have taken days to put all this together. There is information on every girl. A plan of every brothel. One person couldn't do all this.

Dressed in a hoody and baseball cap I went up the stairs to the flat. I was also wearing glasses and a false beard. My James Hecketty outfit. I knocked on the open door to Emma's flat:

- Can I come in?
- Gemma Black looked up and realised who she was looking at:
- Hello? Well.. James Hecketty, well..
- Hello, Gemma, good to meet you at last.

I shook her hand and then John's. Gemma asked:

- How did you do all this? How did you put all this together?
- I didn't.
- Emma then?
- No, it was Alyona and Stanislava. A girl called Margarita as well. They wanted to help. They wanted to be involved... Do you think you have everything that you need here?

- Yes I think so. We'll be able to go into the brothels very soon.
- Please look after the girls. That's the most important thing. It's hard to recover from that. Sometimes it takes years.

She nodded her head slowly in confirmation. She'd already been thinking of that:

- We'll do everything that we can.
- Any problems, just text me... And, John, there is a pile over there that I put out for you. I know you're interested in the Sun House case.

I pointed towards the table and Meehan eagerly followed my direction as I said:

- Goodbye, John. Goodbye, Gemma.

Black was surprised:

- Are you going?
- Yes, I need to.

I left Gemma and John shouting their thanks and goodbyes through the empty doorway.

John looked at a folder that was where I had pointed. The printed label on the front said:

Sun House 2007 -2011

They hadn't said a lot to each other since the discussion about the leaked information. Meehan was sifting through the Sun House data and, not knowing what to say, he concentrated on that. The file contained details on all the girls who worked at Sun House. They had each written a resume before coming to the UK assuming that they were going to a proper place of work. He looked at them all.

- Boss? This is odd. Each of these contains added information on what these girls are doing now. What jobs they have and where they live. This girl, Alina Babina, married an English guy. Lives in Lincoln. Lada

Novosada, injured in the shooting, recovered fully, went home to Russia, lives in Vladivostok and works in a sausage factory. Margarita Pavlovicha had help and a lot of counselling. Not recovering well, four years later. She's still in London.

- John paused. He was visibly upset:
- Do those bastards know what they do?

Black pointed out:

- Hecketty said someone called Margarita helped organise all this paperwork.

John grinned:

- Yes. So he did. I hope it helps her.

He saw another page. He picked it up slowly, with reverence:

- There's a page here on Angelina. There is just one date. I guess whoever did this couldn't find her…

They both looked up. There was a siren howling and a flash of blue light in the street. Meehan:

- What's that?

The siren stopped but the blue light intermittently illuminated the room. Meehan rushed to the window and looked out. He saw an ambulance in the middle of the road with two paramedics swiftly getting out. A taxi cab had stopped too. Lying still on the pavement was James Hecketty, not moving at all. There were three men and a woman around him. One man was looking closely at Hecketty. The others were standing closely around him but looking outwards checking the area. Meehan ran out of the flat and down the stairs. Black followed.

The paramedics were examining Hecketty. One of them went for the stretcher.

Meehan and Black came out of the door to the flats and saw Hecketty placed on the stretcher and carried into the back of the ambulance. The woman and one of the men got in with Hecketty.

Black waved her warrant card and got up into the ambulance to look at Hecketty. She could see his eyes were open and staring. She got out of the ambulance and made a call.
-    I'm arranging for an escort. It'll be safer and quicker.
She made the arrangements. One minute later a marked police car arrived. She quickly spoke to the ambulance crew and then the uniformed police officers in the car. The police car lead the way noisily and with all lights flashing. The ambulance followed.

Black spoke to the eldest man. He seemed to have been directing what was happening when they arrived. The other people wandered off so Black and Meehan were left standing by a taxi talking to this man on his own. The scene had all looked very calm and organised; not the way it would look if these people had just been ordinary members of the public passing by.
-    I'm Inspector Gemma Black, what happened to James Hecketty?
-    He collapsed out here. We called for the ambulance.
-    What's wrong with him? Will he be alright?
-    I very much hope so.
-    Who are you?
-    My name is Timms, Inspector.
-    Who are you people, Timms?
-    We're his protection team.
-    You're his bodyguards?
-    That's correct, Inspector.
She's a little annoyed.
-    How long have you been protecting Hecketty?
-    Inspector I have to go. We're represented by Witter

and Proctor. Please let them know if there is anything that you wish to discuss with us.

Timms started walking towards his taxi as Black thinks aloud:

- Witter and Proctor? I should have known. I guess that answers my question as well.
- Timms got into his cab. Meehan spoke to him through the open door:
- Look after James, Timms. There's a lot more to some people than meets the eye.
- We will, Constable Meehan. Don't worry.

After Timms had gone, Black and Meehan made their way back upstairs to Emma's flat. Gemma busied herself with the paperwork but Meehan's brain hadn't stopped working. He took out his phone and sent a text. He got a response a few moments later:

- Emma Wilkinson speaks Russian with the girls.
- She does? So?
- It looks like Emma Wilkinson may be Angelina. This could all be Angelina's work. I hope so. I do hope so. She's not gunning them down any more but her targets are the same.

John had something more:

- The boffins got a lot of DNA from the trafficker's truck. They got tens of individuals going back years. Mainly just fragments. I.. Well I unofficially checked two women we'd had in the station. I thought Katya Khrushchev might have been on there. There was no match. Then they checked Alex Harewood. It was positive! There was a fragment that matched with her. Why was her DNA on the truck? It makes no sense at all.

Gemma Black shook her head:

- You're sure?

- No. It's a fragment. Not conclusive.
- You're connecting all this to the Sun House case aren't you? You want to find Angelina? That's an interesting idea. Crack that old gnarly nut. It's a good idea. With that and this…

She gestured round at all the brothel data

- …we'd certainly turn a few heads higher up.

Gemma Black looked satisfied as she contemplated future promotion. Meehan hadn't seen it that way:

- I want to know what happened to Angelina. It feels like we're very close to finding out but I don't want to see her caught and prosecuted. She shouldn't be locked up.
- We're police officers John. That's what we do.
- Should we follow up on every crime?
- Of course. That's our job.
- Angelina should be left. She was a victim. I want to help her. I want to know she's alright. I want her to have good things happen to her. Two years she spent doing only what other people wanted her to do. Two years she was made to suffer unwanted men several times every day. It shouldn't be like that for anyone.
- That is so true. But it's not for us to decide right and wrong.
- Yes it is! Today it is. Or I follow up on every crime…

He was threatening her with revealing what he knew about the leaks. A more confident person might have hinted at the threat before stating it, in which case the next few moments might have gone more smoothly and had less of a result.

- John?...My word!

She thought for a moment before asking:

- Would you withdraw that threat, John, for me, for our relationship?

Angelic?

He took a little time to think as well but then said sheepishly:
- Yes..
- So whatever I do you won't carry out that threat?
He didn't look happy and mumbled:
- I wouldn't have done it anyway. You're a victim too.
She looked relieved at his response. Then she paused to look at him for a moment before saying:
- Thank you. Thank you. Now it can be my decision too. Oh God I do agree. You're right. You are so right. There may well be a connection between Angelina and Emma, but they should be left and we should do nothing about what we know. We forget it.
- That's a good decision, Boss.
They both relaxed and laughed together because the tension between them had gone and was replaced with the knowledge that their relationship was now stronger than ever.

A while later Gemma asked:
- Do you think Yak knew? Did he spot a connection? Now I think of it every time it came up he pointed us away again.
- He may have... Do you think he did the same in the original investigation?
- You know the night she killed those men the brothel's guests had all been from another gang. That's why the man she was with had a gun. All eight were depraved thugs. She did the rest of the world a favour as well as herself.
- So you're agreeing? You think he influenced the investigation into Angelina?
She was grinning as she repeated his earlier words:
- He may have.
He laughed in reply and then shrugged his shoulders.

Gemma changed the subject:

- How's it going with Janet?

John was happy to talk about that:

- Oh good, really good. Thank you. I always wanted to be lucky. She's great. We talk for ever about everything.
- That's good. I'm happy for you. That sounds like a proper relationship.

He grinned and nodded. It was harder to say the next thing:

- We talked about you... I didn't know, but she saw it... She saw how you feel about me.
- Oh John. It's OK, I made my choices years ago.
- Is there a parallel universe where things worked out differently for you?
- Maybe, it's possible.
- You deserve good things too.

Their eyes met for a longer than average moment as she silently mouthed:

- Thank you.

They both went back to looking through all the brothel data.

A Private Room
The Royal Free Hospital
London

Source:	James Hecketty/Alex Harewood
Date:	Thursday 11th December
Time:	2.15 pm
Present:	Alex, Eleanor, Katya, The Priest, a nurse, a doctor

Something had gone wrong with me again as I left Azimuth House. I had started to shake. I was James! This was bad. I wasn't safe as James. I fought it and struggled against it. I fell on the floor.

The army was asleep and I slipped out of my tent. Nobody would be asking where I was in the morning. Carpenethes would continue to run things, as he was now, when it became clear that I would not return. I swapped my clothes and became an anonymous young woman. I mingled with the many women who followed the army. I lay awake next to a woman who I had seen dancing and waited for the start of the commotion that I had caused.

The first man started screaming early in the night and I heard him above the normal nocturnal murmurs of the enormous camp. This proud warrior grasped his stomach and tried to be quiet. His screams became moans and sweat poured from him. Then other men found themselves afflicted in the same way. The soldiers looked at each other wondering who would be next. One by one each slipped into his own private agony and then passed on from this world. Many, many thousands died this way during that night.

When morning came and the dying had stopped the few men left tried to organise themselves into ad hoc fighting groups. They knew the Judean scouts would send word of what had happened. The broken remnants of the world's most powerful army had only one choice. Retreat. I watched the cloud of dust surmounted by gold and purple banners that was Sennacherib returning to Nineveh with his retinue and the royal guard. Jerusalem would not fall to this host of men.

There was nothing more to do here so I collected some food, some water, parchment and things to write with and I moved away from the Assyrian camp, leaving behind the sound of the sorrow of the women as they searched out and found the bodies of the men they knew. The hills to the South would have some peace. I was pleased with what I had done. The feeling was not triumph. It was satisfaction.

While climbing up through the hills I ate some of my provisions and had time to think. I knew what had happened yesterday and all the days before while I was in this place. I had planned these events for months. I remembered the days on the march with the army and the time before that in Niniveh with Carpenethes. The person I had been then was not the person that I was now. I found I could recall being other people in other times and places.

London was a cloudy memory too. Though most would say those events were yet to happen it did not seem that way to me. From there and other places I remembered a story told by some priests. The story had been about just these events that were happening now.

I kept moving on but stopped when I came to a small stream among the hills. It gurgled enticingly down the slope and looked clear and cool. I cupped my hands and drank from it. A young man was there, just a few yards away, drinking from the stream and I watched him as I pondered over what was happening. Then I moved towards him and asked the obvious question:

- *Are you Methes?*

He looked puzzled that I knew him and he gave the reply:

- *I am Methes. Who are you?*

I thought about where I was and what I had just done to the army on the plain. I knew what had happened and I knew what was about to happen so I grasped the young man's sleeve as I gave the only response that was true:

- *I have many names. But what I have done they say was done by Uriel.*

He screamed and turned to run away. My grip on his sleeve held him easily. I smiled at him and reassured him.

Everything continued to happen just as it should. Exactly as it was in the story of Methes and Uriel. I gave him the writing implements and said how his life would be. I knew that this would happen because I knew that somewhere else it had already happened.

Then I told him what to write. I told him about the life of an angel. That we struggled through the world not always knowing who we were or why we were there. If we had any perfection then it was not visible to us. Where we found evil we revelled in punishing it using whatever means there were to hand.

At the end of the day I sent Methes back to his life, to meet his beautiful wife and to have their children and grandchildren. I watched him walk away and hide the parchment in the cave.

Right here, right now, this was real. I played many parts but I knew who I was. Uriel.

I heard a voice calling to me. Someone was talking to me, instructing me.

-   Be with us again. Be here with us. It is safe here. Be Alex. Alex has friends here.

The ancient world and the feelings I had there became distant. This voice came from a world where I knew so much less. I felt vulnerable there. I heard the priest once more:

-   Be here with us. Be Alex.

Then I saw the Priest and I heard him talking to me:

-   Don't be frightened of what you are. I know you are Uriel. I know you enjoy doing God's work by casting death and hurt on those who do evil. After so long away from us you will now know of things that you have done before. Are you willing to accept yourself yet?

Words would not form in my mouth but I shook my head at him. He said:

-   Hide as Alex for good people if you wish. I know you find it hard to accept what you are. Embrace it and then be comfortable with all the parts you play. Then

you will want to strike out at evil again.
I still could not find words to answer him. He asked me to
watch for his people, left slowly, keeping his eye on me all
the time and then shut the door. I was alone in a large
private room in a hospital. I slept uneasily wondering how
much of what happened to me was real. I tried not to
remember all the painful things from this world.

When I woke Eleanor was beside me and I was pleased to
have her close and soak up some of her goodness. I was
relieved because I only had to be Alex with her. Being Alex
was easy. She grinned:
- Hi! How are you feeling?
- Much, much better for seeing you!
I smiled and she laughed while wiping the tear from my
eye.

Eleanor started talking, slowly at first then more
animatedly as she saw I was listening:
- When you first arrived... Mum was here too... She
  started saying you were a very special kind of woman..
  but then got really confused after speaking to the
  doctors. She seemed to have thought you were a man!
  As if..! I've never seen her look so wrong-footed. Then
  she just said you were extraordinary. I couldn't
  disagree!
She slowed down again and looked a bit more thoughtful:
- I see now that it may not have been all her fault
  though. Your life is very complicated... But look! You're
  back. You're OK.
She sat by me on the bed:
- You've been away from us for almost two days, like you
  were looking at things that weren't here. Your eyes
  were open but you were just a shell and you didn't
  move. We were all worried. Horribly worried. The

doctors said it was some sort of fit and possibly a kind of epilepsy. They say there seem to be some odd things happening with your hormones and you show signs of exhaustion. They think those things may all be linked. I'll let the doctors explain it to you properly if they can. I asked questions but they didn't seem at all sure themselves, there just seemed to be a long list of options. They want you to stay in for a few days... Are you sure you feel OK?

- I feel fine... Really.

A doctor came in and Eleanor stood back. The doctor asked me all sorts of questions, peered at me through things and instructed me to look this way and that. She attached some wires to my head, took some readings, and concluded that I had recovered but they wanted to do some more tests now that my brain patterns were more normal.

Katya arrived, I thought for the first time though apparently she had been with me for some while earlier. She put down a bag and took out a bundle of things that were familiar to me. I recognised a jumper of mine and some embroidered jeans. She must have been to my flat. I was so happy to see her. She looked good, in every sense, she smiled a brilliant smile and hugged me while I lay on the bed:

- Hi, you're back with us then. And you look well now. Are you feeling OK?
- Yes, thanks, I feel alright.
- That's good. I want my friend to be well.

Eleanor then said something I found worrying at first:

- Do you feel well enough to talk? We... We've kind of worked some things out about you.
- Oh.

There was still real danger. They could see that I was

concerned. Katya plumped my pillows and helped me get upright so I could see them and talk, though I didn't have to say much as she explained:

- Please don't worry. There was a priest here. We thought him a bit crazy at first but what he said seemed to fit you and it made as much sense as anything we've been told by the medical people.

Katya was sitting on the right of my bed. Eleanor was on the left and said:

- He told us a story, though we'd both heard it already, about a boy who does a favour and keeps a secret for Archangel Uriel.

Then Katya explained some more:

- Uriel was always my favourite angel. She likes to help good people but does terrible things to people who are wicked and she is the only angel who appears as both a man and a woman.

This was all going a bit too far towards the incredible but Katya continued:

- The Priest explained that Uriel is often known as more than one person. He said that the people she appears to be often have power far beyond ordinary people and can seem almost miraculous.

This couldn't be happening. My hallucinations were becoming part of my reality. I shook my head but Katya had more to say:

- Eleanor and I talked and shared what we knew. We calculated how much you have done. It's a lot. You've done so much. There may well be more that we don't know about but we do know that you have taken risks and are always in danger. We won't tell. We know it's very serious and that Tavi died keeping a secret for you.

Tavi. I tried to hold it together as I thought of what had

happened. Eleanor noticed and sympathetically gripped my arm. Then she took over the explanation:
- The Priest said you would only want to be Alex with us. That's alright. We want it to be that way too.

There was almost nothing to say. It was good that they knew. I could relax more. I just smiled and took Eleanor's hand in my left and Katya's in my right and gently squeezed:
- Thanks.

Eleanor introduced another idea they had come up with:
- We've thought of something you might like to do while you're in hospital.
- What's that?
- We can teach you some Russian.
- Yes. OK. That's a good idea... Do you think I'll find it easy?

Katya told me the real reason for the suggestion:
- Oh yes. You'll be model student and learn at an astonishing pace. And then, after a little while, you can stop pretending that you don't already know it.

The British Press

Source:	The Press
Date:	Tuesday 16th December

All the papers carried the same story. It featured in the quality papers and the less serious ones. Stories concerning sex will always sell newspapers. This story was also about a major police success.

In the early hours of the previous day the police had simultaneously raided five major London brothels. The police had excellent intelligence that helped them carry out the operations effectively and safely. They made twenty-three arrests and have sixty-three women in protective custody. The women were almost all trafficked from eastern Russia.

The men had already appeared in front of magistrates and charged with a number of offences including murder, false imprisonment, rape and slavery.

Acting Detective Chief Inspector Gemma Black, who was in charge of coordinating the operation, made a statement:
-    In every raid we prioritised the safety and well-being of the women who are the victims of these sickening and inhuman crimes. We have put in place every possible measure to help them recover. We have been able to help most of them to get back in touch with their families. We wish them every success for their future.

The police had handled it well. Teams of female officers

had carried out the raids, they had surprise on their side and there were almost no injuries during the raid. Once the women in the brothels had realised what was happening they had cooperated in every way possible.

The only injury had been to one of the brothel chiefs. He claimed this was inflicted by Helena Guseva who had arrived on the same truck as Alyona and Stanislava with the long red hair. When she saw the police she had delivered a trained karate kick to a point just above the chief's groin rupturing his bladder and leaving him in agony. The police found no witnesses who were willing to corroborate this version of events.

Bond Street
London

Source:	James Hecketty/Alex Harewood
Date:	Thursday 18th December
Time:	14.13
Present:	Alex Harewood, Eleanor Straminsky, David Evans, an SIS officer.

We had been visiting a dressmaker where I had been measured, quizzed and shown all sorts of fabulous garments that I would once never have dreamed of wearing. Eleanor and I had both ordered new gowns for the Mornington Club Christmas Party on Saturday. This was usually a smaller more intimate affair than the summer event but apparently still a good enough excuse to dress up. Eleanor had several gowns already that would do but Ivan's blood had ruined my only good one.

On the way out Eleanor started a new conversation:
- What are you doing for Christmas? Mum said it would be great if you came to us.
- That's kind, really kind. Thank you. I try to avoid Christmas. I worked in a homeless shelter last year.

My attempt to nudge the conversation on had failed because Eleanor asked:
- Is that because of your family?
- My family?
- Well, your parents? I don't know. You never say anything about your childhood. There are things I know about you that don't fit with other things.

I couldn't answer. She put an arm around mine as she saw that I was getting worried.

- Things are complicated for you, aren't they? You helped Katya so much. Mum says how you helped rescue those women from the brothels and I know there's other stuff too. There are so many layers to you. I don't know them all and I'm not prying. I decided a long time ago to accept you as you are now. Just be Alex with me and please be with us for Christmas if you can. I won't say any more if you don't want me to, but tell me if you can.
- I will... You're so good to me. You're such a good friend. Thank you for Timms and his team.

She knew I was talking about providing my protection and cover as Alex.

- They wanted to kill you in the summer. We couldn't let that happen. I'd just made a new friend. A very special and unusual friend we found out. We wanted you to be safe.
- Thanks.

She squeezed my arm to say all was OK, before letting it go.

A car stopped very close and a man got out. He approached us with that police officer air about him, but I couldn't think there would be any reason for the police wanting to speak to us so I guessed he was SIS. I spoke first:

- What can we do for you officer?
- Miss Harewood, I've been asked to take you to a meeting. Would you come along as well please Miss Straminsky?
- What's this about?
- I was told to say that you should "Work it fucking out for yourself" Sorry, ladies, I was told to quote verbatim.

Angelic?

Eleanor looked a bit alarmed. I put a hand on her arm to reassure her:

-    It's OK. We're going to SIS HQ to see the big man.

Eleanor rolled her eyes as we got into the car:

-    David Evans? Oh, well, sure, of course. I mean he's a friend of mine too. Why didn't you say you knew him?
-    Doesn't your Mum know him?
-    I don't think so... I don't know... Does she?

SIS Headquarters

Source: James Hecketty/Alex Harewood
Date: Thursday 18th December
Time: 14.53
Present: David Evans, Alex, Eleanor, Toby

Eleanor was asked to stay in a kind of sitting area with leather sofas and armchairs. I was left in a big plush office on my own. It was a nice office with a good view, high up in the building and all leather and wood panels. A huge fat man came in. He was not at all handsome, but may have been once. I recognised the head of the SIS, David Evans.

- So you're Alex Harewood.
- Hello, Evans. Thanks for helping me.

He waved a hand dismissively.

- You are one clever cookie, girl. Not many people get to screw around with this organisation. Not many get to fuck up a whole mob of evil twats single-handed. But you managed it

This had to be the most obscene compliment I was ever likely to receive. I said nothing.

- Now don't get alarmed. As far as the rest of the world is concerned, and quite a big chunk of it does seem concerned. I'm currently talking to Alex Harewood the estate agent's assistant. I'm telling her that all is well now and she can rest easy. That she can relax and is safe now that the bogeyman has been taken care of... That is so far from reality that I can't believe I even have to pretend that I'm bloody saying it. You are one fucking dangerous woman to cross.

He stared at me for a few seconds with a so-this-is-what-she-looks-like expression. I sat on the edge of my chair trying to look innocent. Mainly because I wasn't.

- If I'd been told there was a clever girl with great technical skills who could hack into any computer system and simultaneously piss off and manipulate clandestine organisations I would say that they were stinking rotten shrunken brain moronic planks for even thinking that such a concatenation of outrageous talent could exist in one person. And yet... here you fucking are.

I had been wrong about the most obscene compliment. He'd just set the new world record.

- That this person has enough high placed friends to get her through any door in the world would be just too much to ask wouldn't it? Right now I'm expecting that overworked phone to ring and the goddamn Prime Minister to tell me that I have to let you go in 77 seconds or the country will be short of oil for the next decade. So I do a little digging of my own. Proper old-fashioned leg work. Talking to people instead of staring at computers. It turns out I'm right. You don't fucking exist! Nobody in the world spoke a single meaningless syllable to Alex Harewood until this year. So I dig through shit loads of stuff and found out enough. Enough to know that you're not quite as mind bogglingly miraculous and that everyone has their little secrets. Anyway I know now. Shall I tell you what I know?
- Do I get a choice?
- No you don't. James reappears occasionally but only to act as bait to draw pitiable mafia thugs into your web. James disappeared but he didn't hide. He just became

someone else and had a bit of specialist help from people with planetary sized connections. Now this is where my brain lacks some fucking thing. At that point they could not have had the smallest pin prick of an idea about the extraordinary nature of what Tavi Mansur had found out. Or how important it was. There doesn't seem to be a single gnat's brain reason why the world's most expensive security service was on your side from day one.

This was intriguing. His mind was so full of plots and counter plots that he had missed something less exciting and far more human. It was also clear that, like Hannah Straminsky, he knew about Alex Harewood's origins. But nothing about where James Hecketty came from. So I kept silent.

-   Hmmm... and still she says nothing.... My head is not quite far enough up into my own intestines to not know that my role here is, in the end, to increase the total volume of happiness in the world, though there are days when this mission is extraordinarily hard to keep in mind. So I went to see some very nice people a few days ago. Very good, honest, hardworking people. I took with me a couple of messages for these people who have suffered and needed to know what it was that their son had done. I turned up in the official car surrounded by little people. I wanted horses and a military band, but some pencil head downstairs muttered some shit about budget cuts. The Mansur family were very good to me. I had to say who I was which kind of took the shine off it, but I wasn't there to polish my ego. It sparkles plenty enough anyway. So I explained to Mr and Mrs Mansur and their family. Proper good people. Did I mention that? I explained what a fucking hero their son was. I didn't give all the details but I said he had done something truly clever and suffered hell for it. They should be bloody proud of him. I'm still not sure they wouldn't rather have been parents to a live idiot than a dead hero but that's parenthood for you.

I made an observation:

- You can't hide it any longer. You only swear to cover up the fact that you're a big soft hearted sweety.
- Quiet! The whole fucking world doesn't have to hear. It's bad enough knowing it without having it advertised. Anyway, just to prove how fucking perceptive you are, like it needs proving, I took a piece of paper with me, signed by a lady I know. She says that Tavi Mansur is pardoned for that little bit of hacking he didn't even do in the first fucking place and the conviction removed from the records. This lady's not so good with her name. Only uses her first. The paper just says "Elizabeth R" on the bottom. There's a lot of folk take a lot of notice of paper with that kind of stuff on. The Mansur family were particularly impressed. Anyway I left those good folk a lot happier than I found them.

This little task had probably taken an hour of his time. It was hard not to like him for it.

- Do your employees know about you?
- Thank Christ, no. Now you don't have to acknowledge. You can just play fucking dumb if you want to. I figure anybody with a brain-box the size of a small house who can save entire fucking countries and bring down multinational companies isn't going to be entirely happy perfecting her tan on a yacht even if it is the size of the fucking moon or shopping at GUM for the rest of her life. She might occasionally want to take on additional projects. Do something a bit different,

perhaps dig her home country out of piles of offal and excrement occasionally. Play marbles with planets, that kind of low key undemanding activity. You'd deal only with me not any of those near imbecile moron turnips who work for me.

- I think you may be overrating me a bit. I got lucky in a few places.
- Don't believe that half-baked nonsense about luck all being down to fucking chance. You had a lot of options. Some of them opened up. Some just croaked. You made it all work.
- Are we done? Can we move on?
- Oh no we're not done yet. You're not the only one in the world that can play mind bending games. We can do a bit of smoke and mirror too. In fact we think we're real dog's bollock good at it and we do hold all the cards. If we want to change the way things appear, they fucking change and you will never know, not even you Miss Ever So Fucking Clever Clogs. So I checked out my theories with the only person who might be able to help. Turns out the key to this riddle is under my nose all along - after hours of fucking leg work. Not many people get the chance to make me look like a tit. There were only two people who really knew James and Alex. Now that we are well and truly out of the shit zone I think reality should be allowed to creep back in again.

I breathed in quickly and thought of Katya as I said:
- Toby!
- You see that's why you're good. You hold a whole menagerie of possibilities in your head all at once. Each new drip of data allows you to re-evaluate them all and come up with a new most probable scenario. I'd been on to that Russian Zombie brained incestuous sadist prick for quite a while. Every time he was in town he'd

leave piles of pooh lying around. I'd been wanting to do something about him for a while. Then I started getting signals that he was drowning in a sea of his own excrement. I had no idea what a whirlpool of manure it was or that you'd be sitting at the middle of it with a ruddy great spoon. It took me a while to see what was really going on. We added our spoon to the mixing process after Arthur Boswell-Clerkson explained where his data about the Novichok originated. That popped a few eyes around here I can tell you. Smithson was too near the middle of it all and clearly at further risk. So we kept him safe for a while.

I grinned:

- Thanks Evans.
- Yes, Toby Smithson is fully conscious, in good health and in possession of the full facts which he, like most normal people, finds about as easy to understand as General Relativity. So there's no security risk because even when he's heard it all he's still no fucking wiser, much like some of the half alive, amoeba brained, imbeciles that work around here... He's also in the room next door.

I got up and raced out of the room and opened the door next to Evans'. Toby was on his own in an armchair reading a newspaper. He looked up, stood up and found me wrapping my arms around him. He hugged me back in a brotherly way.

- Hi Alex.
- Hi Toby. I hoped you'd be ok.
- I was in Australia until yesterday. These guys seemed to want me to take a trip anywhere but London. Something about national security. Seemed like a damn good deal to me, so I didn't ask too many questions. Just a few days ago I got a plane ticket to

London in the post.
- You're OK. Everything's OK?
- Firing on all cylinders now. Especially the important ones. Are you ok? And you look fabulous.
- Thanks and yes I'm well but much, much better for seeing you looking so... alive!

He'd finally recovered fully in a South African hospital and been given some strict instructions about what he could and couldn't do. He went through a list of exotic locations that he had been staying in. Armed with a false passport, a go anywhere airline ticket and a modest allowance. He'd been asked to stick to the southern hemisphere. He'd unsuccessfully argued that as he was only allowed half the world he should have twice the allowance.

I had to ask:
- Do you remember anything about the night of the party? When you were assaulted? The last time we saw each other?
- No complete blank. I've tried. I haven't got anything from that evening. Remembering you as Alex was hard; they had to remind me that I knew a girl called Alex. I remembered James. It was a while before I recalled, you know, the connection.
- Do you remember why you went to the party?
He did remember:
- That gorgeous girl. Still can't stop thinking about her. I met a few others but she just will not   leave my bonce. I don't suppose that she is around anywhere. Did you find her?
- You did. You found her. You met her that night.
- What?
- On the night of the party you found her. You talked to her.

Angelic?

-    I did? Shit! And I've forgotten? Bugger... Did we get on?
-    Very well. She remembers you very well.

His eyes widened some more:

-    She does? How do you know?
-    She's a good friend. She's a good person. You've missed a lot.
-    No bloody kidding. And I thought I'd been on to a good thing living it up in exotic countries at the expense of Her Majesty. So I can meet her?
-    She will be there on Saturday night. For the Christmas party at the Mornington Club.
-    We're going? How did you get the invites?
-    Don't worry about that. Like I said, a lot has changed.
-    Yeah, I'm getting that idea. So I'll see her on Saturday?
-    Yes you will.

Glee was all over his face. Then he looked more subdued:

-    Oh damn... Oh damn... I'm really nervous now.

We started to make our way out. He paused, thinking, saying:

-    Alex...
-    Yeah
-    Well...
-    I'm listening Toby.
-    You look great by the way. How do I say this? I mean I'm sorry about James, but pleased for you. I know this is how things should be.
-    Thanks, that's sweet of you and I'm pleased that you wanted to say it. You helped me, you wanted to make me think again. It was brave of you as well. Thank you.

He nodded and smiled as I continued:

-    It wasn't a swap for me though Toby. James isn't sorry. James is the happiest he's ever been and he's still available to whip your ass at Unreal Tournament any time you say.

- That's good. That's real good. I mean it's good that he's happy. I was always shit at that game.

He thought for a moment. He was still sad. As he saw it he'd lost his two best friends, Tavi and James.

- But, I miss Tavi and I miss James. I knew I was going to lose James from the first time I saw you. Tavi was right. I was selfish.

I gripped his hand and looked into his eyes:

- No, no, it's not like that. You loved your friend James. That's a good thing. I knew that then and Tavi knew that too. I'd be both if I could. Back then I would have gone back to being James for you. But I need to be Alex now, for me.
- Tavi always said he wanted there to be a you that you wanted to be.

We went on to talk about SafeNet. He'd assumed it would be doing badly. I let him know how improved sales were, thanks to some free publicity, and how well our investments had done. He was surprised but also very, very pleased.

I took Toby to meet Eleanor and left them talking while I went back to Evan's office to complete some unfinished business. He looked up and said:

- This better be good.
- The reason I had help. You were looking for a man reason. That's why you didn't find it. The reason I had help was a woman's reason.
- I'm probably a fifty-four double E cup, but I don't use pink phones, paint my nails or use lip gloss. You'll have to give me some more help, I'm an exceedingly useless prick in this dimension
- I made a friend.

Given the clue he worked it out in a few microseconds:

- So you made friends with the daughter of one of the filthiest richest women in the world. She wanted to keep you safe only so you could be friends with her daughter. She had no idea about anything else?
- None at all.
- Just that? That's the only reason?
- There's a better reason? There's a better reason than a mother's love for her child?
- Well roger me till Sunday. Now I'm noddy at my job because I'm a man. Bugger that.

I blew him a kiss:

- You can borrow my lip gloss if you think that will help.

I took out some lipstick and did my lips. Then I put the stick of lippy on his desk in front of him. He picked it up and launched it to the back of his desk drawer:

- Piss off. My daughter's about your age. I'll introduce you to her on Saturday. You can chat about painting nails and wrapping Mossad around hair curlers. You can disappear off now. Waddle off and brighten someone else's day. You've got some matchmaking to do. I'll see you at the Mornington Club.

I got up, kissed my index finger, planted it on his cheek and winked. He put his hand on his cheek and wiped off the lipstick, looked at his hand to see what had come off. His fingertips had a little dark pink on them. He wiped it off disgustedly.

Mornington Club

Source: Alex Harewood
Date: Saturday 20th December
Time: 7.23 pm
Present: Alex, Eleanor, Toby, Katya, Klarra, Imogen

We went up the steps to the Mornington Club Christmas Party. I held Toby's arm the way I had before the first party. Eleanor was on his right arm. We guided him in the same way that I had been guided up those steps in the summer by Toby and Tavi. I offered a little advice:
- You have to be careful with her. She's had some bad times. Be very patient. Be the gentleman. Let her make all the running and all the moves.
- Will she like me?

He looked at me. I felt his stride falter. His nerves had got the better of him for a moment.
- I can't answer for her. But you'll find out in the next few minutes.

Katya, as arranged, was in that impressive entrance hall to meet us, alerted by Eleanor's text just as the car arrived at the club. She stood a little way from the door and dazzled. Every detail immaculate. Every stitch designed to flatter just her. The white dress flowing around her curves showed just enough of everything. Her golden hair fell down from her head in ethereal waves. In contrast to all the glitter and sparkle elsewhere she wore around her wrist a double row of simple coloured wooden beads.

467

Angelic?

Every man stared at her and every woman was envious.
Apart that is from the woman on her left who glowed with
motherly pride. It was good that they were together. There
must have been some meaningful conversations. Imogen
was on Katya' right. If she had done any mourning for her
husband it had been very brief. She wore bright colours
and not one stitch of black.

As we arrived I just caught Katya putting a hand to her
neck; she was nervous. She said a few hasty words to her
mother. Her mother replied. Imogen saw us first, touched
Katya and pointed her in our direction.

Toby saw her and paused. She saw us and started to float
towards him. She was smiling. He was stationary,
transfixed.
-    Mr Tobias Smithson may I present Miss Yekaterinya
     Khrushcheva.
announced Eleanor with a flourish of formality. Katya
simply walked up to him, put her arms around his back and
her cheek against his chest. She fitted neatly under his
chin. It was a this-is a-safe-place hug. He clearly hadn't
been expecting that it would be that easy. He wrapped his
arms around her shoulders and kissed her on the head. She
looked up. He grinned. She grinned back:
-    Hello again
-    Hello
Nervously he touched her hair. Those gorgeous golden
locks. She looked at him. Picked up a lock and twisted it
one way and then the other and handed it to him. It was
OK to play with it if he wanted to. He gingerly ran his
fingers over the waves and curls while she watched the
expression on his face and then hugged him closer.

Klarra looked on holding her hand in front of her mouth.
She was trying not to cry. Then a slow steady stream of

tears started down her cheeks as for the first time she watched her daughter with a man she loved.

Katya turned round and introduced Toby to Klarra:
- Mother this is Toby.
She said it in Russian, but no one needed a translation. Mother was rather overcome and simply threw her arms around the bemused fellow. Toby didn't get all that was going on here and threw me a puzzled glance. Eventually Klarra let him go and passed him back to Katya.

I gave Klarra a formal two cheek kiss. My cheeks brushing her very wet ones. As we drew away she pressed my arm and whispered:
- Thank you.
That told me a lot about the conversations she had had with her daughter and that was why she said it. If there had been anything to forgive then Katya had forgiven. We embraced. I guessed that Ivan had terrorised her too. Why would he not have?

When all the hellos and introductions were complete Katya said to Toby:
- Shall we go to the party?
- Just don't pinch me. I'm afraid that I'll wake up.
Katya let go of his arm and stood back at the same time swinging her arm around to hit him hard on the shoulder, hard enough to make a bruise. He staggered with the blow and looked really shocked. She grabbed him and kissed him full on the lips and wrapped her arms around his back. He was just starting to respond when she drew away. She asked him:
- Do you need any more waking up?
- Not on your nelly. All my senses are fully engaged.
- That's good.
She touched his cheek and slowly kissed him lightly on the

Angelic?

lips. Then stood back and looked at him. He smiled his happiest ever smile and wrapped his arms around the only girl he would ever dream of.

SIS Headquarters

Source: John Meehan
Date: Monday 22nd December
Time: 14.10
Present: David Evans, an SIS research officer and his
               manager.

Evans was sitting at his desk with a researcher and the research manager standing in front of him. They had been trying to find out the history of James Hecketty. They hadn't done too well. There was a sketchy history but they had found nothing certain before he was at college with Toby and Tavi.

Evans looked at the researcher and his manager.
-     Is that the file on Hecketty? Pass the damn thing over
      here.
The researcher reluctantly handed him the file. Evans rapidly flicked through it, taking in what was there and noticing what was not there:
-     What is this? Why do I work with you moronic
      vegetables? What do we serve in the canteen here?
      Baby-bio? Have you two been watered today? You
      can't find any fucking thing? Explain.
The researcher tried to explain:
-     The police didn't look too hard at Hecketty's history.
      There's no confirmable early record of him anywhere.
-     So he never fucking existed. James was not a real
      person?
-     Correct, Sir. We can't confirm any record of him before

college with Toby Smithson and Tavi Mansur.
The clerk saw the expression on Evans face change. He had missed something. The boss was about to go ballistic.
Evans stabbed a large fat finger at the research clerk.

- How much do I pay you?...Too fucking much.

He stabbed the same fat finger at the research manager.

- And if I pay him too much I pay you way too bleeding much. One hour. In one hour I want to know all about the early life of James Hecketty. Or you two guys can cancel your Christmas holidays and I'll cancel your Christmas bonus.
- What? How? We looked.
- No you didn't you half brained, barely alive, semi vegetative fungi. You only looked at half the fucking possibilities.

The two researchers were still perplexed. One said:

- How?

Evans was still shouting:

- Do you know how far it is down to the pavement from that window? Do you know what terminal velocity is? Are you familiar with the hardness coefficient of concrete? Get going. You have 58 minutes left to find the young Hecketty. And this time look for a girl!
- He's a girl?
- Yes! The human brain is capable of one hundred trillion connections. If he's not a boy he's a... wait for it... girl! Perhaps he was always a bloody girl!

He dramatically clasped his shaking head in his hands while looking down at the desk. A single fat little finger on his left hand wiggled twice. It was the only indication required to send the two researchers scuttling from the room. He shouted after them:

- Fifty-six minutes!

Chapter 23
Russia and London
December 2014

The Village of Neshkan
North East Russia

In the far, far North East of Russia are some very beautiful places. Here there are high old, worn, mountains and wide valleys, inlets and bays. There are no trees. Along the shores in winter there are only endless fields of ice. In summer there is the still almost freezing sea. There are few roads. There are almost no people. Where there are people, they cling to the sea for its resources and transport routes.

What people there are tend to be the indigenous Asian people with wide high cheekbones and shallow eyes with the Asiatic fold. They are a beautiful people; thoughtful, intelligent and friendly: fully aware that the world is a harsh enough place without them adding any more sharp edges.

The village of Neshkan sits on the edge of this landscape occupying a narrow spit of land between a shallow bay and the sea. People have lived there for more generations than anyone has counted. It is visited every summer month by a vessel from the whaling company which brings in modern goods and takes out the reindeer pelt and whalebone carvings which have been almost the only source of income.

Traditionally the only building materials were skin, from seals and reindeer and bone from whales. Today people bring in concrete and wood and iron and all the houses are built of these modern materials. They are all the same and built in organised rows. Location would be the only sure way to tell them apart if it wasn't for countless individual touches.

At the middle of the village is the restaurant-bar-hostel-shop that serves as the meeting place for everyone. It is called the village centre in the local Yupik language and no one has thought of a need for any other name. Most houses are too small to contain anything more than their owners and everyone goes to the village centre for everything, but mainly company. If you want something soon and it can't be obtained here, either from the proprietors or from the other people here, then it cannot be obtained.

Things have got easier here in the last year or so. There was some new deal with the whaling company and everything has got cheaper for people in the village. They have put money together to pay for more internet access and some computers.

The young people had started playing games online. It was fun and there was so little to do in the long dark winter months. Then two of the youngsters playing an online game met a character in the game called Anirnisiack, a Yupik name. This character had shown them how to make real money guiding other players to places and things that were hidden. The youngsters found other ways to make money in online gaming and shared their knowledge. They kept notes and learned more. They were starting to develop their own online police force so they could deal out punishment to characters who double cross them. Soon they found they were making more money than their parents. Initially annoyed at the waste of time, the older members of the community now find that this was giving their remote village a future. After a long decline things might actually be getting better.

The wind was strong. It was always strong. It was always cold too. Sally Khabarova went to the village centre. She did so almost every night. All the village went there at some time during a week. Tonight it was as busy as any other night. There were upwards of 100 people in the large cabin. She knows them all. She knows everyone within a two hundred mile radius.

Sally is from Dover, Kent, in the UK. She had come here with her husband two decades ago having fallen first in love with the Russian sailor and then his idea of living in the remotest place. He had died several years ago when their daughter was ten.

Some people don't understand when you say you love a place like this. It's not most people's ideal. She enjoyed the isolation and the way of life many would consider full of hardships. She could always go back to the UK but she would need a good reason to return to all those crowds and busy things. Here she is valued and useful. She is a fixer. If it doesn't work, she makes it work. As more and more technology arrives in the village she gets more and more repairs to do.

By local standards she is wealthy, which means that she has some dressy clothes in her wardrobe and a bank account with roubles in it. Nobody uses roubles here. Coupons from the whaling company are used instead and you can always barter. If you want something you trade it for something else. It's very simple and direct, which is the way most things are in Neshkan.

She has some good friends and they support her. Character is a most important commodity here. If people like you they do you better deals. Everyone looks cheerful all the time. You could be sad for a while and people would be kinder. If it went on too long they would not approve. It is not polite to impose your sorrows on other people for ever.

Sally has been sad for years. She doesn't show it now, and they admire her for that because everyone knows she is still sad. They don't need to be reminded all the time that her daughter has gone.

Her daughter had been precocious. The girl could outshoot the boys and was cleverer than anyone. She'd not had many feminine role models growing up and spent a lot of time with the boys and men who valued her hunting skills. She learned about killing and dying from the hunters and the reindeer. Everyone hated it when an animal was wounded by a shot and not killed. They could see the horrible stress if a joint was hit or worse; a stomach wound. Sally's daughter once despatched a belly shot reindeer from a mile away across a river. They couldn't collect the carcass but no one could stand the injured beast's screams any longer.

She was often mistaken for a boy by outsiders. Feminine curves are not obvious through heavy clothing. The local genes helped too; men here rarely developed facial hair. They saw pretty Western women on TV but they always seemed so alien, a little bit silly, and wore odd, impractical clothes that you couldn't possibly wear here. In her age group she was the only female European.

Her daughter soon learned everything academic that the village could teach her. Everyone knew that she would have to leave one day. After her tenth birthday she was sent off to school. She left on the last summer boat and returned on the first or second boat the next summer. She came back looking bright and happy, older and carrying glowing school reports. There was not a lot of chance to speak in between. Just a short phone call every week.

Sally's daughter should have returned to celebrate her sixteenth birthday at home. She was not on the boat as she should have been, or the one the following month. She had not phoned or written.

Sally took the boat to the city and enquired for her daughter. The school knew nothing. No one knew anything. She sent letters and used the phone but she could get no word. Her daughter had disappeared. There were awful stories of young women being tricked into going abroad to some wealthy corner of the world and being sold there into a life of abuse. She feared that this was what had happened. That was more than five years ago.

Sally always continued the search for her daughter. From her own home she could search the internet and did so every day. She also had two young people, Arana and Artur, who helped her. They used the computers at the village centre.

Today she opened the door to the village centre and said hello to everyone as brightly as ever. Normally she would sit down in her usual place with her friends, sip coffee and talk about very little. Today was not normal. Today was a day she had waited for but almost given up hope of ever seeing.

Angelic?

Arana and Artur stepped forward eagerly carrying printed photographs. The excited expressions on their faces said that they had news for Sally. Word went round the building. People stopped talking. Things didn't often happen here, but something was happening now. The village centre was silent.

Artur had two photographs in his hand. Two pictures printed from the website of Hello magazine. Sally took them and looked at the photographs and read the caption:

> *Yekaterinya Khrushcheva daughter of the Russian oil multi billionaire and her best friend Alex Harewood enjoy a night out in London and eat at the Sentinel.*

She studied the image of Alex, apparently a wealthy young socialite, out for a night with a friend. Sally could hardly speak but said eventually:

- Yes. It is her. It is her.

She held the photographs to her bosom and wept. The village centre was not entirely sure of the appropriate reaction to this event. But Sally was hugged more times than ever before and the village woke slowly the next day with sore heads, uncertain stomachs and happy hearts.

Alex' Flat

Source: Alex Harewood
Date: Monday 22rd December
Time: 09.25
Present: Alex, Toby, Katya

It was Monday morning and I was slumbering. I didn't have to get up for work. I had no meddling to do. I did have to obey my doctor's instruction to rest. It was only 9.30.

There was a knock on my front door. I looked through the spy hole dressed in only my dressing gown. A face was beaming at me. The brightest most beautiful girl. Katya. I could hear her talking to Toby and they already sounded like they had been together forever. I wondered how many milliseconds they had spent apart since the party. I opened the door.

-     Hi!

said Katya as I was hugged. She looked conspiratorial and cheeky like she had looked on the evening that she took me to the theatre. Behind Katya was a massive bunch of flowers that approached the doorway as I stood aside to let them in. They were propelled by Toby:

-     Hi! Where shall I put these?
-     Over by the sofa.

He put them on the table next to the sofa and then hugged me. Katya explained:

-     They're for you. We wanted to say thank you.
-     You helped me. Toby helped me. The flowers are beautiful and I'm so grateful, but didn't we just help

each other?
- You did so much. We don't know all of it. But the more we think the more we realise all the things you've done.

I admired the blooms while Toby talked:
- I told Katya some things about you and me from a while ago. We got the flowers from Louise.
- Is she OK?
- She's fine. She's got a new boyfriend and looked relaxed and happy. I said you looked relaxed and happy too and that you seemed to be very much recovered.

Katya:
- It was just exhaustion?
- That's the best answer they have come up with. They say I was running on adrenaline. As soon as I relaxed I just collapsed. They wanted to know if I'd been doing anything exciting!

Katya had put her cheeky grin on again and was wafting theatre tickets. It was Wicked again.
- Tonight. Is that OK? Shows are always better the second time. You don't have to worry. You just know it's going to be good and you'll enjoy it even more for that.

I was not sure if Katya meant this truism to be applicable to any second visit to a show or if she was referring to our previous visit when I first had to worry if I was going to die slowly and soon or not. She could see what I was thinking:
- We know each other a lot better now.

I grinned at her. Toby saw us and commented:
- Blimey. Look at you two together. One powerful combination of womanhood! Even so being truly representative of your gender I'll bet at this moment you're both far more worried about what you'll be wearing for the theatre tonight.

Katya and I shared a glance and she corrected him:
- Not me I know what I'm wearing.
- Me too. Just the same as the last time. Versace and Jimmy Choo.

They said goodbye and see you later and then left me to get up properly and have breakfast. I didn't do much that day except eat and get ready. I spent a lot of time just staring at the flowers and thinking of all the things that had happened to me and all the things I'd done. They weren't all good thoughts.

Katya and Toby arrived just after five and brought some wine. He grabbed some glasses, opened the wine, poured and then raised his glass.
- To Tavi.
- Tavi.
we responded and drank. I added:
- He was so clever.
Katya:
- He really loved you.
Toby nodded slowly in agreement. I disagreed:
- He was a friend and we only pretended to go out on dates. He tricked you into thinking that he was head over heels in love with me to conceal the password. It was just what he wanted you to think.
I drank my wine as Katya tried to maintain the falsehood:
- Are you sure? He was in the most terrible place. I hate to think about it. It didn't sound like he was making it all up. Chazov couldn't believe it and watched the video to check.
Why was she being so imperceptive about this? Tavi had been astonishingly inventive. He had fooled them all and saved so many. He was still fooling my two friends. I went to sit down in the armchair saying:

Angelic?

- He was clever and wanted you to believe something
  that wasn't true. He saved thousands.

Toby and Katya sat down very close to each other on the
sofa. She still wasn't convinced:

- I'm not sure that people work quite that way.
  Thousands of nameless people just don't tug at you in
  the same way that one person can if you love them. I
  suppose they should but I don't think they do. I still
  think Tavi died protecting you. Thinking of the girl he
  loved.

I put my glass on the floor and then turned to Toby for help
in convincing Katya:

- Please tell her Toby. Please tell her that this is
  nonsense.

But he knew more than I did:

- I can't. It's not nonsense at all. It's true. He talked
  about you, Alex, all the time. You were so different. So
  right as Alex. I had trouble losing James, I said before.
  And so we argued.

He paused, thinking back, and then said cheekily:

- He said he felt you could make the whole world a
  better place. You could multiply the good and divide
  the bad.
- You see! He just stole that phrase from you. You were
  talking about Katya.
- I did say it about Katya and it is so unshakably true of
  her...

Katya grinned and bumped his shoulder with hers in
acknowledgement.

- ..but Tavi didn't steal the phrase from me, Alex. I stole
  it from him when he was talking about you.

The world can be such a strange place. A new reality
beckoned. I made one last attempt to bat it away:

- What? Why are you doing this? He knew who I was

really. He knew what I had been and he knew what I had done.

Toby was about to say something but Katya leaned forward. Quietly, softly she added:

- And he fell in love with the girl that he knew so well.

I picked my feet up off the floor and curled up in my chair:

- He loved me?

They both confirmed:

- Yes.

- Oh! How?

Katya got up from the sofa and walked towards me. She knelt down in front of my chair. Then she held my feet and looked up at me:

- Do you remember telling me I was beautiful?

I nodded:

- Yes.

- She reached up to touch my cheek and smiled, saying:

- Well you're very beautiful too.

I looked into her eyes and she explained:

- Tavi saw you so much better than you see yourself. You've made my whole life better, Alex.

She added something else, it was almost too much:

- Toby let me know who you were before and I understand better than most how hard that is. I also know some of what you've done. I love you more for knowing all that. Not less.

I wanted to say something but I couldn't find any words. Katya found something to joke about:

- It's not easy being an angel, is it?

I grinned at her and shook my head. Toby was grinning too:

- At least you're an angel. Just think of all the far less attractive options. You could have been a witch with a broom, a devil with a forked tail and horns. Or a mirror cracking gargoyle. You might even have been a cherub permanently consigned to infancy, floating on clouds, and wearing nappies... Or maybe a saint? Heaven forbid! All piety and zero sense of humour. No, you've done alright there.

Katya was admiring Toby while we laughed. To me she added:

- You also make a very good cupid.
- You two were always going to look so good together.

Toby followed the biblical theme:

- Amen to that

Katya caught my eye as we both remembered what her aunt had said over the wooden necklace. So we both also said, at the same time, in Russian:

- Amen

as I realised that I had said it that day in Russian too, having needed no translation of what her aunt had said. We laughed together because it didn't matter now but had been important then.

Wicked was as good as the first time. Once again I clapped when everyone else clapped and laughed and oohed and ahhed almost the same as everyone else. But I was thinking about what they had said about Tavi. It was humbling to think that he had loved me. Knowing that should have been a good feeling, and it would have been, if I hadn't also caused his death.

The Village of Neshkan

Every internet capable device in the village of Neshkan became engaged in the search for Alex Harewood and the connections around her. An uncertain history emerged. Sally had noticed things that the rest of the world would not because she had access to a little extra information.

The question that had occurred to Sally was why her daughter had not contacted her. There had to be some good reasons. Looking at the reports on James Hecketty she saw a name that revealed the important connection. James Hecketty was rumoured to be the legendary online gamer Anirnisiack. It was Anirnisiack who helped the village online gamers. Her daughter had not forgotten her.

She looked again at the pictures of James Hecketty and confirmed the connection that so few others were able to make: James Hecketty was also Alex Harewood. She gained a little amusement from the police pursuing her clever daughter on a rape charge. Sally also found mirth in the reports of James Hecketty leading Ivan Khrushchev's men on a pointless chase around London. Ivan's death was reported, but not how it had happened.

There was another connection that was found by the villagers. T. Smithson was a name that had appeared on the new whale company contract. The police had not been able to find what James Hecketty did with all his money. But Sally now knew. Hecketty's money went to help the village of Neshkan.

Angelic?

She carefully examined the reports on the brothel raids after it was pointed out to her that the name Gemma Black appeared as leading both cases. She could make guesses at what all these connections might mean but there were no certain conclusions.

Sally had no idea what was really happening in her daughter's life, but knew it was neither simple nor safe. So when she left for London she had with her Makar Makar. He was twenty-nine, a strong fit and able young man of six feet six and seventeen stone. His consummate hunting skills were, as usual, not finding much employment in the depths of winter. He had admired Sally's daughter as she had grown up, became a good hunter, a great shot and a lively, likeable, girl. He had even developed feelings that were perhaps a little more than admiration. When Sally needed someone to help he had eagerly stepped forward and no one could think of a better choice.

Part 4
Angelina Khabarova

Angelic?

Chapter 24
London
February 2015

Falconbrook
London

Sally and Makar had only had one point of reference for her daughter. The Robert Sefton Estate Agency. Sally had previously rung the number and enquired after Alex Harewood. She had been told rudely not to bother employees at work.

Sally was unsure how best to approach Alex. They arrived on Thursday in time to see her get away from work. They noticed her catch the 170 bus and got on with her. They saw where she got off. Sally decided then to meet up with her the next day on the same bus. It seemed like the best place. It could be a chance meeting, there is little chance of being observed and if Alex did not want to talk she could easily turn away. It had been a nervy and gut wrenching twenty-four hour wait full of questions and few answers. Makar tried to comfort Sally but they had both known that the situation was strange and that the outcome of the meeting with Alex was entirely unpredictable.

Now Sally Khabarova stood third in the bus queue. Makar Makar had been keeping watch and phoned Sally to say that Alex was leaving early. The bus arrived and Sally found a seat towards the back of the single decker. She watched her daughter get on the bus and sit down nearer the front on the opposite side of the aisle. A scruffy young man sat down in the seat next to Alex as the bus set off.

The young man stood up and looked at the floor and a moment later shouted:
- Oh no!
Then he said urgently to her daughter:
- Miss! Miss Alex, you're bleeding very badly.
Sally stood up and also saw the pool of blood at her daughter's feet. The lad helped Alex onto the floor as she was about to collapse anyway. He dragged her into the aisle then knelt over her and applied pressure to the wound in her waist. His hands and knees were covered in blood.

The bus halted suddenly as a taxi stopped in front of it. Two men got out of the taxi and boarded the bus. Sally knelt down next to her daughter and stroked her head. She talked to her as her daughter's eyes turned to a stare and she lost consciousness. Sally screamed silently, mouth open and cradled her daughter's head.

The older man from the taxi took charge of the bus telling everyone to stay calm and stay seated. The second man from the taxi tapped the lad on the shoulder and said to him:
- Good work Steve. Keep that pressure on.
and then told Sally:
- Stay there.
The man deftly put an oxygen mask over Alex' nose and mouth and cut open her clothing. He examined Alex eyes and checked her pulse:
- Shit!

The older man was on the phone and shouted back:
- Ambulance in two minutes.
- Fluids!

A medical bag of crystalloids flew across the bus and the medic caught it. He handed it to Sally.
- Hold this. Up. Like that.

Sally held it high in the air. The medic tried again to feel a pulse in the jugular. Nothing.
- Shit!
- He moved to Alex' legs and cut open her tights. He guessed at the location of a vein in her shin and tried to insert the cannula.
- Fuck!

He tried again:
- Yes!
- Report!

said the older man. The bag of fluid started draining into Alex. The man felt again for a pulse. He nodded and said to the older man:
- She needs to be in theatre, but we could be lucky. Steve here seems to have done it just right.

The lad was still kneeling over her pressing down on her wound. He looked desperate and said, pleadingly, looking at the unconscious Alex underneath him:
- You be alright, Miss Alex. You please be alright.

Sally heard a small reason for hope in all these comments.

The ambulance arrived and the paramedics made some complimentary noises about what Timm's team had done. They placed Alex carefully on a stretcher with the lad still applying pressure and then into the back of the ambulance. The medic got in too. The ambulance drove away with lights flashing and siren howling. The older man got into the taxi that had stopped in front of the bus and drove off into the traffic.

Angelic?

Sally got off the bus mesmerised and shocked. The medic, the older man, the lad. It had all seemed so organised. They knew each other and they knew Alex. Sally didn't know who they were. She just knew they were in the right place at the right time doing the right thing.

The police started to arrive. Then Sally got a phone call from Makar Makar. He spoke in Siberian Yupik, an old language which only a few thousand people in the world comprehend. He said only:
- How is she?
- She's lost a lot of blood and is unconscious.
- The man who shot her is dead. The police will want me. I have to leave. Good luck.

Sally was left standing on the pavement feeling desperate and completely bewildered.

She heard that the ambulance would go to Chelsea and Westminster Hospital. She made her way there but no one would give her any news of her daughter or even admit that she was there. She spent hours wandering around the enormous complex and found nothing. No London hospital would admit to having a patient called Alex Harewood that day. Or the next day. Or on the subsequent day. On the fourth day she went into Lavender Hill Police Station and filed one of the strangest missing person reports they would ever see.

SIS Headquarters

Evans had a newspaper open at the same article Harbinder had shown to Alex. Standing in front of his desk were the senior London Officer and the Head of the Russian section.

- How did this shit get to be printed? Where did all this bloody muck come from? Was someone just lucky putting all this together or do they really know something? If they do this puts a whole group of people, including the Harewood girl, in fucking danger.

He talked to the London officer:

- Richard, you find out where this journalist got his information. I'll then talk to the editor of this fish wrapper and ask him why he's putting this kind of shit in his rag instead of the more usual half-fried nonsense.

The Russian Section chief thought he knew something already:

- We've noticed that Kiril Flyorov has been very busy recently. It's possible that he leaked the story. He was Ivan Khrushchev's solicitor but seems to have filled some of Khrushchev's role in the Arbat group.
- So he's reminding people of the errors that Khrushchev made?
- Possibly. Do you want me to spin a counter story and leak it to a Moscow journalist?
- That's the ticket, Duncan, we'll get a couple of Russian ex KGB types to confirm your story over here.

Evans looked back at the London Officer:

- Can we protect the people over here who were

involved?
- You mean like Harewood? We'll do what we can. It would help if Hecketty was out of the way.
- OK. Find a suitable body and fake his death. See if we can arrange for him to die in a gun battle with Dmitri Chazov. That bastard deserves to die and it would tie things up neatly.

The London Officer nodded:
- Yeah, OK. We'll look into making that happen.

After they had gone Evans sat back in his chair and started talking to himself. He wiped his cheek and checked to see if there was any lipstick on it. Then he was shocked at what he had just done:
- Women! ... Just how did that Harewood kid get to be so good?

He shook his head and looked in the back of his drawer. He took out the lipstick that Alex had left him. He looked at it thoughtfully, twisted it open and tentatively moved it towards his lips.

A woman, his secretary, opened his door and looked in. She saw what he was doing. He stopped and winced with embarrassment. Unable to ignore it she said only:
- That's a nice colour!
- Why are you here?
- Alex Harewood has been shot. I thought you would want to know. She's in the operating theatre at Chelsea and Westminster Hospital. Critical.

The news was clearly painful for him:
- Car! Now!

Falconbrook

Makar was keeping watch on St Johns Hill above Clapham station when he saw Alex leaving the estate agents. He phoned Sally immediately so that she could meet Alex on the 170 bus.

He saw Alex rush a little to make sure of crossing the road ahead of the bus and a car got a little too close. The scruffy lad who had been close behind her had to stop to avoid the vehicle. Then Makar heard the zizz of a bullet whip past him and saw Alex stumble as she crossed the road to catch the bus.

He could tell the bullet had hit her. He looked round and could put together the two points; where Alex was hit and where the bullet came past him and ran an imaginary line back to a building on the horizon. His friend had been shot and he knew where the shooter was. He started to run. He spotted the lights of Transformation House on the skyline and knew where to head for. It took him about the same time to cover the distance as it does to pack up a rifle and get down five flights of stairs.

Makar saw a man exiting Transformation House. He knew what a rifle might be carried in and he knew what a man looks like after making an effective shot like that from a range of 500 yards. Makar stopped running. The man looked in his direction, failed to recognise Makar as a threat and walked off down the road. Makar followed.

The distance between them closed. And closed. The man

with the rifle case in his hand realised he has been spotted and followed. He took out a pistol. Makar saw it happening and launched himself at the man before the gun was aimed. There was a brief struggle but Makar was large and the other man small. In the rain and the dark it didn't even look like a fight from any distance or one of the passing cars.

Makar saw that they were standing on a bridge over a road. He picked the man up and pushed him over the low wall so that he fell onto the road. The fall probably killed him. If not it would have been the lorry that struck him a few moments later. Or perhaps the one shortly after that. In the dark and the rain neither driver was aware of hitting anything other than a bump in the road. Several other drivers would see the unidentified heap by the side of the busy road but it was not a good place to stop. It would be late the following day when a police patrol vehicle stopped to investigate.

Makar waited on the bridge for an open top lorry. He dropped the rifle into a cargo of granite chippings and added the pistol to a truckload of scrap metal. Neither of these two items would ever be reported to the authorities.

Makar made straight for the airport, hoping to avoid speaking to the police, and phoned Sally on the way. He'd not killed a man before. His face showed no regret or remorse.

Chelsea and Westminster Hospital

There was heavy rain, thunder and lightning as Evan's car arrived at the hospital. The black jaguar threw up a line of spray as it pulled up to the hospital entrance. The car had hardly stopped when Evans decided to get out. A man in a suit met him and then guided him through the hospital. Evans, without running, moved his bulk along with astonishing speed. He was stopped at the doors to an operating theatre. Another man in a suit said:

- Sir, they're still trying to save her. It's not looking too good.

He left the operating theatre and went back into the corridor. He took out his mobile phone and shouted all sorts of expletives into it and then some instructions.

- Have those two duffers in research still come up with nothing?... Tell them they're out of a job. Tell them to get their papers and bugger off.

The call ended. He slowed down. Rage was replaced by worry and he plodded his way towards the exit. He looked old and tired.

He passed a room. The family waiting room. Inside was a young man looking drawn and concerned. Evans recognised Toby Smithson and went in to sit next to him. Toby looked at him but said nothing. Evans asked:

- Did you know her before she was James?

Toby looked at Evans, it was not something he talked about. The door opened and Louise Ferryman walked in. Toby stood up to greet her and they embraced:

- You've heard

Angelic?

She nodded and it was clear anyway that she had been crying. She turned to Evans. She knew who he was. He didn't know her. She asked:
- Do you know anything about how this happened?
- Sorry, Lady, who are you?

Louise was surprised at the question and paused. Toby explained to Louise:
- Evans doesn't know anything about James' background.

Louise looked at Evans with some superiority:
- Doesn't he? Well Mr Evans my name is Louise Ferryman and for a few years my mother was married to Thomas Dodson. I was at college with Toby, Tavi Mansur and James Hecketty. Does that clear things up a bit for you?
- It just puts a whole pile of competing ideas in my head. Most of which are probably shit. Why don't you help me clean some of them out?
- No, this doesn't seem like the time or the place. Though I'm a bit surprised to find out that you don't know already.

Evans is not offended at Louise' refusal. Though it didn't happen to him too often. He was impressed with her. He shrugged his shoulders:
- I'm not God, Lady. I don't inhabit every bird that flies.

Katya Khrushchev came in through the door. She hugged Louise. Then Katya looked at Toby, their eyes met and confirmed once more their relationship. She sat down very close to Toby and they gripped each other's hands side by side.

Toby, Katya and Louise all look at each other and Evans knows they don't want him there. They know something that they don't want him to know. Evans looks at Toby and

Katya then goes for the easiest starter question of them all:
-    So how did you two first meet?
They both feel entirely relaxed with this question. They
think they know the answer. Katya tells what she knows
while admiring her handsome boyfriend:
-    Toby saw me getting out of a car and chased after me.
Still thinking he is on safe ground Toby adds some more
detail:
-    James and me were on our way to visit a client when
     we saw Katya get out of a car and I followed her into
     Harvey Nichols. I'd never seen anything so beautiful.
     And she'd said I looked cute.
Katya was surprised. She stared at Toby:
-    I didn't say that! Who would I say that to?
Toby knew what he had been told at the time:
-    You said it in Russian to your bodyguard.
Katya:
-    Bodyguard? You mean Vladimir? He was a pig of a
     man. I wouldn't say that to him.
Toby:
-    You didn't say it? You never said that? Blimey…. So… So
     James made that up? He made up something that put
     you and me together for all time…
Katya interrupted, inquisitive:
-    For all time?
She was grinning at him. He hadn't said it to her before:
-    Yeah, well, not all time, obviously. But for as long as
     the sun rises and the wind blows. For as long as there
     are flowers that bloom and birds that fly. For as long as
     the sky is blue. No longer than that.
Evans was trying not to look too interested while the two
lovers sorted this out. Katya was looking a little soft while
she looked at Toby and said:
-    Well that's OK. That'll do. That may even be long

enough... I remember that day because I was free and escaping from that monster. I was doing Harvey Nichols in the morning and a show in the afternoon. So it was a good day. I could be myself.

She clearly was looking back on the day with some fondness until she got back to the revealing detail of what she actually did say as she stepped out of the car:

- Then that pig started bossing me around in the car, saying where I couldn't go and what time I had to be back, because he thought he could.... I said something about not being a servant... and not being a whore in one of my brother's brothels. I remember saying it because I regretted saying it.

Toby:

- Oh shit. James heard you say that?
- Yes, he could have.

Toby looked startled:

- So you didn't say I looked cute? He made up something that brought you and me together...
- ...for all time.

She interrupted and confirmed with a quiet and cheeky smile and Toby grinned back at her while she added:

- I did see you and I did think you looked cute. But I didn't say it.

Evans had rarely wanted to be small or invisible but this was just such an occasion. Louise caught the eye of Toby and then Katya. They may have said too much. There was a pause. The friends shut up and wondered what Evans would say as he leant forward:

- So this extraordinary girl is playing at being James Hecketty. Then she invents some tosh that throws you to love birds together. Then what? She must have known she risked starting a fucking fire fight with Katya's brother. A gangster who runs brothels. Who

would do that? What sort of brain sapping goddamn
motive would anyone have for doing that?
All three looked blankly back at him.

The awkward silence was broken when a doctor arrived
from the operating theatre and started to explain. Alex had
lost a lot of blood and it was remarkable that she had
survived. She was going to have to spend some time
recovering. She would live, but they didn't know how long
it would be before she regained consciousness.

Evans had no reason to stay longer and got up to leave. He
went out through the door and it closed behind him. He
briefly looked back through the window in the door and
into the room. Katya was talking to Toby and Louise. He
thought back through the police reports. He walked
ponderously down the corridor and remembered the
references involving Tommy Dodson and Ferryman.
Smithson and Tavi Mansur. Then Hecketty. Then trafficked
women. And she spoke Russian.

Evans stopped. His jaw dropped and he stood still for
several moments looking vacant. His mouth moved, saying
nothing. Then he regained some composure and sound
came out:
-    Well I'll be... Fuck!.. Clever bleeding kids.
Evans turned and marched back down the corridor. He
dived back into the family room. The three friends looked
horrified. They guessed he had found what they wanted
hidden and were considering the consequences. Toby
caught Katya's eye briefly then placed an elbow on his
knee and rested his head on his hand. Katya grasped
Toby's other hand and stared at him. She was wondering
just how long he would be in prison. Louise sat bolt upright
and stared straight ahead.

Evans took out his phone and talked into it while looking

round at the nervy people in front of him:

- Tell those two morons in research they're not out of a job. I've worked it out for myself.
  He's Angelina! These kids hid Angelina as Hecketty. Everyone was looking for a girl! Angelina became James Hecketty. Years later Hecketty became Alex Harewood and took on Ivan Khrushchev. He was looking for a guy! Hah! ... She can shoot them. Fox them. Jail them. Red hot genius lass...

He paused for a moment, then, still shouting into his phone:

- Find who shot her. I want them in irons, hung, ... drawn slowly... what? ... Not fucking legal? Who are you? My mother? Just fucking find whoever it was that had that girl shot. And send me the file on Angelina. We'll see what there is in there. One more thing. Get some temporary police transfer papers drawn up. There's a young lad I want to replace those two duffers on this case. Name of John Meehan. He'll make those other two researchers look like dead snails and help keep the police well away. She's a national bleeding hero not a villain and those plodders aren't allowed to tell the difference.

The phone was put away and he turned to Toby and Louise. He knew what they were thinking:

- Now you kids hold steady and don't get all in a bleeding tizz. I can't arrange for you lot to get the medals, knighthoods and pensions you sure as eggs deserve. But I can and will make damn sure no legal, ploddy, half-brained pooh goes flying in your direction for helping that extraordinary girl escape... Jesus. What sort of state was she in when you found her?... Rest easy. Just relax. Give her my best wishes when she comes round and then help her get better.

There was a sigh of relief from the friends. Then Evans phone started ringing. He answered and listened before saying:

- Not Flyorov?... Someone else?... Look into it... Something else. Get these kids somewhere safe, all of them, Smithson, Khrushcheva, Harewood, Ferryman and Straminsky until we know what is going on. Don't let anyone anywhere near them. Liaise with their security teams. Any problems come to me. Find them somewhere safe and palatial to stay in for a while. Don't worry about the cost.

Evans is catching Katya's eye while he adds:

- They can afford it.

Angelic?

The Story of James Hecketty
London
June 2011.

Tommy Dodson was on his night shift. He worked security for a language college. Around midnight, he did his rounds, saw a breathing soggy bundle at the bottom of some stairs by a fire exit and assumed it was a homeless person. He often had to move them on. As he went down the first two steps the bundle moved. In the dim light all he could see was a pair of tired round eyes and a gun pointing at him.

Dodson had seen the reports of the brothel shooting. Eight armed men gunned down in less than a minute was what he had heard. Good-for-you was his first reaction. It had happened early in the day and been all over the news in the evening. Angelina was already infamous and he assumed this was her.

Angelina looked up. She saw the silhouette of a man in uniform and reasonably assumed he was a policeman. She pointed the gun at him but didn't want to go on killing. She didn't want to spend her life in prison either. There were no good options. She couldn't find hope. She was a murderess in a foreign city with no money and no friends. Even if she could get home she would have to cope every day with the shame, the embarrassment, the everyone-knowing and the pity. Or would it be fear she would see in the once friendly eyes that looked at her? She was about to turn the gun back on herself.

Tommy didn't know what might happen. He thought of something to say that might just stop him getting shot. He pretended he hadn't seen the gun:
- Blimey, lad, you look in a bad way. What's your name, son? Can I help you?

Angelina heard those words and assumed she had not been identified. Perhaps this man could help, so she made something up:
- James, I'm James.
- Ok James, come back with me to the office and I'll get you something to eat.

She was hungry and she couldn't see how this closed down any options so she went with Dodson to a small security hut where she eagerly consumed his sandwich and an apple. Later she went back to his tiny flat.

Tommy kept on with the pretence that she was a boy. Angelina maintained it too. She went on being James. As James she didn't have to admit who she really was. The name Angelina was not on any of the news reports. She never used it. She was only ever referred to as James. Her real identity was never mentioned. Angelina would rather not say. Tommy and other people who helped would rather pretend they didn't know.

She hated herself for running away from home and her arrogance at believing she could do better. She hated what had been done to her and that she had pretended that she liked it; that she had smiled and cooed and said how good they were and told them that she loved it. She hated that her body attracted those repetitive, sordid, impersonal vulgarities. As she killed, she had known vengeance. Now she was frightened of herself because she had done it so well, because it felt so right and because it had tasted so good.

Angelic?

Angelina at least knew that Louise was there to help when Dodson introduced her to his step-daughter. Louise brought boy clothes. A grey hoodie, some trousers, trainers, boy's underwear and a baseball cap. They all fitted her OK; the fashion was for things to be baggy. One day she also brought, contrastingly, a beautiful bunch of flowers. She offered them to Angelina who took them, stared at them, realised their meaning and said:
-    I haven't really fooled you then.
-    It's OK. Don't worry. It'll be easier if you don't have to go on pretending so much with us.
Angelina had rarely seen such blooms before and examined them slowly, smelling them and touching them gently. Louise tried to offer some hope:
-    There are other beautiful things in the world.
Angelina looked at Louise and then started to cry. She cried a lot more before falling asleep, exhausted. Tommy and Louise looked at each other and thought things may get better. Crying was better than the screaming she had done in the beginning when she first started to relax and think. When Tommy or Louise had held her and calmed her, talked to her and soothed her.

After another few days they still needed help and money. Louise talked to a friend of hers at college. A man she went out with a few times, as did many other girls. She talked to Toby Smithson. But only because he had money.

Toby insisted on meeting Angelina, though Louise tried to prevent it. He wouldn't provide any money unless he met her. She thought that he was just the wrong kind of man and most people would have agreed with her. When they finally met, Toby talked continuously. He told Angelina stories that filled the damaged girl's head full of new, different and entirely fictional realities. His visits became the only thing that she looked forward to.

The police never got close. They talked to Tommy but it was clear they knew nothing. Angelina had escaped.

Toby bought a computer for her to play games on. He introduced her to imaginary worlds where they played for hours in magical, spectacular, environments and he saw how good she was. She became engrossed in the computer and started to understand them well; primed by the hours she spent at home helping her mother fix them and other gadgets. She couldn't stand to think about herself but she could solve problems, think about programming and play online games for hours.

Toby soon found out she was not a boy and made the connection to the shootings but it was never discussed. He had so many sexual experiences away from his relationship with Angelina that it never threatened to become a part of what they shared. Angelina was a long, long way from wanting to think about sex. She was like a younger brother to Toby and that was how she appeared when they were together.

Finally, Tavi Mansur was brought onto the team. They needed his skills to get Angelina into the real world. They set up a new identity for her using the name James Hecketty. This identity was nothing like as good as the one she and Tavi set up for Alex years later, when their skills were far more advanced; skills they developed in response to the need for a new identity for Angelina. They got her into college as geeky James. Her background helped her easily fit the male persona and she only rarely gave people cause to doubt her pretended masculinity.

For those three years, she stayed hidden as James, squashing flat her breasts, avoiding cameras and people and publicity and any opportunity to be desired. Angelina became the James character. She pretended, even to herself, that she was James and that she was not a woman who had been enslaved and raped thousands of times. She tried to forget that the most satisfying thing she had ever done was to kill eight people.

Then Toby saw Katya going shopping at Harvey Nichols and heard James/Angelina wonder what it might be like to be a girl. Tavi and Toby knew that she could be happier, that she could and should find something more to like about herself. They set her the challenge of being a girl again.

When they first saw her as Alex they knew, long before she did, that she wouldn't be going back. Toby immediately mourned the loss of his friend James and tried to delay the process. He didn't really want the person in the world he valued most to become something that he understood least, a woman. Tavi found that his good friend and business partner was also the appealing Alex. He was overwhelmed by her.

SIS Headquarters

Meehan was equally puzzled and gleeful when he was told by Gemma Black that he was being posted temporarily to work with the SIS. When Evans assigned him to look into the Sun House case and Angelina he was awestruck. He looked and what he found he found to be extraordinary. He discovered all the connections between Toby, Tavi, Louise and Tommy. Then James Hecketty and Alex.

When he was first told that Angelina had become Alex he was delighted and it made so much sense. The trafficked killer girl from Sun House who had intrigued him so much had survived to become Alex Harewood. He remembered Alex from the police interviews and had liked her then. There she had appeared wounded and vulnerable. But he began to realise that while she was hurt and in danger she was also responsible for nearly all that happened in London after the death of Tavi. Now he was in awe of her. More than a little bit frightened.

Alex had initially talked quite freely with him. Then she stopped giving him information other than about Alex. She would just say:
- I was in Canada when that happened.
or:
- That wasn't me. Was it Emma?
And once:
- I read about that. The papers say it was James Hecketty.
Meehan had to respect this. He still learned a lot about

Angelic?

Angelina's history.

He had started looking into the circumstances surrounding her shooting when he got the call to see his new boss.

Meehan walked through the office door. Evans grinned at his most recent acquisition:
- Good to see you here. Perhaps you can help explain to me this little conundrum that's been troubling the contents of my cranium for the last hour or so.
- Err.. If I can.

Evans continued:
- Just yesterday some coppers found a body in the Trinity Road underpass. Completely mashed up by the traffic. Cause of death was multiple repeated squashings by heavy goods vehicles. The DNA says it was Moshe Mandelstam.

Meehan stated the obvious:
- He shot Alex.

and Evans was not impressed:
- What? You can't think I hadn't thought that far. His body was only half a mile from Falconbrook and the timing is spot on. For sure he made the fuckin hit on Alex. Probably some connection from that bloody article. Payback for his god damned brother. Or trying to regain some bloody credibility after shooting himself up...

Evans was grinning and chuckling:
- Hah. Professional assassin shot by armchair. That must really hurt.

Things had clicked together in John's head while he waited for Evans to finish. He could now make sense of what he knew. Relief was all that could be seen on his face as he said:
- So it wasn't Alex. We were thinking that she arranged

the hit on herself.

- Why would you be thinking anything that ugly?
- She was really messed up after Christmas. Struggling to get herself together. We're guessing that in some way she blamed herself for the death of Tavi.

Evans did not look surprised:

- Mental health! Shit! She surely has a lot more crud to wipe off her boots than most people. Do you know how many brave young men I see in here who think they are bloody invulnerable. I've seen them snap like twigs. Nobody knows how much they can take or what the night might bring back to make them scream.
- Alex was getting past that. Her friends thought she was getting better.

Evans was pleased:

- That's my girl! ... So tell me. Here's the puzzle. How is it that Moshe Mandelstam gets to die in a road traffic accident?

There was a brief pause. Meehan was thinking while fumbling inside his jacket. He brought out a small tablet device. Evans face became anticipation. John would have said by now if he didn't know and Evans offered some encouragement:

- Make it good Kiddo.

Meehan showed Evans a picture of a large young Asiatic man. He looked fit, weather-beaten and alert.

- This man, called Makar Makar, killed him.

Evans recognises the man:

- The police tell me he's an accomplice. He alerted the shooter by phone when Alex came out of work. He ran off and got straight on a plane for Russia.

Meehan looked pleased as he asked:

- He got away then?
- Sure. You're happy about that?

Angelic?

Evans was watching Meehan whose face just couldn't hide what he was feeling.

- Jesus. You are bleeding happy. You know more. I need to hear this.

John showed Evans a grainy black and white picture from the security camera on the bus of Sally kneeling over Alex. There was some emotion in John's voice:

- He arrived on the same plane as this woman. This is Sally Khabarova, mother of Angelina Khabarova also known as Alex Harewood. She and Makar both live in the same Eskimo village of Neshkan. The village where Angelina grew up.

Evans looked truly surprised. He sat up and peered at Meehan:

- Well, I'll be a monkey on a stick! So mummy polar bear comes to London looking for her cub. She knows things are screwy in the cub's life so she brings the abominable snowman with her just in case some shit happens, like the shit that did bloody happen. They arrive on the same day she gets shot? What kind of world size bollock breaking coincidence is that?

But Evans could see that Meehan was sure of himself:

- Ok then. Give me the whole shebang. The complete schnozzle. I'll keep my mouth shut as I know nothing. But be warned, smart arse, get this right and you're never going back to the boys in blue. They think you're just a wet woofter anyway.

Meehan ignored the slight. He knew it was true. But he grinned at the prospect of joining the SIS permanently. Evans held up a finger for John to pause and took out Alex' lipstick and twirled it round in his fat fingers:

- Something tells me I'm going to need this. Shoot.
- The person in the whole world who most wanted to find Angelina has to be her mother. Last year a photo

512

was published on the internet of Alex Harewood with Katya Khrushcheva. Her mother found the photo and started searching for Alex, Katya and then James Hecketty on the internet, as did the entire village of Neshkan. A Russian internet agency logged the connected searches and passed the information on. The journalist then added the other information. Hence the article.

Evans was sitting back in his chair rolling the lipstick between his hands, still listening. Meehan continued:

- The only way to find Alex easily is at the estate agency. When she left on Friday both her mother and Mandelstam were waiting for her. It's possible that Mandelstam had her followed. Her mother had been there the day before and chosen the bus as a good place to meet her daughter. She can tell from what is on the internet that things are dangerous and complex for her. For the same reason she brought Makar with her.
- You are sure it's her mother?
- Certain. She booked into a hotel in her own name when she first arrived. Everything else matches too. No doubt.

Evans made a face that suggested he might admit to being impressed:

- Well you sure served that with all the trimmings...

There was a sly grin on Evan's face as he said:

- You know I heard that some woman has been walking into Lavender Hill Police station every day claiming to be the mother of Alex Harewood. They thought she was completely cuckoo, away with the fairies and stark raving. But apparently not. The poor bloody woman. What has she been through?

Meehan was surprised to see that Evans was moved at

Angelic?

Sally's plight and excited by what he heard next:
- John, you know these characters, can you please go and sort out the happy ending? And take a video for me would you? I love weepies.

John nodded:
- Ok I'll do that.
- No, no. That's a joke.

Meehan looked puzzled:
- Ok yes... err which bit, the video or the bit about liking weepies?
- The video. But take notes instead and we'll cry over them later.
- Yeah sure.

Now Evans looked exasperated:
- How can you be so bloody clever and then so damn stupid?
- It's me, Sir. I mean when I'm involved I never get it. When it's other people it always seems so obvious.
- Hah! Well welcome to the human race John Meehan. Now will you go and tell the She-Wolf that her little puppy is fine, all grown up with her own set of razor sharp claws and ...

he tapped the table with a finger
- ... delay the punchline for as long as you can. The bit about her internet search getting her daughter shot. In fact if you don't have to mention it. Don't. Actually... Goddammit! How would I feel if it had been my daughter who had spent two years in a brothel getting...

Evans paused grimacing at Meehan and shouted:
- .... Jesus H! Some things can not be thought about!

He knocked the sickening thought from his head with his palm and then pointed a finger at Meehan.
- If she ever bloody well finds out what it was that got

her daughter shot, I'll throw you out of that ever-loving window behind me.
- Don't worry Boss. If she finds that out I'll throw myself out of that window.

Meehan eagerly left to complete his mission of reuniting mother and daughter.

Evans pressed the intercom to his secretary:
- What did the administrative entry for yesterday say in my diary, Sarah?
- It says shit day,
- And the day before that?
- It says Misery 27. Happiness 0.
- Before that?
- Shit day.
- And the one before that?
- Shit day.
- Okay make an entry for today, would you?
- What should it say?
- Fucking ace day. Good up several points. Evil minus one.

Evans leaned back in his chair with his hands behind his head and smiled. Then he leaned forward, picked up the lipstick from his desk and threw it high in the air.

The Safe House
South Kensington
London

The car smoothly stopped outside the Safe house. Meehan had spent the journey trying to get over the shocks he had at Lavender Hill as well as explaining some things to Sally.

The first shock was discovering that his SIS ID made him the highest-ranking officer in the building. Second was Sally Khabarova spending several minutes letting him know how disappointed she was at being treated like an idiot after he had admitted to being in charge. He had finally found the right words and then the confidence to say firmly:
-    Shall I take you to see your daughter now?
Third was having to deal with Sally collapsing in tears as she realised her long years of anguish, heartache and frustration were within a short car ride of ending.

Meehan got out first and held the car door for Sally. He had explained that Alex was expected to recover fully but had only regained consciousness that morning. She had already been moved to the safe house with Louise, Katya, Toby and Eleanor. He tells Sally that she will first meet Eleanor who will then take her to Alex.

John guided Sally up the steps to the imposing front door. The door was opened by a smart young man who looked familiar to Sally. He was the lad from the bus, the one who knelt over Alex to staunch the flow of blood. He smiled at her. She smiled back. Meehan had explained that the team on the bus were around her constantly.

Eleanor was standing back a little way from the door. She greeted Sally with a warm and excited smile:
-   Hello... Hello.. You do look like Alex. It's so good to meet you. And a surprise!
They embraced and then started to make their way along the hallway where Meehan remained. Eleanor looked round at him and said:
-   Thanks John.
He smiled back:
-   Give her my best wishes.

Sally saw the imposing spiral staircase ahead and admired the cream interior, the quality antique furniture and the fashionable artwork on the walls. Sally looked but hardly took it in. Her anticipation was evident in every move she made. Eleanor said what she thought Sally needed to hear:
-   I've just left Alex. She's been asleep since before we heard you were coming. It may be best not to wake her though the doctor was happy for her to get up earlier. She has a big hole in her side but she hardly seems to notice it.
-   Was she alright?
-   Mmm. Yes. Very much herself. If that makes any sense. We really don't know what will happen when you two meet. She has never admitted to anyone that she was Angelina. She will only admit to being Alex and only talks about what Alex has done.
Sally looked concerned as she started to climb the wide spiral staircase, side by side, step by step with Eleanor.
-   I'm not sure I understand what you're saying.
The imposing chandelier cascaded all the way down from the ceiling four floors above between the spiral of the stairway.

- Oh well,.. well. I'm sorry. I don't know either really. We want to be her friends, not her keepers or her doctors. Things are very complicated with Alex. She is very special. But she's been through a lot. She got very unwell after Christmas, nightmares, dreadful mood swings and cried a lot. We think she felt responsible for the death of a friend. Then she saw the priest and he said what he said before. Just be Alex. She stopped acknowledging anything else and she started getting better. That was fine with us. Everyone likes Alex.

They arrived at the first floor landing. The whole floor seemed to be open plan. It looked like a very exclusive and tasteful nightclub with small tables and circular seating. Sally assumed that the entire floor was just for entertaining. Sally isn't really thinking about the house though:

- She saw a priest?
- Yes. There is a priest who thinks she is an Angel. It sounds really silly, I know. But he seems to understand her and she trusts his advice. It's always worked better for her than what the doctors say.

They started up the second flight of stairs and Eleanor was feeling self-conscious. She looked around at the house:

- It's not ours. We're just renting it but Toby likes it and Katya thinks she might buy it. Katya and I do have a lot of money. But it's not who we are.

Sally nodded in confirmation. She had already worked that out for herself.

They passed the second floor and went on up to the third. Sally was shown to a large bedroom. It could be mistaken for a hospital room. There was a bed, chairs and an array of medical equipment. Sally was briefly introduced to Louise who had been sitting by Alex' bed. Alex was asleep looking a little pale but relaxed and peaceful.

Sally gasped and rushed forward to sit by her. Staring and wiping tears from her eyes. It was clear she wanted to touch Alex but was afraid to wake her up, afraid to break the spell, but also worried what would happen when they met. Sally quietly said some soothing maternal words. Alex moved just a little, frowned slightly and continued sleeping.

A long while later, with Alex still asleep, Sally stood up and Eleanor took her back down to the second floor. Eleanor explained:

- Because of the tight security we have no staff here at the moment so Toby and Katya are cooking tonight. Neither of them have had a lot of practice and we're not at all sure how well it's going to go. We might end up with a pizza out of the freezer.

Sally appeared reassured by the domesticity. She didn't have to worry about anyone getting shot, just the meal being cooked properly.

They went through double doors into a sitting room. It was enormous but it seemed they were still in the more private part of the house. There were three large cream sofas, several armchairs, contrasting cushions, carpet with rugs on top, standard lamps, a grandfather clock and impeccably matching wallpapers. One wall gave a view over the park from two large bay windows. The opposite wall had two large archways so you could see through into the green marble-topped islanded kitchen where Toby was giving advice to Katya:

- You have to peel them first.
- You do?

He opened a drawer and handed her a peeler:

- Well in this country you do.

She was still not sure:

Angelic?

- So how do they get that crunchy skin on them?
- I'm not exactly certain. But you do peel them.

He picked up a saucepan and put it down in front of her.
She got the clue:

- And then you boil them?
- Then you par-boil them. Sort of half cook them.
- I like mine cooked.
- Well after half-cooking them you roast them in fat. I think that's how they get the crispy skin and finish the cooking.
- Does it have to be so complicated? Can't we just put them in the oven.
- That would be baking them.
- I thought it was roasting when you put things in the oven... God I'm going to make a rubbish wife because I don't know why you half cook potatoes.

Toby looked optimistic:

- A wife? Did you have a husband in mind?
- He'd have to have some very particular qualities.

Toby drew himself up and displayed his profile, puffed out his chest and flexed his muscles:

- Tall, handsome, intelligent, English, dark haired, witty, muscular.

But Katya didn't look impressed:

- All highly desirable, but not essential.
- So what's essential?
- He has to know how to cook potatoes.

Katya and Toby laughed happily at each other. Eleanor laughed as well but Sally was too nervous. Toby and Katya realised they had been overheard. Toby asked:

- Damn. Have you been listening to all that?

Eleanor answered:

- Only the funny bits.

and Katya blushed:

- Ohh...I never knew cooking vegetables would be so embarrassing.

Eleanor introduced Sally who then went into the kitchen and took charge, it was better than letting her worry take over. She helped Katya finish peeling the potatoes, worked out how to operate the stove and showed Toby how to cut the potatoes, add some water and put them on to boil. She went over to help Katya with the carrots.

Sally looked up and stopped still for a moment when she heard Eleanor's voice quiet but urgent behind her:
- Sally!
Sally turned round.

Alex had arrived in the sitting room, wearing pyjamas and a dressing gown, seen Sally and was now sitting on one of the large sofas. Louise was sitting beside her.

Alex' legs were drawn up to her chest and she was watching every move that Sally made in the kitchen. Her mouth was open and eyes were wide as she looked from Eleanor to Katya to Toby and back to Sally.
- You're my Mother.
- Yes, I am, Darling.
Sally happily sat down next to Alex who asked:
- You're Angelina's mother?
- Yes.
Then Alex started to look confused and upset. She shrank away from Sally and wrapped her arm around Louise's.

Eleanor motioned to Toby and Katya that perhaps they should leave. Alex saw this:
- Don't go! I need my friends.
They all sat down on the adjacent sofa at right angles to the one Sally, Alex and Louise were on. Nobody knew what to do.

Angelic?

Alex turned to look at Sally and then quickly looked away again. She started to think, her eyes widened and then she started to scream. A high-pitched thin, almost continuous wail with gulps of air taken in the brief pauses. Sally went towards her but Alex screamed louder and waved her arms like a three year old in a tantrum. Sally returned to her end of the sofa shocked at being rejected by her daughter. Alex' screams got louder. Louise wrapped her arms around Alex so that the flailing arms were trapped against her body. She held her and hugged her and stroked her hair saying:

- It's OK. It'll all be OK. Don't worry. Don't worry.

Alex calmed down a little and Louise said to the others:

- She was like this a lot at first. She'd scream all day. We had to hold her down sometimes to stop her form hurting herself. Then she would get exhausted and lie comatose. Just staring. Then she'd be ok for a while. But we had to give her something to think about. Anything but herself. We never asked what happened.
- Alex calmed down and was quiet but very distant. Louise looked pleased. This was a good sign. She spoke to her:
- Alex... Alex will you come back to us?

As soon as Alex became more aware she saw Louise and grasped her tightly. Louise spoke so softly that it was hard for the others to hear:

- It's alright now Alex. You're alright now.

Alex replied equally quietly, but could not do as she thought Sally wanted:

- I'm sorry...I can't be Angelina... I can't be... Not even for her. Too much happened... Don't make me.

Sally urgently responded:

- I won't make you!

Louise confirmed:

- Just be you Alex. That's OK. Nobody else. Just be Alex. Sally stared through wet and desperate eyes at her damaged daughter. Alex shook her head in defeat then stared at the floor.

Eleanor looked from Alex to the stricken Sally who was wondering if she had come so far only to be rebuffed. Everyone was silent. They heard the long case clock ticking in the corner.

Alex then slowly turned her head to one side:
- I can only be Alex now.
She looked determined but still childish. Alex looked briefly at Sally and then back at Louise who reassured her:
- It'll be ok. Don't worry.
Alex expression changed slightly and Sally recognised something. Something from a long time ago. A time when she was raising her only child in Neshkan. She optimistically moved a little way along the sofa towards her daughter. Alex seemed a little more hopeful as she said to her mother:
- I do make-believe a lot. I find it helps. Can we do make-believe?
Sally brightened a little more and perhaps knew now where things were heading:
- I suppose we can... I hear Alex is a lovely girl. Everyone likes her very much.
- Her Mum's dead. She misses her Mum a lot.
Sally had seen the opportunity that Alex seemed to be creating:
- So can we pretend? Can we pretend I'm Alex' mother?
The gap between them closed further as Sally edged along the sofa. Alex said:
- That's a good idea. That sounds alright. I think she'd like that.

Angelic?

- I'd be very proud to be Alex' Mother.
- You would?

Sally started to stroke her daughter's hair and said:

- Yes. Very proud indeed.

Alex looked her mother full in the face and attempted a smile. Sally smiled back through her tears. Alex felt her mother's hair and ran a hand down her cheek, wiping away the tears and reacquainting herself with the details of Sally's face. She leaned forward and breathed in the scent of her mother.

Sally put her arms around her daughter, hugged her like an infant and rocked her back and forth. Alex' sobs were stifled by her mother's bosom. Sally cried quietly, quite overwhelmed at being able to hold her daughter safely in her arms at last.

A short while later Alex sat up, looked at her friends and announced:

- This is my Mum. She likes to be called Sally.

Sally was overcome with happiness again. Alex hugged Sally, then sniffed the air:

- Toby. The potatoes.
- Oh shit.

Toby dashed into the kitchen and took the saucepan off the boil. He came back:

- Everyone likes mash don't they?

Katya was shaking her head slowly from side to side while looking at Toby. He wouldn't do for her. He couldn't cook potatoes.

The Story of Angelina
Sun House
June 2011

Angelina found the gun as she helped her client undress. He had it in a shoulder holster along with two ammunition clips. It was a modern light weapon, one of the smaller calibres, good for a woman. There would be at least ten rounds in a magazine and you could more easily control the recoil.

This guy looked alright. The previous night she'd been given to a group of five men. Groups were not good. They had done all sorts of things with her. Around midnight Anatoly had come in and noticed some blood on her bottom. He had inspected her anus with a finger, found the slight stinging tear and said:
-    Nothing too serious, gentlemen. You carry on enjoying yourselves.

Angelina had started by counting the number of men that she had been with. She lost count somewhere after a thousand. She knew that losing count was a sign that her brain was slipping. So she worried about it all the time. Then she realised that the worrying was the sign that she was slipping. It didn't matter. She knew she was moving closer and closer towards not being able to care at all.

But there was the gun.

The client gasped and grunted his climax. She stroked and kissed his head and said how good he was and how much she'd enjoyed it. He heard her say that he should come back to see her again because it would make her happy. She cared for him and would remember him because he seemed different from the others. These were lines she had acted out with more men than she had been able to count.

She knew she didn't have very long left. There was a limit for everyone and hers was getting closer. She had started by creating fantasies; pretending she was somewhere else, doing something else. Then that became harder and harder to do. Reality constantly broke them. She knew how it would be eventually. She would stop feeling and her eyes would glaze over. In combat soldiers they called it the thousand yard stare. This situation wasn't so very different. She would just become an emotionless automaton. She'd seen other girls do the same. They always disappeared soon after that.

The gun was still there. She got up slowly and took it from the shoulder holster. It was a good weight, a 5.7mm. The client saw her with the gun. She released the safety and put a round in the chamber. He panicked and ran towards her hoping to grab the gun.

Up to that moment the weapon had created several options. Now she had two. She could let him take the gun and go on being a chattelled whore or...

Bang!

His momentum carried him forward and he fell at her feet. A red mess was dripping down the wall behind the bed. What sort of ammunition was this?

Anatoly would be in the corridor, she could just hear his footsteps. He'd have heard the shot and would be arriving through the door, gun drawn, about ... now.

Bang! The back of his head exploded as well.

Two shots. They'd be coming for her now. She didn't want to get stuck in the room. The corridor had more options. She grabbed the ammo and ran out. There would be other men. Perhaps in the office along the corridor. She walked quickly in that direction. A male head appeared round Irina's door exactly at head height. Bang! The head disappeared but the door post and wall had gone red.

There was an alarmed shout from the office. A naked man ran across the corridor from Lada's room and into the office. She heard a short rushed discussion. Now there were at least two men in there. She was thinking about what clues the sounds gave to their location.

Lada ran out of her room towards the office. That was foolish. They shot at her in fear. She was worth nothing to them. Lada was hit in the shoulder and the thigh. Not good shooting, but perhaps a good distraction.

Angelina ran into the office as Lada fell to the ground. Pavel was behind the desk, crouching down. Bang. The naked man was backing away and not shooting. His hands went up. He begged her not to. Bang. She shot him in the throat. This was not a place to take prisoners. And he would have been shooting if his gun had been working. He knelt on the floor and held the wound. The blood flowed between his fingers. He died on the floor.

She ran out of the office. There was someone on the stairs. She jumped into the doorway on the far side of the corridor. Her legs straddling Lada. A shot zipped past her ear. There he was; crouching on the stairs. She didn't know him. Bang. He shot off a second round as hers was on its way. It grazed her thigh. She could feel the air rip as it passed. He fell back down the stairs.

Angelic?

The stairs weren't wide and just a single flight. There should be two men downstairs still. Bronislav, the boss, and whoever was doing the door, probably Daniil.

She went down the stairs screaming and waving her hands in the air. Pretending to be a panicked woman. The gun, high in the air would be the last thing seen as she descended. Bronislav might well be in the office still. He would have heard the shooting. He couldn't know exactly what was happening. Daniil was in the hallway. He would see her feet appear and then her legs and then her torso, finally her arms.

She saw his knee and a foot. He was down on one knee to look up the stairs. Bang! The knee exploded. He collapsed onto the floor. Bang! His right shoulder became useless gristle and he let go of the gun. Bang! Bits of him appeared on the floor behind him as the bullet disintegrated inside the middle of his belly, shredded it and left a large hole in his back. She dropped the empty ammunition clip from the gun and inserted a new one. Only about thirty seconds had passed since the first shot. Daniil died a few seconds later from shock and blood loss and in horrible agony, screaming.

The welcome girl that day was Margarita. She was petrified, just fixed to her spot in the hall.
-    Go upstairs, Margarita. Go to Lada. Go
Margarita did as she was told eventually.

Angelina was fifteen and trusting when they recruited her, from a place where people were always helpful. She had filled out all the forms and shown off the excellent English that her mother had been so careful to make sure that she learned.

The recruiters had said how she would go to work in

London as a waitress. The tips were great. She'd be able to ring home and say how well she was doing once she got there. She imagined calling home in triumph, living in London and earning real money. Proper pounds sterling. Not the whale company coupons. At first she was nervous, not sure if she'd been tricked or not, then she met the other girls on the truck and they had all believed the same story. It must be true.

Arriving in London had been too awful. Lucya, who had arrived with her, was shot straight away. Bronislav had waved his gun and said to her:
-   We have too many. You're not pretty.
Then his bullet had ripped through her heart.

Bronislav was still in his office. The door was open and she stood to one side of it as she talked.
-   Hello Bronislav
-   Is that Angelina? It sounds like your voice.
-   All your men are dead.
-   Are they now? You can't be that good a shot.
-   Seven dead. Nine shots from me. Three of those for Daniil. He died a little more slowly. Did you hear him scream?
-   Shit!
None of her memories of Bron were good:
-   You'll scream the same way, Bron, but for longer.
She hugged the wall and listened to him talking. She pictured where he was in the room. Imagined his location. She moved her head to get a different impression. Yes he was there. Standing up behind the desk, his gun in one hand at waist height. She jumped across the doorway and aimed at the same time. She was moving he wasn't. He shot but had little chance of hitting. Bang. But her bullet was on its way to the nerve that controlled his right arm.

Angelic?

The very spot she had hoped to hit. The gun fell from his hand. She ran into the office and pulled away the gun that had fallen on the desk in front of him before he could recover from the shock and grab it with his left hand.
-    Fuck you
-    That won't ever happen again.
He looked frightened. He should have been. He was still standing up behind the desk. She went round the desk and shot him in the left knee. The joint disintegrated. His lower leg was hardly connected to him now. He fell to the floor. He had felt that one. He screamed and writhed on the plush red carpet. She stood over him. He looked up at her as she grabbed the foot of his injured leg and twisted it. His scream was piercing and shrill. She shot at the computer, knowing where the hard drive would be and that this ammunition would shatter and destroy it. She left Bronislav squirming on the floor and went back up the stairs.

Lada was hurt but she was not going to die. Good. Angelina gave Irina and Margarita instructions to look after her then went back to the room with her clothes in. She got dressed, putting on her jeans, jumper and shoes.

She returned to the office and put one final slug carefully into the stomach of Bronislav. One was enough with these bullets. He would die slowly. She whispered in his ear:
-    Try as hard as you can to die today. If you don't I'll come back. Then you'll die even more slowly and in even more pain.
He looked at her with fear. She smiled back and then twisted his foot again.

She took Bron's woollen overcoat from the office and then walked down the road with the gun in the coat's pocket. She had no idea where to go and found herself walking through the wind and rain of the storm and heading south. The police lost track of her from there and eventually stopped looking.

As far as most of the world could tell, she simply vanished.

Angelic?

Epilogue
Autumn 2015

Robert Sefton Estate Agents

I got in at the usual time. The agency had been picking up some very wealthy clients and we'd been selling some of London's most expensive residential properties. I looked at Harbinder. She had that expression on her face. It didn't worry me anymore.

Robert stood up:
-   I have to go out
He opened the door and left. I wondered:
-   Is that him being thoughtful?
Harbinder seemed to agree:
-   I guess so. That could be.
She arrived at my desk carrying Hello magazine and showed me the centre spread. It was a fabulous picture of a wedding. The bride and groom in the centre and a few guests either side. The confetti was floating down and all five in the picture looked ecstatic.

She pointed at the woman on the groom's right.
-   Nice dress, very nice dress. You look good in it.
-   Thank you. I enjoyed wearing that,
-   So who are these people? This gorgeous hunk of a groom is Toby of course.
-   Yeah, that's him. He is handsome.

Angelic?

- And the impossibly glamorous and happy looking bride, will be the enigmatic and hard to fathom heiress. Miss Katya Khrushcheva.

Slowly, I corrected her:

- That is Mrs.. Katya.. Smithson.

She grinned back at me and pointed at someone else:

- And who's this young lady grabbing her arm and smiling like the world never has worries?
- That's Katya's sister, Asya. She's clever and lots of fun.
- And the other bridesmaid will be Eleanor then?
- She is so good. I could never hope for a better friend.
- So who was the best man?
- I was, kind of, but not really. Sort of an old joke. I did say a few things about Toby and people were nice. They laughed in all the right places.

She looked in a bit more detail at the bride:

- What's this on her wrist?
- Something old.
- Yes, but what is it?
- It's her Aunt's wooden necklace. It holds a dream.

Harbinder glanced at me quizzically but then turned to a photo on another page. There was no caption. Toby and Katya were in the foreground. Behind them you could see me with an older woman.

- Who are you with here?
- That's Sally Khabarova. An old friend of Eleanor's Mum, supposedly.

She peered again at the picture:

- She looks a lot like you.
- Yes she does. Several people said that and we get on really well. She lives in eastern Russia. It's such a long way away, but really likes it there and I can see why. It's so peaceful. Though she was talking about coming back to live in England... Is that place on Fred Wells still

for sale?

- That is a nice place. Really nice. It's quiet for the middle of London. Close to where you are.
- Yes I like it. I think Sally would like it too. Hang on a sec.

I took out my own phone, dialled and for the first time in a very long time I spoke to Sally in the language I had grown up with. I spoke in Yupik:

- Hi Mum! It's Angelina.
- Oh, oh, hello Darling. It's good to hear you. So good.
- It's good to hear you too. There's a property here I think you'll like. It's quite near to me. You may want to see it. Why don't you come and stay with me in London for a while anyway?

There was a pause. She said nothing for a moment so I asked:

- Are you OK?
- Yes, Darling. I'm fine. Never, ever, better. I'd love to stay with you.

There was another pause. I glanced at Harbinder. Her eyes had never been so round before:

- What are you saying? Who are you talking to?
- I'm just calling my mother.
- Your mother? You're talking to your mother?

The expression on Harbinder's face told me I'd be paying for lunch.

Angelic?

Acknowledgments

There a large number of people who have helped me prepare this manuscript by giving advice and finding errors. I am very grateful to all of them.

I would like to particularly mention:

Roger Lindsay, who gave me endless encouragement and advice.

Jan Tozer, whose positive comments were somehow able to outweigh a lot of very useful criticism.

And Jude.

Printed in Great Britain
by Amazon